Dead Wicked

Juliet Bressan

POOLBEG

Published 2010
by Poolbeg Press Ltd.
123 Grange Hill, Baldoyle,
Dublin 13, Ireland
Email: poolbeg@poolbeg.com

1 3 5 7 9 10 8 6 4 2

A catalogue record for this book is available from the British Library.

ISBN 978-1-84223-391-7

Typeset by Patricia Hope in Sabon 10.6/14.5

Printed by
CPI Cox & Wyman, UK

www.poolbeg.com

Note on the Author

Juliet Bressan is the bestselling author of *Snow White Turtle Doves* and *Entanglement*. She was a script advisor with the award-winning RTÉ series *The Clinic* and the BBC series *The Silence*, and is a resident TV doctor with TV3's *Ireland AM*. She lives in Dublin and is married with two daughters.

Also by Juliet Bressan

Snow White Turtle Doves
Entanglement

Acknowledgements

Yet again I am indebted to many. Our muses work in most mysterious ways and the best ideas come at times when we don't even realise that we are open to them. My first word of thanks must go to my wonderful daughter Molly for meeting me so regularly for cups of tea and for providing me with the idea for the story of this book. The island of Inish Rua is entirely hers. To my daughter Jessica for her unfailing loyalty and enthusiasm and for her critical sincerity every step of the way. To my dear friend the writer, television producer and researcher Kieran Grimes, for his invaluable insight and support with this, among many projects, but especially for his very thorough knowledge of the history of the Irish Catholic church and clerical life, and most of all for coming up with the wonderful idea one Saturday night of going to a Taize mass. To my brother-in-law Kevin Homan for his help with the early medieval monastic movement, the history of the Scottish islands and the Church, and particularly for visiting me on a frosty winter's morning when I had the flu and telling me all about the Celtic warrioress Andraste, who became the inspiration for this book.

Deepest gratitude goes to Linda Callaghan, Lar Keogh, David Moore and all the hardworking staff of Astronomy Ireland for their warm welcome and their invaluable help in researching the character of Art Callaghan. It was so wonderful to walk into the offices of Astronomy Ireland on a cold February day, with the mission of creating a gorgeous, sexy, romantic astrophysicist, and find such enthusiastic support for my fictional character from some of Ireland's most important, highly skilled scientists. I only hope that they approve of my Art Callaghan and that he might be an acceptable ambassador for the stars. To the writer Conor Kostick for medieval history and some very good laughs. To the writer Michelle Jackson for so many frankly hysterical moments during the writing of this book. To my dear friend the writer, producer and artist, Marigold Joy for her friendship, inspiration and support. To all at Poolbeg Press and especially to Sallyanne Sweeney of Watson Little for all her patience and expertise. Thanks as always to my father Dino Bressan for his meticulous research into the life of Saint Tristan, and to my mother Jackie Bressan for reading the manuscript over and over again. And to my husband Peter for actually believing that this one could work this time.

A very special thanks goes to my niece Calypso Bressan who gave me the story of Emerald the Dragon. For her superb storytelling, amazing dancing, and her ability to always reassure me by finding something funny in everything I do.

To my favourite artist, Vincent Van Gogh, who longed to paint the starry night because it is so much more alive and richly coloured than the day.

They'd say that when you went out to the island you either turned back and went home again the very same day or you might never leave. Perhaps it was the wet fog that rolled in off the Atlantic that captured you, a fog that smothered the landscape like a ghost, putting all the boats to dock for days. Perhaps the wickedness of the sea trapped you there while it pounded every beach and cliff with waves that whipped the trawlers away from landing at the harbour for a month. Or perhaps you fell in love – with Inish Rua itself, with its solid silence, its empty strands, its ferocious cliffs, its rough hills moist with heather munched quietly by black-faced, tough-nosed sheep. Perhaps you met someone there who needed you – or you needed them. Perhaps you had nowhere else to be. Or perhaps, when you'd been there long enough, you weren't sure why you couldn't leave – but you stayed. To see what would happen next.

Chapter One

The night that Dessie Moriarty officially disappeared was the night that Ciara saw the advert. It was like a little sign. Ciara spent a lot of time looking for little signs. When you've lived your life in a state of complete turmoil, you need to look for signs. When your whole world has been turned upside down and nothing seems to make sense, you attach great importance to the little signs. When you can't make a phone call home without the possibility that it mightn't be answered, you need all the signs you can get.

So the advert was, to Ciara, like a little sign that had been placed there by the Universe to remind her that although Des was indeed at long last gone, she was still alive and had a job to do. It seemed to wink at her from the newspaper like a small beacon – printed in bold font among the plain.

One Desperate Island Doctor Seeks Locum Relief For Three Months. Minor Surgery, Handle Accidents And Emergencies. Minimal Support. Please Come To Beautiful Inish Rua, 25 Miles Off The West Coast Of Ireland.

Accidents and emergencies. Those two words beckoned her, twinkling like a show of stars.

Accidents were something Doctor Ciara Love knew a lot about. Emergencies were all she'd been living for the past two years.

Finding money to pay bills just hours before the electricity got cut off. Having disconnected phones re-started. Finding ways of dodging down a lane to avoid a pack of journalists. Knowing how to find the courage to get out of bed when all she wanted to do was crawl under a stone and never emerge again.

Des had a way of doing things that seemed to turn every occasion into an emergency. Like having to find somewhere you could get alcohol legally on Christmas Day. Finding the Valium hidden underneath the couch. Life with Des had been an all-singing-all-dancing Viennese waltz around the ballroom of accidents and emergencies.

But accidents and emergencies were what love was all about, Ciara had so often told herself. People don't decide *who* they are going to love, and how they are going to go about it. They *fall* headlong into it, they are *struck* by it, they are *bowled over.* Cupid is *armed* – with a lethal bow and arrow, not a clipboard and pen. Life *is* an accident. Love at first sight is *always* an emergency.

Ciara and Des had always said that the main reason they would never fall apart was because they'd fallen in love the very first day they'd met. She was an intern in the A and E, he the handsome driver of an MG who'd been thrown out of the open-topped car and another eight feet across to the other side of the road. It was the work of higher powers, Des said. They would keep on falling in love every day no matter what chaos arose in their lives.

They were meant to be together no matter how much agony it caused, according to Des, no matter how many hours were spent repairing broken doors, replacing smashed plates and re-papering the walls.

Dessie Moriarty – philanderer, gambler, womaniser, drunk – that was his posthumous CV. But of course when Ciara met him he was completely different. He was a law graduate, a solicitor, a businessman. He was an absolute hunk.

She was a surgical intern, straight out of college, didn't know a thing and he was five years older. Bad start? Not at all! Most career women need a maturer, more experienced man. And he came into her life in a most romantic way. She was on duty, saving lives, putting on casts, inserting chest drains, prepping people for theatre and he came into the casualty unit via the windscreen of a car. Well, he came *over* the windscreen to be more accurate – the windscreen of an MG convertible out of whose front seat he had flown. Because he was Dessie Moriarty and he had the luck of Jove, he'd been thrown out of the front seat (where he was wearing no seat belt), across the road and into the ditch on the opposite side where he remained, mildly dazed but quite content (receiving all sorts of attention) until an ambulance arrived. His car was a complete write-off, but the only real injury Des sustained was a blackberry-bush scrape under his left eye. It left a small but very sexy scar. Ciara would soon realise that the reason Des had come out of the car crash in one piece was because he was Des and he was one very lucky guy – until he'd disappeared, of course.

So Des arrived in the casualty unit on Ciara's shift when she was looking just a tad too up-all-night-on-call for her own liking, and maybe that was why when this gorgeous, articulate, funny man arrived into the A&E being all kind and flirty with her, she just melted into mush.

She was the doctor who admitted him to the hospital and she admitted him into her life, which turned upside down and inside out just like the mangled wreck of the car he'd catapulted out of. Des had to be admitted to hospital because he was mildly concussed, for twenty-four-hour observation. They discharged him the next day and he left the hospital with a prescription, a letter for his GP and a new girlfriend. Doctor Ciara Love. That girlfriend within a month agreed to become his wife.

She couldn't resist him. He was the sexiest man she'd ever seen. He undressed her with his eyes, he metaphorically peeled off her bra while she was examining the equal light reaction of his pupils. He breathed heavily in her neck as she tested his sensory reflexes, and he made her heart race like a marathon runner when she auscultated his. When he told her they were getting married – yes, she *knew* how it sounded! – all she could think of asking him at that time was "When?" It was in two weeks, she soon found out. In Las Vegas. So romantic! So spontaneous!

So useful for somebody who hasn't *quite* finalised his divorce.

The *other* marriage became apparent after a year or two – but by then there were so many other problems that it hardly seemed to matter. There was the mortgage on the eleven-bedroom house Des appeared to own – because in the end she had to accept that he didn't actually own anything, and the Bank of Ireland, the National Irish, the Bank of Scotland, the Royal Bank of Brunei – she could go on – seemed to own everything. There were a lot of other people – clients of Des – who thought they owned their own houses too, only it turned out that they didn't either. Their houses were owned by several banks – because when Des conveyanced the sale of all those houses, he forgot to pay the mortgages off. He left seventy-five million euros resting in his client account. He forgot to pay seventy-five million euros' worth of mortgages off, all in one go.

So, that afternoon is where Ciara's story begins.

In retrospect, a lot of people thought that Ciara should have seen it coming earlier. Because there were all sorts of other little signs that happened the same week that Dessie disappeared. There was the seventeen-thousand-euro Visa bill for first-class airline tickets to Brazil that she couldn't possibly have bought – and when Visa rang and told her that they thought that somebody must have stolen her card, she just said "No, I've got it right here in my pocket" and then she wondered for a moment if Des had planned a surprise and used her Visa card by mistake when booking the tickets – but then, other things happened quite suddenly that week that made everything so much worse.

There was the letter that arrived from the Law Society, striking off Dessie. Then there were the letters – lots of them – from the banks. And then on the third day there was the black Mercedes car that prowled along her street with a guy inside wearing dark glasses that she watched with shaking knees from behind a chink in the closed curtains, her heart in her mouth. And, of course, eventually there were the police.

But by then, Ciara was looking for a different kind of sign. A sign that somebody somewhere was going to rescue her – to remove her from all of this. To get her out of the unbelievable, horrendous, ghastly nightmare her life had suddenly become and take her somewhere else where she would never again be recognised. Somewhere small and quiet where nobody read newspapers. Where there was no CCTV. Where nobody took photos for the six o'clock news while you were getting out of your car at the launderette (on the fourth day the CAB arrived and took everything, even their washing machine). Where people were caught up in a completely different world other than the world of the *Daily Press*. "Dirty Des Does A Bunk"; "Legal Crook Owes Mortgage Millions"; "Moriarty's Missing Millions – Where Did He Hide The Cash?"; "Slimy Solicitor Sneaks Away – Police Suspect Dessie In Brazil!"

So, Ciara opened the *Irish Medical Weekly* at the kitchen table and left it open on the back page, the small ads, while she sat in darkness the night she learned that Dessie had disappeared. Given that she couldn't see much in the house, it did seem strange to have opened the newspaper and she often wondered afterwards if there was a reason why she had it open just like that, if the stars were guiding her to the right page or something – but then perhaps she needed something for her hands to do. There isn't much you can do sitting in the darkness waiting for the police.

When the gardaí arrived they sat in the moonlight, all three of them at the kitchen table, and she listened to them tell her that Des Moriarty had disappeared but they had no doubt that he'd be found again quite soon. They had contacts everywhere, the policeman said. A solicitor, even one as clever and as slippery as Dessie Moriarty, couldn't raid his client's account for millions and then up and leave without a trace. They'd let her know as soon as they knew anything. Ciara listened and nodded and waited for them to go. Contacts or no contacts, she knew she'd never hear from Des Moriarty again.

When the gardaí eventually left – the ban garda had insisted on them all having tea, which was difficult without electricity but she'd boiled some water on the still-connected gas – Ciara sat alone again in the kitchen in the darkness and she sat a long, long time, listening to the silence in the house that she no longer owned and the traffic swish outside and then she saw that, the way she'd left the newspaper open, there was a little pool of moonlight lighting up the page just enough for her to read the advertisements for **Locums Wanted**. And the little sign was there. It was staring up at her.

"Staring up at her like an ass in the bog eating thistles," was how Marina would have put it – if Marina had known Ciara at the time. But Doctor Marina de Barra wouldn't get to meet Doctor Ciara Love yet because when Ciara would land on the boat in the middle of the worst sea tides since the Christmas after Elvis died, Doctor Marina de Barra would be on the next boat out.

The newspaper falling on the mat the same morning that Des disappeared, that had been a little sign. The sudden cold snap of weather, the unseasonable November frost. The full moon and the eclipse. The fact that Jupiter ruling Sagittarius was in conjunction with Uranus – all of these little signs did mean that you could expect a major change in circumstances. There are signs for everything, if you look for them.

Doctor Marina de Barra usually said that Inish Rua was

a place where everyone was trying to escape from having to be someone else. The island was a hot-bed of fugitives, was how she'd put it in her emails to her sister Veronica who ran the Las Vegas Desert Springs Hotel. Veronica said, in her emails back, that she doubted very much that any of the beds on Inish Rua were in the slightest bit hot. Which made Marina feel even more depressed, but she had to agree. Inish Rua was beautiful. It was remote. It was romantic, wild, unspoilt, full of characters, it was inspiring, unique, it was magical. But despite being bathed by the Gulfstream which gave it an extraordinary micro-climate in botanic terms, it was never hot. There was a sharp wind that whipped like a blade from the North Atlantic all four seasons of the year, bending the trees into right-angles like famine victims kneeling down to die. It was a wind that lashed the black wintry sea into a deadly foam against cruel rocks, turning grassy hillsides into spikes that only the most feisty sheep could graze.

But Ciara wasn't thinking of the weather when she circled the three-line advert that a Doctor Marina de Barra had put in the *Irish Medical Weekly* to be published on this day, above all days.

She was thinking of the isolation. The blissful isolation. The opportunity to work in peace, to do what she knew best, practise medicine, without jumping out of her skin every time the telephone rang. She wanted to be somewhere that nobody would know who she had been. She wanted to erase the past two years as if they had happened to someone else. She wanted to crawl into bed at night and sleep, or lie awake and read all night without anybody really caring why.

Being on an isolated island, where nobody knows who

I am or where my life has been, Ciara thought as she circled the advert around and around with green biro in the silent kitchen where a clock ticked and the rain tapped against the window pane and Des's burnt-out car lay in a ditch on a road-side in the midst of the Dublin mountains waiting to be found, would be like becoming a new person all over again. It's like re-inventing myself. I can be anything I want to be, all on my own on my island. I can be as miserable, as eccentric or as difficult as *I* want. And nobody will care a stuff. It's the perfect antidote to two long years of craziness. Solitude, stillness, nothingness. That's exactly what I want.

She circled it around and around until the pen made a green and black hole right through the newspaper.

And then she cried. She cried because she didn't know what to do about all the money Des had embezzled. She cried for all the horses who'd lost races that Des had thought they were going to win. She cried because of all the shares in dodgy companies Des had insisted on buying on a cocaine-fuelled tip at the Galway races that had been worth one-hundredth of their value the following week. She cried because her house was dark, and it no longer belonged to her. She cried because the tea the ban garda had made was horrible and because the weather outside was freezing and she was sick of wearing three jumpers in the house. And then she cried because she'd fallen in love with Des in the first place, thinking that he'd never really loved her back.

And then she blew her nose and went over to the sink and washed her face and dried it on a tea-towel and threw the horrible cold sweet tea down the sink. And then she took her phone out of her handbag and she made a call.

Chapter Two

Maggie Hennelly arrived at the Charlotte Street Hotel in London's North Soho just in time. And it was lashing rain. She stepped out of the taxi straight into a puddle and then shrieked because the water had soaked through her brand new Louboutin boots. The boots had been bought half price and so she hadn't minded that they were too tight – and now they were absolutely fucking useless, Maggie thought, cursing loudly at the weather, which the BBC forecast had said with the greatest of confidence would be bright and breezy with some sunny spells. She slopped out of the puddle and turned into the foyer of the hotel. The doorman looked nervously at Maggie's bedraggled mop of strawberry-blonde hair and the trail of water she was dripping in her wake. Maggie, in return, shot him a look as black and thundery as the skies outside.

Maggie Hennelly was quite well known at the Charlotte Street Hotel as she'd been there several times this year to interview the rich and famous for the feature articles she wrote for *Scoop!* magazine. *Scoop!* had cornered a market just prior to the end of the Celtic Tiger years and was now the leading lifestyle and corporate business magazine in Ireland – thick and glossy, it glowed with energy and luxury from the coffee tables of the top hotels, the business-class lounges of airports and the grooming rooms of top beauty salons. Prior to *Scoop!*, Maggie had been a junior reporter with the *Sunday Times* for a year, and was on track for a glittering career in journalism when she was appointed features editor with the *Daily Press*. That is, until Pierce Fox the media and equities billionaire had made a snap decision to shelve the *Daily Press* along with five other of his newspapers that weren't reaching the kinds of profits he usually required, and decided to go into airline investments instead. Pierce Fox had bought up three failing European carriers for a song – making him the hero of the 2009 economic meltdown. But Maggie along with two thousand other journalists had lost her jobs.

Maggie was smart and quick and had worked hard to find a job again and helped Benedict King set up the then fledgling *Scoop!* magazine. Thanks to a dogged attention to detail and ruthless wit, *Scoop!*'s circulation had increased from tens of thousands to several hundred thousand, and it was at long last attracting investment from some serious advertising contracts.

"Maggie Hennelly, from *Scoop!* magazine to meet Gabriel Kelly for nine o'clock?" Maggie said sweetly to Ivana the receptionist who recognised her and gave her a wide-cheeked Slavic smile.

"Meester Kelly has left a message for you, Miss Hennelly," Ivana purred, sliding a note across the reception desk as if it were a Las Vegas playing card. Maggie's wet curls dripped onto the note, and Ivana pretended not to notice that she looked like a drowned rat.

Press Release – Embargo

Gabriel Kelly regrets that he will be unable to attend for press conference at the Charlotte Street Hotel. Mr Kelly will be represented by his agent and publicity advisor Mr Eddie Mannion who will provide interviews. Apologies to all members of the press for this rearrangement which is due to the unprecedented demands on Mr Kelly's publicity schedule.

"Oh bloody hell!" Maggie yelled, ignoring the raised eyebrows of Ivana. "He's not bloody well coming, after all this. I've come all the way from bloody Dublin to interview the sod! Fecking actors!" And she shook her wet curls like a dog.

"Look, I'm really sorry about everything."

Maggie turned to the American-Irish voice behind her. So this was Eddie Mannion, obviously, Gabriel Kelly's agent, turning up to whinge some sort of apology at her. Maggie recognised him from all the New York society pages. Tall and gangly, Eddie still hadn't completely lost his Irish accent although it was Americanised in a rather gentle way. And he was obviously as gay as Christmas, Maggie thought bad-temperedly, taking in Eddie's patent shoes and pale grey Armani suit. Gay men were a complete waste of time, as far as Maggie was concerned. She hadn't got where she had today by being a fag hag. There was only one way to get what you wanted out of men, and it wasn't by discussing interior design.

But this Eddie looked quite sweet, pink-faced and so apologetic that Maggie couldn't help smiling at his helpless despair.

"Well," she said eventually, "at least you've got the decency to look embarrassed."

Eddie grinned. "At least you've got the decency to speak to me," he said. "None of the other journalists even showed up, after they got this morning's press statement. It's really very, very good of you to come."

Maggie opened her mouth and was tempted to say, I'm only here because I *didn't get* this morning's press statement, you thick lanky queen – and then shut it again. There was one way to look at this situation and that was to consider the fact that if there were indeed no other journalists here, then Eddie Mannion was all hers. And gay or not gay, she'd bend him around to her way of thinking and get some sort of exclusive out of him, no matter what it took. She'd come all the way from Ireland to interview the hot young Irish actor Gabriel Kelly, and she was going to get her story, period, even if it meant squeezing this self-conscious poof of a publicist until he was dry.

"Look," Eddie suggested, reaching out a hand to take Maggie's wet coat, "they've made a lovely fire for us in there, and we've got such a lovely little room for us to do the interview in. Wow, is this Marc Jacobs? Mmm, gorgeous. Look, let's go inside and I'll give you the story you need about Gabriel and the film and you'll get the exact same interview you'd have got from him anyway, because he only ever tells the press what I want them to hear!"

Maggie smiled a small smile. "All right," she said. "Only get me a hot whiskey, pronto. And make it a double. Or I'll cry."

Three hot whiskeys later and by a roaring fire, Eddie was making her laugh like a drain. Maggie was seriously enjoying herself. It was true that she would probably not have got a better interview if she'd sat down with Gabriel himself. Garbriel Kelly was notoriously prickly and temperamental with the press, whereas Eddie Mannion his agent was an absolute scream.

"Where did you grow up in Ireland, Eddie?" Maggie asked. "I'm trying to place your accent."

"Oh, for God's sake, don't even try! I've been putting on voices since the day I was born."

"Where?"

"Oh, Galway, then Mayo, then college in Dublin. I spent years pretending to be a woman too."

"Yeah? Me too!" said Maggie happily, waving at the waiter for another round.

"Such a small country, Ireland, isn't it?" said Eddie. "Now, seeing as it's nearly lunchtime, shall we have champagne?"

Maggie beamed while Eddie ordered Veuve Clicquot.

"What did you study at college?" asked Maggie, watching Eddie wolf down cashew nuts.

"Drama," Eddie sighed. "What else? University of Dublin. Isabella Somerfield was in my year."

"Isabella Somerfield? The daytime TV presenter? No! No way!" Maggie shrieked, and clinked her champagne glass against his. "I know her! She and her partner Harry are great friends of mine." Maggie judiciously didn't add that the only reason that she really knew Isabella Somerfield was because she'd once been a very regular booty call for Isabella's partner Harry. In fact, Maggie knew well that Isabella would rather have died than accept that she and Maggie were anything remotely like great friends.

"Well, small world again," said Eddie. "You know, Isabella's the reason Gabriel became famous, in a roundabout way."

"Oh, tell me all about it," purred Maggie, clicking on her tape recorder.

"Well, I was directing *The Playboy of the Western World* in New York and Isabella played Pegeen Mike. And Gabriel was playing Widow Quinn – in drag. It was my idea – and he was a sensation –"

"Oh, so Gabriel *is* gay then," Maggie interrupted.

"*No!* Of course not," Eddie said. "He's single and looking for someone special. And turn that fucking thing off!" He clicked the tape recorder and handed it to Maggie.

"Look, let's forget about the interview and just have a proper chat," Maggie said quickly, shoving the tape recorder in her bag. "You're absolutely right to protect Gabriel's privacy. His sexuality isn't the kind of thing I care about anyway. *Scoop!* doesn't do scandal. And I'm only interested in the film. It's so marvellous to have a Golden Globe nomination for your first leading role. And the press can be such a pain, can't they, making up all sorts of things just to sell copy?" She gave him her most winsome smile. *Scoop!* didn't do scandal – but Maggie had several other irons in other fires, and there were plenty of rags where she was owed favours from editors so she could sell a freelance on without a by-line.

"Oh, well. You know how things are in Hollywood," Eddie said, shrugging his wide shoulders. "There's no such thing as gay."

"Oh, I'm sure that will all change soon. So, tell me more about the connection with Isabella?" asked Maggie, sensing that this might be a way of getting Eddie back on her side again. "I'm so, *so* fond of her," she added, sighing poignantly and pouring him more champagne.

"Well," Eddie began, "Isabella was going through some emotional turmoil that summer –" He looked at Maggie.

"Oh, I know," Maggie said, managing to sound sincere. "She told me all about it, poor darling. I don't know what she'd have done if I hadn't been there for her," she said, lying with aplomb.

"Nor I! Poor little lamb!" said Eddie, finishing the bottle of champagne and waving for another. "But, knowing Iz, she managed to turn it around for herself and played the Pegeen role with so much pathos that the reviews were just astonishing – well, I'm sure you know about all that," he added, and Maggie smiled winningly.

"Oh, absolutely," she said. "But you were saying something about Gabriel?"

"Isabella's performance made the play the absolute highlight of off-Broadway that fall – cue one casting director who comes to the performance one night and spots Gabriel and gives him the part of Johnny Champion in the just-about-to-become a massive hit TV series *Chicago South*, and the rest, as you know, is history."

"So," Maggie said, "thanks to a great theatre director, i.e. you, Eddie Mannion, Gabriel Kelly who is an unknown off-Broadway actor from Offaly manages to get one of the biggest TV roles in America overnight, and then a year later lands the leading role in Martin Scorsese's new film, *Blood Not Tears*. Mmmm. You must be a wonderful publicist to be able to get an actor's career moving that swiftly, Eddie." This was going pretty well, Maggie thought, eyeing Eddie carefully to see if the flattery was working. With a bit of luck she'd get him to talk more and see how thin these gay rumours really were.

Eddie beamed. "Oh, you know. Luck has a lot to do with it. But I am pretty good at my job."

"So, any more directing now?" Maggie looked over the rim of her glass at him.

"Well," said Eddie, "I'll go back to theatre eventually I guess, but for the moment, Gabriel's earning half a million dollars an episode for *Chicago South*, and *Blood Not Tears* earned him two million dollars this year, and as his agent and publicity consultant I'm on twenty percent – so you do the math."

"I'll have another drink then," beamed Maggie. "What a pity that he isn't here. I was so looking forward to meeting him. But it's so lovely to catch up with old friends." This small-world stuff was definitely going to get Eddie out of his box, Maggie decided. There's nothing as shallow as an Irishman abroad.

"Oh, he's in such a pickle at the moment he doesn't know what to do," Eddie said distractedly.

"Ah, God help him!" Maggie sighed, pouring Eddie more champagne. She didn't want to push him too much but she felt that whatever was up with Gabriel was something that Eddie was on the verge of telling her.

"He's got a lot of stuff that he's got to figure out," Eddie said, swallowing back his drink. "Shall we get some sandwiches? I'm starving!"

Maggie thought carefully about her next moves while Eddie ordered a giant plate of smoked salmon with crab claws in garlic butter, and prawn sandwiches with lemon mayonnaise and sweet potato chips. She was going to have to keep Eddie in confiding mode, without him having the slightest clue that she was milking him.

"It's so difficult, isn't it, when you know something desperately private about a friend, and you can't share it with anyone," she ventured. "I do sympathise with you."

"Thing is," said Eddie forking smoked salmon into his mouth, "this is the kind of PR stuff I'm not sure how to handle either. It's a bit of a rock and a hard place."

"About Gabriel being secretly gay?" asked Maggie in a soft voice, dipping a sweet potato chip into the lemon mayonnaise with one hand and sliding the other hand into her handbag at the same time, rummaging as silently as possible for the tape recorder.

"God, no! To be honest, Gabriel doesn't really give a fuck about that. It'll all come out eventually, and neither of us really cares. It's just that we just really need the Golden Globes to be over though, because those selection committees are some really picky bastards. And we'll get a very lovely and willing young lady to escort him up the red carpet and pretend to be in love with him – in true Hollywood homophobic style, as I'm sure you know."

"Hollywood's most eligible bachelor?"

"Exactly. No, what Gabriel's really in a tizz about is some kind of heavy family stuff. About his background. Nothing scandalous to him, but potentially scandalous to someone else, and a tricky PR stunt for me to pull off."

"Gosh! Poor you." Maggie was watching him like a hawk. With one hand in her handbag she'd finally located the button on her tape-recorder, and prayed hard that it was the record button. "I know exactly what you must be going through."

18

"You do?" Eddie looked astonished.

"Well, yes. Of course. I mean, take our mutual friends Harry and Isabella – they've got a little boy, haven't they? But their son is actually Harry's love child, isn't he? A kid that he had via someone else? And so Harry keeps it quiet because of his career in politics. And to protect Iz."

"Oh, you know all about that?" asked Eddie, "Oh, you and Iz are obviously great friends if she's told you all about Harry's child."

"Oh, potential political scandals are so tricky to manage, aren't they? I mean, children by other relationships, very painful." She checked Eddie's reaction carefully over the rim of her champagne glass.

"Well, that's exactly why I'm so worried about this story getting out about Gabriel," he said.

Maggie could see that she had him now. Hook, line, and sinker, Eds.

"A secret shared is a burden halved," she murmured – and a nice little story that will put hundreds of thousands of copies on the shelves, Maggie thought, offering Eddie her most empathetic, eyelash-batting smile.

"Of course I know about that kind of thing," Maggie said in a hushed voice. "I was the *only* one who knew that Harry had had a baby with someone else. It was me who had to tell him that the baby had been born. I'm just so glad," she went on with a sigh, "that he got to hear it from me, and not from someone else."

"The thing for Gabriel is that he's adopted," said Eddie, "which is no big deal. But this week, he received a letter from the adoption agency in Ireland telling him that his birth mother wants to contact him. And, it so happens that his birth mother is someone very well-known – who just happened to be a penniless student when Gabriel was born."

"Oh," said Maggie, trying desperately not to sound disappointed. "Well, I'm sure it won't cause too much of a scandal when it gets out." Tragically for me, she added privately to herself. What a crap secret. It'll be a scoop for about five minutes in Ballyporeen. Unless . . . "Um. Who is Gabriel's birth mother then?"

"Gabriel's birth mother is Nola Connaughton, and his birth father is Pierce Fox."

"Nola Connaughton, the Tánaiste? And Pierce Fox, the tycoon who now owns Leinster Bank and is trying to buy up Jet Éire? Oh, I *see*!" Maggie almost whistled and then remembered that she was supposed to be comforting Eddie. "But," she added dropping her voice by several tones, "I can't see how that might be difficult – for Gabriel. I mean, wouldn't it *help* his career if he were known to be associated with fame and fortune?"

"It might – although Gabriel's always traded on the idea of an impoverished Irish boy from a farm in Offaly who rose to fame through hard work on the stage – so a new story of a guy who was actually potentially born into privilege won't help that image. But the main problem is that it won't suit Pierce Fox or Nola Connaughton in the slightest if the story gets out. Nola wants to be in touch with Gabriel, but she can't be seen to have anything to do with Pierce Fox. It would damage her politically to be connected with Fox. She's married now with several children, as you know, to the director of Jet Éire, and *he* definitely doesn't want anyone to know that she once gave a baby away when she was a nineteen-year-old. He's terribly private about his family and keeps completely away from the press. And as for Fox, he's such a controversial character at the moment with his buying up failing banks and airlines and banning trade unions and sacking all those staff – it mightn't really suit *him* to suddenly become the headline because of a son he abandoned thirty years ago. Pierce Fox trades on nothing if not his personality."

"I see," Maggie said. "And so Gabriel's upset – because?"

"Well, how do you think all of that would make him feel? He's been very happily adopted and adores his parents in Offaly but this potential political stink has raked his sense of abandonment up for him again, and he's having a complete emotional meltdown." Eddie rolled his eyes and drained his glass.

"Yes," said Maggie, her mind whirring as fast as the tape-recorder she touched with electric fingers in her handbag. "It's a painful situation. But hopefully one that's ultimately filled with joy." She eyed Eddie carefully again. "Gabriel's so lucky to have you for a friend, Eddie."

"Yes, he is rather," Eddie chuckled. "Now all I've got to do is to get the big drama queen to put a brave face on things and face the press. I can trust you though, Maggie, can't I, that the stuff about his birth parents will go absolutely nowhere? And I'll make sure you get some gorgeous photographs of Gabriel – nice, intimate ones of him at home – that are exclusive to *Scoop!*. That's the least that I can do."

"That *would* be lovely," Maggie smiled. "And the least that I can do is make sure that the story we write about Gabriel is the one that's absolutely what you want." And she crossed her fingers tightly behind her back.

Now all she had to do was to get back to Ireland as quickly as possible, and do whatever it took to get an interview with Pierce Fox.

Chapter Three

Doctor Marina de Barra figured that she hadn't really been away from Inish Rua in twenty years – not for a proper long break, anyway. Oh, there had been a camping trip in France when the kids were small, when she'd managed to get a locum who'd drunk the pub dry and she'd had to come back early to rescue the island from a man who suddenly became far more dangerous to the people of the island than the wild Black Cliffs where visitors often tumbled or the stormy seas where boats capsized. And there had been a trip to Lourdes with her mother when the palpitations had come back which had been very fruitful as her mother had felt very holy when she'd died – but the trip had been very short. A weekend, really. Marina's mother Bridie had had a heart attack right in front of the Grotto – but she'd gone straight to heaven, Sister Mary Immaculata of the Everlasting Saviour who'd accompanied the trip had assured her.

And so Marina felt, packing a small suitcase (which

needed a good clean, really – up on the top of the wardrobe everything got covered in dust eventually, but on the other hand, why bother? It's not as if anyone would really notice, where she'd be going), that going away for this long *was* going to be a proper holiday, no matter what happened. Three months was a good long break, anyway. Three months – Marina paused, examining a pair of tights that had a small hole.

It was actually a hell of a long time to leave the island. In fact, bar the two-week camping trip cut short by the adventures of Doctor Branigan in Tí Jimmy Seán's pub, she and Gearóid had never left the island together since they'd first married. And, bar the one brief trip to Lourdes, she'd never left Gearóid on his own. Any little trips to the mainland had been made together. Day trips mainly. Like going to Dermot's graduation, or Suzanne's exhibition at the Better Homes.

There was always the problem of getting a good locum. Sam Smith from the mainland would always come over with the life boat, but she hated having to ask. Sam was busy enough in the summer with visitors in the village, and in the winter the weather was foul. Inish Rua didn't have a landing strip for aeroplanes, and the only aircraft that could land was the helicopter that belonged to Pierce Fox. And Marina would no more ask him a favour than she'd eat her own head.

The pair of tights had another hole – just beside the gusset. Marina sat down heavily on the bed and poked her finger through it. The thing was, most of the time she didn't give much of a stuff about things like holey tights – who did, on Inish Rua? Sure, Páidin Mike might get two boxes of tights into the post-office shop all winter, and then you might ask someone who'd be going ashore to get you something from the Spar or even from the big town but most of the time there'd be no call for it. Yvonne Delahunty, who took in Gaeltacht students in her bungalow, was great for the Internet shopping, Páidin Mike said, admiring the frequent boxes with customs notices that said things like *Lingerie*, or *Ladies' Garments* that arrived from England and New York, but Marina wasn't sure. Yvonne always looked quite glamorous it had to be said, and Marina had wistfully watched her serve inedible meals to miserable teenagers in a cashmere twinset from Browns London, washing up afterwards in a floral Cath Kidston pinny with bright pink rubber gloves that swished around the sparkling foam. But Marina's job involved hopping over dry stone walls to visit grumbly farmers on the hillside, or hiking up a blackthorny lane to a thatched cottage where the only water was from a rain-catcher out the back and what good would a good pair of tights be then? It's wellies that you'd need.

Nevertheless, a good pair of tights under her one pair of high-heeled suede boots would be a nice thing to arrive in with that long velvet skirt she had and hardly ever wore. Marina pursed her lips and wondered if a bit of a darn would be out of the question at this hour of the morning. But then the thought of getting out a needle and thread – of course, she *could* ask Mrs Freeman to do it for her but Marina wasn't sure that she could face one of Mrs Freeman's looks again. Oh, to hell with it. She'd wear a good clean pair of jeans and polish her Christmas shoes instead.

She stood up to lift the shoebox down off the top of the wardrobe, and caught sight of her frazzled expression in the dressing-table mirror. Her heart sank again. An open-pored corned-beef complexion that needed more and more foundation every time she went to repair it. Black hair streaked with a sorrowful wintry grey. Hair that was as dry as seaweed on an August shore and looked every bit as attractive, thought Marina glumly tucking a bunch of it behind her ears. Her fingers still shook ever so slightly, no matter how many Xanax she took in the mornings this weather. She stretched out her hands in front of her to see if she could keep them still. Marina hadn't been able to remove her wedding and engagement rings in years so they pinched around her sausage-shaped fingers, making them look like the knuckle-dusters on a bouncer. Brittle nails. Hadn't seen a bottle of nail polish since – oh, for God's sake, stop bloody moaning, woman! She put her hands down out of sight again and inspected her face instead. She tried to smile at herself but the grimace that looked back at her almost frightened her – her teeth looked yellow grey in the wintry light.

"You look like a fecking Hallowe'en witch," Marina told herself, and then reached out to her crumpled make-up bag and took out an ancient Estée Lauder lipstick in a garish fire-engine red. With fingers that she steadied as carefully as if she were performing brain surgery she drew a ferocious-looking cherry-lipstick smile onto her still-generous mouth, and then fixed a black-velvet Alice band around her hair and shook it out. There! A bit better, maybe. She brushed some of the dust off the suitcase with the holey tights and then put them in the laundry basket to wash – no point in darning tights for future wear if they were still all dust.

"Gearóid, I'm off! Give me a hand to the harbour!" Marina roared out of the window to her husband.

Gearóid de Barra turned lugubriously towards the

house from where he was stirring compost at the bottom of the garden.

The wind was icy out this morning, thought Marina, shivering with the window open, and it's only the first of November. We are in for a hell of a winter. Across the fields from her cottage she could see the white horses on the sea. Bloody awful crossing I'm going to have too.

"Did you hear me, you deaf prick? It's freezing out – are you ready for the boat?" she yelled again, and slammed the window shut.

Gearóid leaned his spade against the dry stone wall and tucked his jumper into his jeans.

Three months was a hell of a long time for Marina De Barra to be leaving the island – Las Vegas or no Las Vegas.

Chapter Four

Pierce Fox leaned over towards the window to admire the view out of the window of his private jet as it tilted sharply up and away from London City airport towards the west.

"Gin and tonic?" he asked Gemma, his new and rather tight-lipped legal assistant, flipping open the door of the minibar and flashing her a brilliant smile.

Gemma flushed a delightful shade of pink and eventually replied, "Just a little one, please."

"No such thing as little now you're with your Uncle Pierce," beamed Fox, splashing tonic into three fingers of gin and handing it into her lap, so that he could then drop his hand in between her knees and slide it up her thigh.

Gemma jumped and splashed her drink.

"Aw! Now look, you've spilt it," said Pierce and removed a silk handkerchief from his breast-pocket so that he could rove around her knees again. Such a shame that she was wearing jeans.

"Feeling nervous?" Pierce clinked his own glass against

Gemma's and slugged his drink. She really was very interesting, this new one, with her Oxford law degree and her post-graduate degree in European Studies. Smart women turned Pierce on. He couldn't quite explain it, but they did. They always seemed so – well, so *grateful*. And he just adored these uptight kinds of girls, with their colt-like nervousness and trembling thighs.

And this young one – with her long straight mousy hair and spectacles, oh, it was irresistible.

Pierce turned his face towards her, pinning her with his eyes so that she could lip-read above the noise of the helicopter. "Tell me where you grew up, Jenny."

"Er. Newbury. And it's *Gemma*," she whispered, blushing rosily again.

He loved the way her lower lip trembled when she spoke. "Newbury! Great race meetings. Ever been to Ireland before, then?"

Gemma shook her head, peeking through the windows where the view below was changing from urban grey to green.

"I'm very excited about it. I'm sure it's going to be very special, Pierce," she said.

Pierce swallowed back his gin and watched the carpet of green spreading out between thick clouds. No matter where he lived in the world, he still adored the idea of coming home. "Ireland is a very special place. You'll love it there – only my best assistants get to come out with me. Would you like me to top up your drink? I hope you're not too cold – here, let me stop your hands from shaking." He took both of her hands in his, and lifted them to his mouth to blow on them, holding her eyes with his gaze all the time.

Gemma gulped.

"Such a lovely face – how old did you say you were?"

"Twenty-eight," she breathed.

"Well, I'm going to look after you so well this week. Look, why don't you come out to the island with me this weekend and we can put our preliminary ideas for the Jet Éire proposal together out there, just the two of us? I've got a lovely house on Inish Rua, you see. And you can help me work and meet the residents of Míle Cairde – that's the artists' colony I've set up. Oh, they're an interesting lot." Pierce chuckled. "All the writers and artists and musicians. Very talented people. Lots of fun." He winked at her.

"Famous people?" Gemma widened her eyes. "Like celebrities? Like – Bono?"

"Often. Bands come out to write albums, famous writers come out to write, famous artists to seek inspiration, conductors, fiddle players. All of that." He kissed her fingertips. "I don't bring many of my girls out here. Just the special ones." He hooked his fingers around hers and purred into her hair.

"Just for the weekend?" she said, gasping as his breath tickled her neck.

"Yes," he sighed, thinking how much it turned him on when women squirmed. "Probably. I've got to be in Moscow on Tuesday. And I want you to get this merger deal put together by then." Fox dropped her fingers and swirled his drink idly around in his glass. He'd have to make sure he got the bulk of the work out of her before he bedded her though – this Jet Éire takeover bid was probably his last chance to find a way out of the credit crunch and he was going to have to make it work. At least he wasn't going to get anything wrong in the legalities of the bid this time – this Gemma one, with her background in European law, was definitely the right person to have on his team. And he'd have no trouble getting her into bed when he'd got the legal work sorted out. In Pierce's experience, if you got them too excited too early in the game, they often didn't get the work done accurately at all.

"Anyway. Cheers, sweetheart! Here's to a great working relationship. And to Inish Rua! Bottoms up!" he winked, and Gemma blushed as magnificently as a West of Ireland sunset. The jet lurched into some turbulence and tilted, allowing him to wrap his arm around her shoulders and squeeze them tight enough to make sure he'd got a good handful of her right breast.

"Whoops! Don't worry, we'll be landing soon," Pierce beamed.

The other thing was that it would be lovely to have a few days on the island after all this legal work was completed, even in this mad weather. He was pretty tired, really, sorting out these fucking banking acquisitions and making sure he kept on top of those two government ministers who were a pair of complete wankers but were cautiously supporting him – thank God he had Nola Connaughton the Tánaiste on his side, though, or none of it would have worked. Pierce had never been one to shirk the idea of a nice healthy financial donation to a struggling government that was plummeting out of favour in mid-term office, and till this year his fondness for the Galway Races and a variety of race meetings in Britain, not to forget the golfing tournaments in America, had won him success in pretty much any business venture he had wanted. But this year – oh, everything was bloody different. The coalition government was so much weaker now, and some of the ministers were frankly just a bunch of pussies when it came to taking on the unions and the morons in the press. Pierce found himself wondering sometimes if he'd be better off to run for political office himself. But politics was really premier cru wankology, as far as he was concerned. Politics was where the failures in farming ended up. And as for journalism – that was for failed lawyers. Jesus, in the old days a journalist knew which side his bread was buttered on.

But the fact that Pierce owned a good number of international newspapers and magazines meant that he didn't have to put up with too much bullshit, or too much so-called investigative nonsense made up by some beardy lefty who had a first from Trinity and a fourth in life. Pierce Fox had done Commerce at UCD. He'd left school at seventeen, got a pass degree and had made his first million by the age of twenty-two, selling holes. The holes were an example of entrepreneurship, and they were the example Pierce used now if he ever got to make a speech when he went to collect one of his honorary degrees. He'd say three things, every time those dickhead professors handed him out the next honorary degree, smiling insincerely at him, their lack-lustre eyes full of bitterness. He'd say that he'd never done very well at university so he felt very honoured to receive a doctorate from one so laudable as Professor-whoever-you-are-so-and-so, but that he was delighted to accept it, because the one thing *he'd* learnt that university couldn't have taught him was that no amount of studying and taking exams could compare to the experience of making a profit out of something that someone else wanted and at the same time providing someone else's family with a job. And the other thing he'd say in his speech is that he made his first million selling holes because even in a recession there's a profit to be made.

Pierce had set up his first business, *Spy-door-man* which sold spy holes for people's doors in 1989 on the cusp of a major crime wave and heroin epidemic in Dublin, and he had never looked back.

He'd made his real money out of property speculation in the nineties and buying up state companies that were privatised in the noughties, and then he'd made a killing on insurance claims post 9/11. And then there were his businesses in Eastern Europe after the Balkans crisis, which were controversial, it had to be said – but then, in every crisis there's opportunity was what Pierce Fox always believed. And the contracts for the new Iraqi enterprises were just too lucrative to turn down.

And now there was this situation with Jet Éire that was like a wet dream come true, Pierce thought, enjoying the way Gemma's neck blushed so prettily when he'd told her not to worry about the turbulence in the aeroplane. Thanks to the massive drop in travel from Ireland due to job losses followed by public sector pay cuts, the Icelandic volcano, and then a series of strikes in British airports, Jet Éire was going for an absolute song. It would only take an hour or two to go through the legal documents that Gemma had drawn up for the take-over bid. Pierce did like to read everything he signed. It was what had given him his edge. He trusted no one, especially not those closest to him.

But this one was a peach.

"Would you like to go through your schedule for the next three days, Mr Fox?" Gemma was asking him in a tremulous voice.

"Bring it on!" he said, closing his eyes.

"Well, I thought tonight we could go through the first part of this proposal document from the CEO of Leinster Bank and see what you think of it, and then I wondered if tomorrow morning we should have a conference call with the Minister for Finance, the General Secretary of the Congress of Trades Unions and the Tánaiste about the no-union agreement we've struck . . ."

"Uh. Boring," Pierce interjected. Ugh. He didn't really want to have to deal with Nola Connaughton. If there was one thing he didn't need in this business deal it was emotional baggage. But thankfully Nola wanted to be as hands-off as he did – which was making the whole deal much easier to control too, if the government didn't really get involved.

"Well," Gemma carried on, "would you prefer me to set up a conference call with the American Ambassador and the Chairman of Chase Manhattan Bank –"

"Oh, no, forget about him. I got him sorted out during a squash game. Useless backhand, too. You'd never think." Pierce rattled the ice-cubes in his drink, imagining Gemma might look rather good in a French maid's outfit. That sexy-secretary poker-straight hair was great.

"Oh," she said. "In that case, um. Well, there was another request we got which might have legal implications which is from a journalist called Maggie Hennelly. Apparently she's a great admirer of yours and wants to write your official autobiography. She's requested a meeting with you in Ireland."

"Huh," Pierce grunted. More shite from lefty journalists. And then he remembered that Maggie Hennelly was – well, wasn't she the very pretty redhead who used to do society stuff in one of his Sundays? He opened up one eye. "What does she look like?"

Gemma looked furiously through her notes. "She – er – she –"

"Oh, what the hell." Pierce closed his eye again. "Set her up. Give her a bell when we've hit dry land. Writer, eh? Tell you what. Get her over to Atlantis House. I could do with a bit of a distraction. Autobiography? Mmm. That mightn't be a bad idea at this point in time. Who do we know in publishing? Get me an agent. We'll need a proper deal before I'll consider. Oh, and find her photograph. And then tie her into an editorial control deal so that she has no rights over the final book."

"All right," said Gemma nervously. "So, I'll ring Chase Manhattan first, and then I'll ring her people–"

"No, ring Chase Manhattan later on tonight. It's five a.m. in America now," Pierce interjected. He might be dozing off after the drinks but he didn't miss a beat.

"Yes. Of course I will. Thank you, Pierce. I'll ring her people first, and set something up. Did you say 'get her over to Atlantis'?"

"Yes."

"The house on the island? Now? I mean, during our – your – our stay there? While you – while we're out there?"

"Well, she's a writer, isn't she? And she's going to write a book about me, which I will then appear to have written myself. It's a writers' and artists' retreat. I thought she might like to join the party." He sat up to peer out the window. "Look! We're over the open sea now. We'll be landing in a minute." He smiled and winked again at Gemma's far-too-serious face.

She's so goddamned jumpy now, but I bet I'll be able to

34

persuade her to go for a threesome by the time I've got old Maggie over, he thought happily to himself. And he began to hum "*If I had Maggie In the Wood, I'd Do Her All The Good I Could,*" very softly to himself. If there was one thing Pierce Fox had learnt from business, it was that the easiest way to get what you wanted with a woman was to either make her grateful or humiliated. And with Maggie and Gemma on Inish Rua for a weekend, he could probably do both.

Chapter Five

Amy Shanahan sat in her kitchen in Churchtown in the southern suburbs of Dublin and tried desperately to find the other sock. Amy's kitchen was at the front of the little three-bed terrace, a relatively modern idea in new-builds of the early nineties which Amy and Terence had originally decided to convince themselves was charming when they'd had to move here from their luxury five-bed detached in Foxrock – oh, look, we can sit here in the evenings with the children and look out onto the street! Wave at all the neighbours who pass by, what a lovely idea, and the gorgeous little sitting room at the back with big patio doors straight onto the garden, just right for entertaining!

Nowadays, Amy's biggest nightmare was trying to keep muddy shoes from wrecking the ludicrously pale pink carpet in the gorgeous sitting room that very foolishly opened onto the back garden and not the street. Having discovered that the neighbouring children were an unprecedented variety of bully (the little boy next door had actually tried to *hang*

Amy's youngest child from a tree when she was only one) the over-landscaped tiny little backyard-stroke-outdoor-entertainment-area was the only space for Holly and June to play. Outdoor entertainment, had it ever crossed Amy's mind it would be in any way feasible, would have to have been arranged to coincide with the large-scale removal of a filthy clutter of plastic broken toys, headless Barbies, a paddling pool full of mud and leaves and a rusty swing.

But Amy's main task at the moment was the retrieval of an errant sock – not just any old sock but a Bart Simpson sock. Why do socks always disappear, she thought, whenever you are under pressure to be – and God knows why I do this to myself because at the moment it seems hardly worth it – a perfect mum? Why is it that even though I now have a stay-at-home husband, whenever I try to get the tiniest bit of time to myself to do anything that's just for *me,* something goes wrong, as if to prove the necessity of my being here permanently chained to this bloody front-of-house kitchen?

"How does it happen *every time*?" Amy howled, mostly to herself, but also to the pile of clean laundry she'd just removed from the dryer, to the street, to the Universe, and then she noticed the two small worried faces of Holly and June peering at her from the doorway.

"Don't cry again, Mummy," said Holly, looking rather terrified. "Please don't cry. Have you and Daddy had another fight?"

"Mo more ky. Mo more fight," added June helpfully, offering Amy her salivated soother.

"Oh, darlings, I'm so sorry! I didn't mean to upset you!" Amy crouched down and opened her arms to hug the two girls into her breast. They nestled happily against her neck. "Silly Mummy has just lost a sock, and I'm going to have to find it again."

"Maybe you posted it," suggested Holly solemnly, peering into the empty dryer. "We can open up the machine, I think."

June had had a very problematic experience recently with the toaster when she'd posted all of Amy's credit cards into it – but Terence had sat down with a screwdriver and explained, in a voice that Amy found increasingly tedious now that she had to listen to it all day long, that although you must never post anything into a machine, clever daddies can fix anything if they try.

"Well, darling, I'm not sure it's as easy to take apart as the toaster was, but we'll find it," said Amy, rummaging through the laundry basket in despair. "The Sock Fairy must have taken it and so we are just going to have to ask her to bring it back." How come, even though Terence isn't working, hasn't worked for months, and has single-handedly appointed himself as chief parent – supposedly allowing me, as the only one of us bringing in an income, all the time I need to write my book – how come I'm still the one who has to look for socks?

Holly looked very doubtful. Amy seemed, to Holly, to be rather gullible sometimes. Holly was beginning to seriously doubt the generosity of the Tooth Fairy ever since her friend Kareem's second tooth fell out and the Tooth Fairy forgot to come three nights in a row. It was only when Kareem's granny came to visit from Birmingham at the weekend that the Tooth Fairy had remembered to turn up – and her rate of payment for lost teeth had distinctly come down since tooth number one. And then, there were rumours going around at school about the true origins of

Santa Claus – but Holly wasn't going to go there. She had it all figured out, where Santa Claus really came from, and she wasn't going to have him busted. Not to a bunch of babies in school who thought it was a magical person who lived in Lapland.

Holly had decided to share her insight with Kareem who was a Muslim and therefore seemed to Holly to be very holy. "Baby Jesus was a saint," Kareem explained to Holly once on the quiet, "but he wasn't really a real *god*." Holly had thought that that was fair enough. There was a lot of stuff they told you in school that was a bit of a stretch.

"It's your mother and father who buy the presents," Kareem explained in a hushed but knowledgeable voice. "*My* mother told me that."

"You're wrong," Holly told Kareem over a Marmite sandwich at playtime. "There's just no way my mother and father would buy all of that stuff for us at Christmas time, every year. It costs way too much! They're always fighting about money. My daddy would *never* spend a load of money on a huge big load toys for me and June every year, just like that, 'cos he told Mummy that she'd better stop spending money on shite like hairdressers and Marks and Spencers tights or he'd fucking walk right out. Think about it, Kareem – a Barbie *and* a DVD, *and* a load of bricks and a car for June and clothes and story books. But," she looked about her conspiratorially, "I've figured out where it really comes from." She looked around her and then whispered, "It's the Dublin Corporation. They *deliver* all the stuff."

"Yeah?"

"Yeah. Look, Kareem." Holly began to count on her

fingers. "They deliver the post. They collect the bins. They sent a guy around last month to collect the telly from the sitting room 'cos it was going to the place where orphans live. And so they bring the Christmas presents and they tell you it's from Santa Claus. But don't tell my parents, because I don't think they actually know where it comes from. I wouldn't want to spoil Christmas for them. They get upset about things, a lot."

And that was the end of that.

"Darlings, do you think you can both play out the back for a while? Mummy's got a lot of little things to do –"

Amy was about to finish, "before I go away" but then she stopped abruptly. She and Terence had both (eventually) agreed that she wasn't going to tell the girls.

Amy thought that this was pretty daft – no, appalling really, to try to pretend that she hadn't gone away. It was bizarre. It was all to do with Terence's bloody ego. And so she and Terence had had another blazing row that involved stage whispers in the middle of the night, frozen backs turned to one another in the king-sized bed and swollen eyelids over breakfast. They'd find out anyway if she lied to them, and then they'd feel even more betrayed, surely, she had sobbed. And besides, Holly was far too clever to be lied to any more – she'd spot the deceit and feel doubly hurt that Amy was both going away for a fortnight *and* hiding it from her.

But Terence was adamant that the girls shouldn't be given any opportunity to mourn Amy's departure. He was convinced that they should wake up and find that they were going to have a lovely long day with their daddy, just with him, and then another, and another and so on – and by the time they'd got around to figuring that Amy wasn't actually there, well, she'd be back by then. It was only two weeks that she'd be gone for anyway. He'd take them to McDonald's every night – Amy shuddered at the thought – and to his mother's house, and the park, and the zoo and to a friend's house and they'd hardly notice her being gone.

Amy crossed her fingers and gave in. Sometimes, you just had to know when you were beat.

Privately she knew of course that it was a ridiculous strategy. The girls would figure straight away that she'd disappeared and the fact that they didn't know anything in advance about it would make them even more insecure – but Amy wasn't up to arguing with Terence any more.

It had been so difficult to persuade him to agree to this two-week break at a writers' retreat that she'd been awarded – a prize for a short-story competition in a Sunday supplement magazine! – that she was prepared to accept whatever crazy conditions he wanted to attach to it just to get away. The writers' retreat was called Míle Cairde – 'a thousand friends'.

It was on an island – Inish Rua – the island off the west coast of Ireland owned by Pierce Fox, the equities tycoon who was all over the news for the past two years since he'd tried to buy up several Irish and UK banks that were struggling with bankruptcy during the credit crunch. It was thanks to Pierce Fox that three Irish banks had been rescued by his massive injection of equity capital – but the following year, forty per cent of bank staff, including Terence, had been laid off.

It was thanks to Pierce Fox that the shares in two of the banks had all been bought up at minimal prices and then, following a hatchet job on salaries and a massive government cash injection, publicly floated with an immediate gain of sixty per cent, almost overnight.

For some, Pierce Fox was a saviour – those who had held onto savings that had otherwise seemed certain to end in unpaid pensions without his investment. To others – equity brokers like Amy's husband Terence who'd lost their jobs, and shareholders who'd bought shares in the bank which had mysteriously sunk to an absolute low after Fox had bought it up – Pierce Fox was the devil.

But the most important thing to Amy about Pierce Fox now was that he owned Inish Rua.

Amy had Googled Inish Rua and read everything she could on it. The island was thought to be associated with the Celtic warrior goddess, Andraste, but a monastery was founded there by Saint Tristan in the eighth century – the year 702 approximately, according to Wikipedia. Then, in the nineteenth century, under the ownership of Lord Ardross who'd owned large parts of Scotland and several Hebridean islands as well, the island was populated by almost five hundred people. But the famine tore it apart.

Lord Ardross, however, was a charitable aristocrat who decided to refrain from charging his tenants any more rents during the Great Hunger in the 1840s and instead provided work for them in the form of having a large stately home built for himself on the island – a so-called "famine folly" i.e. an unnecessary building project initiated solely in order to provide work. The house took twenty-seven years to complete, mostly due to ghastly weather that blew several roofs off until they could find the right kind of lead that would stay on in all kinds of wind, and the desperately unhealthy conditions of the builders who were struggling to feed their families and to stay alive themselves.

In the 1880s he became a follower of William Morris's

Arts and Crafts movement and encouraged such activities on the island.

Despite all of that, Lord Ardross never actually lived on Inish Rua. The house remained empty but serviced by a flock of loyal tenants who continued to live and work on the island rent-free, protected by Lord Ardross's will (he died of natural causes during the Great War) that *"no tenant who ploughed or worked the land of Inish Rua or who sang or brought a poem or could fashion a piece of wood or canvas a thing of beauty to adorn the place would ever be charged for his contribution to the peacefulness of the isle"*.

Following the War of Independence, the island had become the property of the Free State and then the Republic – until 1989. Then, in the middle of the worst recession in thirty years, with emigration from Ireland almost rivalling that of the famine years, the government, under the leadership of a prime minister who was desperately fond of Pierce Fox, having been a great chum of his at school and a happy recipient of Pierce's generous political donations, sold him the island.

Pierce Fox bought the island for a million Irish punts – which seemed like a very extravagant thing to do in 1989. The newspapers were full of stories about the romantic businessman who had made a huge amount of money in the Middle East and had decided to "invest it all in Ireland". Investing in Ireland meant, to Pierce Fox, buying up Inish Rua for an absolute song. He would have a home in Ireland but remain a tax exile in the Seychelles.

To date, Pierce Fox had never actually charged the tenants rent, but the mere threat of the possibility that he could at a whim change his mind hung like a menace over the island's inhabitants – and during the Celtic Tiger years with property prices rocketing all over Ireland and twee holiday homes fetching millionaire prices, it hung like a not-too-distant rumble of thunder. But, so far they were still living there rent-free – albeit under Pierce Fox's thumb. Fox visited the island every so often, Wikipedia said, mostly to enjoy the free-spirited atmosphere of the Míle Cairde Writers And Artists' Retreat which attracted international writers, painters and musicians to study and work in a supportive environment. The retreat was housed in the original famine-folly great house built by Lord Ardross, the grandly named Atlantis House. Pierce Fox, when he came to stay, had a suite of rooms on the top floor, overlooking the lake.

The night before she left, Amy had scrutinised the website for *Míle Cairde Artists At Atlantis* once again.

She swished her browser over the pages of photographs of the majestic but terrifyingly steep twin mountains, rising like a dragon's mane out of the wicked sea. In between the ferocious peaks there was a scattering of chocolate-box thatched white cottages and an ink-black lake scowling at the bottom of a kelly-green glen. At the top end of the valley, surrounded by a copse of trees whose growth was only possible because they sheltered in between the hills, Atlantis House sat magnificently like a god.

Swishing her browser through the page marked *Grand House,* Amy sighed for the umpteenth time over the rooms that were sumptuously decorated as a dedication to artistic endeavour. Each resident was given his or her own suite of rooms – a study or studio to paint in, or a music room depending on the profession. Amy was writing her second novel. The first had been a surprisingly fortunate bestseller but she was yet to receive her first royalty cheque. She was finding it impossible to concentrate with Holly coming in from school full of chatter at half past one, and June toddling around at home all day. Her contract was for her second manuscript to be in her editor's in-box in a month, and she hadn't yet written a single word.

Atlantis House, the Míle Cairde Writers' Retreat, was going to be her saviour – with its elegant antique four-poster beds, the marble fireplaces in every room, the dainty armoires, the heavy silk drapes and Georgian shutters on the windows, the long, tiled hall lined with suits of armour, the works of art by famous artists clustered on every wall, the enormous library with first editions going back two hundred years and an inviting dining room where gourmet meals were promised every night. Two whole weeks with no one to cook for, no one's face to wipe or bottom to change, no socks to worry about and no bloody rows with Terence to navigate and nothing to do all day but write, write, write. Her heart leapt again at the thought of it.

She absolutely couldn't wait to get there.

Chapter Six

"Are you sure that it's going to be safe to cross today?"

Ciara looked at the boat (which seemed ludicrously small), and then the sea (which looked like death), and then the captain of the boat who had such a terrible squint that you couldn't really look at him properly because one eye was over there and the other one was looking over her shoulder somewhere else, God knows where – and so she looked at the boat again. *Dancing Lady* was the name of the passenger ferry, which looked more like a bag lady, Ciara thought, with its rusty paintwork and creaking engines and foul-smelling filthy deck. And the sea was absolutely lethal-looking – Ciara didn't have a lot of experience of boats or the sea in general, but she knew what ten-foot waves meant when she saw them.

"Arra, it'll be all right," beamed Mikey Duggan from behind a satanic beard, holding out an oily hand to Ciara from the walkway. "Come on ta fuck and get on board. We haven't all day to be waiting for ya."

There were about ten other passengers on the ferry, all waiting for her. The others mostly sat inside and she could see their impatient faces from behind filthy windows. There were two teenage boys still on the deck, giggling and smoking cigarettes in fingers that were positively blue with cold. Ciara drew a breath. Realistically, she could have turned away. Rang Doctor Marina De Barra and said sorry, mate, but I'm not risking my life by getting onto that rusty tug for the sake of your winter break from that island – so tough luck to you, lady friend. But then. There was the fact that she'd made such a show of taking up this post. And there was the fact that, to be quite honest, she didn't really want to have to go back. Going back meant trying to find somewhere to live without a bank account, a credit card, or any other credit rating whatsoever. Going back would mean a return to dodging phone calls from the press who wanted her side of the Des Moriarty story, hiding every time she saw a press reporter near the Four Courts, walking two blocks out of her way so that she wouldn't have to pass the Law Society offices just in case they might make her pay all of Des's stolen money back. Going back would have been horrendous. There was a reason for her wanting to do this. Rough seas or no rough seas. She was in. She was definitely in.

"Will ya come *awn*!" Mikey Duggan roared at her again.

"I'm coming!" Ciara roared back, and the fellow passengers broke into a cheer when she finally stepped off the walkway and onto the deck of the boat.

Mikey Duggan was hurriedly winding in ropes and slamming fast the bolts.

"We'd better hurry on, you see. We've people to collect

from the island and then this will be the last sailing before the storm."

"Storm?"

"Ah, you know. Rough seas. We'd get them often at this time of year. We only sail once a week in winter time. Sure there's always a storm on Inish Rua."

Ciara nodded, looking doubtfully overboard at the green and grey waves that were leaping up out of icy waters now as the little boat surged bravely ahead like a lunatic surfer desperate to catch the great last wave of his life. Ciara didn't believe in God, but to her intense surprise she found herself praying quite vociferously as the *Dancing Lady* was flung up and over the waves like a bobbin in a stream. She turned back to look helplessly at the last glimpse of the harbour and of land – oh, precious dry solid land! – that slipped away into the mist. *Whoosh!* A massive wave slapped down onto the deck and drenched her and the two teenage boys from head to foot, and she shrieked and tugged her suitcase rapidly indoors. The boys examined the soaking cigarette ends and gave up. The little door banged after them in the wind.

Indoors it wasn't exactly warm, either. The noise of the engine was horrendous, like a whale moaning, and there was a dreadful smell of oil mixed with stale fish. Completely nauseated, Ciara sat down with a small group of three stone-faced women who were obviously returning from a shopping trip. All around their feet and on the hard wooden benches were plastic bags and boxes of tinned food and non-perishable goods. It felt, to Ciara, as if she were on a very tiny coffin ship.

Somebody was playing a harmonica which added to the gloominess and the sense of impending doom – a bearded man, dressed in a filthy snorkel-jacket. The kind Kenny wears in *Southpark*, Ciara thought, and the sudden memory of Des's favourite TV show was like a sting. But he was playing *"La Vie En Rose"*, and she couldn't help smiling back at him when she caught his rather bloodshot eye. He winked at her, and switched to "Moon River". Soothed by the slightly inappropriate but nevertheless romantic music, she closed her eyes and almost fell asleep. It was beginning to lash with rain.

She noticed another woman who seemed to be around her own age, a dark-caramel blonde with kind of mischievous-looking eyes behind black-rimmed glasses. She had a generous face that broke into easy giggles and a sort of haphazard but fiercely intelligent look about her. She was wearing a very city-looking trench coat that made her look a bit more savvy than the others but Ciara noticed that she had a laptop computer with her, in what was obviously a nappy bag.

There was another passenger sitting alone, ignoring the singing, smiling comfortably to himself and reading an illustrated children's book. Ciara wondered if he might be the local simpleton – he was dressed rather oddly in a reindeer knitted jumper and wore a multicoloured bobbly hat – but there was something about him that she couldn't help liking. He had a sort of round-faced, pink, childish look that was kind of cute.

There was a rather elegant blonde in her fifties and two teenage girls who sat in silence and stared out at the sea, studiously ignoring the two teenage boys who'd found another box of fags and were smoking furiously.

The sailing to the island took almost an hour and a half. Halfway there, the elegant blonde sang a song, and Kenny-from-*Southpark* accompanied her on the harmonica. Ciara normally would have cringed but in the circumstances it seemed quite sweet to have the generosity to entertain, even if the song was a bit of an ironic choice, "The Town I Loved So Well". The woman had a very deep and sexy voice. Ciara quietly hummed along with the chorus, just to herself.

The boat was turning around now, the engines groaning like a cow in labour and suddenly, through the thick rain and filthy glass on the windows Ciara saw the island – Inish Rua – and she gasped.

It was magnificent. Rising out of the wild ocean like a great magical beast, it threw its twin mountains up into the clouds as if imploring the heavens with both hands. From this little boat, out in the middle of the Atlantic, it looked like a forbidden, unnavigable place.

"I can see why Saint Tristan thought it such a spiritual place!" she murmured, half to herself and half to the woman who was sitting beside her, whom Ciara had noticed had remained stoically silent during all the music, and was instead self-consciously trying to read a book. There was a very good-looking younger man sitting to the self-conscious woman's right, who had closed his eyes in a dreamy, trippy way as soon as the boat had left the dock, and Ciara, who felt she often had a good insight into people's behaviour, was pretty sure that the self-conscious woman was deliberately remaining silent and avoiding the other passengers to impress *him*. The good-looking younger man was completely inappropriately dressed for the weather – his thick black curls peeked out from underneath a *báinín* beany hat but that was the only weather-proof garment that he wore. Ciara glanced sideways at him – he truly had the most beautiful face under that silly granny's hat, and while the others carried on singing and chattering among themselves she took a good long look at the long, girlish eyelashes, the single earring, and the striped Breton sweater he wore over crumpled pale blue jeans. He slept, arms folded over his obviously well-toned chest, like a beautiful angelic being.

Someone was passing around a bottle of Jameson – it was the Kenny-from-Southpark harmonica player, of course – and Ciara was tempted to see if it would settle her stomach as the *Dancing Lady* took another giant leap into the surf and leaned over so far into the sea under the weight of the wave that slapped down on her that she seemed to almost capsize. Ciara gripped the seat in front of her, and turned to the self-conscious woman, still reading although Ciara couldn't imagine how anyone could hold a book steady and ignore the ferocious weather they were in.

"Aren't you scared at all?" she whispered to the woman.

"Oh," the woman smiled, "we go sailing all the time. My husband is in Dun Laoghaire Yacht Club and we take the boat to France. Don't worry. We're in very experienced hands." She had yellow eyes, like a cat, and a rather beautiful if very pale face under a curtain of very straight, very neatly bobbed mahogany-shiny hair.

Ciara got a chance to see what she was reading and realised that it was music.

"I thought you were reading a book," she said. "Are you a musician? Is that one of your scores?"

The woman smiled again. "Yes." And returned to her reading.

Ciara looked away. So these were perhaps her future

patients. The residents of the island, and some who'd come for the Míle Cairde Writers and Artists' Retreat no doubt – all of them had plenty of luggage with them and there were no day trips in winter, every passage had to be negotiated with a local boatman, so these people were definitely here to stay. She looked around the little group again, clocking every one, trying to imagine what they'd need. The Kenny-from-Southpark harmonica player – well, it didn't take a detective to figure out that he'd be looking for something to help the early morning shakes, sooner or later. And the frosty but beautiful mahogany-haired musician with the self-conscious music score – Ciara had her marked for an appalling hypochondriac who'd probably want all her allergies treated or something before the week was out. The two teenage boys – they'd probably be in to the surgery looking for her to examine their willies or do an HIV test because they'd had a quick snog behind the bicycle shed or something, that's if they could get those two prissy-looking teenage girls to thaw out. And then the glamorous woman who sang the song, with the waist-length blonde hair surrounding a once-beautiful face – she looked like the sort of woman who might need to come in to have emergency Botox.

The mumsy-looking caramel-haired woman in the city trench coat, now that Ciara examined her more carefully (and Mumsy had gladly had a good few glugs of the Jameson's and was giggling with Harmonica Man,) seemed to be quite good fun, actually. Despite her jolliness she had a sort of strong and rather intellectual look about her – glasses always helped, if you were the distractible kind, Ciara thought. Perhaps she might be someone Ciara could be friends with – and then she remembered that she didn't really want to have to make friends. Friends made comments about your relationship, told you things that were for your own good, offered unsolicited advice. Friends were too much work. She needed to be alone.

Still, Mumsy with the laptop in the nappy bag looked all right, even if she did seem to be helping herself to a bit too much of Harmonica Man's whiskey, given the turbulence of the journey. She'll probably be in the surgery tonight looking for anti-emetics, Ciara thought. And as for the white-haired guy reading the children's book in the coloured hat and reindeer jumper – God only knows. He must be at least forty-five – perhaps fifty. Maybe he does have a learning difficulty, Ciara thought.

The only unknown quantity was the beautiful man, two places down from her. Still fast asleep under his *báinín* hat.

They were pulling into harbour now.

"Here we are!" announced the glamorous blonde who'd sang the song, in her throaty voice. "Wake up, Setanta!" She poked the Sleeping Beauty with a pointed ankle boot. Ciara found herself blushing as he opened up his long-lashed eyes and gave them all the benefit of a lazy, unbearably beautiful white-toothed smile.

Inish Rua! The boat banged against the harbour, and the engines churned and the walkway clanged as Mikey Duggan flung it out onto the pier with an almighty clatter.

I'm here at last, Ciara thought, listening to the whistling of the wind and the scream of seagulls as she stood with her one large suitcase on the pier. At last I'm here. And no one even knows me, where I'm from, or who I am.

It's going to be just perfect. Isn't it?

Chapter Seven

Amy had never been on such horrendously high seas before, but she actually didn't care. It was all too much of an adventure. Oh, to be this far away from Dublin! And the smell of clean air, and the taste of salt, and the sting of a wind that blew clouds across a furious-looking sky, full of mists and rain and the promise of magic. And Inish Rua – oh, it was even more wonderful than she could ever have imagined!

It was absolutely bloody freezing, of course, and her little trench coat wasn't half warm enough for this kind of wind – Jesus, were they up near Iceland or something? She'd asked Joy Jackson, the poet with the rather adventurous mane of waist-long blonde hair (like one of Holly's Barbie dolls) whom she'd met on the boat, and Joy had laughed and said, well, they were quite far up north, but nowhere near Iceland really. It was just that it was going to be a pretty cold, sharp winter already, Joy had said. Joy's trees had magnificent foliage on them because of the cold autumn, and the hydrangeas were quite decayed already and that was a good sign of a cold winter. Joy's husband was a very keen gardener – being a man with too much time on his hands, Joy had added in a gruff voice and everyone had laughed. He was a schoolteacher the rest of the time. Joy, of course, was a full-time poet on an Arts Council grant.

"You couldn't have a job and leave any time for poetry – when you're writing poetry, you need a lot of time to think," she'd told Amy in a conspiratorial tone, tapping the side of her head.

Amy had nodded admiringly – privately, she wondered how on earth Joy justified having no job and then swanning off to Míle Cairde for two months of the year to doss around writing a few poems, leaving her husband to do it all. Terence, if she'd had the bottle to try anything like that, would probably put a hit out on her.

"I still do a bit of work as a freelance web designer, as well writing books," she told Joy, and accepted Joy's pitying look. "We couldn't afford things otherwise. Things have been very difficult this year –" And then she reminded herself to shut up. There was one silent agreement that she and Terence had made – well, it was more his agreement than hers, and it wasn't so much an agreement as an exercise in stonewalling – which was that neither of them would talk about why he'd been fired from his job. He was taking a career break. He was going to be a full-time dad! He was not, under any circumstances, an investment broker who'd been fired for encouraging insolvent clients to mortgage their homes against the price of banking shares. And don't even dare to suggest it!

Still. She had two glorious weeks and she was bloody

grateful for it. Leaving the house this morning at four to get on a train to Sligo had been horrendous, of course. Without saying goodbye to the kids. Amy had dressed in silence – even Terence was still asleep – and eventually just said a rather too brief goodbye, pecking him on the cheek. His face had been sharp with morning beard. His breath too morningy to properly kiss. And he'd been too sleepy to care about a proper goodbye, either. She'd tugged her too-large case along the landing and peeked very slightly through the door into the nursery to hear the soft sound of children's breathing in the dark. It had almost broken her heart. She'd desperately wanted to go inside and lift them out of bed and cover their little faces with a thousand kisses – but of course, Terence would have killed her if she'd done that. Instead she moved her suitcase silently down the stairs like a thief, blinking back tears, and without making even the tiniest noise closed the front door and slipped into her waiting taxi on the street.

But now, here she was. At last, away from all of that, on an island out at sea, uncontactable (almost – she'd brought her mobile phone, of course, although she wasn't even sure if they had coverage out here). And with two glorious weeks with all the time in the world to write. In her heart, there was a huge lump of misery without the girls – and already she was missing them like hell. But this place – oh, it was even more beautiful than she'd imagined.

The others were marching up the pier now towards the village, gossiping among themselves, and the harmonica player seemed to know the reindeer-jumper man already from before. And Joy Jackson was striding along, her suitcase on wheels behind her like an air-hostess, stooping as she talked animatedly to the mahogany-haired woman who'd been on board who'd read all the way over and who was studiously remaining silent to Joy's chatter now.

Amy wheeled her case along after them, and behind her a voice drawled, "Do you know your way?" and she turned and it was the beautiful guy with the *báinín* hat, beaming a toothpaste-ad smile at her. Amy felt her heart clang in her chest and wished she'd left her glasses off and put her contacts in.

"I've never been here before," she said. "What about you?"

"Yes. I have. Will we walk together so?" he said.

He might as well have asked her "Will we sleep together so?" with the effect it had on her. Amy hoped desperately that her pinked-up face wasn't too obvious. Still, it wouldn't stay too pink for long in this weather. The wind was like a blade on her cheeks and she furiously regretted the smart trench coat and thought longingly of the horrible fleece that she sometimes wore when she didn't care what she looked like because she'd had another weekend rowing with Terence and all she wanted to do was eat nachos and stay in bed.

They started up the little hill from the harbour towards the few houses that made up the village, silent while they each took in the landscape and the sheer beauty of it all.

"I wonder if it snows here, ever," the beautiful man said in his dreamy voice, indicating the height of the mountain peaks.

"Might be a bit too windy. Aren't the cottages like something in an oil-painting?"

He laughed. "Not the kind of oil painting I do. But I like them. They look like little people, don't they, snuggling into the hills?"

"Do you often think that houses look like people?" she asked him in wonderment.

"Yes. Of course. Especially this kind. Look." He pointed at the thatched-roofed bungalow they passed. "The thatch – like hair, isn't it – growing into the two windows – like overgrown hair growing a fringe into its eyes. The door like a little mouth. Some houses seem to smile, of course, and some look cross."

"That's just what my kids say."

"Then your kids are right."

"You see, that's what I hate about modern buildings," Amy said. "People stopped making buildings that looked like people."

"Ah, but all architecture is political," the beautiful man replied.

"What?"

"It's more democratic to have buildings that don't dominate the landscape, a building that says equality in every floor, offices that are uniformly distributed in a geometrical shape – as if to say, everyone who works here is equally important."

"Well," Amy said, "I like to see the personality in a building. The hawk-like expression of a handsome house. The humble innocence of a thatched cottage."

"You should see the personality of the building I grew up in," he said.

"Was it beautiful?"

"It was a children's home."

"Oh. I'm – I'm so sorry." She felt slightly awkward, but he was being quite sanguine. "But what kind of face did it look like to you?"

He paused a moment tilting his head to one side, which

Amy thought looked even cuter in his *báinín* hat, and then replied, "A jackboot stamping on the face of humanity, I guess." He grinned.

They had reached the little crossroads that marked the village and stood a moment looking around them. The others had all gone way ahead – Amy's case seemed to be a bit too heavy already and it was making her slow. Falling behind meant that she was now walking all alone with the beautiful man.

"It's very kind of you to walk with me," she said a bit nervously and the beautiful man drawled, "My pleasure," which made her tingle in between her legs. Oh, cop on to yourself, woman! You've two kids and you're heavily married, she told herself furiously. Five minutes away from home and you already fancy someone – you are pathetic! You're here to write a book.

The beautiful man was gazing around him dreamily.

There was a little shop, marked *Siopa agus Oifig an Phoist, Tí Pháidín Mike*, and then a few doors up a much larger thatched house sat rather magnificently on a space slightly apart from the street with some benches outside. There was a Guinness pelican sign swinging in the   wind and a hand-painted sign over the door – *Tí Jimmy Sheáin*.

"Do they still speak all Irish here? God, I hadn't thought!" said Amy.

The beautiful man looked at her through lazy eyes. "Do you give a shit?"

She laughed. "No. Not really. We'll get by." She added solemnly, "I'm going to be spending the whole two weeks working anyway."

"Look," he said, walking away from her. "Come and see the little church."

She followed him.

"Give me your suitcase?" he suggested, but she shook her head, feeling like a twit for having brought so much. She could have got away with one tracksuit and no make-up, all fortnight. What on earth did she bring evening shoes and jewellery for? Jewellery! They trudged slower now, her suitcase weighing an absolute ton, and found a tiny grotto with a statue of Our Lady nestling in a dry-stone wall with dog-roses waving madly in the breeze. Some little candles in glass jars were screwed into the railing in front. Our Lady had a most sorrowful expression, eyes rolled up to heaven, hands clasped across her breast in despair. Across the lane was the chapel, a tiny medieval stone building with a slit for a window and a scattering of gravestones in the yard.

"It's Saint Tristan's monastery, the original chapel!" whispered Amy.

"Look," he pointed further up the hill where she could now see a crumbling tower emerge behind the thin, weather-beaten trees. Despite its ragged appearance it was still magnificent, rising out of the landscape like a solemn sword.

They kept on walking past the hillside ancient site, marvelling at the little sign – *Chapel of Saint Tristan. Séipéal Naomh Tristan. PP Father Glen Cassidy. Aifreann – Dé Domhnaigh 11 am. Céad Míle Fáilte Romhaibh Go Léir! Welcome to All!*

And then they eventually arrived, Amy gasping out of breath, to the top of a suddenly steep hill. And there it was.

Atlantis House. Sitting comfortably like a king on his throne in between the hills, the great house spread itself and its outhouses and stables across the valley, on either side of which the brown and green carpet of the hillside swept away like a perfect stage set.

"Oh!" said Amy. "Oh, how wonderful it is. I can't believe we're staying there!"

"Now that's a house that's got personality," the beautiful man murmured.

"Yes. It has. But . . ." she said, although she wasn't quite sure what the "*but*" was for.

"But, what sort of person does it look like?" he finished for her.

"Yes. That's exactly what I'm wondering too."

"Happy or sad?"

"Humble or proud? Defeated or triumphant? It's – well, it's so very hard to tell, isn't it?"

"Yes. It certainly is," he said.

Atlantis was built as a Victorian pile in an H shape, the front door with its pointed neo-Gothic arch sitting rather fiercely in the middle of the bar of the H, and from their position on the hillside they could see all four wings to the front and behind. The sharp, rather jagged Victorian shapes of windows and turrets seemed to give the house an expression of anxiety and surprise. The gargoyles on the roof eaves were weathered and beaten by the wind and salt air, so that they seemed to scream out in pain, '*Help! Help us down from here!*'

There was a series of low outbuildings that had been stables to one side, and in front of the lichen-covered walls and decaying stone lions, an Italianate garden, complete with tiny sculpted hedges encircling a rather rough-looking disused fountain. And then in the distance, beyond the Italianate gardens, some cracked and once-magnificent steps led down to the darkest, blackest and most sinister-looking lake.

"I feel," said Amy, speaking very slowly now, "it's as though Atlantis is a house that is still struggling with its own identity. It's as if it isn't sure why it's here. It's not sure if it even fits in. It knows it's got to perform – it has a duty to others. It needs to show love and to nurture and to shelter and provide authority. And yet . . ."

"Those gargoyles," the beautiful man said dreamily, "those Italian and classical decorations in this simple landscape, the amount of bits and pieces that went into making this house." And he carried on down the hill in what Amy suspected was a stupor of something or other.

"I suppose," said Amy, trotting briskly after him, "the purpose to which it was built, which was to feed the hungry without any real meaning for itself – well, it's as if the house in some way understands that –"

" – that it's as if everybody dressed it up and made it do a job for them, without wondering for a minute how the house would feel about it," the beautiful man finished her sentence for her, then stopped abruptly. He stood as if mesmerised, gazing out across the gardens and down towards the lake.

She looked at him. "It might look neglected," she said, "but it definitely isn't."

"No."

She thought more carefully. "No. I'll tell you what it looks like. It looks as though it has spent a lot of time giving things to others and trying to be all things to all men – and perhaps it doesn't know who it's meant to be itself."

"It was a folly, when it was built."

"Yes," she said. "A building without real purpose. A building for the sake of being built. Oh, poor Atlantis!" Then she smiled at him, suddenly feeling shy. "Don't mind me. I'm just a crazy web designer who'd rather be writing a novel."

"We'll just have to bring her meaning back to her again, won't we?" he said, smiling lazily.

"Yes!" she laughed. "We'll have to make sure she feels that she's one of us! That she's got a place in the world and that all her beauty and loyalty and kindness is still proud."

There was a sudden crunch and they jumped at the interruption to the silence. Reindeer Jumper was ambling towards them across the crunchy gravel drive. He grinned at the two of them standing gazing dreamily at the lake. "What on earth are you doing standing out here in the cold? Come on into the house for goodness sake! Here," he reached out to Amy, "give me that suitcase. And let's hope they've got the kettle on. You must be frozen standing here."

She began to follow Reindeer and then realised that the beautiful man had left her and had walked away from her down a path towards the gardens that led down all the way to the lake.

She hadn't even got around to asking him his name.

Chapter Eight

Art Callaghan threw another bucket of turf onto the fire and listened to the whistle of the wind. Bloody cold for November. Massachusetts was meteorologically much colder than Ireland, of course, but for some reason Art had felt absolutely frozen from the first moment he'd arrived back onto Inish Rua like he'd never felt at home. Home? Well, perhaps Boston was home, now. Only now he was back on the island, and until now it had always been the island that he'd referred to when he'd talked about his home. Home is where you wish you were when you can't be there, Art supposed, watching the blue smoke wisp out of the giant twisted sod of turf as it began to burn.

It was the dampness in the cold, he thought, that made it so difficult to get warm, but he rubbed his hands together quite happily now, watching the big turf fire blaze up. The pub was empty – his dad Jimmy Seán would probably freak when he saw the pile of turf he was wasting on an empty pub, but to hell with that. The fire was jolly.

And if Jimmy was going to sleep all day and then creep around all night driving everybody mad and leaving Art to run the pub, there was no point in running a pub that was as welcoming as a fridge.

In any case, the place would fill up later in the evening, and he'd heard there was a new crowd in the Big House at Atlantis, so they'd be down for drinks later on. Art yawned at the thought of what was undoubtedly going to be another very late night. He knew how to party with the best of them in Boston, but Jesus, these islanders knew how to keep a party going long after they'd outstayed their welcome. Art had been up to almost four o'clock most weekend nights and till at least two o'clock during the weeks since he'd got back home. But he *was* beginning to enjoy his nightly routine, the easy pouring of pints, the gossip, the mad sessions that could get going sometimes, the wiping and the coaxing of the bar-flies out of the pub before the dawn. Tí Jimmy Sheáin didn't open before lunch-time most of the days, and during the afternoon and evening there was a distinct lull in business, when Jimmy Seán would go down for a nap and pretty much stay down until he'd get up in the middle of the night again. And now that Art was there he could do the bits and pieces and make sure the barrels were changed. Looking after his dad, and the bar, was all right. For a while. But ultimately it was moronic work. And the main problem was that Dad was obviously going to get worse.

Art had been horrified when the doctor had told them about the brain tumour that Jimmy Seán had. There was nothing they could do, of course – and the doctor had been very kind. But Jimmy Seán had gone into a complete decline. He was becoming demented. He clung onto Art like a baby for hours and then he'd be off up the hills like a Himalayan explorer and away up to the cliffs like a lunatic. He was afraid to go out alone, he'd say, and make Art come to the *siopa* with him for a packet of tissues – and then he'd suddenly change his mind and tell Art to feck off and go home. He spent a lot of time mooching around the back of the bar and watching telly with the volume on so loud you could probably hear it on the tops of the mountains. He was refusing to go to Mass.

Art loved his dad, and he was pretty glad to be around for him and to have been able to leave his job at MIT to come home and look after him. But it was getting to be kind of tedious being the only sentient adult around the house sometimes. And all the books he'd brought with him were useless as he wasn't getting a lot of time to study – and the Internet access was a problem. Snail-standard dial-up with frequent failure of service. He'd brought his favourite telescope out here with him, his beloved Celestron NexStar, at huge extra expense and extra insurance costs all the way across the Atlantic on the plane as on-board luggage and then on the trawler with Mikey Duggan, fingers crossed the whole way, terrified that water would get in to it. But it had to come with him – he'd have never been able to live without it.

Out here you could see a million stars. Except that it was always cloudy now. Every single night since he'd arrived on Inish Rua seven months ago the skies had been thick with rain and clouds. The stars might as well not exist.

"Well, you can quit feeling sorry for yourself, anyway," said Art to the giant hairy sod of turf that was stinging the crap out of his eyes with the smoke of it. "You came over here because you wanted to. You couldn't wait to get away from her, either. It was an excuse for you. You were happy enough to have somewhere to storm off to sulk instead of having to deal with a thug of a divorce lawyer. And you love your dad. You needed to get back to basics. You need this down time and you're going to make the most of it."

And then he realised that the door to the bar had opened. There was a woman standing in the door.

"Hi," she said in a very doubtful voice. "I wonder if you can help me?"

He realised she probably thought that he was just another crazy islander standing up in front of an open fire having a good old argument with the voices in his head, and so he straightened himself up and ruffled his hand through his hair and tried to look a bit more intelligent. Perhaps she'd think he was reciting poetry or something, he thought, giving her what he hoped was a winning smile. But she was standing looking at him very patiently. She had a giant suitcase behind her back.

"I'm looking for the doctor's house," she said.

"Oh," he said. He was about to add, "Are you unwell?" and then realised that that was a very islandy thing to say, to answer a question with another question and not give the person a proper response at all, and that this woman looked pretty much Not From The Island. Well, the suitcase was a dead giveaway, anyway. Doh. And she was beautiful. She had amazing, glossy fox-fur auburn hair, the kind of colour that grew naturally on Irish women and that costs hundreds of dollars in any other country to get done in a hairdresser's. And her pale face was so sweet. A half-open rose-bud mouth, wide, innocent cheekbones and a tiny slightly snub nose.

"Er. She's just down at the end of the lane. Street. Well, if you can call it that. Road?" he said and then realised he was going off the point again.

The woman looked at him patiently.

She has the most adorable splash of freckles and no make-up, as if someone had just splattered a paintbrush at her face, and her very clean, wind-whipped Titian hair was completely soaked with rain – the way only an Irishwoman would have the naiveté to look when going on holidays – and he couldn't help the sudden comparison with Jade, and then his heart sank as Jade's beautiful, furious image – *Fuck you, Art Callaghan! You're a fucking waste of space!* – filled his head again. Jade would rather have died than go on holidays without a manicure, a ninety-dollar blow-out and full make-up including eyelash extensions.

But this girl – the way she stood there calmly waiting for him to speak. Like the thick sod of turf he was – what the hell had come over him? She was only a visitor come off the boat – just tell her how to get to where she wants to go. No! Offer to go with her! Help with her suitcase!

"Why don't I come with you, show you where to go?"

"Oh, no!" The woman seemed shocked.

"Well, you might get lost," he began.

"On an island? It isn't very big."

She was smart. A bit too smart, maybe. No need to be so prickly, lady. "No. That's true. It's very small. Would you like a drink?"

"No. I'd like directions, please."

Right. Be that way, you icy cow. "Yes. I bet you would." Stony silence. Now I'm being an asshole. Jeez, she's blushing. No, actually that's probably not a blush. She's probably going red with anger. Oh, bollocks. "No – I'm sorry. Look, I'll start again. No, that's not what I meant." Inane smile. "But it's very rainy out. And I could help you with your case," he finished helplessly.

The woman sighed. "I don't need help. I need to find the house. I – can you please just tell me where it is?"

Art opened his mouth and shut it again. This was going from bad to worse. All I need now, he thought wildly, is for Jimmy Seán to wander in and she'll realise how crazy we all are out here. "Look, I'm sorry. I didn't mean to be a smart-ass. Look, please let me show you where to go. Here, I'll take your case –" and he reached out to take the handle but she bent down at the same time to prevent him and he crashed his big thick mop of a head into hers.

"*Ouch!*" she yelled.

"Oh, my God! Now I've hit you – I'm so, so sorry!" He reached out to her.

"Don't touch me!" she roared. She backed away from him, trying to manipulate her over-heavy hard-shell suitcase at the same time. She tugged furiously at the long handle, trying to make a U-turn with the suitcase so that she could make a hasty getaway. But the giant case swayed awkwardly on its axis like a drunk being manhandled out of a bar at night – and eventually toppled over, it's weight too much for her, and crashed to the floor. And the lock burst open. Overstuffed clothes spilled everywhere. Underwear. Bras. Three pairs of high-heeled shoes. Jumpers. Skirts and things. A set of rollers. Art felt his face becoming purple.

"Oh Christ!" the woman groaned, falling to her knees. She began to try to stuff as much as possible back into the case.

"Oh, God, let me help you!"

"Get away! You're crazy! Let me go!"

"I'm sorry! I only –" he paused while he tried desperately to think of what to say.

She was scampering away from him, dusting herself off, getting up from the floor.

He'd frightened her. He'd made an absolute horse's arse of trying to help her and now she was actually frightened.

"Really sorry." He held his hands out towards her in a gesture that indicated that he'd leave her alone from now on, and went to sit down. "Out of harm's way?" He grinned sheepishly from a stool at the other side of the room.

She smiled slightly. "It's all right." She stood a moment and looked at the mess of clothing she'd just stuffed back into the case. "I seem to have brought too many things."

He examined the mess. "Well, you won't need the high heels. Or the jewellery, really. But it's very nice that you brought it along. Where do you come from? How long are you staying? What brought you out here to the island?"

She looked at him sharply. And then her face stiffened again. "Look, I'd better go," she said.

"I'd offer to help you to re-pack, but I'd be afraid of making things worse."

She was kneeling down again, trying to fold her things more evenly into her case, squeezing things into corners. "It's all right. I'm not too good at this either."

"Are you staying a while?"

"I – I don't know."

"Oh." He watched her folding a little lacy bra, her face pinking up as she did, and he looked way. Maybe better to go back behind the bar and leave her to pack her stuff without the audience, he thought. "Look, let me get you a

70

drink – on the house – while you sort that stuff out. The bar is quiet now but I'll be busy later on. And then I'll show you to Marina's house. Only – someone told me she was going away."

"Yes. I'm her locum. But I can find the house myself."

"Oh. Well, that's great, she has a locum doctor. I heard it was a difficult thing to find. Well, I'll definitely be seeing more of you then," he said happily and when she shot him an anxious glance he wondered if he was coming across as a stalker or something. "I mean, I'm not going to stalk you or anything. I only mean I'll be seeing more of you because I'll have to come by the house tomorrow. Because my dad is ill," he ended lamely.

Her face softened. "I'm sorry to hear that." She sat on the case to fasten it. Then she stood up. "So, I'd better go," she said.

"Have just one drink, on me."

She looked alarmed again and shook her head briskly. "I can't. Doctor on call." She dusted herself off.

"Cup of tea?"

She looked at him wearily. He was beginning to sound pathetic now. "I won't tell where Marina's house is until you let me make you a cup of tea. That's the deal. Take it or leave it." He smiled hopefully.

At long last she almost smiled. "A very, very, very quick cup then."

The kettle, of course, took what felt like hours to boil.

Art got teabags out and a teapot – somehow he felt he ought to offer her a pot rather than a mug with a bag floating in it like the other islanders would like. In the silent pub the clock ticked like a hammer on a rock. The turf fire hissed.

"Cheers?" He clinked his mug against hers.

She smiled ever so slightly again.

Art couldn't for the life of him think of what else to say to her. It was as if she'd reduced him to a speechless clod, which made him feel pretty irritated as she wasn't that sophisticated herself. She'd hardly been a fascinating conversationalist either, he thought, watching her sip her tea with a solemn expression.

"So – I took the tea. Now, do I get the directions?"

"All right." He pointed towards the lane. "Just keep going and you can't miss it, just straight on down the hill. I hope you'll be all right," he added, feeling more foolish than ever.

"I can look after myself," she said. Putting down her mug, she said, "Thanks for that." And then she left.

Art sat on a little copy stool beside his roaring fire and watched the flames. He couldn't for the life of him figure out why he hadn't insisted on accompanying her. It would have been a nice, welcoming thing to do. And she had looked a bit pathetic with that enormous overstuffed suitcase on wheels, going up to the doctor's when she'd only just arrived. And, in any case, he was as bored as a pole standing around the bar waiting for someone to come in. His dad was out somewhere pottering around for a change. What kind of an idiot was he becoming out here anyway? He was bored. He was alone. And he was doing nothing about it. He had come out here without an exit strategy.

She seemed terribly pretty, gorgeous actually, but rather frosty all the same. And he was so lonely he couldn't even judge whether or not he was attracted to her, or if he was just desperate for someone to hang out with.

The problem was that he had come to Inish Rua with nothing but pessimism in his mind. It was the perfect way to escape from the impossibly painful end of his time with someone whose love he'd finally admitted he'd lost, and now he was stuck and likely to end up being just as crazy and fucked-up as everyone else who lived here was! He was single now, single once again and hanging around a bar all night – which in any other world would have sorted out everything for him, only here he was in the land of permanent winter looking after his cantankerous dad like an Irish middle-aged bachelor. And meanwhile his ex-wife Jade was living in Hawaii with *her* supposed gay best friend who had turned out not to be gay at all – ha bloody ha.

He kicked a sod of turf that was still smouldering and watched it fall into fiery red ashes.

It was half past three, and beginning to get dark outside already. Sometimes the evenings seemed interminable. What he really longed to do was to get the telescope out and go up to the Black Cliffs and check out the skies – but it was too cloudy now, and there were storms forecast and the seas were looking menacing and the wind would blow you off the cliffs and back out to America – as if.

There's a million billion stars above this island, thought Art glumly – with these kinds of skies you should be able to see from one end of the galaxy to the other. And I can't see any of them any more.

Chapter Nine

Ciara tugged her suitcase back to the top of the pier and waited politely for the group of women who'd been on the boat to say their greetings to the men who met them. That big tall American guy up in the pub talking to himself in front of the fire had been clearly out of his box, and she'd wasted enough time trying to keep him amused by politely drinking his tea. She was relieved to have been able to finally get away from the guy, but it was almost dark now and if she didn't get some proper directions she'd be hopelessly lost. "Straight on down the hill you can't miss it" – what kind of instruction was that? He might as well have said, "If I were you I wouldn't start from here." The easiest thing had been to go back down to where she came from and start again.

She tapped one lady on the sleeve of her tweed coat and asked, "Excuse me?"

"All right," the lady said.

"I'm looking for the house of the doctor, Marina De Barra. Can you help me find it, please?"

The woman looked at the man she'd been talking to. "Take up the messages to Yvonne," she said, pointing to the shopping bags at her feet. "Then come back for me." Then she turned back to Ciara. "Go up the hill to the village and turn right. Go beyond the village after Siopa Páidin Mike and down the hill again. She has a big house and a thatched barn out the back. She's gone away and you'll find Bridgeen Freeman and she'll let you in."

"Oh," said Ciara. "I'm Doctor Ciara Love, by the way. I'm doing Marina's locum for the winter."

The woman looked back at her solemnly. "I know who you are," she said. Then, turning back to the man who was stuffing her plastic shopping bags into the box-carrier at the back of his motorbike, she said something in Irish followed by, "Will you hurry up before the wind slices the skin right off of my face!"

"Chilly, isn't it?" Ciara suggested.

"You'll never be able for it," the woman said triumphantly, and turned away.

Well, thought Ciara. And I thought I might be a bit reluctant to make friends.

She turned to walk away, leaving the woman to mutter half in Irish and half in English to Mikey Duggan about the price of fish and you'd be an awful fool to pay it, and walked briskly in the direction of the village. The cold wind was beginning to feel like razorblades on her face.

What a desolate, miserable place, she thought, taking in the whitewashed walls that would need God knows what kind of maintenance to keep them sparkling like that all summer. And the thatched roofs must cost a fortune to fix, and they'd be full of mice. Ugh! A Honda 50 passed her out with a woman and two children all riding on the saddle behind the man who drove it, shopping bags dangling from either side – it was like something she'd seen in Thailand.

It's beautiful, but crikey, there must be an awful lot of loneliness out here, in wintertime, Ciara thought, with a sudden shudder, turning back briefly just to look at the wide Atlantic sea, and the waves she'd been so relieved to leave. On the other hand, after all the pestering from the media and interviews with the police and avoiding all the pitying looks at work, maybe a little loneliness wouldn't be too bad a thing at all. Would it? At the little harbour, Mikey Duggan was setting off in the boat again into the wild angry sea. This time, there was only one passenger on board.

At the top of the village she turned right as instructed and rolled her case more easily down a lane banked by dry-stone walls over one of which there was a field that led down to a golden beach. God, it's desolate, but how beautiful! she gasped. And then, as the lane turned a corner she came upon the larger, traditional two-storey cottage that was obviously Marina's place. *Dochtúir*, said the little sign painted in black onto the neat whitewashed wall, and there was a tiny tarmacked driveway just inside the gate with a few shrubs and bushes either side and then behind the house a garden with a vegetable patch to one side. To the right of the main house was an outhouse which Ciara suspected was the surgery.

Marina's cottage wasn't thatched – it had a slate roof and nice, solid-looking PVC windows although it was built in the traditional style, double-fronted with a bright green door. There was a little conservatory to one side. At the bottom of the garden behind the surgery building was a small thatched building that was probably a converted cowshed, or what the lady by the boat had called a barn. But it looked smart and habitable – like a tiny little granny flat or something.

She opened the little gate and wheeled her case up the neat tarmacaddam to the door and knocked. And knocked again. There was no reply. She stamped her feet as she waited for someone to answer, and blew on her frozen fingers to try to keep warm.

Ciara stood a moment, knocked several more times, and then decided to go round the back. She tried the surgery door – nothing there. She peered into the conservatory. Quite empty. She was going around the other side of the house to come out the front again when she nearly jumped out of her skin.

"Arrghhhh!"

"Did I frighten you?"

She was face to face with a tall, very weather-beaten man who despite his very polite demeanour, was obviously, having made her jump, barely able to disguise a guilty, worried smile.

"Oh," she said, feeling suddenly faint, "it's all right. I'm Ciara. Ciara Love. The locum. For Doctor Marina."

"Well," he said.

"Um." Ciara looked around her. She was cold. Her feet were like icicles. She was exhausted from pulling the case. It was ghastly weather. She'd been locked out for a good few minutes – and this guy was just standing there like a spade.

"Er, are you Marina's husband?" she asked eventually.

He looked surprised. And then he said, "I suppose I am. Yes. That's one way of putting it, I suppose."

"Oh," she said. Oh, for Pete's sake! What kind of a

place have I let myself in for? It's like a series of mind games just saying hello to someone here. Heaven knows what the surgery is going to be like!

"Um, I'm supposed to be staying in the house. So. I wonder if you'd mind if I went in? It's just that I'm awfully cold, and I really need to get to see the surgery and things."

"Oh! Yes! Of course! Into the house!" he said, as if he'd just discovered something rather special. "Yes! Now, let me see."

"I thought you might have a key," she said.

"A key? Oh. I never thought of that. Hmmm." He began to scratch his head.

Ciara waited as patiently as she could. But she was freezing cold, with the wind biting around her cheeks and her hands so frozen they were in pain now. The guy did look eccentric – but then so did pretty much everybody here. He had rather overgrown greying hair, a lot of it, very thick and in a tangle like a mad scientist and he was wearing a very pre-loved woollen jumper tucked into his jeans which were held up with a huge belt. He was thin and wirey in his body – the jumper which was huge and thick disguised his leanness but she could tell by the bagginess of the jeans and the sort of nimble way he moved about that he was very fit. However, he couldn't for the life of him remember where the keys to the house might be. Had he locked himself out? Or didn't he even know?

"You must think I'm a bit mad," he said eventually.

Although very keen to remain polite, Ciara felt her skin prickle at the back of her neck. But she said nothing back.

"It's just," he carried on, "that I spend all my time in the studio. Painting, you know. And I don't really ever –

well, the truth is that I haven't been in the house in years. I haven't a clue where she keeps the key."

"Didn't she tell you? I mean – you knew I was coming today, didn't you?" Ciara asked in despair.

"Yes. She told me that. But – oh, I know what we'll do. We'll ask Mrs Freeman to come around. She'll know what to do," he said happily.

"Great," she said with relief.

"Now," he said. "Let me just think. Where would Mrs Freeman be at this hour of the day?"

Ciara wanted to cry. She couldn't stand the cold any more. Her hands, in thin leather gloves, felt as though they were about to drop off. Her nose was cold. Her teeth were beginning to hurt. She wanted a hot bath and a cup of cocoa – no, a hot whisky, actually, a great big one and to get into bed and never get out of it again. And even if she did manage to get into the house tonight, God knows what kind of a state Marina might have left it in. If her husband was this potty, Marina might be an absolute nut-job. Doctors who lived in these desolate places might go seriously round the bend, Ciara thought in despair. The place might be uninhabitable. But yet. She looked hopefully at the little conservatory that did seem quite cosy with its wicker chairs and a bookcase and some well-fed plants.

And then, like a gift from heaven, across the whistling of the wind she heard another voice.

"Gearóid de Barra! Is it you and the lady doctor there beyond? Would you not let her into the house at all?"

Ciara turned and clocked the little plump woman, with a round, jolly face underneath a bright headscarf, who was marching down the lane.

"Ah. It's Bridgeen. Well, thank God for that. Have you the keys?" said Gearóid in relief.

"The door is open, ya thick plank! What kind of person keeps a set of keys on this island? Marina de Barra would no more lock the doctor out!" said Mrs Freeman, marching past him up to the house.

"Are you Mrs Freeman?" Ciara asked, offering her a gloved hand which the woman ignored in favour of flinging open the front door.

"Come in out of the cold and get beside the range and we'll have a cup of tea I've your room ready for you were there many on the boat did you meet Peigeen she was beyond in Sligo getting messages go on now Gearóid and I'll take care of the lady I'd had meaned to make a tart but Páidín had no cookers a soda cake will do Marina would have killed me but there's plenty of blackberry jam although the hedges were quite empty this summer in account of all the cold . . ."

Mrs Freeman carried on talking without the slightest pause or punctuation as she moved through the house, as if she expected that there were people following her wherever she went.

"Oh. Thank you so much, anyway." Ciara turned to the now redundant Gearóid who still was standing outside the house. She stood a moment in the hall and wondered what else to say to him. He had such a kind face, heavily lined but full of expression, with rather sad eyes like an old, beloved dog.

"Well," said Gearóid, "I'll be off. And good luck to you," he added rather awkwardly and then loped off.

"Close that door and come in to the warm inside!" Mrs Freeman yelled, banging a kettle onto the range and furiously stoking the turf fire inside the stove.

Ciara closed the door, shutting the wind and the weather and the world away. She stood a moment in the doorway of the kitchen taking in the warm smell of turf and a damp tea-making smell from the range, and admired the large scrubbed pine table with a simple dresser and some nice pottery and a jug of flowers. Behind the large Belfast sink with a row of pottery vessels that held wooden spoons and scrubbing things was a small window, through which she could see the now black sea. She wandered out into the corridor again and went upstairs. At the top of the stairs she found a bedroom – that was an absolute tip. She closed the door rapidly. Well, which was obviously Marina's room and she hadn't had a chance to tidy up. Oh well, she might have been very busy before she got away.

On the other side of the landing was another bedroom, this time very neat with just a big, white-covered bed and a simple wardrobe. Underneath the window was a single chair. And through the window – oh, wow! The bleakest mountains rose up into the heavens and in between the wildest-looking valley stretched and meandered out of sight. And right in the middle of the valley sat the magnificent Atlantis. Ciara stood and stared at the view for a while. This was obviously her room.

She felt, with this kind of view, she'd never want to close the curtains again. The big house looked intriguing – and as twilight was beginning to fall, it was lighting up with lamps and even the flickering of firelight could be seen through the big bay windows. Atlantis looked, despite its grandeur and austerity, as if within its stern grey walls there might be quite a lot of fun going on.

Mrs Freeman was chattering like a flock of seagulls in the kitchen when she went back down – most of it to

...elf, as Ciara felt incapable of conversation. It was a bit of a worry, she thought, having to live at what was obviously going to be very close quarters with a quite over-verbose lady-help. And then that very strange man Gearóid painting away all the time at the end of the garden.

Yet, there was something about Marina's big, comfortable home, with its abstract paintings on every wall, its bright colours in the curtains and slightly faded but very clean, floral loose-covered furniture that she knew she was going to like. And even Mrs Freeman, gabbling away while she flung china teacups and saucers out and rattled spoons to a running commentary about every little thing that happened on the island. Ciara hadn't used a saucer in decades.

And so despite the sudden extraordinary demands of the rather sudden and unexpected intimacy of country life, Ciara felt quite suddenly content. The great thing about Mrs Freeman's stream of consciousness as she buttered scones and poured tea and generally flapped around and gossiped like a hen, was that she talked so much and managed to cover so many subjects in one soliloquy that there was absolutely nothing else that Ciara would ever have to say.

Chapter Ten

"Hello?" Amy called, standing in the hallway.

Reindeer Jumper had marched knowledgeably off in some direction to another part of the house, and she could hear his voice laughing uproariously now from the far end of it where he was chatting to the other guy she'd met on the boat – that nice old thing with the whiskey. From the same direction she could hear the deep growling voice of Joy Jackson, who seemed to be very much at home there too. The beautiful man seemed to have slipped away somewhere. Reindeer Jumper had left her suitcase at the bottom of the stairs.

The stairs were magnificent, though, reaching up and winding their glossy banisters around the landing into rooms and corridors and secret places. There was a giant hallstand covered in coats and hats and umbrellas, and a very tiny suit of armour with a sword. The floor was a gorgeous red and green Morris-patterned tile, and the walls were panelled in oak.

"Hello?" she called again, and was beginning to wonder if she ought to just get on with looking for when a tall, flustered-looking woman appeared, ...g her hands with a tea-towel. She wore a gingham apron over a long floral skirt and polo-neck jumper, and had long, dark-blonde fairy-princess hair surrounding a rather heartily complexioned but gentle face.

"Oh, you poor darling, you must have been waiting ages, let me help you with your case! I'm Trish Lenihan, I'm the director of Míle Cairde. You must be Amy! Oh, it's so lovely to meet you at last. I absolutely adored your book!" she added, in a suddenly hushed voice. "I can't tell any of the others that, of course," she muttered conspiratorally. "All artists are equal here. Oh, Amy, don't tell anyone but I couldn't put it down! Now," she snapped again into hostess mode, "let's get you to your room and then I'll show you round the house. I've put you in Lady Ardross's room at the top of this landing . . ." Trish was off with a gallop, long legs leaping up the staircase with Amy's ten-ton case in one hand.

Amy nipped up after her, panting as she took two steps at a time.

"I thought you'd love the view up here," Trish breathed, flinging open the door to a room that seemed to have come right out of a Barbara Cartland novel. It was decorated entirely in pink, with a magnificent four-poster bed in the middle and on two walls were bay windows with window seats to admire the view of the lake from the front and the gardens and greenhouses from the side. There was a giant marble fireplace, a chaise longue, a lady chair, a mahogany desk and an enormous wardrobe.

Amy felt suddenly quite pleased she'd brought so many clothes. There would be nothing worse than landing in this sumptuous room with its magnificent wardrobe and having nothing but a rotten fleece to put in it.

"Oh, God, Trish, it's so wonderful! Oh, thank you for this room!" she gushed, and pranced about from the view at the front, to the side windows, to the bed where she couldn't resist bouncing, to the front window again.

Trish giggled. "It *is* the loveliest room, isn't it. And it's the only room that's got a ghost."

Amy froze. "*What*?"

"The ghost of Lady Ardross," Trish said importantly. "She killed herself. She drowned in the lake. Because Lord Ardross didn't love her any more. The story is that she came here to meet him as a surprise to celebrate their wedding anniversary, walked in unannounced, and found him bonking someone else and so she drowned herself in the lake." Trish giggled, but Amy's hairs were standing up on her neck. "Lord Ardross couldn't sleep a single night in the house afterwards and died of a broken heart."

"Oh, God," Amy groaned, "why did you have to tell me that?"

"Oh, for God's sake, it's only a story! Don't be such a silly-billy!" Trish hooted with laughter and whirled out of the room again. "Setanta is in the room across the corridor," she added with a mischievous smile. "He'll ghost-watch for you."

"Who?"

"Setanta Lynch. He came up from the boat with you, didn't you notice him? Don't be late for supper. Come straight as soon as you hear the gong. Mrs Freeman hates people being late."

"*The* Setanta Lynch?" Amy was beginning to feel very faint.

"Of course." Trish beamed. "See you for supper!" And she drifted out of the room and down the stairs.

So *that* was the beautiful, dreamy man who loved

houses for their personality! Setanta Lynch – the only Irish artist to have been nominated for the Turner Prize this year! – of course, being from Derry all the British Sundays pretended they thought he was Scottish. Famous for his abstract nudes, Setanta Lynch's Turner entry had been a series of large-scale interactive multimedia installations. Since his nomination, however, Setanta was known most importantly for his commissioned portrait of the UK's Prime Minister. He had replaced the face of the PM with that of a Derbyshire speckled pig. Rumour had it that Number Ten had not been amused. Nor had the pork farmers of Great Britain.

Setanta Lynch had happily returned all of the money he'd been offered for the commission, and sold the copyrights to a T-shirt factory. The portrait had become a simultaneous icon of both the anarchists and the BNP.

"Oh, God, what a bloody hunk," moaned Amy to herself as she unpacked her case and tried to decide what on earth she was going to wear for dinner. "Just my luck to be parked next to him, so's I won't be able to sleep a wink all night."

She sat down on the bed and spread a low-necked top out on the duvet, wondering if it was too tight. She then examined a low-necked wrap dress in front of the mirror, and then almost jumped out of her skin. From the darkening skies just outside was the most terrifying noise, like thunder only much more rhythmical. Amy leaped off the bed and glued herself to the window at the side of the bedroom that overlooked the gardens.

A giant navy helicopter was descending onto Atlantis like a hawk.

Chapter Eleven

Ciara had woken to the sound of singing. Loud, tuneless bellowing might be a better description. Halfway through the second or third verse of the song she recognised the tune. "*Báidín Fheilimí*" – a sea shanty she'd learned in school. Age four with thirty snotty noses and a melodica. An ice-cold classroom and a cheese sandwich for lunch.

Outside the wind was whistling around the gables of the house and a seagull had joined Mrs Freeman's song.

"Báidín Fheilimí, d'imigh go Toraigh!
Báidín Fheilimí, 's Feilimi ann!"

Ciara slid out of the bed. She stood in front the window which she'd left uncurtained, despite the wintry night. At the top of the valley Atlantis greeted her in all her solemn grandeur, the two wings of the castle on either side like a pair of open hands.

Mrs Freeman had switched the song.

"An bhfaca tú mo Shéamuisín, mo Shéamuisín, mo Shéamuisín?"

Ciara winced. Perhaps it would be easier to join her, than to try to weather it out. And it was only nine o'clock in the morning. Surgery wasn't due to start until eleven, but she could breakfast and maybe get a little walk – although heaven knows where she'd walk to. Up and down the lane, round the village and then back – it would be pleasant enough and very blustery and fresh but a bit pointless when she thought about it.

On the other hand, it was impossible to sit inside this house all day. The landscape seemed to beckon her, despite its hostility. And as for Atlantis – the thing about Atlantis was that the house seemed to have its own voice, almost louder than Mrs Freeman's. A booming but silent voice, as if that were possible, but nevertheless it seemed to speak to her from its seat above the valley – *"My name is Ozymandias, king of kings, look on my works, ye Mighty and despair!"*

For a moment she thought suddenly of the warning that Professor Maurice Hanly had given her before she left – and then swiftly put it away. Delayed grief reaction – depressive symptoms – give me a break, Ciara briskly thought. This place is marvellous. Just what I needed. Post-traumatic stress disorder, me bollocks!

She opened her suitcase and found a pair of tweed trousers to put on and a black cashmere jumper. Then she went out to the kitchen from where there was a good smell of something baking.

"Hi, Mrs Freeman!" Ciara yelled. And then, *"Hi, Mrs Freeman!"* until the singing stopped.

"Well, there you are there's a nice soda cake for you although I suppose you'd have a porridge for your breakfast and do you take tea or coffee Marina is always one for the coffee and she has a lovely expresso machine only it's an awful devil to get it going but we could have a go did you see the wind and there'll be no ferries until that's died down again and they are saying there's more storms on the way would you like some fruit?" said Mrs Freeman with a generous smile.

Ciara blinked. It was a bit of a Joycean stream of consciousness, but she did like Mrs Freeman. On the other hand, it was disconcerting that this woman could be found in the house pottering around at any time. And yet – she was a guest, of sorts, even if she was replacing Marina in the surgery for the winter. And it was Marina's house. This is how Marina lives, thought Ciara, with Mrs Freeman popping in and out and putting soda bread in the oven and then Gearóid hovering out the back – she obviously likes the coming and going of it all. She's probably a lively, sociable old thing. Not like me and my introverted city ways.

It's just that Ciara wished she had known how close the living with Mrs Freeman was going to be before she'd picked up the phone – or would that have made a difference? She *had* been so determined to come here. And looking out the kitchen window now at the angry black sea and sea horses that needed tranquillisers to get them to come back down, she couldn't help reminding herself exactly why. It *was* the roughness that she had longed for. The bitterness of the sea. The cruelty of the wind. And the mercilessness of the island. And yet all of that looked terribly uninviting now.

But the kitchen was warm and very cosy. And the soda bread delicious – Mrs Freeman had just taken it out of the oven.

And as for Gearóid – whom she could see now gathering a bucket of turf from the pile at the shed – Ciara wasn't quite sure yet what she was going to have to do about him. It was definitely disconcerting, the thought of living here and working here and having this man hovering out there, watching her all day and all night too. So much for being alone, thought Ciara, beginning to feel slightly glum. I've never been so closely supervised in all my life.

She was sure that Gearóid meant to be kind, and she waved back now at him as he saluted her with a solemn hand before returning to the turf, but it was very strange, the feeling of living in a fishbowl observed as though one were an exhibit at the zoo, and at the same time one is put in the rather disturbing position of having also to observe someone else.

"Thank you. This is delicious, but there is really no need to come round all the time. I can look after myself," she told Mrs Freeman who was pouring tea and talking non-stop about the history of terrible storms that had destroyed Inish Rua in the past.

"It was in nineteen twenty-eight that the original pier was destroyed and it took several years for them to mend it back again many of the islanders died in that winter well the cold and lack of food they had no helicopters in those days well my father grew up on the island and his father and they lost a load of sheep and then the fishing boats could not go out . . ."

Ciara deliberately zoned out again now that the clackity monologue had resumed in the background. Zoning out to the background of someone else's monologue had become an easy habit to her now. At the worst of times, she had discovered eventually that it had been the only possible way to cope with Des and his episodic flights of ideas and what could become hours and hours and weeks of crazy trips around the country to race meetings, sudden flights to Portugal at the drop of a hat, horrendously foul moods and then manic exuberance that would result in a ten-day drinking binge. I've got to the stage, she thought, of not even being motivated to get into conversations any more. I've got absolutely no idea what to say to her. When Des was like this, only of course that was very different, I just blanked out and waited for him to take enough Valium again.

Perhaps I've lost my own ability to speak, she thought, watching Mrs Freeman's mouth continue to move. What do other people do, in order to engage? Is this normal – or am I the one who's mad?

She cleared her throat, and pointed at Gearóid. "I was wondering . . ." she began.

"Ah, don't mind Gearóid he stays out in the barn for painting there was a time Marina couldn't stand the smell of paint and oil in the house and turpentine and made him go outside and told him never to come back but well you know between you me and the wall there is a lot more to that story but it's none of my business how's your tea I put three spoons into the pot as Doctor Marina likes but I never asked you do you take it strong . . ."

Ciara decided to leave well enough alone. You had to laugh really. In the beginning she'd have laughed with Des too. How long does the laughter last, normally? Before you only want to cry?

Only another hour and then she'd have to start the surgery anyway.

"What does Gearóid paint?" she interrupted.

It had the desired effect. Mrs Freeman stood still for at *least* five seconds.

"Well, pictures, I suppose."

"Oh. Yes. Picture. Um, what of?"

"Pictures of things."

"Ah. Um – is he successful?"

"They say he would get over a thousand for them on the mainland if he would sell them but he never does and in the summer when the visitors came to the island a few years ago he did sell one but that was to an American and he was pure mad but then there's those who would say that you wouldn't pick them up if they were scattered on the ground." Mrs Freeman examined Ciara's look of astonishment carefully. "He wouldn't show them to you even if you wanted though because he keeps them in the barn and there's a lot of men have left the island already for the winter."

"Really? Why?"

"To work in Scotland that is what they do and is your own husband coming over in the summer months?"

A lump of concrete had just landed in her stomach. The porridge turned to cement in her mouth.

"No," she said.

Mrs Freeman made a hissing noise through her teeth.

"He'll be over next summer so. Some men work for all the year round."

"I'm only staying for three months, myself," Ciara replied. "And my husband has just died."

Mrs Freeman crossed herself swiftly as if Ciara might possess a sort of evil spirit that killed husbands left right and centre.

"There's too many widows on this island," she said

ominously. "May the Lord have mercy on his soul now eat your breakfast and I'll be leaving you to go on up to the Big House and so we'll see you at Mass."

"Oh, no. I don't go. To Mass, I mean."

Mrs Freeman stopped in her tracks and then crossed herself again. Muttering darkly to herself, she made a hasty exit.

Now, thought Ciara. I may well be the Antichrist, but this is nice and quiet. Silence at last.

She sat at the quiet table drinking tea that was as strong as stew and through the window at the back of the kitchen watched the sea which seemed at times to want to swallow the island up. There were waves that seemed to be well over twenty feet high crashing over the pier in a great wallop of water that made the tiny harbour look as if it were a toy. And all around her, despite the hissing of the range and the cluck-clock of the over-mantel clock, there was the constant low-pitched hollow moaning of the wind.

Mikey Duggan, the boatman who'd brought her over, had threatened a storm. The island suddenly seemed to be rather vulnerable and very far away.

Just then the back door banged open. Gearóid? Ciara sat up alertly at the table and waited for him to enter. A solid-looking elderly man walked in wearing a cap and carrying a pipe. Rough ancient skin folded over on his face like a crumpled towel.

"Hello?" she said.

The man took a slight glance at her and then shuffled over to the range, where he turned his back to it as if to warm his backside and proceeded to light his pipe.

"Can I help you?" Ciara said. "Did you need to see the doctor?" She paused and waited for the elderly man to speak, but he said nothing, just carried on chewing his pipe. "I'm the new doctor for the next few months. While Doctor De Barra is away," she added.

Silence. The sweet, bitter scent of tobacco smoke. The tocking of the clock.

"Cup of tea?" she suggested.

The man grunted something incomprehensible which she took to be a refusal, and continued to smoke his pipe. There being nothing left to do, she continued to watch the sea.

An hour later, as silently as he came in, he left.

She watched him leave. Through the window she saw him shuffle past. He nodded slightly at Gearóid. Gearóid, who was stalking the garden and pacing about the little path and all around the house as if he had lost something, did not react.

What on earth, Ciara thought, have I let myself in for coming all the way out here?

"You need *what*? A fucking helicopter? Are you out of your tiny mind?"

Maggie took a deeper breath. "The boats can't go out – the weather's too severe. There's no other way of getting out to him. And he's promised me an interview and if I can persuade him to talk properly I've got a massive story. If we play along by his rules it will pay off, I promise. From Heathrow I can get a plane to one of the mainland airports in Ireland, but after that a helicopter is the only way of landing on the island. They've no airstrip and the seas are rough. The mainland's only twenty-seven miles away – it's a hop, skip and a jump for this helicopter company and they do it all the time for stroppy actors and musicians who are going out to Míle Cairde at Atlantis to sulk. Look – it'll pay off in the long run. I know it will. Trust me on this one, Ben. We've got a private interview with Pierce Fox, in his home, on his island tax-haven retreat. I've told him I'm going to help him ghost-write his autobiography too. He's so vain he's actually going for it. What could be more perfect, Ben? We've got him cornered. The Fox is trapped. If I can't squeeze him for his side of the story in this location, when all his guards are down, then I'll – oh, I'll resign from *Scoop!* All right?"

"Huh!" roared Benedict King, Maggie's editor-in-chief at *Scoop!*

"Look, I'll talk to you tomorrow. Hold the front page! I'm going to bring this home, Ben. That I promise you!"

"Don't spend any money at the airport," Benedict King roared and slammed down the phone.

Maggie beamed. She was going to Atlantis. She was going to meet Pierce Fox. She was going to have to use every inch of sexuality that her vast experience could muster, in order to get him to talk. It was going to be the story of a lifetime.

Chapter Twelve

The morning was so green. A sky that was a pale, pale clean blue behind the hills. The ancient trees thick with whispers. Amy knelt on the window seat of the bay-window and let the view of the lake and trees and mountains wrap around her and soak their moodiness into her until she almost ached. Oh, if I can't write beautifully here I'll never write again! she thought, and then caught the sudden tang of frying bacon from downstairs. Oh, wow!

Amy had had a failure of nerve the evening before and hadn't gone down to dinner.

Amy washed her face quickly, found a nice tight pair of faded jeans, a long-sleeved T-shirt, chandelier earrings and a rope of beads, and brushed her hair. Make-up? Hard to know what was the best thing to do in this place. In that majestic landscape with this overwhelmingly beautiful house, to attempt to add adornment to one's face seemed almost like pollution – and yet. She hadn't been out of the house without make-up for twenty years, and the thought of having to go downstairs and greet strangers over breakfast *au naturel* was just a bit too scary. On the other hand, coming down at nine o'clock in the morning with a party face on might look – well, pushy or something. She dabbed some blusher on her cheeks, found a very pale lipstick, and then drowned herself in Ysatis.

Following the scent of bacon she walked very slowly down the stairs marvelling at the giant sweep of banister, the little stained-glass window on the return, the polished oak steps that were each as wide as one of the rooms in her suburban Dublin house and then the sudden chill of the entrance hall as the stairs met the tiled ground floor. Through the huge double doors at the front of the house she could see the lake, brooding like a cauldron. Amy turned, in the direction of the all-too-wonderful bacon whiff and the sound of chatter and morning kitchen noise that was coming from the rear of the house. The long corridor was paved in tiles and pretty nippy to walk down too, she thought, missing her cardigan now and folding her arms in front of her to keep warm. She passed a giant drawing room with big bay windows and window-seats that overlooked the lake in front and then the wonderfully lush gardens on the side and the giant Victorian greenhouse that was rusting helplessly behind the trees.

The drawing-room walls, just like every wall in Atlantis, were panelled in oak and hung with magnificent works of art, and the art was all mixed up everywhere. There were giant landscapes, traditional cows and fields and trees and then garish abstracts and cubist shapes, nudes and portraits and minimalist charcoals. And then she passed the dining hall, with its endless glossy oak table and candelabras and a fire in the fireplace which had already been lit – obviously they had to keep that going all day long in this weather, Amy thought, sniffing the mild smell of turf and pinewood in the air. But the bacon smells were beckoning. She paused a moment at the doorway before entering the kitchen to watch the little group who sat at the table deep in conversation, just to get a sense of what was going on.

The kitchen was an enormous high-ceilinged room with dozens of cupboards and shelves at the back, and then on the wall closest to the door a giant dresser the size of – well, two of the wardrobes in our house, Amy thought, but it was warmed wonderfully by an enormous range. Over to one side beside a big window was a round table at which several people sat. There was the smell of fresh, pungent coffee, scenting the air like a delicious perfume and the smell of toast, the rashers frying, and oh, something warmly stickily hot and sweet . . . Scones! she thought, spying a pile of freshly baked wonders on a cake rack steaming by the range. Somebody gets up early in this house and bakes fresh scones! I have absolutely died and gone to heaven.

"Hello, everyone," she said cautiously and ventured in.

"Hi!" came back a chorus of reply.

"We met yesterday on the boat," said Reindeer-jumper man. "I'm Zack Rowley. Come on in. Sit down!"

She sat down beside him in the window seat of the bay window where she could turn back over her shoulder and still see the lake. Now that his woolly hat was off she could see that he had hair that was completely silver-white and in thick, cherubic curls like one of Botticelli's angels.

"Hi, Zack. I'm Amy – hold on a minute – Zack? Not – oh, you're *Zack Rowley*! Oh my God! But my children love your books!" she gasped, and everybody laughed.

"Aw. Thank you! That's awfully sweet of you," Zack replied, his face pinking-up delightfully. "Do you know anybody else here?"

"Let me guess!" Amy said, but she still couldn't help beaming at him. Zack Rowley! Who'd have thought! Oh, Holly and June would be so excited if they knew that he was here! Oh, bloody Terence. If only she could phone and talk to the kids.

"I absolutely love *Emerald Finds Her Pants!*" she said, unable to get over the fact that she was actually sitting beside the guy who'd written it. Zack looked at her as though he was a kid who'd just met Santa Claus.

The harmonica-playing snorkel jacket with the whiskey bottle on the boat was at the table too, with a very lurid complexion and a morning-breath that she could smell from the other side of the room – but it was a toothpaste-modified whiskey morning breath, and she didn't mind it too much.

"What's your name? I'm Amy Shanahan," she said to Harmonica Whiskey Breath.

"Well, I'm Aiming-for-improvement," Harmonica Whiskey breath replied with a still-drunken smile.

"He's Wolftone O'Neill, ex-punk rocker now a drunken poet and a thundering disgrace to literature – and he is much more civilised in the evenings. Aren't you, Wolf?," smiled Joy Jackson, the blonde-haired glamour-puss poet that she remembered from the boat. "I've got a place out here because I won TS Eliot Award," Joy added, simpering a little.

"Oh, well done, Joy. That's wonderful!" Amy turned to the mahogany-haired woman who'd been reading on the boat. "I bet you're a writer, too," she said to her.

Mahogany Hair tinkled a little laugh.

"Oh, gosh," she said, looking around her at the group with an amused face. "Tell me more about myself, *please*!"

"Well," Amy took a deep breath and looked around her at the group, sensing the beginning of a game, "I bet you're a chick-lit writer," she went on, beaming at the others who nodded encouragingly.

Mahogany Hair looked as though she was about to hit her. "*Excuse* me?" she barked.

"Well . . ." Amy quavered.

"That's a compliment," interrupted Zack. "Amy's a very successful chick-lit writer herself. Aren't you?" he added doubtfully.

"Oh! Have you read my book?" Amy said, desperately hoping that he had. She was beginning to feel like a schoolgirl among some very cranky nuns.

"Er, not exactly. But I do know who you are. And you've done very well. You must be very proud," Zack said kindly. "She's been on the bestsellers list," he added to Joy.

"Well, you won't get there with poetry," said Joy in a gruff tone, but Amy knew she was trying to be kind.

"A *chick-lit* writer? How on *earth* could she possibly think . . ." Mahogany Hair was shrieking hysterically.

"I write women's fiction books," Amy said, drawing up her shoulders. "And I suppose the reason that I thought you might do too is because you look . . . oh, I don't know . . . glamorous, I suppose?" She raised her eyebrows at Mahogany Hair and cocked her head to one side. "And interesting. And witty. And fun. So, obviously I was wrong. Mind if I have some tea?"

Mahogany Hair recoiled. "Well," she said, watching Amy pour tea with eyes that were as yellow as a cat's, "I suppose when you put it that way. It's just that I can't

100

think of anything that is *less* like my profession." And she tinkled her little laugh again. She shook out her fan of hair and shuddered and wrapped her silk pashmina tightly around her shoulders. Underneath she was wearing a rather eveningy black cashmere dress.

"So, what *do* you do?" Amy asked her lightly, helping herself to toast.

"I'm Marguerite Coyle," Mahogany Hair said.

"Oh." Amy looked desperately at Zack.

"Marguerite's a very well-known cellist," said Zack.

Mahogany Hair gave him a feline smile.

"Oh, that must be lovely. What a gorgeous instrument. My husband used to play the drums," said Amy with enthusiasm. "When we were students," she added.

The others nodded back politely. Mahogany Hair was rolling her eyes.

"What sort of music do you play?" Amy carried on, tomato-faced. "Um – on the cello?"

"I'm *Marguerite Coyle*," Mahogany Hair said, tossing her sleek bob like a colt. "You will have seen me on the cover of CDs. Or in a concert, perhaps? And on television, of course." She sighed and gave the gathering a little look of mild fatigue, as if the burden of her famous existence was just a bit too much to carry sometimes.

"Oh," said Amy. "Well, we don't get to go out much nowadays. Two small kids, you know," she added, looking helplessly at Zack.

Marguerite smiled her feline smile again. "How lovely to have children," she purred. "My darling husband and I have not been blessed. But we have so much love for one another I must say," she turned to Zack, batting eyelashes like Bambi, "that we simply don't seem to need the distraction of children." She turned to Amy. "We are both musicians, you see, and so our relationship is in such harmony that we seem to grow deeper in our love for one another almost every day." And she sighed again and poured herself a cup of thick black coffee, dumping three sugars into it.

Amy wasn't sure whether or not to laugh – on the one hand, it might be a piss-take, given that she'd announced herself as a chick-lit writer and Marguerite was clearly underwhelmed. And on the other hand, she had a very strong feeling that Marguerite was actually being serious about herself.

"So," Zack was saying to her, "tell me all about the book *you've* come here to write."

But Setanta Lynch had just drifted in through the door and was eyeing the group dreamily from under his báinin hat.

Amy's heart began to thump.

"Grab the scones from over at that range, Setanta!" Joy barked at him. "He might be beautiful," she added to the others, "but by Jesus he'd better make himself useful, that's all I can bloody well say."

Amy laughed. They were an extraordinary group. She was surrounded by some of the most lauded artists in their fields. Although she'd never heard of Marguerite Coyle the cellist before – but then with two tiny kids at home it wasn't always easy to get out to listen to classical music, was it? But Zack Rowley was actually sitting next to her having breakfast! And he was nothing like she'd imagined him to be. Zack was obviously making a fortune from his children's books – Holly had read every single one of the *Emerald The Dragon* series and couldn't wait for the next one to come out. But Zack seemed to be just an ordinary guy, a bit shy in fact, with absolutely terrible taste in clothes, she thought, noticing the faded purple flared cords underneath the reindeer jumper and the battered brown lace-up shoes. And the cherubic silver curls of hair – wasn't he a bit too young to be that rather startling shade of all-over white? Zack only looked to be about thirty-five. The completely white hair was kind of fun though, if you liked that sort of thing. He was, she supposed, a bit magical looking, almost. A bit like a Christmas elf might look, minus the pointy ears. Oh, if only she could phone Holly and tell her that he was actually sitting here beside her! Oh, if only Terence wasn't such a plank with his stupid ideas of fatherhood!

And then Joy Jackson – Amy didn't read much poetry but she'd heard of Joy. She was even on the school curriculum. But then one of her friends was a secondary teacher who'd told her that Joy Jackson was total crap and that the only reason she'd got onto the schools' curriculum was because she's written some poetry in Irish. Joy seemed to be a reasonably warm person though – albeit with a strangely masculine strength of character that, coupled with her waist-length golden hair, plunging neckline over a slightly crêpy décolletage and lacy almost see-through top was beginning to make Amy wonder if Joy was in fact a man in drag. But the perky boobs with jewel-like nipples at right-angles through a flesh-coloured bra were real enough. And her face was kind, even if her heavily pencilled eyebrows were a bit too inclined to scowl sometimes.

Wolftone O'Neill – now that she could get a proper look at him and he didn't have his harmonica in front of his face, she recognised him from his early days as a London-Irish punk. Wolftone had headed up the raucous punk band Niall and The Nihilists, and Amy, in her student London days, had been an enthusiastic fan. But poor old Wolftone had obviously taken a battering over the years, she thought, taking in the frazzled complexion, the swollen eyes and the nest of hair that not even the most desperate cuckoo bird would sleep in for fear of what he'd catch. She'd heard that Niall and The Nihilists had broken up due to the usual combination of heroin, alcohol and general bad behaviour. Wolftone O'Neill had gone solo in the nineties with a neo-punk folk-ballad band, The Irish Lunatics. The Irish Lunatics were bringing down the houses all over London and New York in the nineties, but Wolftone himself had been unable to put a Manhattan down. His ever-deepening levels of drunkenness had eventually put The Irish Lunatics on ice for at least a decade. He'd had some poetry published since then, but mostly out of kindness and in the kinds of Sunday supplements that give you free copies of Jordan's calendar on CD ROM for Christmas. Given the content of Wolftone's poetry, however, most of it would make a pretty good background to an evening spent with Jordan's CD ROM, Amy thought.

Wolftone had released one poem as a Christmas record with a background of punk rock guitar called "Get Your Knickers Down Or Santa'll Never Come" – the record was, naturally enough, banned immediately, so it became an instant Christmas Number One download – and at least poor Wolftone and The Irish Lunatics had got back into the charts.

And then there was Setanta – the beautiful man who'd

slept the whole way over on the boat. He was pouring himself some tea and lazily buttering a scone, listening through half-awake eyes to something Joy was telling him about the death of metaphor. God, he was an angel, Amy thought, kicking herself for having decided against make-up and a plungier or at least more glamorous top.

"What sort of work are you doing here, in Atlantis?" she asked Setanta quietly when she could get a word in edgeways between Zack, who was giggling at a filthy Limerick that Wolftone was reciting, and Joy who was furiously refuting that that kind of jingo could be called a poem.

"Sculpture," replied Setanta dreamily. "It's something that I've never done before. I'm trying to stretch myself as an artist, to become more tactile. Until now I've always loved to paint. And then I drifted into conceptual art – but that's a load of bollocks really. My hands are telling me something now, that it's time to make them feel again." He looked at them stretched out in front of him. Amy marvelled at the beauty of his fingers, their perfect length, the neat rounded nails, the roughened finger tips – oh, just imagine those fingertips feeling *me* –

"Well, if you ever need a model, Setanta," Joy was saying in her growly voice, and Marguerite laughed like a drain.

"Yes. You never know," Setanta smiled his tantalising smile at Joy, who winked at the others.

"Well, I'm going to have to go and play some music," Marguerite purred, slithering away from the table, her pashmina coiled around her shoulders like Venus de Milo. "I find that if I don't manage to start my hands warming up by ten o'clock in the morning it can take forever for the blood to circulate. It's a very physical thing, musicianship," she said dreamily, and then drifted out of the room as if she were a Greek chorus commenting on the world.

"Wouldn't fancy your chances of getting her into bed," Joy muttered to Setanta, "if she has to start warming up at ten o'clock in the morning to get her blood to circulate."

"It's a very physical thing, a hangover," sparked Wolftone, splashing his coffee with the contents of a hip-flask.

"I don't know how you can write when you're drunk," Amy giggled. "I'd be a complete wreck. I can hardly hold myself together after two glasses of wine nowadays."

"Well, perhaps that explains the difference between my writing and yours," Wolftone said, tipping the hip flask into his lips. "What did you say your book is about, anyway?" he asked her, trying to focus his eyes.

"It's – oh, basically it's a romantic novel. A woman who falls in love with two different men, brothers – and she marries the wrong one," Amy replied. "It's called 'My Two Lovers And I'," she added anxiously to Joy – who was clearly trying very hard to look pleased.

"Is it a bodice ripper?" asked Wolftone, snorting with laughter.

He's not laughing at me – he's just drunk, Amy told herself.

"Could be," she lightly replied. "But that's a bit of an old-fashioned term, isn't it?"

"Oh, pass me that bodice ripper," began Wolftone in a theatrical voice. "Where did I leave my glasses? Ah, here they are, underneath my bodice ripper. Perhaps you might allow me to place my bodice ripper here while I tie my shoelaces?"

"Wolftone's a performance poet, really," Joy told Amy whose cheeks were stinging.

"*I'm not a bodice ripper, I'm a bodice ripper's son, I'm only ripping bodices till the bodice ripper comes,*" Amy quipped back, and the others roared with laughter.

"That's great!" said Zack.

"See?" she said to Wolftone who'd shut up by now. "Now I'm a performance poet too!"

The others grinned at Wolftone who was scowling into his tea-flavoured whiskey.

Amy stood up. "Well, I'm afraid I'm going to have to go and do some work as well. I've got a deadline and another novel to write by the end of the month." She smiled shyly at everyone. "Excuse me, please."

"See you for dinner tonight?" said Joy. "We all dine in the dining hall at seven. It's compulsory and the food's astonishing. Mrs Freeman's a genius."

"And then afterwards we can all play games," added Zack.

"Games?"

"Oh, absolutely," beamed Joy.

"Can't wait," said Amy. But privately she was rather terrified.

Setanta's eyes were as green as the hills of Inish Rua, and as sulky as the bog. God knows how she would get any work done, with a ghost of a suicidal woman in my room – and with him in the studio next door, Amy thought, smiling bravely before going back to her room.

Chapter Thirteen

Yvonne Delahunty, Bean an Tí, was set to have a very busy day. There were four teenagers after arriving yesterday off the boat and staying in the house for a fortnight, all of them from Dublin – which was far more trouble than it was worth really because teenagers nowadays had no manners and the Dublin ones were worse. Atlantis House had an annexe which was a conversion of the old stables, where students for the Coláiste stayed. Yesterday, Yvonne got the beds ready and made sure the children – well, you couldn't really call them that, the girls were wearing make-up, which was appalling. They shouldn't be *allowed* to wear that kind of make-up at that age. *And* one of the boys seemed to be growing a beard and Yvonne could have *sworn* she smelt cigarettes off the other one – and then today she'd had to spend ages explaining the breakfast and dinner arrangements for the week because their Irish was atrocious. In Yvonne's experience teenage girls didn't eat at all, whereas boys ate far too much. This group were two boys *and* two girls – which was the worst possible combination, of course, but nobody ever asked her for her opinion, they just sent the children over and she had to make what she could of it and keep them out of danger, although any danger they might come to on Inish Rua would clearly be of their own doing.

Yvonne had put in an order with An Siopa for two sausages for each boy and one for each girl for their evening tea for the next four weeks, and they would have porridge for the mornings. Two sliced pans per week which would go into the chest freezer. A four-stone bag of potatoes. They would have frozen burgers or fish fingers for lunch. Yvonne knew well that there was no point in serving fresh fruits or vegetables to teenagers. On Sunday they could have a tin of prunes.

Yvonne had woken early, fed the teenagers and practised her Pilates so that she could be quite prepared for the weekly class that Trish Lenihan taught at the Halla Oileán – although Trish was so dreamy that Yvonne was usually several paces ahead of her, but what could you do? If Trish's Pilates was the only exercise class on the island then so be it. Then, having arranged for the deliveries to be made from Siopa Pháidín Mike, Yvonne put a silk scarf (which Pierce had sent her from a trip to Venice, it was Giorgio Armani no less) around her neck and went up to Nóirín the Gruagaire to have her hair set. Holding her scarf loosely around her golden curls to keep out the furious wind, she went up to the church for confession, it being Saturday. Confessions were heard for everyone in Inish Rua on the first Saturday of the month.

Yvonne slipped quietly into the little chapel and blessed herself, noting with dismay that the contents of the holy water font were looking a bit stale – really, Father Glen didn't have a lot to do now in the winter months and you'd think he could make sure the holy water was changed daily. But he was new to the parish and perhaps he hadn't got around to noticing. She genuflected before the altar and knelt down in her usual pew, waiting for Father Glen to open the door of the confession box.

Most of the islanders went to confession every month, except for the drunken has-beens that would stay up all night in the pub banging away at their bodhráns and tin whistles (thank God there was the retreat at Míle Cairde or the cultural possibilities on Inish Rua would be unbearable altogether, Yvonne often thought). But Yvonne went to confession every month and you could time the moon by it. It was one of the main reasons, she felt, that she lived with such inner peace. Each of us is capable of sinfulness and daily life puts all sorts of temptations in our way. Monthly confessions were a beautiful way of committing to God once again and it was a pity more people didn't take advantage of it.

In any case, Yvonne felt something of a coup in the notion that she was probably the most frequent confessor of all of Inish Rua.

And today, so far, she was the only confessor. The chapel was empty, the howling wind and promise of more freezing rain keeping other sinners away. Yvonne prayed for their forgiveness, and said a decade of the rosary while she waited for Father Glen.

Eventually, the side door of the sacristy opened and Glen Cassidy appeared. Father Glen was a very neat man, with a soft, round face, lovely pink cheeks and an expression of very great holiness indeed.

"Well! Just yourself, is it, Yvonne? Well, there's no need to step into the confession box if it's just yourself that's in it," Glen said. "You could come up to the house instead."

He looked a bit flustered today, she thought, thinking that it was a shame that Sorcha the housekeeper had left the island with the last priest – and everyone wished them well but with a child on the way there was no way really that Father Máirtín could have remained on the island and continue as the parish priest *and* live in what had clearly become an active sin with Sorcha – because that left Father Glen with no housekeeper at all to help him with that collar which was clearly not quite right. Yvonne would have loved to offer to fix it up for him but you couldn't be an involuntary housekeeper to a priest as well as a personal assistant to Mr Pierce Fox, even if *he* was a very infrequent resident on the island, *and* a Bean an Tí as well.

Yvonne liked the fact that Glen was only just after being ordained – his newness and lack of cynicism glowed from every pore.

"Well, I'll step inside, if you don't mind, Father," Yvonne said. "I'm an old-fashioned girl." And she smiled to herself at the thought of it.

"Well, you're very welcome now, Yvonne."

Yvonne slid into the oak-smelling confession box and knelt down.

"*Bless me, Father, for I have sinned,*" she began in her most demure voice.

Father Glen Cassidy wasn't quite sure what to make of Yvonne, but he was at least very appreciative of the amount of time she tended to spend in church. She was definitely a dedicated Christian – which was a wonderful thing, Glen felt. And she did seem to care a lot about the appearance of things, commenting on the flowers he picked from the hedgerows and the little cottage garden if he'd made a special effort with their arrangement (which in fairness, he put a great deal of thought into), and mentioning the sorts of hymns she'd like to add to the church services. Nóirín the Gruagaire played the little electric organ for Mass and often hit the wrong notes or played something that wasn't even a hymn, and Glen didn't really mind but he appreciated it that Yvonne Delahunty was the first to notice when Nóirín was playing the theme from Robin Hood instead of *"Glór Sna hÁirde"*.

Glen hadn't been disappointed to be given Inish Rua as a parish on his first gig – in fact, he was delighted. The idea of a monastic settlement thrilled him. He'd often felt that if he could have chosen to live in any other time in history it would have been as an early medieval saint out on a secluded island in the middle of the ocean with a crowd of other monks, nothing between them and God but the beauty of nature to battle with. And now, here he was on the most beautiful of all the North Atlantic islands, with nothing between him and God but a slightly over-lethargic congregation of islanders and a residence of the discontented rich and famous to contend with. As a philosophical challenge, Glen found it to be bracing. So Yvonne was something of a treat for him – she was, at least, very enthusiastic about her presence in the church.

"Tell me your sins, my child," Glen said now in his most holy voice. He closed his eyes. On the one hand, he couldn't help feeling slightly intrusive asking anyone to confess their innermost conflicts with him, even though he was God's priest. And he did know that it was his most

holy calling to help. To serve those who needed God most. But he couldn't help feeling like a bit of a sneak sometimes. All of the time, in fact. There was something slightly discomfiting about hearing confessions, the intrusion into people's private lives, Glen had discovered, and this discovery had alarmed him greatly. He had prayed very hard to a quite disinterested God for some strength and wisdom on the matter. But it hadn't worked – not yet.

Glen liked sacraments in general – he adored Fist Holy Communion for example, all those little white dresses like mini-meringues, a froth of lace and white taffeta in the sunlight, well, he would almost clap his hands in glee! He liked baptism, as long as the baby was very small and didn't whinge at all and the couple weren't too demented with lack of sleep – and he especially loved marriage, but there wasn't going to be much opportunity of that on Inish Rua, unless of course he could advance his plans to encourage mainlanders to the island to celebrate their weddings there.

Glen had, since coming here three months ago, hatched a heretofore secret plan to make Inish Rua known internationally as a very special place in which to get married. It was so wild and romantic, the little medieval chapel was very holy indeed and full of history and Glen felt sure that it was the kind of place a truly romantic couple (a couple like, say, Brangelina for example) would like to come and have a quiet but superbly glamorous and *extremely* spiritual wedding. He had a catalogue of wedding gowns from Vera Wang among his personal books, as well as a copy of *Vogue Bridal Valentino Collections* which he looked at every now and then and found to be truly inspirational. But for now, confessions were the only sacrament other than Holy Mass that he got to administer on a regular basis, and that brought him out in a slightly prickly, itchy state of unhappiness. So he liked to hear confessions with closed eyes. It made him feel less voyeuristic, and closer to God.

Yvonne was never bashful, of course, which was a help.

"Father, I confess that I have taken the Lord's name twice in vain, when I heard that the Gael Scoil were sending me two sets of teenagers – but really, my pleas were entirely in their interest I have to admit so perhaps the sin was not intended. Teenagers nowadays need so much dicipline. And, as you know, I am a woman on my own, since my husband passed away."

"Yes. I know Yvonne," said Glen in a spiritual voice. Rumours of the sudden disappearance into the afterlife of Yvonne's husband had, he gathered, been greatly exaggerated.

"And I *have* felt tempted by the sin of vanity when a particularly lovely parcel arrived in the post last week from Mr Pierce Fox thanking me for getting his apartments at Atlantis ready for him. Pierce is coming over shortly to work privately here with legal colleagues and spend some time at Míle Cairde." Yvonne lowered her voice. "Pierce is very kind to me, as I'm sure you know, and the silk pyjamas he sent from America were wonderful and so I couldn't help feeling the tiniest bit spoilt when I tried them on – but you know, it's not often a girl gets such a lovely treat like that!"

"No. Yes. No. I mean, well. Er. I'm sure you deserve the gifts he sends. You are a very – um – dedicated housekeeper."

"Oh, I'm not a *housekeeper*, Father! Oh, good heavens, I wonder what made you think I was?"

Glen felt his heart sink. "No, I'm sure that it's really a lot more work than that," he said hastily.

She carried on. "I mean, Mr Fox has a lot of very specific requirement when he comes to stay, around his privacy of course. He works long hours at his legal work – now, don't *ask* me what that is about, because I wouldn't have a *clue*, but I know it's very important he has everything set up for him. Of course Mrs Freeman leaves the meals cooked but he'd need me to serve them in the apartment and make sure he has the kind of wine he needs and all the right chocolates. He has them sent specially over from France."

"Yes. How lovely it all sounds."

Glen was sure that at some point he ought to suggest a penance for the sin, but he had begun to lose track of where Mrs Delahunty's sin had happened in the first place. Wasn't this something to do with vanity? Or – perhaps he'd better listen a bit closer and pay more attention.

"Carry on," he suggested.

"Oh, and Father Glen, I'm not sure that Mrs Freeman can manage all the catering for Míle Cairde as well as for that new doctor. Now, I saw the new doctor today going up the lane when I was coming out of Tí Nóirin the Gruagaire and she really looks far too young to be a fully qualified doctor, and a bit – well, unkempt, I thought. I mean I'd be worried that she is only just out of college."

"Oh, I'm sure Doctor Marina would have made sure her credentials –"

"I hear they work them very hard nowadays and you just can't be too sure. As you are no doubt aware my own health is quite delicate especially in the winter months. At least Doctor Marina did look her age – well, and a lot more sometimes I often thought, especially first thing in the morning, only I wouldn't want to hurt her feelings but there were times when I really felt that Doctor Marina mightn't take the best care of herself at all – do you know what I mean, Father?"

"Er," said Glen.

"But I *had* hoped that we would be getting a doctor who would have had at least the same experience as Doctor Marina has!"

"Yeeees," Glen said, wondering if he ought to ask her to start over again with the sins, but knowing that it wasn't really a runner at this stage in the game.

"And in fact," she continued, "I was really hoping that we'd be getting a doctor who had a lot *more* experience. Like Doctor Sam Smith from the mainland who came over a few years ago, Father. Do you know, he was the only doctor who's ever been able to find out what was the real cause of the pain in my chest?" and she sighed heavily.

Oh," said Glen. "And are you feeling better now, Yvonne?" And then he winced. *That* wasn't the right thing to say in confessional – he was supposed to be listening for repentance.

"Well, in the frosty mornings I do get a dreadful pain still right here, under the solar plexus and it travels right around my back and into my spine and up the back of my neck into my hairline – really, there are times when I feel that I'm going to have to lie down again and never get up." Yvonne sighed very loudly now.

Outside in the chapel there was the sound of a little cough.

"Ah. Well, perhaps you could say three Hail Marys then, Yvonne –" Glen began.

"Only three?" Yvonne was clearly insulted.

"Er. Yes. Well, say four or five then. If you'd prefer."

116

"I would!"

"*And I absolve you in the name of the Father . . .* "

It had been a rather odd confession, Glen thought, but he'd get used to it – hopefully. The seminary hadn't prepared him for a whole lot of real life, when you thought about it. But that is what he was here to minister to.

As Yvonne Delahunty slipped out of the confessional again, he sort of felt he ought to come out and say goodbye – he still couldn't help feeling odd just sitting there with the door closed. It was a bit claustrophobic, actually, sitting in here just smelling the woodwork and the dust. Like being in a coffin, only sitting up. It sort of reminded him of a tanning booth he'd liked to visit sometimes up in Dublin, only that was different.

Glen smoothed the pale grey linen of his trousers out, and hoped that there weren't too many more confessors to come today because he was getting a bit hungry and there was a nice smoked salmon and asparagus quiche in the fridge that Mrs Freeman had sent over from Atlantis House last night – and then he prayed quickly for forgiveness for that thought.

The door of the confession box opened and a man stepped in.

"*Bless me, Father, for I have sinned,*" the man began, and then filled the little box with loud productive coughing.

Nowhere, not all the seminaries of Rome nor all the missions of Africa, would prepare you for this, Glen thought, closing his eyes tightly and zipping closed his lips. If only he could have zipped his nose too. You can't exactly cover up your face when you are in a confession box – even though there's a little grid between you and the confessor, they can still see what you're doing, especially if you start putting on a balaclava or a paper mask or something. Well, he'd been asking for it now. Imagine the gush of germs that whirled around in that tiny space!

Glen squeezed his nostrils and asked in a small tight-lipped voice,

"Hello there, Jimmy. Would you like to speak to God and ask him for forgiveness for your sins?"

Jimmy Seán from the pub shuffled and wiped his nose and coughed a good bit more.

Glen was aware that the man was sick – but actually, he didn't know Jimmy Seán too well at all really. Jimmy Seán hadn't been to Mass since Glen had arrived on Inish Rua and become parish priest of St Tristan's three short months ago. He'd been asked to pop up to see Jimmy Seán at the house – Jimmy Seán's son Art who was very tall and a bit too good-looking in a kind of rangy, broad-shouldered American way if you like that sort of thing, had asked him to come around when he'd first come over from Boston and found his dad all lonely at home and not wanting to go to Mass – and Glen had blessed the house and tried to find some comfort for this poor man, who had told him he was dying. But Jimmy Seán had burst into tears and told Glen to go away. Actually, what he'd really said was "Fuck off, you dirty paedophile, and get back to your filthy magazines, ya bollocks ya."

So it was definitely a good development to see him in confession now, despite the shower of phlegm, Glen thought. He decided to say so.

"Great to see you, Jimmy. I know you can't always make it to Mass, and so I really appreciate you coming down today in the wet and the cold. The Lord is always here for you."

Jimmy Seán hacked loudly again. Glen made a mental note to take a thousand milligrams of vitamin C after confessions and to have a nice long Tea Tree Oil soak in his bath tonight.

"Indeed and He is not," said Jimmy Seán, coughing again and sucking catarrh back through his throat. "That feckin pipe needs cleaning again."

"Um. I'm sorry?" said Glen. "Take your time, Jimmy. There's no need to rush. God has all the time in the world for you." Lavender and Eucalyptus with the Tea Tree Oil was best, he remembered, and it would be a lovely treat listening to some music too. He had a new CD that his mum had sent – *Mamma Mia*, the movie soundtrack.

Meryl Streep had such a gorgeous voice.

"There is no such thing as God," said Jimmy Seán.

Glen wondered for a moment if he'd better ask him to say that again – but it sounded like such a terrible thing to say that he wasn't sure if he really wanted to hear it. And then again, silence wasn't really going to help matters. His collar pricked again. He wondered if Jimmy Seán would notice if he took it off. Really, what he shouldn't have worn today was the Abercrombie and Fitch vest, as well as the stiff shirt over it.

"Jimmy," Glen began. And then he didn't know what to say. "*An bhfuil tú all right?*" he asked. Are you all right?

"I am dying. And I don't believe in God. Does it sound like I'm all right?" sniffed Jimmy Seán. "What would you do if you were me?"

Glen opened his mouth. And shut it again. What would he do?

Dying. What on earth did he know about that? The Sacrament of the Sick – well, that *was* Glen's most realistic experience of dying.

He had done a short stint in the hospice in Dublin for three months in the summer time and he had enjoyed it thoroughly – serving daily Mass to some very enthusiastic nuns with a scattering of grateful relatives and one or two patients in wheelchairs who were very blissfully out on post-op drugs. He had felt quite at home there, administering the last rites and confessions to people who smelt of soiled clothing masked with incense and candle-scent, whose morphine trip to heaven was only hours away and who had very little left to trouble them – this is what dying meant to Glen. It was the beautiful, floral-scented journey that brings us finally to God.

So what *would* he do?

Glen felt, as he had often felt during that quite pleasant if slightly unidimensional stay in the hospice, that dying was a very *precious* human state. He had rather imagined that when *he himself* reached the final journey into God's arms he would be deep in prayer, in a state of mesmeric semi-consciousness in which the troubles of the material world would slip away from him and he would enter the kingdom of heaven peacefully, in a state of joyous perfection.

On the one hand, he could have told Jimmy Seán this – that death is the end of our life on earth and the beginning of our journey to meet our God. And yet, something told him that the kind of foul mood Jimmy Seán was in wasn't going to be amenable to this idea.

"I would pray," was what he eventually suggested to Jimmy Seán, and Jimmy Seán hurrumphed and spat up lots of phlegm. Glen winced again and almost covered his head.

"That's exactly the kind of answer I'd expect from a

priest. And I'd have thought, you being a young lad, you'd have been a whole lot better than the last one," said Jimmy Seán lugubriously.

"Well, we must all do our best to serve the Lord," began Glen and then sensing Jimmy's immediate reaction he changed tack. "Look. Why is it that you think you can't pray to God for guidance?"

"Because I don't believe in God!" roared Jimmy Seán. "My things keep going missing! There are ghosts and things being stolen! And you wouldn't know who gets into the house at night!"

Glen cringed again. Outside the confession box he could hear shuffling, and muttering of voices. Midway through a confession, one doesn't normally open up the door and check out the state of the queue – and so Glen didn't, but something told him that the parishioners who had gathered after Yvonne and Jimmy were by now making a quick exit.

Glen panicked. It was as if the church was being hijacked by this one foul-tempered man who was renouncing God, and at the same time the good and the faithful were being driven away. This is the way temptation and sin work, Glen reminded himself, and he told himself to hold his nerve. The good parishioners would be back. And in any case, he'd see the entire population of the island at Mass tomorrow and he could offer anyone who felt a desperate need to have an extra quick confession then.

"Why would you say such a thing, Jimmy Seán?" Glen whispered, cringing again as he felt the door slam and heard the voices becoming distant outside. Now there were more people leaving!

"Because God doesn't believe in me!" Jimmy Seán

roared. "If he did then why has he left me in this state? My son has come home from America to take care of my pub for me, and it's ruined his life. He has no wife, he'll end up here living as a bachelor forever. And I've lost my glasses," and Jimmy Seán burst into tears.

"No, no, no, no, no," said Glen, his sense of panic mounting.

"Arra, for fuck's sake!" huffed Jimmy Seán, and Glen cringed again.

Oh dearest God All Mighty, nothing in the seminary had prepared him for this!

"What use is it living a life like this? I might as well be dead. *Death, I welcome it!*" Jimmy Seán roared.

"Oh, God!" said Glen.

"Father," Jimmy carried on, lowering his voice to a growl, "I have decided that the only way I can face this is *to take my own life into my own hands*."

Glen felt his head beginning to throb. "Jimmy Seán –" he began.

"If I were a Swiss man I'd be taking the cowardly way out and ordering a doctor's euthanasia. So I'll do it like an Irishman, and I'm saving anyone the bother of having to do it for me," he announced triumphantly.

"*What?*"

"I have it all arranged with the doctor. Only, she doesn't *know* I have it all arranged. I'll collect my morphine tablets until I have enough to kill myself. And the poor doctor will never know. Isn't it a fine solution, priest? And no trouble to anybody when I go."

"It's horrendous!" flustered Glen. "It's appalling! You can't do that! It's suicide! It's a mortal sin! And in any case," he added very quietly, "won't the doctor figure out what you are up to and be very annoyed? You'll put her in an awful spot." He felt cold sweat trickle down his neck.

"Well, you're a fecking lot of use, you are," Jimmy Seán replied, and exploded into a fit of wet coughing again.

Glen was beginning to feel faint. How much longer could he survive in this confession box without taking a breath, if the man kept spraying germs everywhere?

"Jimmy," he squeaked through a tiny gap in his lips, "perhaps we should end this confession now and perhaps the best thing would be for you to come up to the house during the week and we could talk about this again properly? I really feel that this dark confession box isn't quite the right place to discuss something as important as this . . ."

"Yeah, yeah," Jimmy Seán was shuffling around on his side of the box to leave. "That'll be the day. Good day to you, Father, and don't be bothering yourself with me and my troubles. I'll let you get on to your dinner."

And he left.

Glen's first instinct was to open the confession box door as quickly as possible and get some air. He flung it open, but there were two old ladies still sitting at the back of the chapel looking animated and so he didn't follow Jimmy. It was so difficult to keep private things private on this island, Glen reminded himself. He watched the man walk with hunched moody shoulders out of the chapel.

What on earth was he going to be able to do about this? Nobody in the seminary – nobody! – had prepared him for a parishioner who wanted to commit suicide, had disclosed it in confession but didn't want a priest involved because he didn't believe in God.

He waved a shaky, beckoning hand out to the first of

the two old ladies who was crossing herself enthusiastically with a set of rosary beads.

The best thing to do, Glen decided, when this lot was done, was to spend as much time as possible praying. Then his stomach rumbled loudly. He was dying for a bit of that quiche.

Chapter Fourteen

From the moment Liam MacDara had stepped off the trawler onto the soil of Inish Rua six months ago, after ten terrifying years of teaching in Inner City Dublin, he knew the island was his home. His pace had fallen into the rhythm of the land from the first footstep he'd taken. His feet had crunched on the sandy path and the slow steps that he'd walked up towards his thatched cottage, on a hill beside the stone grey school that was to become his new life, were like the stairway up to heaven for Liam MacDara. The island was a blanket of green and grey, moss and stone, and the whitewashed houses of the village beamed back at his delight. The pub was quiet, solid, run by a gentle solid type called Jimmy Seán who took his time and polished glasses and let him talk for hours about the trauma he had suffered at the hands of eleven-year-olds in the Inner City for ten years, and how relieved he was to be away from it all now. Liam bought a button accordion and was learning how to play. The nice thing about bringing an instrument out on the island was that nobody really minded how it sounded.

Sometimes, when the weather was fine, he'd go on up to the Black Cliffs and lay on his stomach on the cliff's edge and watch gannets and the seals through his binoculars. Or he'd go to Puffin Rocks and watch puffins waddle and fall over and dive into the waves. He'd chat up friendly Americans who came over on day trips, and sexy Germans with long brown legs in shorts. He was thinking of investing in a polytunnel.

The thing was, that Liam liked the little teaching job and his cottage and vegetable patch but what he really longed for was a group of other adults to hang out with.

At night-time, he would often walk along the beach and count the stars and then walk back the hill towards the village and think about the Míle Cairde retreat at Atlantis and wonder what they were all up to in there. Every so often a helicopter would come and go from the helipad at the back of the big house, and Liam would observe these giant birds with a hump of disapproval as they bobbed into place on the Atlantis lawn while he hoed carrots or rotivated potato beds. Every now and then, one or two of the artists or writers would make their way down to Tí Jimmy Sheáin and listen to a session or have a gin and tonic at the bar and sit wide-eyed on a stool and then go back again. Liam was tempted to chat to one or two, but that was all really.

The Big House was a very separate place.

Trish Lenihan had shown him round the island and was very courteous to him, but that was all. Trish was kind of sexy, in a hairy-armpit sort of way. She worked her ass off for the house and didn't seem to be appreciated at all by any of the people who stayed there. Liam suspected that Pierce Fox didn't even know how much work she did to keep the place in order. Fox seemed to arrive whenever he felt like it and would waltz around the island for an hour and say hello to the natives or gaze up at the mountain with a triumphant grin on his face and his hands in his pockets before going back to his rooms. Or he might be seen with his Barbour jacket on, marching up the hills with a rifle to shoot rabbits. But that was rare enough. Most of the time, Liam suspected that Pierce Fox's only interest in Inish Rua was as a tax-deductable shag pad.

Fox always seemed to have a woman with him, or running after him, or getting things arranged for him. There was Trish who ran the house like a five-star hotel for a gang of people who came and went and wrote and painted and were fed like lords and didn't have to pay a cent. Then there was Yvonne Delahunty, Bean an Tí, who seemed to think that Pierce Fox was some sort of god and spent all her time running up and down to the big house to work as some sort of personal assistant whenever he was there, and even when he wasn't. Yvonne's task, as far as Liam could make out from what Trish had told him, was to personally deliver his supplies from the boatmen, personally make sure that the shipments of wine he had delivered from Fortnum and Mason were carted up the hill and across the land at the correct speed and with the correct amount of gentleness of carriage, and to personally make sure that the apartments at the top of Atlantis house were aired, heated properly, and had fresh flowers arranged every day just in case Fox turned up.

It was a load of pretentious crap, as far as Liam was concerned. But Pierce didn't particularly bother Liam directly. What upset him the most was the way Pierce treated everybody else. Trish's fingernails were broken from working the mangle in the laundry. And her hands were reddish purple with folding sheets and peeling spuds. She did all the gardening herself, and although what turned Liam on most about Trish was the way she loved nothing better than being up to her elbows in muck, he wanted to help her out as much as possible when there was heavy stuff to be done. But she'd never let him into her greenhouse, no matter what. She was very self-sufficient when it came to her herbs.

The greenhouse was beautiful though. It was an original Victorian structure, and Liam was often asked to do repairs to it which he loved doing, sanding off the rust, finding the right kind of bolt to fasten something down. Trish had a kind of mild eccentric side that intrigued him, if truth be told. She was Aquarius with Virgo rising, she'd once told him with a giggle, which was why she was tall and statuesque and bone-thin no matter what she ate. As he watched her stalking around the gardens with a giant spade, marching up and down the lane to the Siopa for her monthly shipments of bleach-free washing soda and starch, or lugging huge buckets of turf in from the sheds, Liam found her slender, athletic, almost masculine figure to be desperately sexy.

Still, he'd never have the courage to "ask her out". Even the phrase seemed faintly ridiculous, here on an island where there was nowhere to go out *to*. He'd sometimes thought of asking her to take a walk with him when he went up the hills and around the walkway built in famine times towards the back end of the valley and then out across the top of the island towards the Black Cliffs. But he couldn't imagine Trish having time to do something self-indulgent like this. And as for going up to the pub for a drink – well, everyone did that. It wouldn't be what you'd call a date. It was the only place to go on the island after dark. Unless you stayed at home. And he wasn't going to invite her to do that. You didn't invite people to your house on Inish Rua. You just accepted that they dropped in. Or not. If you'd actually asked somebody to visit you, they'd have thought that you were ill.

"Sir, what's the Tuiseal Ginedeach of *seomra*?" asked one of the teenagers who was busy picking her spots. Liam thought her name was Lauren, although she pronounced it as Lorren. She was from Dublin. From Blackrock. Pale skin, a thick black shiny bob and a little nose-ring.

"*An tseomra*," said Liam. The good thing about teaching this tiny number of teenagers, four in fact, two boys and two girls, was that they were easy to control. The bad thing was that they knew no more Irish than he did.

"So, have you finished that essay, then?" he asked them, noticing that the boys were politely looking bored. Lauren was still ruling two red lines into the margin of her copy book and putting little circles in above her i's. And Niamh was biting her fingernails. Niamh was the one with the spiked blonde hair like Annie Lennox.

The two boys were called Stiofán and Luke, but Niamh and Lauren had rapidly nick-named Stiofán *Stiffy*, and Luke *Puke*. Stiffy and Puke were both slightly acnified, Stiffy more so than Puke, Liam couldn't help noticing, but Puke was slightly shorter and had still got that pre-pubescent bum-fuzz look about his face that was obviously going to get him nowhere with the girls for another few years yet, whereas Stiffy had shot up to almost six feet tall and had a full, sulky mouth and long, floppy brown hair and deep brown eyes. Liam was convinced that Niamh, behind the fist whose nails she was now furiously paring down with her perfectly retained teeth, was smouldering at him.

Stiffy was oblivious though, or at least putting on a very good show of it. Actually, Liam thought, noticing the packet of Dunhills poking out of his satchel, Stiffy was probably just dying for a fag.

Of the two boys, Puke seemed to be the more craic, and was, despite his juvenility in appearance, perhaps the most popular with the two girls. Even Lauren was giggling now as Puke did an impression of Mrs Doyle from *Father Ted* for them, encouraging her to finish up her essay quickly.

"Ah, go on, go on, go on, go on, go on, go on, *go on*!"

"Can we get a break now, sir?" Stiffy suggested, his fingers itching at the cigarette packet by his thigh.

"Yeah, go on. Take twenty and I'll meet you back here then for poetry. And it's Liam, Stiofán, not 'sir'. You can call me Liam."

Stiffy nodded one brief nod and slid silently out of the room.

"Leem, would you not come outside with us for a fag?" Niamh batted her eyelids at him wickedly.

"Aw, no. I don't smoke. And neither should you. I'll just have a cup of tea."

The students all smirked but not spitefully.

"Sir, do we have to go to the dance?" Lauren asked doubtfully as she gathered up her coloured pens.

"The céilí. Yes, you have to go. What's wrong with that? It's part of your Irish Language and Culture course. what's not to like?"

"It's lame!" exclaimed Niamh.

"It is a bit," added Lauren. "We don't do Irish dancing any more in school," she added confidingly.

"You'll learn," said Liam.

And I'll be playing the accordion, so I'll expect all of you to dance plenty. The whole island will be out and you'll have the time of your lives.'"

"Sir, do you need ID for the pub?" asked Puke.

"Luke, you are seventeen. So, you're underage anyway, and there isn't anyone on this island who doesn't know it, so no, you don't need ID because you won't be served drink anyway."

"Load of crap," muttered Puke, raising his eyebrows at the girls. The girls smirked again and drifted out to have a fag with Stiffy.

A few jigs around a good céilí would probably put manners on them, thought Liam dolefully, and then reminded himself that he'd got to go up to Atlantis after school today and speak to Trish. He'd heard there was a musician staying at Mile Cairde for the month of November and he'd see if Trish thought she might like to play something at the Céilí. It hadn't happened yet, of course. Of all the musicians who'd come over all summer and into the autumn, none of them had had the generosity to bring their instrument out and give it a bash up at Tí Jimmy Sheáin at night or in the weekly céilí at the Scoil Oileán. But you never knew. But it was well worth going up to Trish again to find out.

Trish Lenihan sat on an ice-cold wrought-iron garden seat in an eye-wateringly low winter sun to enjoy a little smoke. This was a nice sheltered spot at the back of the house in between the two wings, where the kitchen garden nestled and the sun flowed in long luscious curves from the south west. The sun seemed to be of very generous spirit this morning, sparkling through the trees, dancing across the wet grass into the pond. It *was* a bit too cold to be sitting out here in a floral summer dress, despite the wellies underneath and the giant Shetland cardigan on top, but Trish didn't mind the cold. There was something rather bracing about having a smoke through icy purple fingers, the combined energies of the foggy morning breath, the pale gold sunlight and the sharp acrid smoke she inhaled. Trish didn't often smoke in the mornings but she had a lot on her mind at the moment and so from time to time she had a nice long solitary one, just sitting here outdoors for a treat. She squinted up at the long fingers of morning spreading through the trees and let the sunshine bathe her face – not too long before that would be down behind the hill and the day would be already over.

Trish enjoyed the darkness of the winter, the battening down of hatches, the hibernation of nature, getting ready for the storms. Opening one eye, she glanced across at her greenhouses sitting like mirrors in the low morning sun and reminded herself to go around them carefully and check that the joints and fixtures were in good condition before the weather got too rough. There were some very wild storms forecast. Stubbing out her rollie underneath her welly boot, she stood up and made her way over to the greenhouse, sniffing the air for pines, enjoying the damp crunch on gravel under her boots.

The greenhouses were lovingly painted and maintained every year by the teacher, Liam MacDara, who came down from the Scoil Oileán to help her in the summer with the damage that was needed to be repaired after every winter. And thanks to Liam, the door didn't sway off its hinges like it used to, and she opened it without too much of a bang this time. Every time you banged something in here, you always worried that one of the fragile windows might crack and break again.

It was damp and pretty cold inside the greenhouse this morning, but the scent of the tomato plants still lingered, and she touched their dying furry leaves as she wandered among them, finding the last of the summer fruits and putting them in the pockets of her long floral dress. And then the spinach was still good to eat. And the winter cabbages were robust this year. And there were plenty of carrots and turnips in the field, and the potatoes were beautifully floury now. Trish took a knife from the rack and, fastening her long blonde fuzz of hair behind her neck, she crouched down to cut three cabbages out for dinner that night.

She took her time pottering around the greenhouse, conscious of the fact that she could be observed still from the house – and moreover, that she could be completely observed from Mr Pierce Fox's apartments on the top floor, from where he and his new lawyer had a bird's eye view through the glass roofs.

Trish couldn't quite believe the new woman was actually his lawyer. She seemed far too young and inexperienced to be working for him – which led Trish only to conclude what she had often concluded before about Pierce Fox, which was that working for him might involve several non-curricular duties. But God knows, that young woman, Gemma, with her glasses and her poker-straight hair and her flawless powdered-smooth

133

complexion, well, chances were she knew exactly what she was up to by getting involved up there. Trish stood up for a moment to survey the remaining cabbages and beetroot plants, and to decide from which of the special plants she grew in between the vegetables she was going to cut a few leaves to dry out in the hot-press where she kept a little drying rack behind the tank.

The thing she loved most about living in Atlantis and running the Míle Cairde Writers and Artists' Retreat was the opportunity it gave her to be with real writers, poets, playwrights, musicians, sculptors – she simply glowed in the presence of people who created works of art.

Trish had always wanted to be a writer herself. In her teens she had written several volumes of poetry. At university, she had dabbled in DramSoc. After graduation, she had attempted (several times) the first five chapters of a novel while wondering how long she could survive on a Tesco checkout-assistant's salary, staring out of the window of her bedsit in Rathmines. And then she'd gone back to university, done a Master's Degree in the history of art and found a job at Míle Cairde.

Of course, the money here was absolutely nothing. She got to live in this luxurious house, live like a governess-stroke-Victorian-housekeeper, and grow vegetables for a living. There was a stipend attached to the management of the retreat, but it was embarrassingly small. Trish charged a small amount for her weekly Yoga and Pilates classes in the Halla Oileán, but half the time the islanders forgot to pay. Given the stupendous wealth of the owner of the house and island, Trisha knew that she really ought to feel more disgruntled at the size of her own salary and the conditions in which she had to live – as a permanent hostess who never really got a holiday because, well, there wasn't really anywhere to go and her salary certainly didn't support foreign travel – and a baby-sitter to what amounted to a bunch of spoilt show-offs who thought that they were stars.

Those were her most private thoughts, anyway – and ones which she didn't really like to express, not even to herself. Trisha kept a diary, in which she wrote quite beautiful prose – thoughts about the sound of the waves at the Black Cliffs, or ideas about the whereabouts of a heron's cry on a rock, the rush of a gull's wing, the burnished dew on fir trees in the morning, the magnificence of the sea. But she had never shown anybody what she wrote.

That was the difference, Trish had once realised, between those who get to make a living from the arts, and those who don't. Everyone who came to Míle Cairde had succeeded somehow, in proving themselves to others – a selection committee of one, in most cases. Pierce Fox, for example, who liked to see himself as a patron of the arts, had all sorts of odd ideas about what was going to be the next big thing and what wasn't, and very often got it completely wrong. Like the time he had decided to invest a million euros in *Thin Lizzy, The Opera,* and it had backfired completely and nobody had bought tickets and so he'd simply closed down one of his newspapers to pay the debts and thirty journalists had been let go. But, nevertheless, all the residents of Míle Cairde had to *prove* at some stage to someone that the work they had done in the arts was worthwhile. It wasn't always a matter of quality, Trisha privately thought. It was a matter of brass neck.

Still. If you hadn't the brass neck yourself, then you

couldn't really feel bitter and twisted about those who did and who stuck it out at every available opportunity. And there were some people who came to Míle Cairde who did write some jolly good stuff, she thought. Amy Shanahan, for example – Trisha would never have admitted it to any of the other writers but Amy's racy novel about a woman who has a lifelong affair with her husband's brother was a fantastic under-the-covers read. And Joy Jackson was all right, even if she came across as a bit of a flower. And Wolftone O'Neill was a sweetie pie, even if he was out of his box most of the time. And Zack was kind.

And as for Setanta Lynch – well, with eyes that beautiful you could forgive him anything, even his tendency to spend all day up in his studio lashing the plaster of Paris around and come down to dinner in an appalling mess and then his irritating habit of not really talking to anyone, just sitting there smouldering all the time.

Actually, when you thought about it, the crowd that were there at the moment were all pretty much all right. There was no one too demanding. Not yet anyway.

There was one more writer who was on her way – a Maggie Hennelly, whom Trish had never heard of. But she was coming over by special invitation from Mr Fox, that stuck-up little Gemma had told her, so Trish had instructed Yvonne to organise extra stationary, wine, chocolates and roses for the apartments, and made sure Mrs Freeman knew the right numbers for dinner.

Trisha glanced up surreptitiously to check if she was being overlooked from Pierce Fox's top-floor apartments, but there was no one looking out that she could see. He had said, when he'd arrived late last night, that he'd had a lot of work to do on some major legal contracts he was preparing with Gemma – ha! – and they didn't want to be disturbed. Which was fine by her – Trisha didn't particularly want to be disturbed either. What she liked to do most in the evenings was to get away from the residents after dinner and have a nice long bath, smoke something and read a book. And the last thing she wanted to do was to have to disturb Pierce and Gemma the so-called lawyer at anything they might be up to. She cringed again at the bloody awful thought of what that might be.

And now this other woman was supposed to be coming over by helicopter, this Maggie Hennelly who was ghost-writing an autobiography only she was coming at the special request of Pierce and his so-called lawyer. Very unusual, Trish thought, that she should be bypassing the normal selection process that she, Trish, would usually so painstakingly apply.

Sometimes, just every so often, it really bothered Trish that her entire life was being dedicated to the upkeep of a beautiful, inspirational, internationally reputed artists' retreat on a remote monastic island off the magical west coast of Ireland, that was in reality just a knocking shop.

Chapter Fifteen

"There's a card for you from Marina," Mrs Freeman said – well, yelled, actually, from the kitchen where she was pottering about.

I am getting used to this already, Ciara thought, swinging her legs out of the bed and looking down at her toes at the end of her pyjamas. Mrs Freeman let herself in and out whenever she felt like it. At any particular point in time you might find her in the kitchen leaving in some scones, or a bit of a chicken pie, or a goat's cheese roulade. And then other people seemed to just wander in when they felt like it too – like that old man who mooched in and stood by the range saying nothing and then left, just like that.

Marina De Barra's house was clearly a sort of pit-stop for the islanders, Ciara had decided. In fact, the only person who never seemed to come into the house was Marina's husband Gearóid.

She padded over to the window where the rain danced

against the glass. The view was thick with mist. She could barely see Atlantis through the trees.

She found a pair of thick socks and put on her navy trousers and a green blouse and clipped her hair up. It was difficult to know what to do with her hair nowadays – it was thick and getting long and the fringe was too short to sweep back and too long to be a fringe. But it seemed to be such a very long time since she'd cared about her looks. In the beginning, when she'd first met Des, she'd gone to the hairdresser's every week, twice a week. She'd spent hours getting her nails done, fake tan all year round, pedicures, she'd even contemplated just a touch of Botox when a slight creasing began to develop between her brows and she'd only just been twenty-five! But that was the effect Des had had on her. She'd been acutely aware from the moment they'd started dating that the quality of her appearance on his arm was extremely important to him, much more important than her having a job or a career or a degree in medicine. Pretty soon she realised that she was an important accessory in his life and pretty much on a par with his top-of-the-range BMW, his yacht and his second home in the Algarve. So by the time Des had started not to care too much about what she looked like because he was far too interested in where the next bag of cocaine was coming from, a trip to the hairdresser's wasn't on the agenda any more.

Ciara had had some wonderful clothes in the beginning – designer things Des had bought her in Las Vegas, furs, Armani straight from Italy, shoes bought on the Champs Élysées. But then, after several years with Des, she'd got to the stage where she actually felt like dressing down. Anything to avoid drawing attention to herself – well, to them as a couple, actually. Towards the end of their relationship, Ciara would attend race meetings with Des, but often in her oldest trousers with the plainest possible jacket and a shirt. She'd wear nothing on her face but just a smear of lip-gloss and wear her hair scraped back into a pony-tail rather than a glamorous hat like every other woman in their circle. The last thing she wanted was for Des's outrageous attention-seeking behaviour to draw any more attention to herself.

She looked at her reflection in the mirror now and wondered who she was. This person with a pale, freckled face who frowned too much. With thick, once-shiny auburn hair that was growing out all over the place that she couldn't even be bothered to brush any more. Who would I brush it for? Ciara thought. And then she thought, perhaps I should get it cut? She suddenly remembered the little hairdresser's she'd seen in the village on the first day. *Gruaig Deas by Nóirín. Gruagaire.* Hairdresser. Well, I haven't had my hair done in months. And it'll probably be dead cheap out here. And I could do with a treat! It'll pass the time anyway, after the surgery one afternoon.

In the background, Mrs Freeman was still talking to herself but appeared to be leaving as the voice moved from kitchen to backdoor and then around the outside of the house in a muffle that then emerged by the front again where Ciara's window overlooked the path. And then Mrs Freeman was off, scooting up the hill towards Atlantis house.

Alone at last.

Ciara went into the kitchen with caution – that old man could be there propped up against the range again, or even someone else perhaps, sitting on the loo or something. Lying in the bath. But the house was definitely empty now, and so she made a pot of lovely strong fragrant coffee and cut a huge slice of the apple pie that Mrs Freeman had left out on the table. She might be intrusive, Ciara thought sinking her teeth into soft, buttery pie crust, but she's a genius cook.

On the table just beside the pie was a postcard. From Las Vegas. Ciara picked it up and read the message on the back – in a very neat, almost child-like handwriting, Marina had written: *Weather marvellous. Thanks for looking after everything. Getting a great rest, best regards to all, Marina.*

Weather marvellous? In November? But then, perhaps compared to horizontal rain, it was. She looked at the postmark and the front of the card. It was a picture of the Las Vegas Desert Springs Hotel all right. But the postmark said October. This was really very, very strange. Marina hadn't even left the island till November. There was absolutely no possible explanation for Marina having sent a postcard in October from Las Vegas when she was still on the island and wouldn't leave till November first. Marina might be eccentric but she was definitely not a time traveller. And how could a postcard arrive so rapidly in any case, when Marina had hardly set foot in Las Vegas yet?

Ciara put the postcard carefully on the mantelpiece in front of the clock.

She washed the dishes, waving from the window as she did at Gearóid who waved a very slight, shy wave back, and then she wiped her hands on a tea-towel and turned around and stood a moment to survey the kitchen from the sink. It was really very cosy here, quiet, silent actually, just the sound of wind in the chimney and the ever-present hush of the sea. It was the peace and solitude she'd longed for, and yet she felt intimately surrounded by people and

141

over-looked in a way that she'd never felt before in all her life. Gearóid for example, at the bottom of the garden, pottering away, in his little shed, painting goodness knows what – but he was sweet, really. And then she suddenly realised that she felt more comfortable being over-looked by Gearóid than she'd felt living with her own husband. She'd only just met Gearóid, he was quite clearly as mad as a brush, and yet she was actually quite happy to hang around the house on her own with him pottering around observing her but never actually speaking to her.

Des had done nothing but talk excitedly a thousand miles an hour at her from the moment he'd first met her, a stream of jokes, gushing remarks, wild stories, mad ideas. She'd been so excited by his outrageous thought-processes in the beginning. In the end, they had terrified her completely.

It was time she went to work. She had barely glanced into the surgery the day before as no one had turned up for treatment. Unlike the house, the surgery was kept locked but the key, a huge, old-fashioned thing that looked like something you'd use to lock up a jail, was hanging on the kitchen door, under a little sign that said *Surgery Key*. She took it down, and then opened the back door into the wind.

Five yards across the garden to work – how lovely, she thought, and she opened up the surgery with the key, sniffed the slightly damp stale air and went inside. There was a little hallway with a tiled floor that led into a tiny waiting room, sparsely furnished with six hard-backed chairs and a little coffee-table with some magazines. A door off this led to a loo, and then there was another door with a sign on it saying *Surgery*. She opened it.

It was a largish room with a fireplace on one wall, the only furniture a giant desk, a battered leather examination couch, a few chairs, some bookcases and a filing cabinet in the corner.

Ciara went around the little surgery touching everything. It was cluttered, messy and full of unexpected stuff, but it was colourful. There were lots of paintings on the walls with little cottages and clouds and child-like figures cutting turf or making hay. She touched the blobby thick oil paint on one large canvas above the fireplace. It was a beautiful painting of a group of children fishing for winkles on a summer strand, the water sparkling with sunshine. The painting was unsigned. On another wall, a giant clock that ticked loudly.

There was a persistent cold dampness in the place though, and she shivered and decided to plug the little electric heater in as Mrs Freeman had instructed. The room began to warm up quickly and Ciara sat in front of it, warming her hands. The heater emitted a scorching heat that would burn your legs if you sat too close to it. But it did nothing about the fog on the window pane and despite the cosiness in the room that developed quite rapidly once the heater was switched on, there still was a kind of mouldy smell.

Marina was desperately untidy, too. Ciara had discovered that as soon as she'd arrived in the house. But in the surgery her untidiness reached a different dimension, Ciara thought, examining the scatterings across the desk. It was as if Marina was determined to defy the fact that the surgery was a place of medicine.

She would tidy up, Ciara decided. Right next to the fireplace was a nice big sink with elbow taps and Mrs

Freeman had left a pile of fluffy towels which was a help. She'd get everything ship-shape for when Marina came back, and she stood up from the baking hot electric fire and began to figure out how to best organise the desk. The only problem was that she wasn't sure how *much* she should tidy up.

Marina's desk was littered with pens and notepads and copies of the MIMS and bits and pieces of examination equipment, so it was easy enough to put these into order and clear a space to work. But the floor was covered too all round the edges of the room, with piled-up boxes of syringes and patient's notes and bundles of correspondence from hospitals. There was a dusty miniature skeleton hanging on a display hook by the door. Ciara wiped it down with the damp edge of one of the towels, then decided to have a look through some of the piles of papers and patients' notes. Nothing was in any sort of order. It was as if the floor was a sort of permanent in-tray for Doctor Marina De Barra.

Well, that could be her task then, to impose order on Marina's office and her life and make sure that by the time she got back from Las Vegas, the house would be ship-shape and the surgery would be sparkling. She began to stack the papers and the charts more neatly into just one pile and put them all on top of the filing cabinet, and decided that she'd go through everything that wasn't yet filed and file it all in alphabetic order and make sure everything was beautifully catalogued. There was a dead plant on top of the filing cabinet, so she removed that and looked around for a bin. Then she realised that there probably wasn't a bin. Where would you dump a bin on Inish Rua anyway? You'd have to recycle the plant. Feeling pleased at the idea of this, she took the decayed thing outside and, pulling her jacket around her against the spray of rain that was coming in off the sea in a razorblade of a wind, she waved at Gearóid who was mooching around in the doorway of his shed, spade in hand.

"Hi, Gearóid! I thought that we should throw this out!" she yelled across the roaring of the wind. "It's probably dead and it's taking up space, and I'm hopeless with plants too. Would you like to bury it?"

She reached the end of the garden and handed him the plant, then joined him in the shelter of the doorway. Gearóid took the plant and looked at it with what Ciara thought were tears in his eyes. Or perhaps that was just the wind.

"Is it Marina's?" he asked her gently.

"Well, yes. It was in the surgery. Only it's obviously dead, so we should really throw it away. It's taking up space."

"Ah. I'd be afraid to throw anything away that was Marina's," he said, handing the dead plant back to her as if it were on fire.

Jesus! Ciara thought. This man is difficult. She took a breath.

"Well," she said, "I'm not afraid to throw it away. But I don't know where to throw it. And you have a compost heap." She pointed. "Over there. Don't you?"

Gearóid looked very doubtful.

"It would be disintegrated by the time she gets back," Ciara said. "And she'd never know it was gone. We could grow something else for her to replace it."

Gearóid looked even more anxious.

"Oh, for God's sake, Gearóid! It's only a bloody dead

busy lizzy!" she cried. "What on earth are you afraid of? If we keep the plant in the surgery like this it'll begin to rot and stink the place out! Look!" and she marched past him and tossed it on the compost heap, and then threw a lump of seaweed over it. "There!" She smacked her hands off each other. "Now, that's the end of that." She beamed at him and handed him the pot.

Gearóid grinned. "How are you settling in, anyway?" he asked.

Ciara smiled in surprise. That was the first normal thing she'd heard him say. He leaned on his spade and looked at her with innocent pale-blue eyes.

"I'm fine, Gearóid, thanks very much," she said. "I like it here. But I'm afraid I can't work in the same kind of mess Marina works in. I'm going to have to tidy up the surgery." Gearóid instantly looked extremely alarmed. "Look, don't worry," she said hastily. "I'm sure she won't take it out on you. We'll tell her it was all my fault. And I'll make sure we don't lose anything. I'll put things in alphabetical order and make things much easier for her when she gets back."

"*If* she gets back."

"What?"

"Nothing." He was looking shamefaced.

"What did you say?"

He shook his head. "I'd better get back to work. You'll be all right." And he smiled a sad and crumpled smile.

"All right," she said, and watched him turn away and prop his spade up outside the little shed and bow his head to go inside the door again.

If she gets back?

Across the dry stone wall the seagulls screamed with

laughter and the black sea roared and the horizon was a million miles away. Ciara shivered in the rain, and then turned and marched quickly back into the surgery.

At least the little electric heater had warmed the place up thoroughly, and she hung her jacket up and shook her wet hair out like a dog. Then she heard footsteps, just outside the window. Someone had arrived. She opened up the door to the waiting room.

To her astonishment, the first visitor to the surgery was Pierce Fox.

Doctor Marina De Barra swallowed down the five pills they'd given her with a glass of water and cursed. She cursed the sleepless night she'd had. She cursed the sweat that was pouring out of her. She cursed the purple face on her in the mirror and she cursed the trembling in her legs that she couldn't control, and the nausea in her stomach and the irregular thumping in her heart. But most of all she cursed herself.

"Group work, now, Marina," the cheerful attendant said. "Come along now, hurry up."

"Oh, for the love of God!" roared Marina, and burst into tears. Could it be that despite herself she actually missed the island? At least out there she could be herself. She didn't have to pretend.

Be herself. Herself? She didn't even know who that was any more. She didn't know what she wanted. When she sat down, she immediately wanted to stand up. When she stood up, she wanted to lie down. When she watched TV, she wanted to have a bath. When she was in the bath, she wanted to go out for a walk. When she walked in the grounds and marched briskly along the river bank she only wished she hadn't bothered coming out. This was hard. So much harder than she'd ever imagined. And the worst thing was that she couldn't run away. There was nowhere she could go. This was it – for better or worse. She had to do it now. She had to survive this, she had to come home in a better state than she went out or she might as well never go home again. This was her one chance to fix herself, and she was determined to do it, whatever it might take.

Ciara knew it was him as soon as she opened the door and found him there. Tall, black hair flecked with grey, deep-brown eyes, thick eyebrows as sharp as blades and a Barbour jacket and shoes that were so beautiful and yet so unsuitable for rainy, windswept country life that Ciara almost wanted to ask him to take them off so that she could put their pale golden soft leather up on a high shelf out of harm's way. He looked incongruously glamorous, standing there in the tiny waiting room where the only magazines were ancient copies of *St Martin's Magazine, National Geographic* and the Christmas *RTÉ Guide.* Christmas two years ago, that is.

"Good morning," said Ciara.

Pierce Fox turned around from where he was standing looking out of the window, to face her.

"Hello, darling," he replied, leaving Ciara open-mouthed. "Glad I caught you first. Bloody cold in here. So, how's Chez Marina treating you?" and he marched past her into the surgery.

Ciara followed him and slid nervously around the big oak desk into her chair. Pierce Fox had settled himself down comfortably in the other chair and started playing with her stethoscope.

"Er," she began. "Nice to meet you, Mr Fox. I'm Doctor Ciara Love. What seems to be the problem? I mean, how can I help you?" She watched him twist the bell of the stethoscope round and around and then leap out of his chair and onto the weighing scales.

"Phew!" he groaned. "Gained two point four kilos. Must speak to Mrs Freeman about that!" He turned to grin at Ciara. "Everything all right for you here, sweetheart?"

"Er, yes," Ciara replied. "It's very nice. I'm – well, thank you for asking." She felt astonishingly foolish. He'd only come around to see how she was settling in, not for a consultation. To her horror she found herself blushing – which was ridiculous of course. Pierce Fox had a foul reputation for being very arrogant, but he was bloody good-looking with it.

"So," Pierce stretched his hands out and cracked his knuckles. "Want to play doctor and patient today then?" and he chuckled.

"Play?" Ciara was aware that her voice sounded faint. She looked around the surgery with its desk, and saw two uncomfortable chairs, a broken filing cabinet, chaotic bookshelves, the cracked leather examination couch that Marina had repaired with a giant piece of elastoplast and the one window that overlooked the laneway and it suddenly all seemed to be much smaller and more wretched to her now.

"Just kidding, darling. No need to look alarmed. Just came to pick up my usual," Pierce replied, cracking his knuckles again.

"Usual," Ciara replied. "Yes. I see. Well, let me get your notes out, Mr Fox . . ."

"No need," he replied. He was beginning to look bored. "And it's Pierce, Ciara. Always Pierce."

"No, well, it's just that I need to see what your past medical history – um, let me see –"

Ciara got up and went to the filing cabinet to find his notes and became acutely aware that he was actually grinning at her. To her further humiliation he began to hum.

And the filing cabinet was – well, it wasn't exactly a filing cabinet after all. Ciara opened the top drawer and found a box of tissues, another dead plant, a pair of wellies and a – yes, it was. An empty bottle. Cork Dry Gin. She opened up the second drawer.

The second drawer was a bit more hopeful. There was a hanging rack of files, but they didn't seem to be in alphabetical order. Actually, they didn't seem to be in any sort of order. They contained letters about patients going back decades that were completely over-stuffed into each of the hanging envelopes, lab results and other correspondence, but nothing was in alphabetical order, nor were there any particular note-keeping arrangements of any kind. It was a complete mess. And there was something rattling underneath the rack of hanging files and she knew just by the rolling sound of it on the metal of the filing drawer, the familiar roll of glass in a drawer, the eternal murmur of an empty bottle of – ah, of course. This time it was vodka. Stolichnaya, to be exact.

She slammed the drawer shut.

"I can't seem to be able to find – um, your case notes, Mr Fox," she began, peering very cautiously into the third drawer which was packed. With what looked like a pile of jumpers, a very old handbag and an anorak.

"Marina doesn't keep notes – not for me, anyway," Pierce Fox grinned.

She was aware that he was enjoying this thoroughly and it made her feel even more stupid.

"Look, she keeps things in the dispensary," he said, smiling heartily now. "She just orders things for people and they get sent over and we pick them up. Perhaps you'll find it there."

The dispensary was a sort of walk-in cupboard at the back of the room. Ciara opened it up and found, among the boxes of drugs and medicines, a log book of records sitting on a shelf. There were thirty or so names in it, listed alphabetically like addresses – only Marina had listed them alphabetically by their first names, M for Mikey Duggan, J for Jimmy Seán, N for Nóirín, and so on. Under P for Pierce Fox she found *Viagra 100mg tablets thirty* written in arachnid, trembly handwriting.

"Oh," she said.

"That's her list of orders from the mainland. The pharmacy only delivers every now and then." He winked at her. "So I get her to make sure she's well stocked up for my visits. You wouldn't want the boss to run short of anything," he added solemnly.

"No, of course not." She blushed the colour of the Merlot whose empty bottle Marina had also carefully filed in the dispensary cupboard in between boxes of antibiotics and dressing packs. The boxes and contents of the dispensary cupboard weren't in any particular order either but it was easy to spot the box of Viagra, sitting there among its mundane companions.

"Um, how many does she usually give you?" Ciara asked, her face on fire.

"Darling, the whole box is for me," Pierce replied, smiling through very white teeth that had just a slight gap between the front two which made him all the more sexy.

He took the box out of her hands and fished six packets of tablets out of it, popping them into either side of his Barbour jacket pockets. "Although there'd be no harm in passing these around the island every now and then. It'd be a positive act of charity," he said, and stood up to leave.

"Do you – I mean, I was thinking perhaps you'd like me to check your blood pressure, while you're here?" Ciara said and then felt her face becoming purple again. It was ridiculous. He was making her feel like a medical student again.

Pierce grinned. "Go on, for the craic!" he said, sitting down again and rolling up his Barbour sleeve. "Let's see if you can give me hypertension." And he twinkled his deep brown eyes at her while she pumped the cuff.

His heart rate was relatively low, Ciara noticed, watching the mercury fall. Her own heart rate was approximately twice the rate of his, and her heart seemed to be thumping right in her mouth.

"One ten over eighty. Well, I suppose that's pretty healthy, really," she muttered putting the stethoscope away.

"Great!" Pierce stood up and thumped his chest. "Glad to know I'll live a while. Anyway, wonderful to meet you. Delighted Marina's found someone so pretty to take her place. Not before too long though." He thrust out his hand. "What did you say your name was again?"

"Ciara. Ciara Love."

"Ah! Doctor Love. Well, Doctor Love, come on up to the house sometime. Yvonne will tell you when I'm home, she keeps all my arrangements for me. She'll let you know when there's a slot free.'" He winked and then turned to go.

"Slot?"

"Yes. I'm not on the island a lot, but I've got a few days at the moment to put some contracts together and relax a bit." And he strolled out of the door, his right hand raised at her as he left in a sort of presidential salute, and marched through the waiting room and out the door again.

"Bye," she heard her voice saying in the empty room. But there was somebody else coming down the little path – she could hear their footsteps just outside and hear voices. A woman. And two men.

She brushed down the front of her green blouse and navy trousers and pushed her hair back before she fixed her face into a smile as they came in.

"Well, you're *very* welcome to the island, doctor," the tall blonde woman was saying and smiling rather over-enthusiastically at her as she came through the door.

Ciara smiled back in relief and extended her hand. How lovely and friendly people on the island were!

"Come on inside."

She opened the surgery door to let the woman through, and indicated to the two men to sit down in the waiting room. And then she realised she'd seen the elder of the men before – he was the strange, silent visitor she'd had on her first day in the house, who'd come in and just stood there and then left again and had said nothing! And he was with the other guy, the only other guy she'd met since coming to the island – the tall American guy who ran the pub. The awkward kind of guy who'd been standing in front of the fireplace talking to a sod of turf.

She smiled at both of them, and the turf-sod-guy smiled back.

"How's it going?" he said.

"Great," said Ciara. "Nice to see you again." Because it kind of was, even if he was a bit, well, distractible or something.

And the turf-sod-guy actually blushed! And then the auld fella looked sideways at him and looked back down again at his feet.

"Be with you shortly," Ciara said, and followed the woman into the surgery room.

"Now, what's your name? I'm Doctor Ciara Love," she began, sliding around to the other side of the desk. God knows how she was going to conduct a surgery without any case notes or computer files to go on, but she'd do her best, and she took a blank notepad from the pile of stuff she'd made at the corner of the desk and a pen to write.

"Mrs Yvonne Delahunty, Bean an Tí," replied the blonde woman, patting her curls. "And I'm sorry for your troubles."

Ciara blinked. "Date of birth?" she said, ignoring Mrs Delahunty's remark.

"Excuse me?"

"Um. Your birthday? The day that you were born?" Ciara looked at her. She'd try it in Irish. "Um, Lá, lá – bhreithe?" she beamed, thrilled with herself.

Mrs Yvonne Delahunty was looking quite put out. "Doctor Love, I'd rather not get into that much detail. I've only come for my reflexology."

"Oh," said Ciara. "Oh. I see. Oh, Mrs Delahunty, I'm so sorry. I'm afraid I'm not a qualified reflexologist at all, you see. Marina didn't say – I mean, she didn't tell me – I'm afraid it's not something I'm trained in." She tried to smile at Yvonne but Yvonne was looking very disappointed indeed.

"Oh. Oh, dear. Well, that's a shame. I was only saying to Father Glen that I thought it was a mistake for Marina to be replaced by someone who's so *young*. Even if you are a widow like myself. Mmmm. Oh dear." She looked around the surgery helplessly. "I wonder what I'm going to do about the pain in my chest now."

Ciara felt very bad. Useless, in fact. She was used to working in a big city hospital where if you couldn't do something for someone, you'd refer them on to someone who could. She felt ashamed of having judged Marina's chaotic style of practice. Marina was obviously very skilled and was able to be all things to all people on the island, and had been for many years. And Mrs Delahunty was obviously very sensitive, and dependent on a good doctor-patient relationship with Marina.

"Could I examine you and perhaps see what's wrong? Then perhaps I could help, even with conventional medicine?" she asked timidly.

"Oh, dear, no. Oh, that wouldn't be a help at all. I've been examined by the doctors over and over again and they can't find what's wrong. Oh, perhaps I'll just have my acupuncture and be on my way." And she began to remove her gloves.

"Er. Does Dr De Barra do that here?" Ciara asked and tried not to let her voice squeak. Acupuncture too! Oh, man oh man.

"Every month. Will I go to the couch and lie down?"

Ciara took a breath. It was a challenge, acupuncture, that was all. It was just a challenge. No need to panic. Nothing she couldn't figure out herself. She used to be an A&E doctor. She was used to thinking on her feet. Needles, pins, that was all it was, wasn't it? And there was always the placebo effect – at least thirty percent of every recovery in casualty is due to the placebo effect of being in a therapeutic environment, her boss Professor Maurice Hanly used to say. Well, she could give it a bloody good go, couldn't she?

"Certainly, Mrs Delahunty. No problem at all. Now, tell me, which acupuncture points does Doctor De Barra use, when she treats you?"

"Well, there's one point here on the tip of my ear, another on my wrist, and the third is on the inside of my elbow," Yvonne Delahunty said, rolling up a silk patterned sleeve. "She's very good, you know," she added, scrutinising Ciara.

"Great. Now you close your eyes, and I'll get the needles in," said Ciara brightly. Nothing ventured, nothing gained, she thought. God knows, I might even learn something out here.

Chapter Sixteen

Maggie Hennelly gripped the sides of the seat inside the chartered helicopter as it twisted sideways to make its descent onto the island, and squealed with excitement. After a slightly sickening helicopter flight across a very windy sea, the island was now visible beneath thick clouds like a black and green dragon rising out of the ocean. And she could see Atlantis! Pierce Fox's legendary house was now at right angles due to the tilt of the helicopter but nevertheless it was an astonishing sight from the air. The house was so bleak and Gothic and yet desperately glamorous, nestled in between the hills that were scattered with sheep, and then bowing gracefully down to the lake with its surrounding trees. The helicopter swept over the thatched houses of the village, that tumbled down a hillside to the sea, and then circled the house before landing gracefully on the slightly muddy lawn behind the greenhouses. Maggie waited for the purring of the helicopter blades to stop and then the pilot opened out the door for her and let down the ladder. And she was here!

The gust of fresh, wet Atlantic air hit her like a slap in the face and blew her hair everywhere – but it was exhilarating. And it was so green and damp and wonderfully clean! She pulled her bag out and descended the ladder cautiously, while the pilot helped her with the luggage, and then stood, heels sinking slightly into the very soggy lawn. There was a woman standing with a spade as if she'd been digging. Maggie shivered, glad to be at last on solid land, even if the fine soft rain was absolutely soaking down. The woman who'd been digging had set her spade aside and was walking over to her now, and Maggie wheeled her little case behind her, making her way over to her.

"Trish," the woman said, offering a mud-caked hand.

"Maggie," Maggie said. "Fair play to you gardening in this rain!"

Trish smiled. "You're the writer, aren't you? The one that's ghostwriting his autobiography?"

"Yes."

"Marvellous!" said Trish. "Absolutely marvellous to have you here. Come on in, Maggie, and meet the others. They'll be thrilled that you've arrived."

How charming, Maggie thought, following Trish into the big house through a French window. And oh my God, there's Setanta Lynch, in that studio room there! I can't believe it's him – and plastering something with no shirt on too! Crikey, he's much more gorgeous than I'd ever imagined. And she almost tripped over the suitcase she was pulling.

"I've put you on the ground floor near Gemma's apartment," Trish was saying.

"Yes. That sounds lovely. Who's Gemma?" Maggie asked, craning her neck to maintain the view of a half-naked Setanta crouched over his sculpture.

"Pierce's lawyer. She'll be working with you on the book. The ground floor is where the artists' studios are as well, but it's very peaceful and quiet and you'll barely hear a thing because Setanta works such very long hours. He barely ever leaves his room, poor lamb," Trish was rattling on. "He's been working like a demon ever since he got here, obsessed with his new sculptures. He could do with someone fun like you to get him out of his shell." And she turned to beam at Maggie again.

Oh, ho ho! Jesus, thought Maggie, I'm going to have such a brilliant time here!

Amy couldn't write. Not a thing. It was torture. The sun was out – for an hour, probably, and then it would slip back down again behind the lake when the next shower burst and drenched everything in mud again and she'd have done nothing all day but stare out of the window at the rain and tear her hair out of her head. Two hours she'd sat here and all she'd written was a paragraph and that was crap. She couldn't decide who her main character was. She couldn't decide if she was going to write in first person or third. She couldn't decide if the book was a tragedy or a comedy. She was in an absolute knot.

The real problem was that she was completely out of practice. She'd written one book while pregnant with her second baby, June, which had seemed easy – the book had almost written itself. Resigned to bed under doctor's orders as Baby June had not been able to decide whether she was breech, transverse or head-first, she'd rattled at the keyboard all day long and out had come a bestseller. No bother. But now? The truth was that since June had been born she'd discovered that having two children under the age of four is very much more than twice as many as one child – even if that doesn't make sense in maths, she thought glumly. She hadn't read a single thing since June had been born. She hadn't written a thing either. She'd been so convinced that writing was a piece of cake because the first book had been snapped up by her publisher and had sold so well that it hadn't occurred to her that there might be any difficulty with the second. And now here she was – out here on a flipping island with two precious weeks ahead of her and not a word written and a contract that had to have a manuscript in by next month. She rubbed her fingers through her hair furiously and then burst into tears.

Amy sobbed loudly and without inhibition, cradling her head into her arms on her desk. The worst thing was that she'd spent the last two years blaming Holly and June for not being able to write and now here she was, on a remote island with absolutely nothing to do *but* write, and she was paralysed. And she missed Holly and June desperately.

Terence had been so adamant that she shouldn't ring – that she should leave him alone to be an über-parent and spend the time throwing herself into her writing and earning them some money, but she just didn't think that she could do it any more. Being away from the girls was like having a hole in her heart. She couldn't write with them – but she couldn't live without them! Perhaps if she just rang and spoke to Terence, that might help. He mightn't let her talk to them, but even if she could hear their voices in the background, that might help a bit.

Sniffing back tears and rubbing her nose with her sleeve, she picked up her mobile phone – thank God, there was reception! – and dialled home.

"Jesus, Amy, I thought I told you not to ring!" was how Terence answered the call.

"Oh Terence! I'm so lonely out here! I miss you all dreadfully. And I can't bear to be away from the girls. Can't I even talk to them for just a little bit?"

"The girls are fine. I am coping perfectly well. We are having a great time. We've been to McDonald's. They played at the playground. I got them an ice cream. And now they are outside on the street going up and down on Holly's tricycle. We're getting along perfectly without you. You can't keep supervising me like this, Amy."

"Oh, I know, Terence. I'm not trying to suggest that you can't cope. I just mean that I miss you all."

"Amy, don't try to make *me* feel guilty."

"Terence, I didn't mean –"

"I'm not as useless as you think. My children are happy with me. You wanted to get on with your writing and your book. Well, I'm getting on with parenting my children."

"Please, Terence," she said, trying not to let new tears fall.

"Oh, I've got to go. Holly's just taken a tumble off her bike!" he said.

"Oh, Terence, is she all right?"

"Of course she is. You think that I can't cope, don't you? Well, I'm getting on extremely well," he said, and hung up.

"*Arrgh!*" she howled, and then noticed there was a very soft tapping at the door.

"Oh. Um. Come in?" she said, dabbing her eyes and fixing her hair. She found her glasses quickly and slapped them on.

"I heard you crying. I was worried about you." It was Setanta Lynch.

"Oh God!" Amy felt her neck becoming beetroot. "I'm sorry. I didn't mean to disturb you. I'm – I miss my kids," she finished lamely.

"Aw," he grinned. "You poor thing. How's the writing going?"

He wasn't wearing a shirt. He was standing there, Setanta Lynch, looking like a gay men's garage calendar in a pair of ragged, holey, faded jeans, bare feet, plaster caked into his hands like a construction worker, and flecks of plaster through his dark curls and even in his long eyelashes – and if Amy hadn't been thick-nosed with tears and blurry-eyed behind her glasses she'd have probably been having an orgasm by now.

"The writing?" she said faintly, cringing as her voice came out in a clot of tears.

"Yeah." He wandered into the room and sat down on her bed. Her *bed*! Setanta Lynch was sitting on her bed. She was probably going to pass out.

"Your book. What's it about anyway?"

She swallowed hard. "Well." She looked at her computer, then turned back to him, trying to remember to breathe. "It's about a woman who has a relationship with her next-door neighbour's son –"

"Is she an older woman?" Setanta asked, stretching out his bare feet in front of him.

"Yes, well, she's older than her neighbour's son, of course."

"How old is he?"

He was leaning on her bed now – no, he was lying on her bed! Setanta Lynch was reclining on her bed, his long legs stretched out lazily down to his bare feet with adorably rounded, slightly hairy toes that were splashed with pale grey plaster too, and he leaned onto one elbow with his head in his hand, watching her.

Her throat was dry and she licked her lips to try to make them moist again, and then realised that that might be misconstrued. Oh, man! "He's –" She cleared her throat. "The boy she has the affair with – well, he's – how old are you?" she asked.

Setanta smiled his lazy smile. "Twenty-eight," he replied.

"No way! Oh, I mean, you look so young!"

He raised his eyebrows.

"Oh, no, I mean, I didn't mean to insult you. That's a compliment, actually. A huge compliment," she said, flustered.

He was actually batting his eyelashes now. "So, how old's the guy in your story?"

"Um. Well, I was thinking that he'd be about seventeen – or nineteen, twenty, twenty-one or two, something like that? Or is that a bit too pervy? For the forty-two-year-old?" she asked, tomato-faced.

"Nah. I think it's pretty hot."

"Oh, God! You're fantasising this, aren't you!" Amy gasped and burst into hoots of laughter.

"I like to visualise," he said. "I am an artist." And he spread one of his paint-spattered hands out in front of him to examine it.

She giggled. "How's *your* art work going?" she asked him.

"Good. But. I need a model. And I was wondering. Would you like to pose? For me."

She felt as though her heart had just fallen out of her chest, and then wondered if she was actually going to be able to draw another breath.

"Oh, God," she said. "I – I – I – just don't know. I really need to write, you see," she mumbled.

"Ah. Yeah. I see. Ah, I was just wondering, you know? You've got a beautiful body. And I'd love to sculpt it, see. Ah, no bother, though. I don't want to take up too much of your time." He sat up, as lithe as a panther, and leapt off the bed, padding across the carpet in his bare feet like a ballet dancer. She watched him open-mouthed.

"The story sounds great, though." He grinned at her from the doorway before he left.

Amy cringed as the door clicked shut. Then she rushed over to the bathroom where she found her face in the mirror was blotchy and swollen with tears, her dark-blonde hair was a tangled lump of rats' tails and her glasses made her look like a bad-tempered schoolteacher. Oh, crap. Oh, crappity, crap crap crap!

But she had a beautiful body, he had said. She looked at her reflection sideways in the mirror. Her tits weren't *too* bad. Maybe. As long as she wore a good bra. And she was nice and curvy, with decent legs and a not-too-flabby tummy. And a pretty pert little arse. She'd make a pretty hot sculpture. Maybe. Hmmm.

What the hell am I thinking? She stared at herself. This is insane. This is bonkers. I'm married. I'm completely married and I adore my kids.

In the mirror, her pupils were wild with delight.

She returned to the computer and opened up the lid. Taking a deep breath, she began to write.

He was an artist, a sculptor, whose hands were rough and grasped her with a passion that she'd only ever dreamed of until then . . .

Chapter Seventeen

Mrs Yvonne Delahunty was delighted with the result.

"You know," she said, wrapping a silk scarf around her throat while Ciara made a note with a little drawing of where she'd placed the little needle in her ear, "I wouldn't have thought that I could have expected to feel so well as soon as this."

"Oh, I'm so pleased!" said Ciara, smiling very genuinely now, and crossing her fingers very tightly behind her back.

"I'll have to spread the word around the island that you've got a real knack, Doctor, for acupuncture," Mrs Delahunty murmured and smiled benevolently before she left.

Christ, thought Ciara. And then she thought, oh, well. At least I didn't fill her with a load of pills she didn't need. So which is worse – fake acupuncture or fake medicine for hypochondriacs? None of us are perfect. And at least I'm making case notes, she decided, filing Yvonne's new file away carefully under Y.

Ciara watched Yvonne go past the little window in the lane, and then got up to call the next patient in.

"Hi." The tall guy reached out his hand. "I'm Art Callaghan. And this is Jimmy Seán, my dad. Small world I guess."

She smiled at him. "So, which of you is the patient today?"

Jimmy Seán was standing at the window looking at the two of them in distrust.

Ciara looked at Art. Here, in her surgery, his height and his confident stance made him seem a bit less distracted than he had the last day.

"Dad's got – er – a terminal illness. And he has a lot of pain. In his hip and back too, don't you, Dad? Jimmy?" Art said, but Jimmy scowled and said nothing.

"We – er. We just wanted to pick up the tablets Doctor De Barra gives him every month."

She smiled again at Jimmy, and then gave up. Miserable auld fella! She slipped out from behind her desk again and went to the dispensary. Jimmy Seán, under J, morphine tablets, ninety, one three times a day. There was a date beside the last dispensing which was – well, it was last week.

"Jimmy," she said, coming out to the surgery room again, "I think Doctor Marina gave you your morphine last week."

Art looked at him.

Then for the first time Jimmy spoke. "Aren't you the widow?"

Ciara bit her lip. "Do you have enough tablets?" she said very carefully to Jimmy Seán.

"That's funny," said Art. "I checked today and he's run out."

Ciara nodded.

"He never comes down himself," Art added.

Are you the widow! Ciara's head buzzed, Jimmy Seán's words still hanging in the air. It was clear that Mrs Freeman had been all over the place with her story and she'd only just set foot on the island!

She steeled herself to concentrate on the task at hand. Dispensing Jimmy Seán's prescription.

But something told her that with the filing system, and the postcard that she'd sent dated before she'd left the island, her dispensing system was probably quite arbitrary as well.

"Will you look after the tablets for him?" she asked Art, counting them out.

Art prickled. "I've been looking after Dad for several months, now. We're getting along real well."

Oh, all right. Lanky string of shite, Ciara thought. And then felt some remorse. Christ knows how anybody could get along with poor old Jimmy Seán.

They left. And then she thought of something else.

She tapped on the window and Art Callaghan turned around. She opened the window and leaned out.

"If you ever need me to do a house-call, that would be all right," she said. "Only, sometimes elderly people are more comfortable in their own home." And, she thought, if I did a house-call then perhaps the old guy wouldn't come marching into my house whenever he feels like it.

Art smiled. A huge, friendly smile like a happy dog. A smile of – well, thought Ciara, it was probably a smile of sheer relief.

"Great," he said. And he took his father by the arm, who shrugged him off immediately.

She opened the surgery door to let the next patient in.

Art walked slowly up the lane behind Jimmy and wondered why on earth he'd just told Ciara that he and Dad were getting along real well. For Pete's sake, there was no reason to hide the truth from this young new doctor. Although the *real* truth was that he'd been dying to find an excuse to pop down to Ciara. After meeting her that day, he'd felt such a clod, and yet he couldn't stop thinking about her. There was something so, well, mysterious about her. She was so quiet, so shy, so – well, stand-offish, actually, that he'd been attracted by her beauty and yet at the same time utterly repelled by her frostiness. But after what he'd heard about her in the pub that everyone on the island was saying, that her husband had just died, he was intrigued. And then he felt guilty, of course, for having judged her. And the more he'd thought about it the more he'd realised he couldn't wait to see her again. He hadn't been able to stop thinking about her, come to think of it. And so going down to the surgery today with Jimmy Seán had provided the perfect excuse to see her again. On her own territory. Where she'd be relaxed and he could get to know her a bit – only it had all gone all – well, fuzzy around the edges. The truth of the matter was, he suspected, that Ciara had probably been rightly put off by the disgraceful behaviour of Jimmy Seán.

But she had been kind. And that was so sweet of her to offer a house-call. Art cringed again at the thought of how crazy he must seem to her. She'd only met him as a guy who works in a pub. She had no idea he was a scientist, no idea he'd worked in NASA, in MIT, had a degree in astrophysics and had done a PhD with Stephen Hawking.

Standing there talking to himself in front of the fire that day he hadn't looked remotely intellectual – he'd looked as though he'd just come down in the last shower and there wasn't a lot he could do about it now. He could hardly run off back up to the surgery and burst in on her and say, 'Ciara, I know things look a bit wild around here but I'm actually a very interesting astronomer, so, how about it?' In any case, Art reminded himself glumly, as Jade had so often remarked as she'd waltzed out of the door into her new life, astronomy isn't exactly the kind of thing a woman wants to talk about all day.

But Ciara did seem to be a very different kind of woman. She was so quiet, so solemn, almost paralysed with shyness, he thought, to the point of being stand-offish and yet she had this way of suddenly doing something very sweet – like flinging open the window and offering to do a house-call for Jimmy Seán. God knows how she was managing Marina's jumble of a surgery, never mind trying to cope with Jimmy Seán! But she did look, to Art, as though she was going to fit in. It was almost, he thought, as though she fitted in a bit *too* well on Inish Rua. She had that wild look about her. The spontaneous, ungroomed, lack of self-awareness look that he couldn't help finding attractive in Irishwomen. But it wasn't the same as the wild, unaccountable look that some of the other women around here had – Trish up at the big house, for example, she was one crazy bird. He'd once come upon Trish on his walks about this island with her wellies and her nightie on, pottering about in the garden talking to the frogs. But Trish was tough.

Ciara, on the other hand, had arrived on the island and struggled all the way from the boat on her own with a suitcase, even though she was the doctor and could easily have arranged someone to transport the luggage for her. Half the prima donnas at Atlantis house refused to lift their own luggage up the hill and Art had often given Trish a hand wheeling some opera-singer's cases up the hill, or seen Liam dutifully driving cartloads of Louis Vuittons on the back of his tractor. So he took his hat off to Ciara for at least rolling up her sleeves and getting on with it. And yet somehow, standing there in the rain, with her unsuitable suitcase and her desperate shyness, she'd looked a bit *pathetic*. But there – he'd said it now. A bit pathetic was what she looked. And then he scolded himself furiously for thinking that about someone whose husband had just died. I mean, who wouldn't be a bit pathetic? he thought, feeling desperately ashamed – I'll probably be completely pathetic myself by the time Dad pops off.

Jimmy Seán was away with the fairies most of the time. It was probably just a matter of time to see how crazy things would become eventually, before he'd have to ask Ciara for a lot more help. And although part of the reason he didn't want to burden her too much with all the crazy stuff when she'd only just arrived was because he thought she looked pathetic, the other and possibly bigger part was the fact that Art just didn't want to have to accept how absolutely pathetic the entire situation made him feel either.

"Trish Lenihan," the woman said. "Just came to bring you some herbs. Marina uses them for her remedies. Oh, and I just wanted to say how sorry I am to hear about your husband's death."

Ciara cringed again. But she decided to keep her eyes

tightly glued on Trish. "That's very kind of you. I'm afraid I don't know what to do with the herbs. I'm not a herbalist." She was beginning to feel increasingly inept. How could she have misjudged Marina! The surgery might be cluttered, the note-keeping might be eccentric, but Marina had obviously got all sorts of skills that she herself didn't have! She felt useless. Absolutely useless without her stethoscope and prescription pad.

"Oh, never mind. The herbs do help me though. Sometimes I can't sleep because of the ghost, you see," said Trish.

"Ghost?"

"Yes. The ghost of Lady Ardross. She drowned herself in the lake. But she – oh, she stomps around the house at night and drives me crazy sometimes, keeping me awake." Trish smiled a happy smile.

Ciara smiled back. She couldn't help it, she liked Trish.

"You must come up one night," Trish said. "To the Big House. To Atlantis for dinner. Mrs Freeman is a wonderful cook."

"I had her apple cake for breakfast."

"Well, come on up for dinner, I'm sure Pierce wouldn't mind. You'll get awfully lonely here on this island in the winter time, you know."

"I could go to the pub," Ciara said. She was determined to stay away from Pierce at all costs.

"Yes. Yes, that's what people do. Yes, well, whatever you like. But you can just pop around too, and see the place. Liam the schoolteacher comes in sometimes. So, do come if you're free."

"That would be lovely, sometimes," Ciara said.

There was one more patient in the waiting room.

"Marguerite Coyle," the woman said. She wore a tight, black dress over flared trousers, and chandelier earrings. Ciara recognised her as the mahogany-haired musician from the boat.

"We sat next to each other on the boat," she said, smiling as she took out her writing pad.

Marguerite raised one eyebrow. "We did?"

"Yes. You were very brave. You were reading a musical score while everyone else was praying we weren't going to capsize."

Marguerite smiled a prim smile. "I find the sea to be very therapeutic, you see. My husband and I do a lot of sailing in the south of France."

"Oh, yes. Lucky you. Well, what can I help you with today?" Ciara asked.

Marguerite eased her shoulders back and flexed and extended her wrists, curling then around in a circular motion and then stretching her neck like a lizard. She had a lovely long neck, Ciara noticed, and with her almond-shaped yellow eyes it gave her the appearance of a rather elegant snake.

"I've come for my colonic lavage," Marguerite replied.

Ciara's heart sank.

Chapter Eighteen

Pierce Fox's lawyer Gemma had arranged a meeting for the three of them in his private drawing room and Maggie was a bag of nerves. It was only just early afternoon but already the darkness was beginning to fall and the rain didn't help to lift the persistent gloom that seemed to hug Atlantis like a weeping child. God, if we have a thunder and lightning storm out here it would be terrifying, Maggie thought, applying black eyeliner carefully in an unhelpful light.

Trish had given her a gorgeous set of rooms at the back of the house which looked onto the lawn with its lichen-covered ornate walls and the greenhouse that looked as though it was about to blow down in the gale. Outside her window the trees bowed down, humbled by the weather, and Maggie felt a shiver go through her once again. The house was warm and cosy though, big turf fires in every room and a giant range in the kitchen that was like toast. She hadn't bothered with the arty-farty crowd much –

Trish had introduced her to a crowd of odd-looking poets and writers – earnest cry-into-your-pint types, Maggie knew. People who'd left college and couldn't hold down a job, pure chancers milking an Arts Council grant. Thank God she had a proper writing job. And now this potential autobiography.

In the down-turn in publishing, Maggie was smart enough to know that what the big publishing houses wanted wasn't more poncey literature, it was a honking good read. Publishers would pay good money for sure-fire auto-biographies of controversial celebrities, much more than you'd ever make by writing toe-curling prose or crappy romance novels.

And so this was it. Her big chance to get a break, to get a book on the shelves and make a name for herself as a bestselling author, and have a hot piece of news to sell about Pierce Fox on the side as well. Writing the story about Fox's abandoned son for a tabloid without a by-line would give Maggie all the ammunition she needed. The anonymous story about the missing son would come out on the eve of the Golden Globes – Maggie would time it to happen just like that. That scoop would catapult Pierce Fox into the realms of journalistic gold dust. But by then she'd have signed a contract with him for his autobiography. And Pierce, furious that some unscrupulous journalist had outed his past, would be desperate to repair his image. And by then her pitch for the autobiography she was about to negotiate with Fox was going to be so hot that publishers would be at each other's throats for it.

Maggie's held her hand very steadily as she applied a smokier layer of grey eye-shadow and then mascara, layer over thick layer until her lashes framed her eyes like

Bambi. Then she drew a very careful line around her lips, exaggerating very slightly her natural cupid's bow, and filled in each of her lips with a bright cherry gloss. Maggie's mouth was very sexy anyway – she knew by the way men's eyes were drawn to it, the way the bottom lip was slightly thrust forward in a bee-stung pout, the way the perfectly formed twin peaks of the top lip made it full and the margin seemed to turn outward, opening her mouth slightly like a venus fly trap. *Blow-job lips*, was how one of her lovers had described her mouth, and Maggie layered another coat of gloss on top, licking her teeth carefully afterwards.

She had decided to wear a dark pink shirt – which could have looked demure, but with Maggie's strawberry curls instead looked, well, confident, she thought. She left the top two buttons of the shirt open, and slid into a pencil skirt and a pair of black knee-high boots. Then she realised that the look wasn't exactly *writerly* – it was more sexy secretary. Well, good, she thought. There's enough hippies and fleece-wearing anoraks hanging around in the kitchen here. Pierce is probably dying for a bit of skirt. Smoothing the front of her pencil skirt she checked her appearance for the last time, and then drowned herself in Opium.

"Come in!" It was a woman's voice.

Maggie creaked open the giant door. Fox was standing in front of the window with his back to her, jangling change in his pockets, and the lawyer was sitting at the little round parlour table in the centre of the room with a laptop, a calculator and a legal pad and pens. Gemma Goodbody, the lawyer, looked like a right old stick-in-the-mud, Maggie thought. Time to convince her to see the dollar signs – that'll probably get her interested.

"Hi, I'm Maggie Hennelly," she beamed, entering the room.

Pierce turned around. He was older than she'd imagined, with a good-night-on-the-tiles sort of bagginess around the eyelids that couldn't disguise wickedly sexy brown eyes. But he was every bit as hot as she'd expected him to be. Dark hair only just beginning to show some silver. Sharp, clean eyebrows. Smooth chiselled features, high cheekbones and a tiny dimple in his chin that was very cute. He was dressed in a sort of country casual style with an open-necked shirt that revealed just enough of a hairy chest peeking up above the breast-bone at his throat to make Maggie long to see more.

He didn't smile. "Very good of you to come," he said, pulling back a chair. "This is my legal advisor, Gemma. Gemma, Maggie." Then he looked at both of them sitting at the parlour table and he grinned. He had the most adorable little gap between his two front teeth that made him sexier than ever. "Ladies," he said, clapping his hands together, "shall we have some drinks?"

"We could have coffee, or tea, or something. It's half past two in the afternoon," Gemma began.

Pierce waved a hand to dismiss her and marched over to a sideboard where there was a full bar. "She's always trying to look after me," he said over his shoulder at Maggie, "But it doesn't work."

"That's so sweet." Maggie smiled demurely at Gemma who'd begun to bite her nails. "I'll have a whiskey, please," she said briskly to Pierce. Never a bad idea to start an interview with a drink and settle everybody's nerves.

Pierce winked again at Gemma, whose face was on fire. "Good girl yourself. A stiff one down your throat always makes things much easier for everyone, doesn't it?"

Maggie couldn't help snorting with laughter. Gemma looked aghast.

"So," said Pierce, handing Maggie a Waterford Glass tumbler the size of a plant pot, full of Tullamore Dew, "this autobiography. I'm very excited about it. It's going to be great fun. Can't wait to spill the dirt on everyone – politics, filthy business, all the people who've fucked with me –"

"Women?" butted in Maggie with a winning smile.

Pierce looked at her with scrutiny. "Aw, no, let's not get personal," he said. He glanced at Gemma who was busy scribbling in large loopy handwriting on a legal pad. "Nothing personal," he added for her benefit.

"Pierce," Maggie lay a delicate freckled hand on his, "it is an autobiography. It's supposed to be personal."

"Aw, Jesus!"

Maggie shook her head and licked her lips. She could have sworn that Gemma scowled.

"It's your personal journey through life," Maggie said. "That's what people will find inspiring about it. You've had such an incredible story – growing up in rural Ireland, getting expelled from school, starting your own business while you were still at college, becoming a millionaire in your twenties – people adore that kind of stuff. You've taken on the giants and you've won. You've been a patron of the arts, you've sponsored major charities, and now you're breaking all the rules by investing in toxic banks and buying bankrupt airlines with the money you've made from the Celtic Tiger." She smiled warmly at him. "Your personal story is a legend. So people will also long to read about whom you've loved and lost. Think about it. You watch the Biography Channel, don't you?"

"Nope. I only watch pay-per-view." Pierce topped up their glasses.

"That's enough!" Maggie never had a problem knowing what to do with a bottle, but four fingers of whiskey before dinner was enough to polish anyone off.

But Pierce was looking very frisky. "Gemma." He bore his eyes into hers. "Go on. Treat yourself. To please me?"

"Maybe later," Gemma murmured, watching Maggie and Pierce clink glasses.

"So," continued Maggie, noticing Pierce's eyes switch their focus from the plunge in her pink blouse back up to her face. She leaned forward slightly so that he could have a better view. "What readers will really want is your personal story. Parents, teachers, siblings, loves, rivals, friends, enemies – the business stuff they can get in the Sundays. Or in magazines like *Scoop*! But the real story," she lowered her voice, "is what's in here." Maggie tapped her chest.

"I'll say it is." Pierce grinned at Gemma. "So, Maggie, what makes you tick?"

"Tick?"

"What turns you on?" he smiled wickedly.

Gemma stiffened.

"Drink, Gemma?" Pierce said again.

"Actually, I think I might," said Gemma in a brittle voice.

"Good girl yourself. Let me just pour Gemma a drink, Mags. And then why don't you tell me all about yourself."

"Oh, there's nothing much to tell," Maggie began, twirling ice around in her glass.

"There's always something to tell," twinkled Pierce. "Isn't that right, Gem?"

"Probably." Gemma knocked back the whiskey and went to pour herself another one.

Maggie winked at her. Poor kid, she didn't know how to play the game at all. God help her with her pink legal pad and her lovely natural uncoloured hair and her expensive fountain pen. Which reminds me –

"Pierce, do you mind if I begin taping at this stage? It's probably early in the whole writing process but I feel that a lot of insight can be gained into your persona in these informal sessions which I might need to listen to later on to inspire me to write in your own unique voice."

"I've got a better idea," said Pierce, leaping up and prowling over to the other side of the room. He pressed the oak paneling and the paneling immediately revolved, like a magician doing a trick, opening up to reveal a video camera pointed at the room.

"Oh," said Maggie. Feck him and the helicopter he came in on, she thought – he's got every angle covered. "Well. There's no need to *video* all the sessions for the book, is there?"

"Security," he said. "The whole house has got camera wiring and CCTV. You don't think I'd run a palace like this in the middle of the ocean and not think that someone might like to pinch the silver, do you?"

"Er, no. Well, of course not. But surely – don't you trust the staff and residents?"

Pierce laughed. "Actually," he said, "I do." He shrugged his broad shoulders. "In all the years I've owned this place nobody's stolen as much as a sausage and as to the likelihood of anyone breaking in – well, if you can brave that sea and organise your own transport out here and rob the place and manage to take anything away with you, good luck to you."

"So why the cameras then?"

"Force of habit. I like to watch. I like you. Like to watch you, Maggie. Like to keep on top of my game. I like to replay. Fast forward and rewind. More whiskey?"

"God no! Oh, go on then. Perhaps a smidge." Her head was definitely getting a bit fuzzy now. "Throw a splash of water in there too," she added, wondering if the carafe of clear liquid he was pouring into the glass was actually water.

"Gemma?"

She shook her head.

"You'll catch up later, won't you, sweetheart?" He raised his eyebrows at Gemma. "But, sensible girl, you'll need to keep a good head on your shoulders for your legal notes. But we'll get a proper party going tonight, won't we?"

"We will?" Maggie said. Well, now – this mission out here was beginning to look like it was going to be very well worthwhile indeed.

"Ah, we'll go and meet the other residents," said Pierce. "I like to relax after a hard day's work."

If this is his idea of a hard day's work, thought Maggie, watching the view of the lake through blurred eyes, then I'm a fucking poet. I'm plastered already and it's only lunchtime! I need something to eat.

"Do you think, Pierce, that we could send for sandwiches or something? I feel I need a bit to soak up the alcohol."

"Ah yes, didn't Yvonne Delahunty leave something in the drawing room?" He looked about him vaguely. "Gemma, you organised Yvonne to get us something, didn't you?"

"Of course."

"Well, bring it in then, there's a good girl. Fucking famished actually, myself," he beamed.

Gemma stood up like an obedient servant and Maggie instantly felt sorry for her again. Pierce was bossing her around like a junior PA, not a lawyer.

"Here," Maggie said, standing up as well, "I'll help you get the food. I'm a bit tiddly though so don't mind me being clumsy."

In the drawing room next door Mrs Delahunty had left a plate of prawn vol-au-vents, a platter of smoked salmon, a duck liver pâté, a venison terrine, some soda bread and a giant goat's cheese. There was also a rosy tomato salad glistening with olive oil with the most beautifully fragrant basil torn over it, and a cut-glass giant bowl of plums.

"God, what beautiful food!" Maggie stuffed a plum into her mouth immediately. "Who prepares all this?"

"Trish grows vegetables and herbs in the gardens, and Mrs Freeman cooks. Then Pierce has a sort of assistant, a kind of PA if you can imagine that sort of thing out here, Mrs Delahunty, who makes sure he has food, liquor, whatever he needs sent up to the apartments when he's here." Gemma looked at her sternly.

"So where is she now? The kind-of-PA?" asked Maggie through a full mouth. Her stomach growling with alcohol at the sight of the food, she'd been unable to resist throwing down a vol-au-vent as well, unable to wait till they'd brought it through to Pierce.

"She's not allowed up here when he's doing business," Gemma replied. "Mrs Delahunty, Yvonne, well, she's a rather twee country lady, a widow apparently but nobody really thinks her husband died, he just disappeared and never came back. But she's convinced Pierce is in love with her so she treats him like a god – which suits him, of course. He makes sure she gets lovely presents sent every time he's here – my task, apparently, to choose a suitable gift to thank Mrs Delahunty for being his de facto butler and keeping his apartments warm and aired while he's away – but other than that he tries to keep the islanders out of his life as much as possible."

"Wow," said Maggie, taking up the tray. He sounds like Mr Rochester in *Jane Eyre*, she thought, keeping a full house of servants and butlers and fires burning and food ready for him just in case he might turn up. And now the crazy lady in the attic too. She looked sideways at Gemma who was unrolling silver cutlery in linen napkins. "Even Trish, say? She seemed so lovely and warm when I met her downstairs."

"Trish – well, she isn't really an islander, but yes, I guess Pierce probably thinks she's a bit hairy for his liking. A bit rustic and unsophisticated. He likes women to be more – a bit more –" Gemma paused, flushing slightly.

She's really very pretty, thought Maggie, behind that booky, schoolteachery look. If only she took her specs off and did her hair up a bit and put on a bit of lippie – and maybe a better outfit. God, she's probably got great legs too. She glanced down at Gemma's long colt-like thighs in tight black trousers.

"He likes women to be *a bit more like us*?" Maggie smiled very sweetly at her.

Gemma turned to her, puce-faced with humiliation. "You may think I don't know what you're up to, Maggie Hennelly, but I am watching you like a hawk," she hissed. "And Pierce isn't fooled either, you know! We'll tie you up in a legal contract for this book that'll make you sorry you ever came out here. You might think you're digging for gold, but you're only digging yourself into a career-hole you'll never come out of. Oh, you'll make a bit of dirty money for yourself from this book – and Pierce will come out of it smelling of roses too. But don't think you'll get anything more than one book out of this adventure – Pierce is very clever and he's right on to you and if you play one false move he'll make sure that you'll never work again – except for him. I know where you work right now. I know who your contacts are. I know all about what happened to your job as vice-editor at the *Daily Press* when Pierce dropped the paper, and why you're just doing celebrity features now. I know you're out here for *revenge!*" She finished with a spray of spit.

Maggie's jaw had dropped. "Jesus, Gemma, the thought never even crossed my mind. Why would you think a thing like that?"

"Oh, for God's sake, I'm not born yesterday! Autobiography – of your number one enemy? Give me a break!" Gemma snarled.

Maggie stared at her. And then the penny dropped. "You're in love with him, aren't you?" she said very softly.

"How dare you!"

"No, honestly Gemma, it's all right! He's a fine bit of stuff. No, he's a ride. And a half. In fact, he's the dog's bollocks. I'd fancy him myself if I didn't know any better. And there's nothing wrong with wanting to get – I mean, there's nothing wrong with fancying your boss." Maggie put the tray back down on the sideboard and took poor Gemma's trembling shoulders in her hands. "Jesus, Gemma, look at me, will you? I'm a journalist – was a journalist – I should know how these things work! The casting couch is a well-respected method of getting what you want in life, and don't let any woman ever tell you differently. In any case – *ouch!*"

Gemma had just slapped her across the face!

"What the *fuck*!" she yelled. "What the hell are you doing, you mad bitch!" She nursed her stinging cheek. "Are you crazy or something?"

Gemma burst into tears.

"Oh, for Pete's sake!" Maggie sat down on a lady chair that was upholstered in a beautiful pale-pink silk damask and watched Gemma put her head into her hands and sob her heart out. Then she put a hand out and patted Gemma roughly on her back between her shoulder blades. This time Gemma didn't flinch.

Gemma turned to her with reddened eyes. "Can't you see? You're going to ruin everything! You're so much prettier than me! You're so sexy and tough and confident and you can write – which he admires no end. Look at all the trouble he goes to for writers and poets and playwrights and things. He adores the arts! It's all he cares about! He pretends to be all rough and ready but he longs for poetry and drama and he would have given anything to be able study literature – but he didn't have the patience – and so he gives everything he's got to artists and writers." Gemma sobbed and gulped back tears. Maggie handed her a linen napkin. "And nobody knows him like I do – he doesn't talk to anyone the way he talks to me, just to me, when we are working alone. And now you come along with your big ideas for how to get him to talk about his life –" Gamma's eyes flared suddenly, "– but he never will!" She rubbed her nose defiantly. "He'll never talk to you. You've got all the wrong approach – thinking you can get to him by talking business and playing quick tricks. He despises business. Business and politics – that's the way he uses to punish the world for how he is! You'll never know what he really loves!" And she stood up.

"Wow," said Maggie. This is the most bizarre business meeting ever, she thought. Bloody lunatics, the pair of them. Pierce pacing around the room, skulling back Tullamore Dew like it's Pepsi cola, getting me as drunk as a skunk before we've even discussed a single word of the book, and now this melt-down from the lawyer. "Wow," she said again. "He's really got into you, hasn't he?"

"He understands me," said Gemma through gritted teeth, "And I him."

Maggie's mind was racing. She knows about Gabriel Kelly! She knows! He's told her! And if I can't get to him, then I'll bloody well get it out of her if it kills me.

"Well," said Maggie, "good on ya, girl. And so let's help him to write the best autobiography ever written, shall we? Let's give him the story he deserves."

"You know what, Maggie," said Gemma in a stony voice, "For as long as I can help it, you'll never know what he deserves."

From the next-door study room Pierce watched the cat-fight with amusement on his CCTV monitor. No, amusement wasn't actually what it was. It was lust. It was hard, horny lust. Jesus, those two girls were hot. He sat down in front of the bureau where he kept the monitor for the CCTV and watched Gemma bawl at Maggie, and then watched Gemma cry and Maggie's eyes open up with amazement and then take Gemma by the shoulders and stare into her eyes. He unzipped his flies.

Fuck, that's good! Christ, this was a lot better than pay-per-view! God, she's beautiful. Jesus, she's just slapped the other one across the face! Oh, fuck, that's beautiful! Pierce Fox watched agog, unable to peel his eyes away from the screen where all his favourite fantasies were coming to life in his very own house.

Afterwards, he chucked the antique linen napkin that had been carefully laid out on a silver tray with the china breakfast things by an utterly devoted Mrs Yvonne Delahunty, Bean an Tí, into a dustbin.

Chapter Nineteen

Amy had been writing all afternoon and her neck ached, her shoulders were in agony, her eyes swimming from the computer screen – but she'd done ten thousand words! It was a miracle. The words were just flowing out of her fingertips before she'd even thought of them – they were on the laptop screen before they'd even been made up by her brain. Hot, sexy stuff, steaming with emotion. Oh, and it was real, proper, good writing too. The characters were alive! The emotions were heartbreaking! She finished up a paragraph and sat back to look at it sitting proudly on the page. It was going to be a cracker!

Bong! The dinner gong again. She tugged her fingers through her hair and then suddenly realised she hadn't washed that day. She hadn't dressed. She was still in a smelly tracksuit and slippers and her unwashed hair was like stiff hay! She had no make-up on and there was a dinner being served downstairs and she was ravenous.

Bloody hell. *Bong!* Again. She looked at the clock. Five

minutes should do it – ten at max. She pulled her tracksuit off, flung it anywhere and snapped the taps on. Quick leap into the shower. *Crap!* Scalding hot. *Ouch!* Freezing cold! *Shit!* How the hell does this work? *Yowza!* Shampoo in eyes! *Hell, hell, hell!* Blasted useless unresponsive shower controls! How on earth do you get conditioner out of your hair with ice-cold water? – it hardly seems worth trying. Should I skip dinner altogether and sneak down later with hair in towel to make sandwiches? But no. That would seem so anti-social. And besides, I absolutely can't wait to meet Pierce Fox.

Water better now. Luke-warm better than freezoid. Much better. Hot even. Jesus! Scalding! Help! Conditioner glued to scalp like molten plastic! *Yow!*

She leaped out of the shower and decided to fill the sink with water instead, dunking her head into it like a Hallowe'en apple bob. Conditioner out. Hair in towel. Hairdryer? Shit! Forgotten it! Oh, for fuck's sake! Two weeks on a remote island with an utterly desirable man next door without a blow-dry – nightmare of worst-case scenarios possible in the canon of all nightmares!

Bong! There it was again. They'd be all sitting around rattling their knives and forks waiting for her.

In the mirror she caught her agonised expression complete with wretchedly wet hair and florid complexion from the over-heated shower. Fuckity fuck fuck fuckity fuck. Need to calm down now. *Bong!* Dinner gong again, going like a burglar alarm now. Ten past seven already. What to wear? Shit!

She flung open the beautiful wardrobe and surveyed her clothes. Six skirts, six long-sleeved jersey tops and a pair of cigarette pants. Long-sleeved top with skirt best choice. But which colour? Red? – too likely to clash with her scalded complexion. Navy? – a bit demure? Black – funereal. The navy top was looking like the best option – low-necked, and she could wear it with the flared gipsy skirt and some lovely beads at her throat. Sexy, actually. But with just-out-of-bed hair? Or more accurately just-out-of-towel hair? Wrong look altogether! Perfect for skinny lank like Kate Moss with denim jacket and high boots. On me, with just-fell-out-of-a-bush-backwards-hair – mental patient on a manic bender, Amy thought. Jeeeeeezus!

Bong! Bong Bong Bong!

She sat down on the edge of the bed again and wondered if she was going to cry. And then a little tapping at the door.

"Yes?" she whispered.

"It's only me – Zack." A cherubic head popped in. "We were wondering if you – oh."

"Oh fuck! I mean, I'm sorry. I'll get dressed." She tugged the towel that had fallen onto her lap rapidly around her breasts.

So: he's seen my tits already and I've only just arrived. Oh, what the hell. Like I'm anything to look at anyway. I mean, Terence hasn't bothered in months. What was I thinking earlier? I could never be an artist's model! Tits so droopy from breastfeeding they look like mandarins in the bottom of two Christmas stockings. Although, Zack looks quite turned on, actually. Funny, that. Don't care though, to be quite frank. Can't handle this many decisions in one day.

"Would you like us to wait for you?" Zack gulped.

"Nah. I'll be down. Let me just pull something on."

"Gotcha. It's quite informal here, you know." He was

189

smiling so sweetly now and his pinked-up face went so well with the whiter-than-white hair. Like a marshmallow.

"Jeans?"

"Perfect."

"Jumper?"

"You'll look fab."

"Thanks. You are a pet."

"Big glass of wine?"

"On my way."

She could hear the chatter from the dining room and it sounded buzzy and quite fun. And her jeans were clean at least. She grabbed a bottle of Ysatis and sprayed it vigorously into her armpits. And the jumper – well, at least it was cashmere, even if it was a little worn around the armpits.

Oh, God, she thought, fluffing her wet hair in front of a giant gilt-edged mirror in the hallway, it's been so long since I've been able to afford new clothes – wouldn't it be wonderful to have something unmended and all crisp and neat – or a cashmere jumper that's non-bobbly to wear sometimes?

"Hi, again," said Zack who was at the sideboard pouring wine. "Have a nice big glass of that and come and sit by me."

Zack was wearing a pin-striped suit with a T-shirt underneath that made him look even more incongruous than the reindeer jumper had done – but he had obviously scrubbed up and had a shave. She took the giant Waterford Crystal jewel-like glass of ruby-red wine from him and slugged down a great big gulp of it.

"Come on, we're all starving!" He led her to his end of the table and sat her down opposite Setanta.

Amy looked about at the others. Marguerite Coyle was wearing a feathered clinging black evening dress with a crystal choker around her neck and had her mahogany hair coiled up in a grand chignon on the top of her head. She looks like a heroine in a Brontë-novel period drama, with little sexy snakes of tendrils caressing her perfect little ears, thought Amy, feeling suddenly hideous in her jumper and jeans. Joy was wearing a scoop-necked salmon-coloured T-shirt over black palazzo pants that looked both comfy and elegant at the same time. Trish was wearing a rainbow-patterned maxi-dress that was straight out of Abigail's Party. Wolftone was wearing what appeared to be his anorak.

"Oh, Amy. How clever of you not to bother dressing up!" cried Marguerite, turning her smile immediately away towards Setanta. "You're so brave – it must be wonderful to be so Bohemian," she purred.

"Setanta didn't dress up either," Amy began, and realised immediately how childish it sounded.

"Yes, I did," grinned Setanta who was wearing a *Never Mind The Bollocks Here's The Sex Pistols* T-shirt over his holey jeans.

"Have some lamb, it's just delicious. And the duchesse potatoes are divine." Zack started passing plates to her. "And have you met the others yet?"

She looked around them at the table – Joy, Marguerite, Setanta, Trish who was looking a bit glassy-eyed and seemed to be talking to herself, funny that. Zack was beside her; Wolftone, who was drinking something that was clearly not wine, sat next to him, and then she noticed that there were two other women at the other end of the table whom she hadn't yet met.

"Hello," she waved at them. "I'm Amy Shanahan."

"I know," said the pretty redhead with a very plunging neck that showed off her voluptuous breasts scattered with freckles like daisies on two ripe hills. "I interviewed you for your book. Remember? I'm Maggie Hennelly from what used to be the *Daily Press*?" She rolled her eyes at the others and then smiled at Amy.

"Oh, Maggie! Gosh, how lovely to meet you here again! And what a lovely surprise!"

"And Gemma? Pierce's legal advisor?" said Maggie looking pointedly at the other woman with the poker-straight hair and glasses sitting next to her. There was a sudden prickle in the atmosphere at the table. It was as if, Amy was quite sure, the body language of the entire group had shifted slightly.

"Gemma, hi. Are both of you here to write and paint too?"

"I'm writing a book," Maggie sweetly replied. "Taking a break from the journalism. Although it's all churnalism these days. It's so – soul-destroying, isn't it, Gem?" She beamed again at Gemma by her side.

Gemma said nothing.

"Marvellous," said Amy, helping herself from a giant bowl of asparagus glistening with Hollandaise. "God, this food is delicious! What's your book about then, Maggie?"

"About this wonderful island. This beautiful place. The history of – um – Atlantis." Maggie waved a hand vaguely while Gemma stared solidly at her plate. "Pheasant?" she offered Gemma the dish. Gemma shook her head.

"Not a pheasant-plucker, then, Gemma?" Maggie smiled sweetly at her again and passed the plate to Joy.

Amy giggled and looked quickly at Wolftone – but he

hadn't noticed. He was too busy adding huge curls of butter to his duchesse potato before hoovering it up.

"Vegetarian," Gemma snapped.

"Oh, you'll soon crumble after a few days of Mrs Freeman's cooking," Zack said happily, tearing half a lamb's shank off the bone with his teeth like Henry the Eighth.

"I tried to be a vegetarian once but then I got pissed and ate a cheeseburger," said Wolftone, topping up his glass with something he'd produced from a bottle in the breast pocket of his anorak.

"Don't you drink wine?" Amy asked him.

"Wine. Well, it's not really a drink, is it? I mean, I drink whiskey. And vodka when I'm driving. But for some reason if you put a bottle of whiskey out on the table here it draws attention," said Wolftone gloomily.

"How's the poetry going?" Amy asked him, pouring herself more wine.

"*Whiskey is poetry. Wine is song. Love is music. Are you going to play along?*" He grinned at her through a pile of misshapen teeth.

"Did you write that this afternoon?"

Wolftone gazed away into the distance. "No, just thought of it now. It's good though, isn't it?" he beamed, produced a pencil from his breast pocket and began to write on the tablecloth.

Joy seized the pencil from him. "Don't do that, Wolftone, ya big thick eedgit, get a piece of paper!"

"She only has my best interests at heart," he explained to the others, slugging back his drink.

Sitting directly opposite Setanta had a horribly distracting effect on Amy's appetite. The food was wonderful, every mouthful like ambrosia – the pheasant was so rich, salty and meaty, the lamb was garlicky and marinaded in a wonderful red wine and cognac sauce. But the mere idea of being seen to chew, swallow, drip gravy on her chin was an absolute nightmare. I bet I've got red-wine stains all over my teeth, she thought miserably. I must have. If I try to pick up those peas with my fork they'll roll off under the table. If I have more duchesse potato I'll look like a complete pig. And I'd love another helping of lamb but then I'll stink all night of that delicious garlicky marinade!

It was impossible to keep her eyes on her plate with him sitting opposite her. And yet – if I look up at him – Argh! All she could think of every time she looked at Setanta was the sex scene she'd written that afternoon – the vivid, gloriously erotic and shockingly arousing scene, completely and shamelessly inspired by a shamefully filthy fantasy about giving oral sex to Setanta Lynch! What the hell is happening to me out here? she thought to herself in despair, picking away at her lamb's shank. I can barely concentrate on food – I haven't spoken to the girls in two days – but the writing – oh, the writing! At least something is working out for me. I might be turning into a mush just sitting here looking at Setanta, but at least he's inspiring me to write!

Marguerite had refused duchesse potato but had taken a tiny mouthful of the pheasant and was painstakingly scraping the Hollandaise off her asparagus – stalk by stalk.

"So," Amy turned to Zack in a whisper, desperate to distract herself from Setanta who was being lionised by Marguerite, "where's Pierce Fox tonight?"

"Dunno." Zack shrugged. "He's a law unto himself. Sometimes he eats with us, sometimes not. He might turn up for dessert or liqueurs or something. So, tell me how's the writing going? What have you been writing about all day?"

"Um," said Amy, quickly filling her mouth with bread. She chewed slowly, trying not to think of the images that had her computer positively steaming all that afternoon. What have you been writing about? Well, let me see. Setanta's big hard cock, as I imagine it to be. Oh and then there's Setanta's strong thighs and the way he might wrap them around my waist, Setanta's six-pack, Setanta's tight balls, Setanta's musk-like smell, a scent off his armpits like moist hay, the way Setanta's fingers would rove inside me –

"Amy?"

"Oh! Er. Yes. Well, actually, Zack," she dropped her voice to a whisper, "I've actually been writing a very steamy sex scene!" She giggled. "For one of my characters. You'd have a laugh." She checked his face.

Zack was blushing, eyes dilated, face like a teenager who'd been caught under the duvet. "About?"

"Can't tell. Literary indiscretion. Buy the book." She grinned.

"Can't wait!" Zack raised his eyebrows. "Are you finding Atlantis house and Inish Rua inspiring? Sexually?" He blushed.

"Don't be so outrageous!" She laughed heartily. "It's a work of the imagination." She shrugged. "I've only got two weeks away from the kids. You've got to just put your head down and do the work." She'd clocked Marguerite dabbing gravy off Setanta's chin. Bloody slutty little cow! All that crap about missing her husband – her husband, poor devil, is probably demented with insecurity every time she goes away, she's such a flirt. "Are you finding it inspiring, here at Atlantis, Zack?" she asked as he splashed her out more wine. "I mean it must be very fairy-taley, mustn't it? Those dark mountains and the lake and the wild sea and everything. It's all so sinister and mysterious."

"Yes, I am actually," he said, looking very pleased she'd asked. "I'm writing a story about an island which is actually an undersea dragon." His face lit up as she turned to face him. "Andraste the dragon lies under the ocean," he began to explain, "and on her mane and shoulders live the people, thinking they are on an island. The poor dragon can't move too much or it will frighten all the people. She has to stay still and hope that they'll never notice that they are actually living on a dragon's back. But she's very lonely, you see. Because Andraste knows that all the people who live on her back are having fun and living lives, and she's just underneath the sea and she can't play with other dragons because she's got a whole population living on her back."

"Can't she just shake them off?" asked Amy, fascinated. Holly and June are going to adore this story! And to think she'll be able to tell them that she sat next to Zack Rowley at dinner while he told her all about it!

"Sometimes she'd love to shake them off, because it's so much responsibility. But the truth is that Andraste loves them. They are little and vulnerable. They depend on her. She gave them a world to live in. They tie her down but she'll never do anything to hurt them."

"Oh my God! It's so sad!" said Amy, her nose began to burn, signalling tears as she imagined Holly and June sitting up in her big bed at home reading the story with her. "Oh, shit!" She hiccoughed. "I'm getting a little bit drunk." She put down her wine. "Tired and emotional, I think." She sighed and sat back to enjoy the sight of the magnificent banquet. The long candlelit table, the moonlit view through a Gothic window of wild trees dancing in the midnight wind. Then she saw Marguerite leaning towards Setanta, deep in conversation with him so that her magnificent moon-like breasts heaved out of the feathered plunge of her dress, glowing like disco-balls in the candle-light.

"No, you're right," Zack said, handing his empty plate to Joy who was clearing the table. "It's terribly sad. I think about Andraste the dragon all day long and I wake up in the night worrying about how sad she is. And I can't think how I'm going to finish the story. What can she do to get out of her dilemma? If she goes anywhere to find some other dragons she'll destroy the lovely little town of people who live on her back. But if she stays there under the sea to keep them happy, she'll die of loneliness herself."

He's as mad as a brush, thought Amy happily – but he's terribly sweet. "Oh, I can't wait to get that book for my little girls!" she said, and the thought of that brought another horrible burning feeling again to the back of her throat and to her nose. Oh, Holly and June! Oh, God, I miss them so much.

"I miss my kids dreadfully," she confided quietly to Zack who nodded sympathetically.

"Tell me what they're like," he said.

"Well, June is the baby, and Holly's –"

And then suddenly eight heads simultaneously looked up. Pierce Fox had just walked into the room. No, that was absolutely not what had happened. Pierce Fox had *slid* into the room. He had *skulked* into the room. Like a panther stalking his prey he had appeared as if out of nowhere, in a black polo-neck sweater under a suede jacket, his dark brown eyes black as coals in the candle-light.

"Well. Good evening!"

Everybody murmured something inaudible in reply, except Maggie who purred in a low tone "Hi, Pierce" from the other end of the table.

He sat down at the head of the table.

"Well," Maggie piped up while the others sat very still, "You must be starving after the day we've had." The others stared politely at their food. "Have some woodcock, Pierce." She picked up the platter and passed it up the table to him. "It's wonderful."

"Pheasant," Amy giggled, passing the dish to Pierce.

"Thank you, angel." Pierce winked very slowly at her. "Although woodcock is probably delicious too. Or any sort of cock, mmm?"

Amy felt her neck becoming as pink as Maggie's shirt.

Pierce helped himself to a giant portion of pheasant and then smiled broadly around the table. "Well then, Maggie! Do the deed, there's a good girl. Introduce me to my newest and most beautiful guest."

And Amy felt her neck burst into flames.

Chapter Twenty

As Amy was being introduced to Pierce over dinner, Ciara was sitting in an empty surgery and wondering what to do for the evening. It was pitch black outside. Going for a walk was out of the question. Where should she walk to? Out to the pub? She shuddered at the thought of it, trudging all the way up the hill in the terrifying darkness to sit in that gloomy thatched pub with two auld fellas listening to the clock tick. Nothing else to do then except go back to the house for the night. Have a read, perhaps. Peace and quiet. Solitude. Well, that was what she'd come here for, wasn't it? She sat in the silence for a while and listened to the wind buffet constantly outside, chewing over the memory of her day.

What the hell had she been thinking, telling Mrs Freeman on day one that her husband had died? It was all over the island now, they were obviously talking about nothing else! She'd thought it was the perfect answer to the question of why she was alone – she'd assumed that a dead husband was the last thing anyone was going to ask her about. But she'd been so wrong! Widowhood was positively making her a celebrity here. Mrs Delahunty, despite having a rubber tube up her bottom at the time, had been unable to stay away from the subject of widowhood and the lonely, tragic life it was. Ciara had come out here thinking that the only thing she'd want would be to be left alone with nobody remotely interested in her past and she'd been landed in it. The whole island knew her business – no, they knew more than her business, they knew things about her that weren't even true, stuff she'd made up. The silly lie she'd concocted to explain the whereabouts of Des, the little white lie that had seemed such an easy get-out-of-jail-free card when it had tripped off her tongue that morning had escalated into an absolute soap-opera! The whole island was talking about the Merry Widow above in the doctor's house and there was nothing she could do about it now. She couldn't exactly go about knocking on the doors and tell them all, "Oh, remember I told you my husband had died, well, he hasn't exactly died, it's just that he's sort of disappeared and we're assuming he's staged his own death or done a runner because he's wanted for a very serious amount of fraud. Have a nice day, now!"

Oh, God oh God oh God oh God! Oh, well, the worst thing that they'll think about me is that I'm pitiable. Which perhaps I am, if I can't even face the truth about my own life and I'm making up stories about my husband being dead. The funny thing is, making up a story like that is exactly the kind of thing Dessie used to do, only he did it to get attention rather than to avoid it. And I hated him for it in the end.

It was an interesting first day on the job, though. And not a single accident or an emergency, mind – just a very odd series of requests, and some very routine prescriptions. So maybe this job was going to be a doddle after all. But no matter how hard she tried to put it out of her mind, she couldn't help thinking a lot about one thing in particular – which was the absolute mountain of Viagra Pierce Fox had collected.

Crikey, what kind of a sexual appetite did he have anyway? Although perhaps he was just very, very impotent, she thought, trying to put her most Hippocratic medical hat on again – but then she quickly put that particular image right out of her mind as well. There was something about Fox that she did not want to impinge on her consciousness at all. He'd set off some sort of alarm bell for her – like an antibody reaction, as soon as he'd come into the surgery, almost as soon as she'd heard his voice. It was almost physical, her response, as if a warning was going off inside her head: *You've met this enemy before. You've been hurt by this. Turn away! Walk away! Abort! Abort! Abort!*

She suddenly felt very small and alone in the little surgery, and the memory of Pierce's presence in the room made her feel even more vulnerable especially as she couldn't see anything out of the windows and into the black night. She stood up, shook herself briskly, gathered up her things and switched off the light.

She locked the surgery door in the howling wind and scuttled across to the unlocked house and slammed herself inside. She stood by the kitchen door for a moment, listening to the clock tocking loudly in the silent house.

She decided she was going to fix something to eat. In

the kitchen there were some tins of soup and so she heated up a large tin of tomato while she hummed to herself and tried desperately not to think about Pierce Fox at all. Then she sat at the table and ate her soup in the silence, and some more of Mrs Freeman's delicious bread, and then put the dirty dishes away and had a cup of cocoa while watching *Ros Na Rún*. And then she wondered what to do. There was no point in going out. It was pitch black outside and she'd never find her way around. How do people go out at night round here anyway? she thought. Do they all go to the pub? Visit one another? You can't see a thing if there's no moonlight. The moon was just about visible tonight but it was so windy and there were great big thick clots of clouds that made everything seem so much darker. She'd walk out the door and fall straight into a ditch.

She went to the window in her bedroom that overlooked Atlantis house and noticed that the big room was all candlelit and flickering with silhouettes of people moving about – and it all looked so lovely and jolly, from over here, anyway. And although she couldn't see any of the people properly as the skinny little Gothic windows were really very small, you could make out that there was definitely a bit of a party going on.

Pierce Fox.

Ciara felt her heart thump again at the memory of him smoothing his way into the surgery. The way his body, his masculine-scented presence had seemed to overpower the whole of the room as soon as he'd stepped into it. The way she hadn't been able to take her eyes off his face, no matter how disdainfully he'd talked to her. The way he'd got exactly what he'd wanted without even a proper medical consultation, and waltzed out with all that Viagra! She shivered slightly as she realised she could still smell his aftershave – Obsession for Men. She knew it all too well.

It was exactly what Dessie Moriarty had always worn.

It was the smell that had turned her on so much in the beginning that she'd associated it with muscular arms, a stiff proud cock, *unbelievable* sex – *Oh my God!* – sex that would make you want to lie down forever beneath it and die right on the spot! Sex that would leave her whole body shaking with one orgasm after another.

It was the scent that she'd associated for several months with overwhelming love and adoration. And then after those few short months she'd begun to associate the scent with a growing sense of anxiety. Then with incomprehension. Then jealousy, insecurity, and bewilder-ment. Then dread. And then within a year, with a feeling that she were going insane. She'd associated it with screaming, yelling, bawling her eyes out, crying, feeling utterly demented with grief, and eventually she had associated it only with nausea, terror and throwing up.

She quickly pulled the curtains and closed off the view of Atlantis.

Actually, the surgery had been pretty unorthodox today, no matter which way you looked at it. It wasn't just Pierce Fox. There was the disastrous mess that masqueraded for a filing system. There was the lack of alphabetical order to anything – all right, the population of patients was small and at least Marina kept the dispensary in alphabetical order even if Ciara suspected that her records of dispensing mightn't be too tight. But then there were several other signs that Ciara had recognised all too well.

She desperately wanted to feel at home here. She desperately wanted to feel as though she was in charge of her own little kingdom – where she could do a little job and go home and watch TV and go to bed and get up in the morning and for it to be the same easy, gentle, painless routine with no surprises and no challenges for the rest of her life. But there were little signs that Marina had left all over the place that pricked at her because of what she knew they meant.

There were empties. Empties in the filing cabinet. In the dispensary. In the drawers of the desk. There might well be no bin collection on Inish Rua, and maybe no bottle bank – but if there were empties in the filing cabinet there were probably empties all over the house.

Empties were something that Ciara knew a lot about.

When she had eventually moved out of the house she'd bought with Des Moriarty which had now been repossessed by the bank – several banks – she'd hired removal men. They'd offered a packing service. Which seemed at the time to be almost as good as having had a guardian angel coming down from heaven to offer to do the laundry, make the bed, phone her mother, bring her a nice cup of tea and take over her life. "Yes, please!" she'd breathed in sheer relief when the removal company had offered to empty every cupboard and shelf, label the boxes and pack her stuff away and then unpack it later. There wasn't much that she still owned, but she needed somewhere to keep her clothes and books and personal items. So she'd arranged to put all her personal things in storage. The removal company labelled everything they put into boxes for her – "clothes", "books", "kitchen utensils", "ornaments" – and there were only seven boxes of these. Seven boxes – my life has been reduced to seven boxes of stuff! Ciara marvelled. But there were also *seventeen* boxes which the removals company had labelled "miscellaneous".

The miscellaneous boxes were tightly sealed but Ciara found that there was a curious rattle from all of them that defied logic and so she opened one labelled "miscellaneous, airing cupboard". Inside she found twelve empty bottles of a mixture of interesting and various Eastern European vodkas. She found pretty much the same in the other sixteen. She had paid to have seventeen boxes of empty bottles professionally packed and sealed and stored until she found somewhere else to live. Thankfully their rattliness had given them away and so she dumped the whole lot as quickly as she could get them out of the house. But the mere thought of the removal men finding well over two hundred empties in various corners of the house, under beds, in wardrobes, airing cupboards, in the study, under the stairs, down the back of the enormous white, leather-covered squashy sofa (no wonder Des had spent so much time lying down on it) and carefully packing them and sealing them into boxes which they then labelled *miscellaneous* filled her with beetroot-faced shame.

And now, Marina's empties in the filing cabinet told the very same story. A secret life. A hidden personality. What else was there around the house? Ciara began to rifle through pots and pans and cupboards with packets of things – nothing particularly in there, but Mrs Freeman would probably notice things hiding away in the kitchen presses. No wonder Mrs Freeman had to come in every day and make sure there was food on the table.

She paused a moment and thought about the one room

where she hadn't yet ventured. Marina's own bedroom. Bedrooms are a private place – and although Ciara was pretty sure that Marina was hiding more than a drink habit that would explain her absence and the crazy situation of Gearóid living at the end of the garden and not seeming to know what was going on in the house – womanly solidarity kept a slight grip on her burning curiosity. So Marina had secrets. So her life was a mess. That was no reason for Ciara to go rooting through it without permission – was it?

On the other hand, it was getting to her. There was no two ways about it. Living here with Gearóid at the end of the garden mooching around looking all paranoid – and every Tom, Dick and Harry walking through the house and into the surgery – there was something weird about Marina that she had to get to the bottom of. On the one hand, she couldn't resist the temptation to start looking for more evidence of the kind of woman Doctor Marina de Barra was. But on the other – she didn't really want to know that there were more Dessies in the world. Especially not in this world. She'd come all the way out here to forget that there'd ever been such a thing as Dessie. She'd left everything she'd ever known – and good riddance to all of it – to be alone, to find herself. To see if she could wipe out all the pain and embarrassment and disgust she felt for herself and what she'd tolerated for the last two years of her life. She had come to somewhere where she would be left alone.

And yet, since she'd come to Inish Rua, she'd been bombarded with people – the surgery just beside the house meant that people wandered in whenever they felt like it, and Marina, of course, didn't bother with appointments.

People just turned up. And the house itself was rarely empty either. Despite the fact that she was inhabiting it on her own, she woke up every morning to find Mrs Freeman in the kitchen or some neighbour who'd wandered in like Jimmy Seán – and then there was Gearóid who lived at the bottom of the garden like a sentry on duty! It was as if she were alone and yet completely over-looked. And the way people who came into the surgery knew all about her – Mrs Freeman had obviously gossiped up and down the island and in the space of a couple of hours everyone knew all about her! It was very weird.

And now the discovery that Marina was obviously living a secret life herself – perhaps that was why Ciara had the sense of being over-looked all the time. Perhaps people were used to keeping an eye on Marina.

Evidence of chaotic drinking was the last thing that Ciara wanted to find in her new life and yet an uncontrollable curiosity came over her as well. She was alone in this house, this remote house that belonged to another woman – it was impossible not to wonder what was inside every cupboard, under every shelf. The airing cupboard, for example – she opened it up and had a quick sniff around, and found a naggin in between the sheets. Well.

And the bookshelf in the living room – yup, Cork Dry Gin again. And the piano stool – naggin again this time. Again, another Cork Dry Gin.

Her curiosity had beaten her hands down by now. She opened the door to Marina's room and marched straight in. It was an unholy mess. Marina clearly had a problem with tidying up. So she would never notice if Ciara disturbed anything. She had a little look inside the wardrobe just to see if – yes, just as expected. Three pairs of knee-high boots in the cupboard with a bottle in each boot keeping it upright. Full bottles in two, empties in the other four. The underwear drawers were chocka. As was the laundry basket.

There *was* a reason why Marina had left the island. She hadn't been running the surgery with any kind of method at all. And there were bottles of drink stashed everywhere. She was using her own house as a bottle bank. If Doctor Marina de Barra was in Las Vegas where Ciara knew the drink was free as long as you were gambling – and oh, boy, did she know it, Dessie Moriarty hadn't wanted to get married in Las Vegas for the weather report – then there was a very distinct possibility that what Gearóid had hinted at yesterday might be true. What if Marina *didn't* come back? What if she had done a Dessie and just ran away? And although it was pretty unlikely that Marina could ever have run up the kind of financial problems that Dessie Moriarty was now famous for, if Marina had an empties collection in the house and had gone travelling, the chances of her coming back all in one piece were slim.

Ciara stood at the kitchen sink and stared at the reflection of herself in the window, through which she could see nothing but the thick black starless night, and a most unpleasant thought came to her.

She could be stuck out here forever.

There was only one thing to do. She would have to speak properly to Gearóid. Gearóid who had been nothing but reticent since she'd arrived here, was going to have to speak. He might live in a shed at the bottom of her garden but he was Marina's husband and he must know what sort of woman she was and why he feared she might not come

208

back. And Ciara needed to know. If Marina was never coming back, well, she'd deal with that. She'd do her locum here for three months as agreed and then she'd see what to do next. It wasn't a disaster. It was just a thing she needed to know about in advance.

She felt a hot prickle of anxiety crawl up her neck.

What the hell exactly was Gearóid doing anyway, living in a shed? The thought of having to live in the middle of a marriage based on fear – of one partner studiously avoiding the other – there was something about it all that made her feel desperately uncomfortable.

Marina hadn't left her any notes, or any communication other than the very odd postcard from Las Vegas that had arrived astonishingly early. And, when you thought about it, if Marina's boat going out of the island was the last to leave and the boats only ran once a week, then how on earth did a postcard get out to the island? Hah!

Ciara went to the mantelpiece where she'd left the postcard of the Desert Springs Hotel and examined it again. The handwriting was very neat. It was clearly spelt and written with a very steady hand. The handwriting in Marina's dispensary records was atrocious, like a drunken spider had crawled out of bed and limped across the page. Doctors do write quickly on the job but Marina's job was hardly busy, Ciara thought. There was only one thing to conclude. This postcard had been written by someone else.

In her two-year experience of having had a series of very large rats to smell and having denied every one of them until she had to face up to them, Ciara was not going to ignore another rat.

There was only one way to sort this out. She must, must speak properly to Gearóid.

She pulled on her anorak and a pair of wellingtons and trudged out into the rain. Gearóid's little shed was lit up at the end of the garden like a star. She ran across the path, pulling her hood tight around her face, and arrived breathless on his doorstep. She knocked and then jumped out of her skin when Gearóid flung the door open as if in shock.

"*Arrrgh!* Oh, God, sorry, Gearóid, but you're always making these sudden moves! Can I come in?"

He stood there looking very puzzled. He craned his neck out past her to see if there was anyone else standing outside with her in the rain and then stood back to let her in.

She shook her hair out of her hood. "Sorry to impose."

"Oh."

"Er. Any chance of a cup of tea? I just thought that – well, seeing as we are neighbours and all, we could – you know – have a sort of chat – or something?" she ended lamely.

Gearóid looked as astonished as if she'd suggested that they rob a bank and elope to the Seychelles.

"All right," he said eventually. "I'll make the tea."

She looked around her at the interior of the little cabin. It was spotlessly tidy. There was a ladder reaching up into a loft, but the downstairs was all one room with a stone floor. The tiny makeshift kitchen was really just a Belfast sink, a kettle on a pot-bellied stove and a table with a few jars and things on it. There was no fridge. There was a door on the other side of the room leading into what she assumed was an out-house. Gearóid must wash at the sink, she thought, wondering where he slept. There was a long rather tatty, squashy-looking sofa – but surely that wasn't it? And yet – there wasn't any room for anything else. And presumably the upstairs loft was for painting in.

"Do you do your painting upstairs?" she asked, watching him carefully pouring water into a teapot. He had a sort of child-like methodical way of opening tins and pouring milk from a little jug, she thought, wondering if the milk would be foul without a fridge. And then she watched him putting the jug back into a bowl of water and covering it with a cloth. It's as if he just steps back fifty years in time living in this little shed, she thought. No, sixty or seventy. And he's only about ten years older than me. What a weirdo! What a freak! And he's wearing sandals – in this weather! Without socks. And he sleeps on a sofa and makes tea on a pot-bellied stove.

He's a psychopath, she decided. He's a hermit and a crazy guy and Marina's run away because he was going to kill her and now I've let myself in and he's making me tea and then he's going to stab me in the shower –

"Sugar?" said Gearóid looking at her with the most plaintive expression on his crumpled face.

Except he doesn't have a shower. He's got a loft and an outdoor loo, and a Belfast sink. He's a crazy eco-hermit who probably makes his own loo-paper out of recycled seaweed or something.

"Two, thanks." She took the teacup and it looked perfectly fine.

"I've no biscuits or cake but Mrs Freeman left some pie," he added.

They sat down on the sofa together, each with a piece of pie in their hand, sipping tea, listening to the wind.

"Gearóid," she said eventually. "Why do you live out here in the shed?"

He stared at her.

"I mean," she looked down at her cup, "you've got that lovely house. And it's cosy but it's very small in here. And if Marina's gone – well, I don't want to be nosy but would you not want to live indoors?"

He looked away. "I don't know where she's gone," he eventually said.

"I thought Las Vegas?" Ciara began to feel the prickle up her spine again.

"Well, that's what she said."

"She isn't in Las Vegas, is she?" Ciara asked.

"I don't know where she is."

More prickles began to crawl up her neck. "Gearóid, is there any chance – I mean – is she still alive?"

There. She'd said it. And now he'd either take up a hammer and smash her head open, or he wouldn't. He'd either pull out the large kitchen knife he kept for these kinds of situations, or he wouldn't. She held her breath.

He chuckled. "She's alive all right. Alive – and living somewhere. But I'm not sure where she's gone. She just upped and left."

"Left? Didn't she tell you where she was going?"

He shook his head. "She said Las Vegas – but I know that's a lie."

"Why?"

He shrugged. "Because of the postcard."

"Ah." Not as dozy as he looks.

"So – what do we do now? I mean – I'm running her practice and we don't know when she'll be back. And you're her husband and you don't know when she'll be back. What do you think we should do next?"

"Do you want to see the studio?" he said.

212

His eyes were such a soft pale blue and the baggy folds around them made him look so meek – if he *had* chopped Marina's head off and thrown her body out to sea then at least he was making a very good job of *looking* innocent.

"All right," she said. "Lead the way." She let him go ahead of her up the ladder to the loft.

The cloud had cleared in the windy night and Gearóid's loft was so full of moonlight you could almost see colour. Almost the entire back of the roof that overlooked the sea had been replaced with a giant Velux window so that he had a magnificent view – and in the unlit night-time she could see the sea heave and rock with foam in the pale moonlight and the rainy sky over the Atlantic tossed with clouds.

"Wow!" she said. "This is amazing."

"I like it here."

"Those are your paintings?"

"Yes."

"Can I put the light on?"

"Of course." He struck a match and lit a candle, and the place took on a Gothic atmosphere. Okay, if Gearóid was going to stab her to death and bury her underneath the same compost heap where he'd buried Marina, now would be a good time to do it, she thought, glancing quickly at him out of the side of one eye. But Gearóid was standing very still holding nothing but a little candle in his hand.

There were canvasses piled everywhere. Ciara walked slowly around the studio loft examining each one – they were little landscape scenes of people thatching, cows grazing, dry stone walls and haystacks and currach boats and children on a beach. The figures were stick-like, almost as if a child had drawn them, but they had so much energy about them, so much life. They actually seemed to *move* in the candle-light. She blinked, wondering if she were seeing things. Their almost cartoon-like quality made them all the more real. She reached out a hand to touch the figures in one – a painting of a haymaking day with children riding on the back of a tractor, drinking lemonade in the sun – and then checked Gearóid's face again to see if he minded her touching them. His face was soft and tender as he watched her. It was almost as if he wanted her to touch his art. The little figures of the children were full of innocence, drama, life – and to her intense surprise she found her eyes filling with tears.

"Do you have kids, Gearóid? You and Marina?"

"Grown up and gone now."

"These paintings are wonderful."

Gearóid's face softened into a smile. "She never likes them much. She thinks they're foolish." He looked down at his toes.

"Oh, Gearóid! Oh but they are perfect! This one, of these two little children paddling in the strand, oh, it reminds me so much of my childhood on beaches in County Clare! I can just feel the way the waves wash cold over your feet and the squelshy sand in your toes and the smell of the sea and rock pools and warm seaweed and the sound of gulls – oh, it's beautiful!" She looked at him. He had painted a magic place. "I can't believe she doesn't like this one," she said, crouching down to touch the thick blobs of paint on a gloriously sun-filled painting of an old man in a bog bending, simply cutting turf. "How come you're painting down here and not involved in all the artists who go up to the Big House up there? I mean, you've got such a lovely gallery here and nobody knows about it."

Gearóid shrugged. "I'm not a trained artist. I haven't been to Central St Martin's or had an exhibition on the Green. I started painting because it was something to do. I go to the mainland every year and buy my paints and canvasses and I sit up here. I sold a couple of paintings once to some tourists but sure they were mad. I'd say they just felt sorry for me and they thought they should oblige. And that's all."

She touched another one, blobby with thick paint. A solemn cow staring across the cliffs – solitary in a rock-strewn field high above the sea on an island in the Atlantic on a summer's day, contemplating her cud and just staring out to sea as if she were the most content creature in the world. It was as if he'd captured a sort of human quality in the cow's expression that was so innocent it was almost comic, and yet at the same time it was an expression that seemed to represent everything she felt about why she'd come out here.

"This is the place where people can be just themselves," she said very quietly, touching the blobby paint on the canvas that was the rump end of the cow. "Just humans and nature and nothing else. It's very simple but it's true."

"The tea is getting cold," said Gearóid.

She followed him back down the ladder to the ground floor again and sat down beside him on the sofa with her mug in her hands

"Why don't you live in Marina's house?"

"Because Marina doesn't want me to."

"Aren't you lonely, out here all the time?"

"Isn't everyone?"

Ciara thought about this one. "I don't know. To be honest, Gearóid, my life's been a bit crazy for the past two years and I sort of came out here because I *wanted* to be lonely." She looked at him. "I kind of needed to be alone. But it's a bit scary too, you know. Trying to get over things, trying to start again. Trying to figure out who you really are, when someone else's life has been deciding everything for you because of the crazy way their life has been." She looked down at her tea mug. "I need to see what kind of person I really am. To get to know myself – doesn't that make sense?"

"Loneliness," he said, "is the downside of getting to know yourself."

"Are you lonely?"

"Would you like to draw?"

"Draw?"

"Yes. When you've got something big you need to figure out, that's what I do. I draw." He reached up to a shelf and brought down a sketch pad and a packet of oil crayons for her. "Here. These are nice and colourful. Just draw, and it seems to tell you the story you need to hear. The picture will give you the answer."

She looked at him astonished. And then she said, "Well, all right then."

And she began to draw.

Chapter Twenty-one

Amy had drunk far too much wine but she was having a whale of a time. Zack was very funny and, she suspected, completely besotted with her, gazing into her eyes when she spoke, telling her little stories about dragons and sea witches and making her peal with laughter. She was finding it very flattering. And she was quite grateful that he was distracting her from Setanta as well as Pierce.

But the more wine – and eventually a very expensive cognac – that was being passed up and down the table, the more flirtatious and sexually charged the atmosphere was becoming.

Marguerite was leaning close to Setanta telling him how much she missed her husband. Joy was busy smouldering at Pierce. Maggie and Gemma were obviously in hot competition for Pierce's affection. And while Trish was glaring at Pierce and studiously ignoring his occasional commands to her for more wine or another decanter of cognac, Amy couldn't help noticing a sexual tension between them too. When Zack suggested they play a party game, Amy felt almost relieved that the emphasis of the evening might shift.

"Spin the bottle?" growled Pierce. "Strip-poker?" he said, gazing longingly at Marguerite's magnificent bosom. At least she had the decency to blush.

She slapped him playfully on the arm. "My husband would die if he thought I was having such a wicked time out here."

"Strip Twister?" suggested Zack and everybody laughed.

"Why don't you all just take your fucking clothes off and get on with it?" slurred Wolftone who was nodding off into his anorak.

"Wolftone, don't be so crass," said Marguerite. "I adore party games! But I'm very bad at remembering the rules." She smiled at Pierce. "I always have to get my husband to cheat at poker for me."

"Well, you could just cheat on your husband and play strip-poker with me," Pierce winked at her and Marguerite looked around her at the others in mock-astonishment. Out of the corner of her eye, Amy caught Joy rolling her eyes at Setanta.

"I know a fun game," began Zack. "It's called Humiliation."

"What's so fun about that?" Joy growled. "Some of us are already being humiliated."

"What you do is think of an experience you haven't had – which everyone else has had. The more other people who've had that experience, the more points you get. I'll start –" he cleared his throat. "I've never been up in a helicopter." He smiled at Pierce. "That's an easy one, isn't it?"

"Guilty," Pierce raised his hand.

"Me too," Maggie and Gemma replied.

"Setanta?" Zack looked at him.

"Well, only as part of a charity parachute jump," replied Setanta in a distracted, bored voice.

"It's still a helicopter!" the chorus came.

Zack counted all the raised hands – Pierce, Maggie, Gemma, Setanta – "Four points to me. Great. Anybody else? Wolftone!"

"Wolftone?" asked Joy. "You were in a helicopter? When?"

"I used to be a famous rockstar. Has everybody forgotten Niall and the Nihilists? I was a fucking American Number One, and in Germany and Japan. *And* I played at Live Aid!" Wolftone roared and everyone made murmuring sounds of approval.

"All right," said Zack. "Five points to me. Amy – you next."

"I've never – um – I've never – um – I've never been to New York!" Amy blushed, thrilled with herself. It might be humiliating, but she was definitely going to get points for that one.

"Hmmmm. Clever girl." Zack counted the hands that were going up around the table. "Pierce, me, Setanta, Joy, Wolftone, Marguerite, Maggie, Gemma, the only other hand that isn't up is Trish. Well done, Amy, you're way ahead. Eight points."

Amy beamed. "Now I get to choose?"

Zack nodded.

"In that case –" she looked at Setanta, "it's you." She felt her neck flush again but in the dimness of the candle-light nobody would notice. She felt a tingling between her legs begin again. Oh, say something, Setanta! Just say *"I've never fancied anyone as much as I fancy Amy Shanahan now"*, she willed him desperately. Setanta softened his big brown eyes and smiled at her. If she didn't breathe now she'd probably pass out.

Everyone was staring at Setanta, dying to see what he'd say. Oh, you idiot, thought Amy, get a grip, she scolded herself and she steeled herself to look away from him again and instead forced herself to smile at Zack.

And then Setanta switched his gaze to Pierce. "I've never," he said, staring straight at Pierce Fox, "taken money from anyone for work I wasn't proud of."

Pierce hooted with laughter. "That's a good one!" he began.

"Jeez, Setanta, where do I begin?" gasped Maggie and everybody laughed. "Taken money for work I wasn't proud of – have you seen the company you're in?"

Everyone was grumbling that it was an unfair question. Everybody has to make a crust at some point in their lives – nobody's perfect! Even Joy was grumbling that she'd once taken a job writing information leaflets that go inside pharmaceutical products, till the products had to be discontinued because they caused liver failure.

"Well, Pierce," said Setanta, glaring at him. His deep brown eyes had hardened like stones. "Do confess."

Amy held her breath again. It was as if Setanta had become a different person all of a sudden. From the sleepy-eyed detached dreamy artist to Jeremy Paxman in the twinkling of an eye. What the hell was he up to, glaring at Pierce Fox like that? The atmosphere was electric with anticipation.

"I thought we were playing Humiliation, not

Confession," smiled Pierce but his eyes were as sharp as blades.

"All depends on whether or not you find your confessions humiliating," Setanta said.

"Lighten up, Setanta," growled Joy, nudging him with her shoulder.

"I've never been more serious."

"It's a very abstract notion, isn't it, shame?" asked Pierce lightly, passing more cognac around the table. "One man's shame is another man's enterprise. Some of us take more risks than others, don't we? Some of us get our hands dirty – and some of us just wash our hands." He shrugged and splashed a generous measure of cognac from the crystal decanter into his own glass. "Don't know how many points you're going to score out of this one, Setanta."

Amy was desperately trying to think of a way of answering Setanta's challenge – had she ever worked at something she was ashamed of? She began to quickly tot up all the jobs she'd ever done – waitressing while at college, a summer recruiting donors for a charity, web-designing, being a mum – God, she was definitely ashamed of that one, given the state she left the house in most of the time and, as for some of the meals she gave the kids, she often let them have crisps in front of CBBC for breakfast. Perhaps Terence was right. Perhaps they were better off with him being the house-parent after all. But, of course, she hadn't been *paid* for being a mum.

"Well, let's make it simpler, then," said Setanta. "I've never used my political connections so that I could buy up a toxic bank, then dump my shares on the stockmarket as soon as they'd increased in value, destroy the entire bank overnight and then buy it back again via another company through another major government bail-out when it was worth practically nothing."

"Setanta!" barked Joy.

Setanta didn't flinch. In the silence, all eyes were on Pierce whose face was rock solid – but there was a tiny muscle flickering just below his temple.

"Do enlighten me," drawled Pierce. "You obviously have some private information that you're itching to share."

Maggie's eyes were glistening, and even Gemma was sitting up looking all animated now.

"There's a reason for Fox Enterprises buying up Jet Éire now, and it isn't just because Pierce loves to fly," Setanta murmured.

"Economics expert, are we now?" said Pierce. The muscle in his cheekbone twitched again.

"How *did* you get to invest in Leinster Bank, Pierce?" Setanta carried on.

Wolftone had suddenly woken up and was rather crookedly eyeballing Pierce now. "Jeez, Pierce, he's got a point," Wolftone began. "No other industrialist would have touched it with a ten-foot pole. All the economists in the country were warning government not to accept private equity investments – but they accepted you. You managed to get the government to support you. How did that happen?"

Setanta's eyes from underneath their long lashes were watching Pierce like a hawk. "He took over the majority of shares without anyone even knowing that it was Fox Enterprises behind the deal."

There was a very long pause. And then Marguerite said, "Gosh, that sounds awfully clever, Pierce. You buy the shares when they are really cheap and then the government shores up the bank so the prices go up – and sell them all in one go to make a great big profit and then you get a different company to buy them up – and you still own the bank! Oh, isn't the world of finance so tricky to understand?" She looked around her at the others in admiration.

Pierce lifted his whiskey to his lips. "Conspiracy theories are usually as full of crap as most fiction," he said.

Amy frowned at this one.

"And as for your abstract talent for art, Setanta, it doesn't quite translate into a talent for imaginative thought. Although," he looked at Zack, raising one eyebrow, "it makes a nice fairy tale." Pierce turned to Wolftone. "And as for your drink-sodden poetry –"

"Oh, you think you can speak to me of poetry?" said Wolftone in a prickly tone.

"Well then. Let us converse in verse," Pierce smirked.

"Shall we give somebody else a go?" Zack butted in swiftly. "Somebody else choose a humiliation instead?"

"Yes," said Pierce, brightening up. "I'd like a go." The atmosphere froze again. "Wolftone, I've never been a member of an illegal organisation. Have you?"

"Fuck off," Wolftone replied.

"Wolftone!" barked Joy. "What the hell are you playing at?"

"Yes," smiled Pierce. "What the hell are you playing at, Wolftone? And while you sit there drinking my whiskey and eating fine food in my house, remind us again why you are here? Is it to create a work of art? Or are you just stirring up more shit for yourself because you haven't coated yourself in enough of it yet?"

Amy felt her skin becoming cold. This was horrible! Everybody had clearly had too much to drink but what on earth was going on between Setanta and Pierce? And Wolftone – Jesus, what was he up to? Everybody knew Pierce Fox and Fox Enterprises was a controversial issue – and she above all people had a major axe to grind if you were really going to be picky about who'd lost jobs and who hadn't when poor old Leinster Bank went down the toilet. Because when Leinster suddenly didn't seem to have any funds to manage – well, Terence's life as a fund manager had gone from working twelve hours a day and running a company Jaguar with an expense account, long lunches in the Bentley and a nice fat bonus at Christmas time, to being a stay-at-home-dad who was underneath her feet all day. They'd had to sell their dream home in Foxrock and move into a terraced shoebox. But it hadn't been Fox Enterprises that had sunk the bank – had it? Everybody knew that the government had tried to hold the bank up for a while and that there had been some private equity investors – but everybody had thought that the money had come in from a property company in America. Hadn't it?

"I thought an American property company had bought up the bank," she said in a very quiet voice.

"Because that's the official story," Setanta looked at her.

"Gosh," Maggie said, giving Pierce a very meaningful look, "that's an interesting take on history, isn't it? So, where were we with the game anyway –"

"Membership of an illegal organisation." Pierce's voice was loud and clear.

"And again the answer is – fuck off." Wolftone's eyes were full of rage. "You won't make scurrilous allegations against me, not now, and not ever," he growled at Pierce.

"And for the record," Wolftone turned to Maggie, "Dax Properties Texas is a subsidiary of Stanaway Oil which is a major share holder in Torquel Oil, a co-owner of Gestate International which owns the Washington Scope which has recently invested in Zetter Point Fuels. Which is based in Northern Ireland and which funnily enough, is a major client of – wait for it – Fox Enterprises! Ah well," Wolftone reached out for the decanter, "funny old world, isn't it?"

"Funny enough for you to be involved in a ridiculous scheme to have Zetter Point Fuels closed down – surely that's something to be ashamed of, Wolftone, in a world where jobs are like gold," snapped Pierce. "Wolftone donated money to defend the anarchists who broke into Zetter Point Fuels and wrecked the computer systems," he added to the others in a mock-bored voice.

"I care about the environment!" Wolftone yelled back at him. "I'm an artist! I'm a local celebrity in my home town! If multinational American weapons manufacturer are going to set up in my home town I've a duty to complain."

"Oh, it's the suffering artist then, is it? On a crusade to save the world?" snarled Pierce.

"I don't like nuclear weapons. I don't like what they do!" barked Wolftone.

"I don't think Nuclear Arms is the right industry for Northern Ireland either, and I sure as hell want to know the truth about where this factory gets its political support," Setanta said frostily. "I think we'd all appreciate some inside information, Pierce."

Pierce glared at Wolftone. "Well, your IRA friend here would appear to agree."

"How dare you, you fucking poncey bollocky prick! I

am a member of a legitimate left-wing republican organisation!" Wolftone was roaring now.

"Please!" It was Trish, in despair. "Can we please stop this horrible row! We only wanted to have some fun and games – this is appalling! Pierce! Stop fighting now!"

"Absolutely," Pierce gave her a winning smile. "So, where were we, Trisha? Playing games, weren't we? My apologies. Yes. Let's get back to our game. What was the name of it? More cognac, Amy?"

"Humiliation," said Zack in a meek voice. "That was the name of the game we were playing." He smiled nervously around the table, trying to lift the mood again. "Trish, why don't you go next?"

They all looked hopefully at Trish. "Oh, all right," she said.

Wolftone hiccoughed loudly and Marguerite shuddered.

"I'll go," Trish said. "I've never –" she paused and looked around the table with wicked eyes. "I've never –"

Amy held her breath. *If she doesn't bloody think of something I'm going to burst. This is painful! Agony! Say something, Trish! Say anything. Anything to get things back in harmony again.*

"I've never," said Trisha, "been so *humiliated* in all my life."

They all burst out laughing. Even Setanta.

And then Amy screamed.

"What the fuck?" Wolftone roared at her.

"Jesus, woman!" Pierce jumped. "What the hell!"

"Amy!" Zack put a hand out to her. Setanta and Joy stared at her. Marguerite was cringing away. Maggie and Gemma's mouths were open. Everybody's eyes were on her.

"There!" Amy's voice came out like a squeak. She pointed

at the window where she'd seen it. It was the most horrible thing she'd ever seen – a pale white face with hair sticking up like a mad thing! Glaring in the window straight at her! She must have come straight out of the lake!

"The ghost of Lady Ardross!" Amy whispered. "It was at the window! Staring in at me!"

Ten pairs of eyes swivelled around immediately. The window was bare. There was nothing to be seen but the blackness of the night and the flickering reflection of the candle-light.

"I'm so frightened!" Marguerite began to whine.

"There's no ghost," Joy said, pouring herself another glass of cognac with a trembling hand. "Don't try to frighten people, Amy. Stick to the fiction writing."

"I saw it too!" Maggie whispered, and everyone looked at her. "I saw it as it just slipped away." Her face was white in the candle-light.

"Ladies! Get a grip," said Pierce and then there was suddenly a very loud creak.

"*Arrrgggghhhh*!" Amy, Maggie, Gemma, Marguerite and Trish all screamed together.

Wolftone pulled his anorak over his head.

"It's just the door!" snapped Pierce and they all turned to look towards the back of the dining hall. And sure enough, a head had popped around the door – Amy wasn't looking, she was covering her eyes and had hidden behind Zack's back – but it was just a human man. Not a ghost. Just an ordinary chap. Sticking his head around the door to see if he could come in.

"I don't want to interrupt," said Liam MacDara cautiously, "But Trish suggested I pop by to invite you all to the céilí tomorrow night."

Chapter Twenty-two

Amy didn't sleep a wink. The house seemed to creak and groan and moan all night long and she lay awake most of the night with the light on, terrified. There were footsteps up and down the landing at all hours. Doors creaked open and slammed shut. Window shutters snapped. Voices muttered, groaned, moaned, whispered, yelped – even though everyone had said goodnight and gone off separately to their own suites, it was as if there were all sorts of comings and goings all over the house.

By morning she was exhausted and her face was puffy from lack of sleep and her hair looked like it belonged on the inside of Wolftone's anorak.

At breakfast time, everybody was making a tremendous fuss about the céilí. And of course, despite the all-night-long creaks and groans all around the house, nobody was admitting to having been out of their beds.

Trish was insisting they all go to the céilí because it was important to be seen to be taking part in the social life of the island. Marguerite was making a song and dance about the horrible proposal of having to sing and dance, which Amy thought extraordinary given the fact that Marguerite was a musician. But the others seemed to be relatively sympathetic to the idea that Marguerite's delicate ears shouldn't have to be exposed to rough, traditional music thumped out by an enthusiastic amateur like Liam MacDara on an accordion, nor should she be expected to tolerate what she was convinced was going to be very unmusical singing. Wolftone was the only one who was looking forward to the céilí but then Wolftone was more or less happy as long as there was a reasonable expectation of being legitimately drunk, and he brought out a bodhrán which he then insisted on practising during breakfast which sent Marguerite off in an enormous huff. Zack listened politely to the bodhrán for all of five minutes before slipping out to walk around the lake. Left alone with Wolftone and the bodhrán, a thumping hangover and the growing possibility of no escape as he burst into song, Amy nipped out leaving him happily thundering away, oblivious to Trish who was screeching at him from two flights up to stop before she murdered him.

Amy went to sit down in the peaceful emptiness of the large drawing room that overlooked Trish's herb garden and wondered what to do. She was too hungover to start writing, but everyone else was going to be busy for the day. Maggie was busily organising a legal contract with Gemma. Gemma seemed to have thawed out a bit and was at least getting on much better with Maggie now, Amy noticed – the palpable tension between the two women seemed to have thawed a lot after Wolftone and Setanta had stirred it up so much last night. Joy was going to walk in the hills contemplating poetry and would visit Setanta's studio later on, she'd said – being around the sculpture would help to allow her to identify with the poetry of ancient Greece from which she took her influence. Trish was bustling around her garden with bunches of herbs and a brace of wild rabbit that Pierce claimed to have shot – although the thought of eating them was making Amy shudder. Thank God Mrs Freeman was preparing something vegetarian for Gemma!

Setanta had gone up to his studio straight after breakfast and was absorbed in clay. The extraordinary thing, Amy thought, is that during breakfast nobody had mentioned the mad row that had erupted last night. They didn't even seem to care. Either that – or they were all up to something even more dramatic.

Amy's head thumped from lack of sleep. She decided that the best thing to do today was to get out of the house. And the only thing to do about her hair was to find a hairdresser.

She remembered passing a little shop called *Gruaig Deas by Nóirín* on the way up from the boat, and although the shop had looked a bit old-fashioned, well, Nóirín was bound to have a hairdryer at least. She started walking briskly to the village, marching down the hill in the morning sun. The wind had died down completely and there was barely a rustle in the trees. The air was still damp and thick with dew and sea promise, but it was so clean and so beautifully quiet. A lonely cow bleated on the wind from a faraway field. Amy marvelled that she could hear it all the way over here. On the stony path her feet crunched loudly – every squeal of every bird could be heard in the silent landscape, and in the distance there was the ever-present swish and rumble of the sea.

It was parky though. She rubbed her nose to warm it up, and walked very briskly towards the village, thoroughly looking forward to a hot blow-dry and a nice hairdressery chat with Nóirín the *Gruagaire*.

Ciara smiled nervously at Nóirín. "Just a little trim, please. Nothing too dramatic – Ooh!"

Nóirín had just slammed her head into the sink and started scrubbing as if she were trying to rip the scalp off her. Ciara squealed as the hot water scalded and then froze almost instantly and then scalded her again.

Nóirín completely ignored her and scrubbed away like she was trying to get baked-in custard off an oven dish.

Ooh! Oh! Ow! Christ, she's rough!

Then she took a towel out and rubbed her head before pulling a comb thorough it like she was raking a garden. She whipped out a pair of scissors and without even asking Ciara what she wanted done, began to snip away with abandon as if she were pruning a hedge.

Ciara butted in over Nóirín's monologue. "Er – I'd like a bit off at the back and not too much off the layers and then blow-dryed with the ends turned out and lots of body on the top!" she yelled.

"Oh, only gorgeous!" said Nóirín appreciatively, clipping away with enthusiasm. Ciara watched long Titian locks fall to the floor and gasped in agony. Nóirín was taking far too much off the back! And the fringe – what the hell was she doing there? But it was too late to do anything – and besides, the woman had a pair of scissors in her hand and she was prepared to use them.

Snip, snip! Ciara buried her head furiously in a copy of the *Farmer's Journal*. What the hell had possessed her to come into the *Gruaig Deas* and let this lunatic at her head with a sharp object? *Snip snip snip*!

Nóirín took out the blow-dryer.

"Lots of body on the top and flicked out –" Ciara piped up again without any real hope.

Whooooo! Nóirín's blow-dryer blew and Nóirín continued to yap. Ciara succumbed to the idea that her hair was being dried in the manner in which you might dry a kid's hair after a swimming lesson. Nóirín rubbed her scalp with one big meaty hand and moved the dryer back and over with the other. Shouldn't she be – um – curling it or something with a brush, putting a shape into it? Ciara thought helplessly to herself. But Nóirín blew and rubbed her head and then when it was dry, combed it out again, just dead straight.

Ciara blinked. She looked very carefully at herself in the reflection of the rather grubby mirror. And she realised she'd never looked better in all her life.

Amy stood outside the *Gruaig Deas* shop for a moment and checked out the photographs in the window. There was a picture of Princess Diana, circa 1985, and one of Madonna, circa 1982. And there was one other photo – of the Pope.

Hmmm. Well, at least it's indoors, Amy thought. And it's warm. And there will be hot water and towels. And, she thought, catching sight of her damp rats' tails for hair in the mirror above the sink from where Nóirín the *Gruagaire* was standing yapping to another customer, it's the only place I'll get a blow-dry on this island so I'm going in.

"Ah, how *are* ya?" said Nóirín the *Gruagaire* when

Amy walked into the shop, as if she'd known her all her life.

"I'd like a blow-dry please," Amy said, smiling shyly at the other customer. She recognised her instantly. It was the woman who'd come over on the boat with them – with the long, wild Titian hair blown all over the place in the sea wind, who had a sort of sad, pinched look about her freckled face. The one who'd been a bit scared about getting onto the boat in the first place but who'd eventually jumped on and they'd all cheered. She'd had her hair done though, and Nóirín the *Gruagaire* had softened her look completely, bringing down the wild look to a gentle bob around her pale freckled face. She was terribly pretty, Amy thought, in a very natural, wholesome sort of way.

"Hi," she said to her. "I'm Amy. I'm staying at Atlantis House. I'm a writer."

"Ciara. I'm the doctor on the island."

The woman looked nice but very shy. Amy sat down in the chair beside her. "Gosh, your hair looks so lovely now!" she marvelled. Old Nóirín must be a genius! "You came over in the boat with us, didn't you? How are you finding the island?"

Ciara paused. And then she said, "Actually, I'm beginning to think I like it here."

"Oh, me too. Are you going to the céilí tonight?" asked Amy.

"Sure what else would ye be doing?" asked Nóirín.

And then Nóirín twirled Amy around rapidly in her swivel-chair and yanked her head back into the sink.

"Oh!" said Amy, without any real effect. Because Nóirín had begun to vigorously wash her hair, splashing water everywhere and rubbing shampoo in as if she were scrubbing a floor. It suddenly occurred to Amy that she hadn't actually told Nóirín what she wanted done.

"See you later then," she heard Ciara say, and the little bell of the door went *ping* as she left.

Amy opened her mouth to tell Nóirín how she liked her hair blow-dried: plenty of styling product scrunched through the roots to give it lots of body on the top with a side split and the ends dried straight with the large-roll hairbrush and then slightly flicked out but not too much and then a touch of serum just to separate the layers round her face, some spray shine products or a very light hairspray – but Nóirín was yapping away in Irish. And then a giant blob of shampoo suddenly washed into her mouth. "*Bleuagh!*" Amy tried to spit out the side of her mouth with her head tilted backwards in the sink but found that it was easier to swallow the shampoo. Oh, my God, this is horrendous! But Nóirín carried on rinsing and splashing – her shirt was quite soaked through now and Nóirín hadn't even put an apron on her, had she? Jesus, this is like being in a car wash!

Nóirín splashed and sprayed and scrubbed and kept a fascinating although incomprehensible monologue going. Amy closed her eyes very tight and tried to think about how lovely and clean she'd look at the céilí. Oh, God, going to the dentist was less painful than this! Eventually Nóirín took a very threadbare towel and briskly rubbed her head with it. She looked up from the towel at the mirror to see what was going on – but Nóirín had the blow-dryer out and was talking above it now, battling with its roar.

Amy closed her eyes. Perhaps she'd just catch up on

some sleep. The dryer roared and Nóirín yapped and remarkably, thanks to the sleepless night she'd had, she dropped off.

Half an hour later she woke up. Well!

She patted the back of her hair. Well! She twirled around a bit to see what the sides were like. Well, that looks beautiful, she thought. Really lovely. What a fantastic hairdresser! Nóirín was as rough as a fisherman reeling in the nets – but wow! Nóirín had blow-dried her caramel-coloured bob dead straight so that it hung around her shoulders in a soft, shimmering curtain. God knows what she'd used for shampoo – it could have been Fairy Liquid – her hair was so shiny now it positively glowed – but she looked great. Younger. Happier. Different. Beautiful, even.

"Oh, *go raibh míle maith agat*!" She beamed at Nóirín.

Ciara walked away from the *Gruaig Deas* with her mouth still open. What an extraordinary experience. Okay, she hadn't exactly been to the hairdresser on her own in several months. Years, perhaps. In fact, she couldn't actually remember when the last time had been that she'd done something like that, that was just for herself. Just about her and her appearance. Even when Dessie had wanted her to look nice he wouldn't have entertained her just going off into town and getting her hair done – he'd have brought her to a salon himself and told the hairdresser what to do. She touched the soft clean bob that Nóirín had given her. She looked different all right. Younger – and at the same time kind of more mature. A bit – well, perhaps a bit sexier even.

Chapter Twenty-three

Father Glen Cassidy was very excited about the céilí. He spent the day arranging flowers for the altar on Sunday and deciding what to wear. Glen liked to be a little bit casual at night-time – the image of a priest was one he adored, but perhaps in view of the fact that this was a céilí night and there would be dancing, he decided on his Ralph Lauren Polo jeans (the ones he'd got at Century 21 in New York, what a bargain – the prices were unbelievable!). With his dog-collar on top, he'd look very much the part, he decided. Then he went out to collect flowers for the Mass.

Glen's dream was to have a Taize Mass at St Tristan's chapel one of the Sundays – a prayer service with chanting and songs and free prayer. "A pilgrimage of trust on Earth," was the phrase he'd been rehearsing for when he got to pitch the idea to the islanders. And Atlantis was so full of creative people – and musicians, like the gorgeous cellist Marguerite Coyle, and that bodhrán player

Wolftone O'Neill. The bodhrán could be a very spiritual-sounding instrument, it was so plaintive, so innocent, Glen thought, as he climbed the little lane behind the chapel. He'd had such a wonderful time on his own pilgrimage to Taize in France last year with a group of French monks – Oh, Fabien had such a wonderful baritone! – and the chanting was so moving, sure who couldn't be absolutely moved by it? Wouldn't it be wonderful to get the artists and writers into the chapel and have a real community Mass?

There was very little left on the hedgerows now, but he gathered a bunch of the viburnum from the little chapel garden and then climbed a little way further up the hillside to find some winter heather from the hills behind the house. And then he thought about the irises that he knew Trish had in the gardens at the back of Atlantis.

What if he popped up there now? He could try to meet Marguerite and Wolftone O'Neill and bounce the idea off them of playing their instruments in the chapel if he had a Taize mass. And in any case, it would be good to show his face before he met everyone at the Halla Oileán. And he ought to get to know Trish a bit better anyway.

Climbing onto his bicycle, he fastened his pale grey scarf neatly around his neck and peddled down the little lane.

"Morning!" called a deep, masculine voice.

It was Pierce Fox, with a rifle across his back, stalking off into the fields! Glen wobbled so much he almost fell of his bike trying to get a good look back at him.

The legal contract Pierce and Gemma had prepared was like the Lisbon Treaty it was so complicated. "Look," said

Maggie, "There are so many clauses in this it's making my head spin. Can't we just forget about all this legal stuff? Then I'd have the biography written by tea-time and you could rip this contract up and we'd just get on with getting a book out on the shelves. Why does he have to complicate all this with this big legal document? Why can't we just rummage through his stuff while he's off deer-stalking or pheasant-plucking or whatever it is he's doing?"

Gemma giggled. "He's shooting hares."

"Makes a change from splitting hairs," grumbled Maggie. "Jesus, Gemma, do I really have to sign this big contract? I mean, what on earth is Pierce Fox trying to get out of me? I only want to write his autobiography – and he's trying to turn it into a game of sleuth."

She looked at Gemma. They were getting along much better now – last night's screaming match between Pierce, Wolftone and Setanta had broken a lot of ice. But she was dying to know what Gemma knew about the issues the two men had raised. "Gemma, aren't you a bit curious about where all his money goes – I mean, there's a lot he doesn't tell you, isn't there? And you're his lawyer."

Gemma said nothing, but her mouth was pursed.

She probably makes sure that nothing Pierce had ever done in all his adventures on the stock market or in acquisitions and investments is actually illegal, Maggie thought, and he pays her enough to make sure of it. But if Setanta is going to stir up trouble for Pierce's reputation, and the campaign against Zetter Point Fuels is going to be shored up into a massive political campaign by local heroes like Wolftone, then Gemma needed to have a proper look at Pierce's private papers too. Didn't she?

"Look, Gemma," Maggie said, "we both know that

Pierce has secrets – even from you – about his investments in Zetter Point, for example. I bet you didn't know about that."

Gemma blushed. I was right, though Maggie triumphantly. He doesn't keep her fully in the picture at all.

"I mean," she carried on, "it's humiliating that the first you heard of his interests in that plant were over a drunken dinner party – and the research was done by a poet wearing an anorak that looks like it doubles up as a night-shelter. I don't want to pry but don't you ever wonder if he's pulling the wool over your eyes sometimes? And if he ever pulled off anything that was corrupt or even mildly dodgy in the political sense, he'd ruin your reputation."

"I don't have a reputation without Pierce," Gemma sulkily replied.

"Well, he'd make sure of that. He practically owns the press. He likes to keep his enemies very close." "Don't you ever wonder why he's hiding things from you? Aren't you afraid he'll get you into hot water by getting you to find legal loopholes for him – or, you know, loopholes that are a bit of a stretch?"

Gemma shook her head. "He's got very powerful friends."

"Nola Connaughton, the Tánaiste?"

Gemma's eyes widened. "You know about that?"

Maggie drew a breath. "Yes. Of course I do. Nola's a very good personal friend of mine," she lied. "And she adores Pierce, of course," she added lightly, praying that this was the right line to take.

"Yes," Gemma nodded enthusiastically. "She's very good to him – although, I have to admit, I'm not sure exactly why."

Maggie took a breath. This story about Pierce was obviously going to be so much bigger than she'd ever imagined. The fact that Pierce and the Tánaiste, Nola Connaughton, had had a love-child together and that she, Maggie, was the only journalist who seemed to know about it, was one thing. But now, knowing that Pierce was receiving political favours from Nola Connaughton, was up to his neck in dodgy banking and had links to arms manufacturers, she realised that this was a much more complicated story now. Gemma was Pierce's lawyer but she didn't know the truth of what she was letting herself in for. Maggie looked at Gemma, her doe-eyes creased with anxiety. He's taking her for a ride, Maggie thought. She's just a kid, in out of her depth, and he's taking advantage of her inexperience to get her to cover up for whatever he's up to. She's letting him lead her into disgrace with his political wheeling and dealings. She doesn't deserve that. He'll ruin her. He'll ride her to hell.

Maggie couldn't help herself – she wanted her scoop and her big story, but she didn't want to see poor Gemma getting crushed in the making of it. Perhaps if Gemma knew what she knew, just that small piece of inside information, that she'd received a tip about Nola Connaughton and Pierce having had a love-child, she might see the truth behind the connections between Pierce and the Tánaiste and she might be more cautious in her undying loyalty.

Maggie didn't want to alienate Gemma completely. She didn't need to tell Gemma that she was only on the island because she was planning eventually to run the story in the newspapers. But she could drop a little hint, just to protect Gemma from fastening herself so closely to Pierce.

"Gemma. There's something that – well, something I heard recently – something rather sensitive." Maggie lowered her voice. "Something that might – um – something which I think you might need to know. About – about–" and she mouthed "*Pierce*". "And it's rather private, actually." She raised her eyebrows at Gemma.

Gemma looked very carefully at her. And then she nodded slowly. "All right," she said. "But, don't forget," she lowered her voice, "this place is very – um – secure." Then she said much more loudly, for the benefit of the CCTV that pointed at them from the corner like the barrel of a gun, "I wouldn't mind getting out for the afternoon, to work on the book, would you, Maggie?"

"Oh, that sounds lovely! Let's go to the pub!" Maggie loudly replied, and beamed at Gemma. "And then," she added, "we need to get ready for tonight."

Chapter Twenty-four

Amy couldn't believe how gorgeous she felt. Her hair looked amazing! Good old Nóirín at the *Gruaig Deas!* And it was going to be so much fun tonight. So what about the ghost – she'd have a good old hop around the floor and sing a few songs with poor old Wolftone and have a bit of a dance with Zack and then she'd be able to sleep like a log. And, besides, the day was glorious, she thought, taking a few moments to relish the view from her desk.

There was an incredibly blue sky and yet over at the edge of horizon, growing out of the sea like a strange creature, was a shelf of thick black cloud. Then she turned back to her laptop and had a quick read over what she'd written since sitting down. Shit, this is good, she thought happily. This is very good. In the studio next door, she could hear the odd scraping noise while Setanta worked. She closed her eyes and imagined his hands again. Imagined his naked body as he sculpted. Oh, for God's

242

sake! she thought, furious with herself again. Get a grip, girl! Think of your husband and your kids!

She closed her laptop lid again. This is hopeless, she decided. I'm either distracted by ghosts now or distracted by Setanta – I've got to get him out of my head. Except that – she opened it up again and had a look at what she'd written today.

He was young and tender in her arms, and her heart soared as bright as a lark . . . Oh, all right, so Setanta is my muse, she thought, chewing her bottom lip. That doesn't mean I have to spend all day fantasising about him. I can turn it on and off again as I want. Can't I?

Fingers that touched her with electric passion . . .

There was only one thing to do to wash the guilt out of her right now. She would ring Terence again and see what was going on at home. Tentatively she lifted up the phone.

"Just wanted to see that everything is all right."

"Yes, well, the kids don't miss you at all," Terence laughed. "They're having a great time."

"Oh, Terence! I miss them. Terribly. You've no idea."

"Well, they're having a ball so you just get on with your work and forget about us. We are going to the shopping centre later on. Holly, eat your tuna fish. No, June, you can't leave your sweetcorn you have to eat it all. Well, then if you don't eat it you can't come out with Holly and me."

"Can't I just talk to them for a little moment?"

"No!" he hissed. "They are fine as long as they don't know you aren't here. They've almost forgotten who you are."

"What?"

"Oh, you know what I mean. It's so much better for them like this."

"Terence, are you sure?"

"Of course it is. They're actually getting on very well now. They're eating better too without all those yoghurts and biscuits you let them eat all day. They go to bed on time for me too, and neither of them wake up during the night. We read a story and then lights out, straight to sleep. I've got a great routine going with them now and we're having lots of fun. Actually, I think in many ways it might be a real advantage to them to have all this time alone with me. They just seem to be more calm, more disciplined. And they seem much happier now too."

Her heart sank as low as a stone.

She said goodbye and then sat there for a long long time, looking at the phone as if it were the enemy. Never in her life had she felt so far away. Here in this beautiful room surrounded by all this luxury – and with all the time in the world to do what she cared about most – writing. And yet it was painful to think that the people she loved were quite happy without her. She blinked back tears again and then stood up. She needed to talk to someone. Anyone. Otherwise her heart would crumple up and she would die.

Briefly checking her appearance, she reassured herself that her hair looked bloody fantastic and then very quietly went to knock on the door of the room next to her.

"C'mon in!"

She creaked open Setanta's door and found him crouching on the floor in front of a giant, bulbous female-shaped sculpture – he was naked from the waist up, of course, in his increasingly plaster-caked faded jeans with bare feet. He rose when she came into the room.

"Feeling lonely?" Setanta smiled at her.

"You can tell?"

He nodded. "Your face is like a book."

She walked over to his work table and reached out to touch the sculpted head he had made. A woman's face with wild wild hair like Medusa's snakes. Her mouth open, her gaze upwards, she had the appearance of being care-worn and confused.

"Beautiful," Amy murmured. "Who is it?"

"Andraste," he replied. "The spirit of the island. The Celtic warrior goddess."

"Oh, just like Zack's dragon!" She was thrilled to have spotted the reference.

"The Celtic warrior goddess Andraste is associated with this island. You know that ancient Celtic cross in the churchyard? That isn't really a cross – it's a Celtic standing stone. I believe that it's the burial place of Andraste. The Christians tried to fashion it into a cross but once you see it you'll see that Andraste's spirit wouldn't let them – the stone won't yield. It's as if Andraste keeps a hold on us."

Amy shivered despite the warmth of the sun-filled room. "She is a force to be reckoned with, isn't she?"

Setanta smiled. "Depends," he said. "But I feel protected by her. Look." He took Amy's hand and made her finger trace the hollows and ridges of the sculpture's hair. "See how soft she really is, even if she's made of hard plaster?"

He was right. It was as if the undulations and rhythm of Andraste's angular features became tender under her touch.

"She's like all women," murmured Setanta. "Cold and hard and tough on the outside but full of love inside."

Amy felt her heart skip a beat.

But he was gazing out of the window at the blackening sky. "There's going to be a storm tonight," he said.

"Can you sleep at night, Setanta?" she asked. "Doesn't all the noise the house makes keep you awake?"

"You get used to it. It's only a house. The dead don't mean us any harm. It's the living that cause us all the real trouble."

Amy smiled. "Yeah, you're right. I need to take a break, I guess. I'm a bit lonely without my kids and I'm a bit overtired from lying awake all night listening to the ghosts."

Setanta broke into a grin. "There are no ghosts."

"Oh, but I can hear them."

"Look," he said gently, "why don't you have a good old wander around the house while it's bright? Get to know the place. Look into all the rooms. See what you find. It's just not knowing all the rooms that has you scared. Once you walk around the place you'll see that it's the floors that creak, or the wind in the eaves that whistles and moans. You won't be scared once you've figured all the noises out for yourself."

"All right," she said. "That's good advice. I'm going to thoroughly explore the house. And I won't stop till I've examined everything that could possibly move and make a noise!"

Chapter Twenty-five

Liam MacDara lined up chairs along one wall and then realised that he'd run out of chairs to line along the other and you couldn't have the whole island all sitting along one wall, so he evened them out a bit. And then he fixed the microphone for his PA system and checked the sound. The piano accordion wouldn't need amplification but he liked to have a little PA system anyway for the raffle – livened things up a bit. One, two, one two, he tapped and blew into the mic. Tonight's prize was a bottle of whiskey from the pub – fair play to Art for offering that because Jimmy Seán had looked daggers at him when he'd asked and Tomás had just snorted at the idea. But good old Mrs Freeman had donated a Christmas cake.

Liam stood a moment and took in his kingdom – the dusty, musty smell of the Halla Oileán. The little disco ball that still hung there since the late seventies. The hard rows of school-furniture chairs.

Is this what my whole life has become? he wondered. Is

this the extent of my spirit of adventure? Is this scruffy little hall my most glorious hour?

He needed to break out of this shell, socialise a bit. Trish Lenihan was always telling him to pop in anytime, but last night when he'd gone up to invite them to the céilí the women had screamed the house down, thinking he was a ghost. He'd felt such an eejit, in front of all of them.

With the céilí on tonight, Mrs Yvonne Delahunty decided that she'd take the opportunity to tidy up and replenish the rooms for Pierce Fox. Yvonne wasn't going to waste her time on a drunken céilí when Mr Fox was in residence. Although he hadn't contacted her since arriving at the house, Yvonne knew this was because he needed time to settle in. She stood at the bay window of his apartments that overlooked the lake and watched his tall, dark figure in the distance stalking up the damp hillside and across beyond the lake.

Mr Pierce Fox shouldn't have to be at the céilí tonight. It was beneath a man of his station to hop and leap about with the drunken yokes that lived on the island all year round.

Yvonne turned away from the window and carefully rolled up the sleeves of her silk blouse. The cream silk blouse was from her collection that Pierce had been sending to her over the years from New York, Italy, Paris and Spain. She had a tiny pair of jewelled earrings that she liked to wear with it. Pierce was always so good to her. She'd give the room a good polishing and replenish the coffee for the machine and lay out his chocolates for him. Perhaps he'd need her to come up to the house tonight when everyone else was busy dancing. Perhaps he'd need her to help with his paperwork by then.

Maggie and Gemma discovered that the pub was empty but they were welcomed with a huge smile by its very attractive owner Art Callaghan. He was six feet tall and very broad-shouldered with thick, dark hair that was slightly overgrown around his ears and the nape of his neck, designer stubble, and heavy-framed glasses that made him even more attractive as they had the effect of drawing attention to navy-blue eyes and a full, sexy mouth.

They sat outside in a weak midday sun and drank hot whiskeys and then had a couple of pretty decent cups of coffee with Art who made them hoot with laughter with stories about his dad's increasing forgetfulness and bad temper, while Tomás, the lugubrious bartender, mooched about inside.

"So let's talk," Gemma said to Maggie when Art had popped out to check up on his dad.

"I guess Pierce is having a pretty big effect on all of us," Maggie began, eyeing Gemma cautiously.

Gemma sighed. "He's got a lot of problems at the moment, really," she said. "He's up to his neck in it financially. I mean, I shouldn't be telling you this, but I'm quite terrified of what's to come. All his companies are majorly in debt. He's completely over-stretched." She lowered her voice. "He borrowed hugely from Leinster Bank, you see. And then he bought back all those shares – with money that he'd borrowed – his finances are all over the place. It's very complicated keeping up with him. And it's been very stressful for me."

"You've been a very loyal friend to him, though, Gemma," Maggie said.

"Well, to be honest, I don't know what he'd have done if it weren't for me." Gemma crossed and uncrossed her legs on the little wooden bench. "He's taken huge risks with this Jet Éire investment. But I am worried that there's a lot more that he's not telling me."

Maggie took a breath. "You still love him very much, don't you?" she murmured. "And he trusts you completely, doesn't he?"

Gemma nodded. "He does trust me. But he's taking huge legal risks – moving money in between different companies to buy up equities because he can't resist the bargains in the current economy. But he owes millions. And there are big holes in his financial portfolio that I can't seem to make sense of at all."

Dirty bastard has dodgy cover-ups going on all over the place, thought Maggie.

"Weren't you always worried, Gemma, that he might be getting you involved in something illegal?"

Gemma looked strained. "He wouldn't do that – would he? I mean, he's got too much of a reputation riding on his political contacts."

"What do you mean?"

Gemma shrugged. "Nola Connaughton the Tánaiste is a very old friend of his and she means a lot to him. He'd never let her down."

"Gemma, have you ever thought they might have anything else in common – besides money and politics, I mean?" Maggie gripped the edge of her seat while she wanted to see what Gemma would say.

Gemma paused a long long time. "They were friends

around thirty years ago – when she was a student, it seems," she eventually said. "She always looks out for his interests – even now. She's very good to him – placing contracts his way for big government projects – and she makes sure that he gets to see the programme for government first, and the budget, even before most of the cabinet do. But," she turned to look at Maggie to check her reaction, then lowered her voice, "I suppose, like you, I can't help feeling sometimes that," she shook her hair as if almost trying to dispel the unpleasant thought, "as if perhaps she's more than just a loyal friend." Gemma blushed.

Maggie looked carefully at her again. She felt very sorry for her. She was so bookish and earnest and *bewildered*-looking.

"I think you should be more assertive, Gemma. I mean, you are his legal advisor for some pretty major stuff. This little-boy lost act he puts on all the time only goes so far. You should think about having a look through his private things."

Gemma gaped at her. "*What?* I wouldn't dream of it!"

Maggie took a breath. "Gemma," she began, "I got a tip from a publicist recently who represents an actor, Gabriel Kelly. And it's a very long story, but I think I know how Pierce manages to wrangle political favours out of the government, and how he's always been able to get what he wants politically, and how he's been able to wheel and deal his way into buying up those shares in Leinster Bank, dumping them, then re-buying without an ounce of policital controversy – just like Wolftone said."

Gemma looked scornful. "What on earth has a tip from an actor's publicist got to do with Pierce? And me? I mean – you've no right to accuse me, Maggie, of –"

Maggie held up her hand. "Gem, I'm not accusing you of anything. I know you've worked your butt off for him and that you've always worked within the law. Which I admire no end. But you have to admit that there are things he hides from you. And you'd be better off knowing the full story, wouldn't you? Before you get yourself in any deeper with him."

Gemma looked furious, but she softened. Maggie was being genuine, it was obvious. And Pierce *was* as slippery as a snake and there was no point in trying to deny it.

"Gemma, there's something that I've discovered – and it's a long story, but the bottom line is that I think that Pierce is blackmailing the Tánaiste," Maggie said.

Gemma opened her mouth in horror, but Maggie put up a hand. "Honestly, Gemma, I know it sounds horrific but I wouldn't make this up. Look, apparently he and Nola Connaughton had a love-child twenty-eight years ago whom Nola put up for adoption. I bet he's been blackmailing her about it since she became Tánaiste, holding the secret against her in exchange for political favours."

Gemma's face had become very white. "You – are – oh, Maggie. How can you be sure?"

"It all adds up, Gemma. He's got a love-child that I know about who's just traced his birth mother and found out she's Nola Connaughton and Fox was his dad. And, meanwhile, Nola's been doing political favours for Pierce and landing sweet financial deals in his lap for absolutely no reason. Nola's desperate to keep her past with Fox a secret, which is how I came to find out about the son. I know Pierce's son's publicist, who says the pressure of it is ruining his client's life. The son is completely disraught because he feels it's a double rejection – rejected at birth, and now he can't have an open and public relationship with his birth father because it would bring Nola into disrepute. That's what Pierce is holding against her. He's destroying his son's life and blackmailing Nola – all for political and financial gain."

Gemma sat very silently for a while before speaking. "This is awful. If anybody found out, this would be – I mean, blackmail's –"

"Illegal?"

Gemma nodded wordlessly.

Maggie waited.

Then Gemma said very slowly, "He's got me in a bind. He's ensured that – that I've been a party to his blackmail . . . oh, Maggie! You ought to see the letters he's made me write to her! To Nola! Oh, horrendous, threatening stuff! All full of hints about compromising government position and balance of political endeavour versus fiscal responsibility – oh, he's so cruel, now that I know what was really behind those letters! But he'd given me the impression all the way along that she was just another thick, dodgy politician who couldn't resist his charm and was stupidly flattered into thinking that he was remotely interested in her political party. He told me she'd taken huge bribes from him in the past like all the others, and that he was just holding that against her! Oh, God, poor Nola! How horrible he's been to her!"

Maggie nodded.

Gemma sat furiously biting her bottom lip. "The bastard!" she said. She began to bite her nails. "He's told me so many lies – oh, Maggie, you've no idea! He told me such a cock and bull story. We are going to have to outsmart *him*!" she hissed. "We are going to have to blackmail him back." She stared at Maggie. "Maggie, see this contract he's tying you into over the book? Don't sign it! I'll get you a much better deal. And I'll get a clause put into it that will guarantee you all the world rights and adaptation rights you want, because we'll have information on him that he'll *never* want Nola Connaughton to find out. That way, Nola becomes more powerful than him. And he'll never blackmail her again."

"Yes! How?"

Gemma looked very carefully at her now. "I think I know how to get what I want from him."

"Good girl. How?"

"We need to give him something that he wants from us. Something that he can't refuse. Something that we'll hold against him forever."

Maggie's jaw dropped. So! Little innocent, bookish Gemma with her long poker-straight hair and her unmade-up face and her horn-rimmed specs. Gemma removed the specs and pulled her hair out of its clasp, shaking it free. She smiled at Maggie.

Maggie winked back. "Yup," she said, grinning at Gemma. "We need to give him something very special first. And then, I suspect, we'll get exactly what we need from him."

Pillow talk. The only route to the truth, thought Maggie.

"Gemma, we are going to have so much fun at the céilí tonight." She squeezed Gemma's hand. "I'm so glad we've become such good friends."

Art examined the sky. It was far too blue for a north Atlantic winter's day. Funny how he didn't even listen to the weather forecast any more – the forecast was a bit arbitary up here anyway, they couldn't predict more than a few hours of weather really. But that blue, blue sky – there was something almost sinister about its tranquillity.

"It's a calm before a storm," he heard his father grumbling to Tomás the barman as he came in from the kitchen. He was probably right – there were heavy rainclouds gathering on the tip of the horizon.

"Dad! Great to see you up. How's the back? Do you want to have some lunch?"

The pub was empty apart from the two very pretty girls who'd come up from Atlantis House, who were talking conspiratorially outside and drinking coffee in the wintry sun.

"The calm before the storm," said Jimmy Seán again. "The calm before the storm. I'd like a storm to eat, please. What did you say your name is again? Can you make me a storm?"

"All right! It's Art, Dad. Art. Your son. And I'll make you a sandwich." He looked around for Tomás to see if he'd finished with the barrel, to get him to offer more coffee to the girls. God, Tomás was useless! Three customers in all day and he still couldn't manage to be around. And the pub would be very busy tonight with the céilí on next door at the Halla Oileán. And if Jimmy Seán were acting up and needing attention . . .

"Tomás!" Art stuck his head out of the back half-door to look for him out there. But Tomás had mooched off again. He was a law unto himself. It was charming the way the island was such a casual workplace but Art wasn't sure how much longer he could cope with running the pub this way, with a father who was becoming increasingly bewildered and a barman who was next to useless.

God, if only he could just get away with his telescope for a few hours and set it up and sit underneath the night and just watch the stars –

"Art! Who are those women sitting outside there drinking my tea?" his father roared from inside the pub.

"Don't worry, Dad. They are customers. You own a pub. They are paying customers. It's not your tea, we sold it to them. Coming with your sandwich now, Dad." He left the bar and went into the little kitchen at the back to open up the bread.

Chapter Twenty-six

The cross stood on a little knoll of grass and rocks that held it upright. It was about four feet high and chiselled in a strange form of a very crude cross, as if someone had started making a cross out of it and hadn't got it right. Ciara examined the confusing pattern of lichens to try to figure out the face that was underneath and realised that it was much more than a cross. The flat stone was cut into relief with raised squares and shapes but she couldn't make sense of them, they were so worn and speckled with the white blotches of lichen. She stepped back to see if the image would appear more easily from a slight distance and then stepped closer again. It was like a psychological game of trying to see a mind puzzle. Out of the pattern of lichen the images reappeared, mysteriously as before, and then she realised that a face was staring out of the pattern with a gaping wide open mouth and eyes that were hollow with death. It was like a warning.

She looked around her at the bleak little churchyard,

now becoming darker as the mists gathered from the Atlantic. A sacred burial ground. Spirits all around. Ciara looked up behind the stone to the sheltered hollow where the small chapel nestled like a prayer, among stones and lichen-covered graves, its gable ends hugged with overgrowth.

She had read that some of these burial sites might have been laid by the Celts, hundreds of years earlier than the seventh-century monastery chapel she was looking at. The other stones and crosses climbed up into the arc of the hillside behind the chapel, silhouetted against the blackening sky and there were other standing stones among the crosses; as bleak as primitive children fossilised into the island's soil. Stones that knew a million days like this – that had watched hooded monks move about and till the land and milk the goats and pray and sing. Stones that had guarded a thousand years and a thousand lives of solitude. Stones that had listened to the wailing of the sea and the raging of the wind and the anguish of the gulls and had heard the whispers of saints and sinners and confessors in the chapel walls.

"They say it's the burial stone of Andraste, the spirit of the island," a deep voice behind her suddenly said.

She almost jumped out of her skin. Turning to the man's voice, she found Jimmy Seán's son, Art Callaghan, standing watching her.

"Crikey, you frightened me! You shouldn't skulk about in graveyards like that!" she gasped.

"I'm sorry. Do you like the standing stone?"

He looked so pleased to have found her looking at it, she couldn't remain cross.

"It's mystical, isn't it?" he beamed. "I often think it almost seems to be alive."

She smiled shyly at him. "I can't seem to move away from it. It's as if it's warning us about something." She frowned and peered at the standing stone again.

"I know it's kind of scary-looking, but I like to think it's protecting us." He came up closer to her. "I like to come down here a lot when I need to feel something bigger than myself. I mean, normally I'd go and look at the stars but it's always so cloudy and rainy here at night." He grinned. "So, I like to come and see the standing stone instead, and think about the way she watches the island."

"She does?"

"Some people think Andraste has blessed the island to protect the women here and keep the men under control."

Ciara smiled. She liked the sound of that.

"And," he carried on, "some think she rules this place. They tried to change her burial stone into a cross but she wouldn't let them. The story is the stonecarver was struck by lightning. If you trouble her spirit you'll suffer for it. You have to respect her authority here."

Ciara looked at him. He was very flaky, really. All that American spirit-speak. And yet – it was funny, but she'd never met a man who talked about spirits and superstition the way she liked to.

Art looked at the sky now. "There is a storm coming, you know. It's going to be very rainy and thundery later on."

"How can you tell?"

"I watch the skies. I'm an astro-physicist – *was* an astro-physicist before I came back here to look after Dad."

Ciara stood amazed. "You were?" She'd always assumed he was just a barman.

He nodded. "I worked for NASA. And then for MIT.

But when Dad got sick I had to come back here to look after him." He looked meek again.

"How –" She was about to say "How unbelievable that as you could be a scientist", and then realised how insulting that sounded. "You're very superstitious for a scientist," she said instead, and then cringed because that sounded even less polite.

He smiled. "You're a scientist too. Doesn't stop you believing in the unbelievable, or the power of the universe though, does it?"

Ciara looked at him for a long, long time. What she was thinking was, it's unbelievable that someone as fascinating as you could end up in this remote and lonely place, and so there has to be a catch. But she didn't know how to express something like that without sounding even more rude. And in any case, she felt as though her mouth had just turned to clay. And then she said, "Do you believe that when people die they really die? Or do you find their spirit somewhere else? Can you find their spirit inhabiting another life?"

Oh, Jesus, what am I saying? I sound as flaky as anything, she thought. Yet there was something about this guy that made her realise that he probably wouldn't mind talking about this kind of stuff. He might find it interesting. And that he mightn't even mind the fact that sometimes her greatest fear was that there might be an afterlife and so even if Dessie *had* died, even if his body was dead, his spirit would haunt her forever. In Marina's empty bottles. In Gearóid's lonely art. In the way she felt watched all of the time despite the fact that she was in a place where nobody knew her.

"Maybe." Art smiled. "There's a lot about physics

that's pretty magical. I often think that more we find out about the universe, the more magical is seems. But I think it's getting dark and cold and you could do with a cup of coffee. Will you come up to the pub and let me make you one?"

She followed him down from the burial mound and he took her hand to help her with the last few steps.

"How's your dad today?" she asked.

Art rolled his eyes. "Giving out as usual – he's having a little sleep at the moment so I took the opportunity to get a bit of a walk. I was kind of hoping to get my telescope out tonight seeing as the skies were so clear earlier – but now look at that." He pointed out to sea.

"You've got a telescope?"

"Yes. Would you like a go some night? If we can get a night without rain!" He laughed.

"Yes," she said. "I actually think I would."

"Maybe when this storm is over. Are you going to the céilí later on?"

She shook her head. "I – I'd better just stay in. In case something *happens*. You know."

He laughed out loud. "In this place? You're kidding – right? What kind of thing could *happen* here?"

Chapter Twenty-seven

Amy walked cautiously along the landing of Pierce Fox's private wing, listening out for creaks and moans but the house was silent. Comfortable, really. Nothing scary happening here, she decided, and knocked on every door along the landing to make sure that everyone was out. The place was empty all right. Setanta was the only one in the house and he was up to his beautiful neck in plaster at the other end of the enormous house.

She opened up each of the doors she came to, and checked for ghosts. Nothing. Of course not. What an idiot I've been.

There was another staircase at the side of the landing going more narrowly up to a third flight – and this, she knew, was where the private rooms of Pierce Fox were, at the very top of the house. Only she probably shouldn't go up there at all – I mean, what if somebody came in? Somebody – like who? Trish was at the back of the farm for the afternoon. Joy was out walking round the lake.

Marguerite had gone up to the chapel to talk to the priest about playing the cello for some sort of folky mass. She'd spotted Maggie and Gemma walking down the lane towards the village. Wolftone had gone up to the Halla Oileán to talk to Liam about music. Zack had gone for a walk. And that left – well, the entire house was empty then, wasn't it? So nobody would mind really – would they? If she just peeked in a tiny few seconds to make sure there were no ghosts? Just a minute was all it would take. Just a quick peek and then – oh my!

Pierce Fox's apartment on the top floor of the house looked straight out over the lake.

Amy stood very still in the doorway, taking in the giant bay window with its magnificent view, the beautiful curly-legged table with antique chairs, the marble fireplace, the book-lined walls, the crystal decanters, the artwork on the walls – a Jack B Yates and a Paul Henry! Oh my! And – yes – she ventured a few steps further into the room – Crikey, that is an original Picasso! And jeez – that's actually a Cezanne! And a Jackson Pollock too! Oh my!

She touched the drapes in softest silk and caressed the polished wood of the panelling. The carpet was probably silk too – she bent down and touched it lightly – oh, beautiful, Afghan silk! – and then she noticed the doorway into the bedroom. Pierce Fox's bedroom. The bedroom of Pierce Fox. And nobody in the house.

Would it be so awful just to have a peek? Just a tiny little peek? I mean, who would really mind – if they didn't know, that is.

She crept in. Oh, the most magnificent four-poster splendid oak-framed bed covered with a – yes, it was a real fur spread – on one side of the room. There was another magnificent marble fireplace with an enormous canvas over it. A stag's head on the wall in front of the bed – what else? Amy thought, trying to avoid the solid stare of the creature's deep black eyes. Over by one window, a crimson silk-covered chaise longue with a matching lady's chair beside it and a cocktail cabinet. Above the cocktail cabinet, on the silk-patterned heavy gold-embossed wallpaper, hung a rifle.

She stood a moment taking in the sheer luxury, the chocolate-box views through the twin bay windows, and the overwhelming scent of *decadence*. You could run a *Scoop!* magazine feature on this room alone, Amy thought. Pierce Fox welcomes us to his magnificent home. *International man of skulduggery and charm, Pierce Fox, has decorated his beautiful island home in his very own personal style – cruelty and wealth.*

Money and power. Sex and death.

She went to examine the painting above the fireplace. She peered very closely at the signature on the canvas. Without her glasses she had to check twice but – no, she was right the first time! The signature was unmistakable.

Setanta Lynch.

Well! So Pierce Fox sleeps underneath a painting by Setanta Lynch! So Pierce *was* a Setanta Lynch fan, despite the bollocking he'd given him last night after dinner! And the painting – Amy cocked her head on one side and examined it for a while – but it's subject was unmistakable too. It was a well-recognised, well-known painting from Setanta's early heyday as an emerging artist that had caused outrage amongst art collectors because it had been withdrawn from auction, having been sold for an undisclosed but presumed-to-be-enormous sum to an unknown bidder, around about the time Setanta was nominated for the Turner Prize. It was a magnificent abstract nude – Setanta's painting of Andraste, the Celtic Warrior Goddess, the same goddess that Setanta was still sculpting in his studio now.

Either Pierce Fox was obsessed with Setanta, or Setanta was obsessed with Andraste.

She stood back and looked about the rest of the room. There was a beautiful bureau in the bay window as a sort of study desk. She went over to the bay window to look. At the view, of course.

I mean, if Pierce Fox is going to leave his bureau open like that – well, as a writer, she told herself, I'm bound to have a natural curiosity.

I mean, he's an interesting man, isn't he? And – this is research. So his computer wasn't exactly turned on when I arrived – but I can turn it off again, can't I? I mean, it's only a laptop, isn't it? There can't be too much of a big deal going on there. I mean – maybe if I had a quick little look at his email account or something – just a tiny peek, of course, just to see if there's anything I really ought to know about. For Terence's sake. It might even help Terence. It might help all of us to understand what's really going on. I mean, if Setanta and Wolftone are right, then maybe it wasn't completely Terence's fault he lost his job. Maybe there are bigger problems with corruption in Leinster bank that Terence needs to know about . . .

She flipped up the lid and the laptop sprang to life. She quickly scanned the folders that were on the desk-top: LEGAL. PHOTOS. VIDEOS. PRIVATE. Lots of others with unrecognisable titles. Intrigued, she clicked on the folder marked VIDEOS.

And then something leapt out at her.

There was a file in the menu that immediately drew her attention to it. She stared for a moment, not sure whether or not she was seeing things, but no, she'd read the name of the file all right. She felt her heart jump into her mouth. She was beyond curiosity now. She was on a mission. Nothing, not all the ghosts in hell, would have stopped her from opening up that file now.

Reaching out a trembling hand to the mouse again, she clicked upon the file that bore her name.

And then Amy found herself looking at something that was so utterly, completely horrible that she thought she was probably going to get sick.

It was really much, much worse than seeing a ghost.

"Amy – Amy?"

"Where are you – aren't you – ? God, she's in a hurry!"

Gemma and Maggie watched Amy hurtle down the path towards the village, and she was gone.

"Funny that. Do you think she's all right?" Maggie said.

"She's probably getting inspiration for her book," Gemma replied.

Chapter Twenty-eight

Mrs Yvonne Delahunty popped back up the stairs with a new can of Pledge and a fresh duster. There were far too many new drinks stains on the cabinet. It was a thundering disgrace. She would never dream of speaking to Pierce about it but that lawyer should have more sense than to put a drink down on a piece of polished furniture. Pierce, of course, would never be so unmannerly as to tell her not to, which was why that lawyer was getting away with such appalling behaviour. Yvonne pushed open the door to the apartment, but then something struck her as being a bit odd.

That's funny, Yvonne thought, pausing a moment on the landing and looking swiftly around her. I could have sworn I locked the door behind me. I wouldn't go out of the apartments and downstairs to get something without locking Mr Fox's apartments first – would I? She felt a pang of anxiety and guilt. But the door was open all right.

Yvonne Delahunty blushed at the thought of her

forgetfulness. But in all her years of taking care of Mr Pierce Fox, she'd never left his doors unlocked before.

The house was completely empty – wasn't it? She'd made sure of that when she'd arrived. Everyone apart from Setanta was out – and there was nothing of course that Mr Fox wouldn't share with Setanta Lynch – not that Setanta would ever show the slightest bit of interest in poor Pierce's life anyway.

She reassured herself that the unlocked door was absolutely no harm whatsoever in the whole of the ten or fifteen minutes it might have taken her to go downstairs to the back kitchen and find a new can of Pledge and a duster and a fresh batch of coffee for the machine. There was nobody in the house anyway. She'd seen them all go out – Zack for his lakeside walk, that slut Maggie the biographer gone out with the lawyer, that dizzy young writer Amy gone off to the hairdresser's, Setanta busy of course – he never left the studio. Marguerite was in the chapel, Joy was walking, Trish was gardening – there was no way that anybody else could have come in. Reassuring herself that all was safe for Mr Fox, Yvonne Delahunty set about dusting the room. She flicked her duster over the furniture, the little wine tables, the four-poster-bed, mantelpiece, and eventually the bureau, carefully avoiding touching the laptop computer.

Mr Pierce Fox was very fussy about his laptop, and Mrs Delahunty wouldn't dream of ever, ever touching it.

Amy walked as fast as she could away from the house. She marched with her arms folded in front of her chest, trying to hug herself as if to protect herself from the thing she'd seen. She had come out without a coat too and it was freezing. Absolutely Baltic! An icy wind and the beginnings of a very certain promise of rain – but she walked on and on regardless. Bad and all as she'd thought sleeping with a ghost might be, the thing she'd seen on Pierce Fox's computer was ten times – no, a million times worse.

She sobbed a little sob to herself, shivering in the wind. She'd reached the sea which was absolutely pounding the shore with big gulping, crashing waves. It was quite magnificent and in some way reassuring to watch – as if nature itself was empathising with her turmoil. And so she crunched down over the stones and began to walk along the beach. The gale was thundering in across the Atlantic now and there was a clot of black black clouds sitting very low on the horizon sky. A storm. That's what it looked like was coming. Her hair flapped around her face in the ferocious wind and she stood there hugging herself and watched the crashing waves. It was as if the sea was punishing the island.

God help us, all of us, she thought. On this tiny island out at sea. And that monster. That absolute monster, bearing down on all of us!

And then suddenly a finger tapped her shoulder and she screamed.

"Amy! What on earth's the matter?"

It was Zack. She burst into tears.

"What on earth happened? Are you all right?"

"Yes," she sniffed. "You just gave me such a shock. I've had a kind of emotional day. Oh, God, I'm freezing though!" she laughed and sniffed at the same time.

"What are you doing out here without a coat? You'll catch your death. Come on." He wrapped his arms around her.

"Stand on my toes and walk," he said, holding her arms back around his waist so that she could lean her face into his neck, "and I'll keep you warm. We'll go up to the village and have a coffee in the pub and you can tell me all about it."

"Stand on your toes and walk? This is what children do!"

"It'll keep you warm. Look, we'll sing a song as well. That will keep you warm. Do you know – um – 'Octopus's Garden'?"

And so they sang, as loudly as they could, all the way up the beach and to the top of the harbour and then all the way to the village till they got to Tí Jimmy Sheáin's pub.

"Miserable old plop, isn't he?" said Zack, indicating Tomás who was scowling from behind the bar.

Amy nodded. "The other chap seems nice though, the American-sounding guy."

Zack handed her a hot whiskey. "Why were you crying when I met you?"

She said nothing. Just sat and watched the turf glowing in the fire. Watched the flames. "Better than telly, isn't it?" she eventually grinned.

"Missing your kids?"

She nodded. "But I'm going to be fine. You can take my mind off things."

"Singing always helps. Something else upset you though," he probed.

She said nothing again. There wasn't really any point in telling Zack what it was she'd seen. It was too horrible to speak about really – she felt hideously ashamed just thinking about it. And she couldn't really tell anyone that she went up to spy on Pierce. Because that would mean explaining why she was interested in the first place. Because the truth was that although Terence had lost his job and she'd accepted it in the turmoil of the meltdown at Leinster Bank, he'd never really explained why. And what kind of wife has a husband who comes home one day and tells her he's going to be a full-time dad from now on and never even tells her why? The kind of wife who doesn't even demand to know why he's lost his job in the first place. The kind of wife who's a complete coward. The kind of wife who goes away to a writers' retreat and starts fancying the wrong kind of man. The kind of wife who is so nosy and curious that she'd sneak up into the bedroom of her host and spy on his computer. And then – well, she thought. Then she'd get what she deserved.

She shivered.

"Still feeling cold?" he asked, giving her a little hug.

She shook her head. "Let's sing another song," she suggested.

Five hot whiskeys and plenty of songs later, Amy was feeling very much better. From behind the bar, they could hear Art Callaghan joining in, and Amy cheered loudly when he did.

At one stage, Art's dad Jimmy Seán came out and asked, "What is it you call this bloody thing?" and Art replied, "It's a spoon, Dad. It's called a spoon." And Amy and Zack looked at one another and giggled. You couldn't be miserable for long on Inish Rua.

"You guys not going up to the Halla Oileán?" asked Art, in the middle of singing 'Ain't No Pleasin' You'."

"Oh, bloody hell! We almost forgot! The céilí! Let's go! C'mon, Zack! Aren't you coming, Art?"

Art shook his head and grinned. "Gotta keep an eye on

Dad. He gets very active at night-time. You'd never know what kind of mischief he'll get up to, left alone."

Ciara stood in the stillness of her house and listened to the wind roar and the thunder crash in the hills. It was lashing rain. The whole island was being battered by the storm. Her little house beside the sea seemed particularly vulnerable too. Everyone else was up at the céilí and she was here. She looked out of the window at Gearóid's little candle-lit cabin. Poor Gearóid, all alone down there. Another clap of thunder whacked the sky. And then the lights went out.

Oh, crikey. The generator has probably taken a tumble in the storm, she thought, fumbling to the dresser. She found a box of matches and lit one, then a candle – in the candle-light, the cottage seemed to shrink into an even deeper loneliness. And then there was a sharp knock at the door.

Oh, crap. Who the hell is this?

"Jesus, Gearóid!" she gasped as he appeared to her in wind and rain. "It's like hurricane Katrina out there!"

"Ah," said Gearóid. He seemed to be at a bit of a loss.

"Are you coming in?" she asked.

"Oh, God no! No, not at all."

"Right," said Ciara. She waited patiently. "Gearóid, you're going to get awfully wet just standing there."

"Ah. Yes. Well, you see, I was just wondering – do you fancy coming up to the céilí – for a half hour? Just for a bit of a twirl?"

She paused a breath. And then she grinned at him. "Yeah, go on. Why not? Just let me get my wellies and wet-gear."

Chapter Twenty-nine

Amy was having a whale of a time. Zack twirled her around the dance floor like a dervish, and the whole room thundered with the sound of their feet. The band was fantastic – well, if you could call them a band, but fair play to old Wolftone he was hammering away on the bodhrán and then he'd pick up the guitar and have a go at that, and then when the other fellow played the guitar, Wolftone would whip out the harmonica again.

Liam MacDara was thumping out the polkas on the piano accordion. The lights were flickering and the generator was probably going to cut out altogether due to the storm, but nobody cared. There was a gas-lamp over near the band and plenty of candles on the little tables all around the hall. Poor Liam's PA system was a bit hit and miss, but what the hell! Between the claps of thunder and the thumping of feet on the dance floor Liam pelted out jig after reel on the accordion and Wolftone battered the lard out of the bodhrán, and somehow or other it just seemed to work.

Pierce Fox slid into the Halla after the dance had started and was dancing rather daintily with both Maggie and Gemma at the same time. Amy turned her back on him and let herself be led around the floor by a delighted Zack. Then Liam MacDara played a waltz. Zack took her in his arms and steered her around the floor rather drunkenly to "Spancil Hill", which they both sang along at the tops of their voices.

Marguerite was dancing with the priest which was really rather sweet of her, Amy thought.

Joy and Setanta were solemnly lining up with the other islanders in "The Walls of Limerick".

"*Yeehaw!*" roared Wolftone as the dancers galloped by.

They moved into "The Siege of Ennis". Amy had to swing around with Pierce Fox as the partners were passed along. His hands felt like ice in hers. He danced her around but she avoided his eyes at all costs. The couples were passed along again and eventually she ended up where she'd started. She had never felt so relieved to be landed in Zack's arms again.

Setanta was looking gorgeous, though. He'd scrubbed up and changed into a dark pair of jeans and a pink T-shirt which in the candle-light made his dark skin and green eyes look even sexier. When Amy found herself coupled with him as they danced with each other, his hands around her waist were like electricity. Oh, God, why do I have to keep on fancying him so much? she asked herself furiously, breathing in his bitter scent as they danced around one another. She smiled warmly at him as he danced away and back to Joy again.

Torture, that's what this is, Amy told herself miserably. Torture.

The only thing to do was to have another drink.

"Amy!" Zack was waving at her happily from the bar.

There were two teenagers who were leaping around as if they were at a rave.

"Probably think they are – I caught the two lads popping E's around the back!" giggled Zack.

Overhearing him, Liam cringed in despair.

"Isn't Marguerite elegant?" sighed Amy, watching her waltzing around with Setanta much too slowly for the fast polka that Liam was belting out. And then she noticed Marguerite sliding her hand down the back of Setanta's jeans. Bloody little slut! Amy gawped. Elegant, my bottom! She's just a flipping tease. Pierce meanwhile was polka-ing with Joy, her blonde hair bouncing along behind her like a circus pony. Trish had her skirt tucked up into her knickers and was pogo-ing with the two teenagers who were high on E.

Amy spotted Ciara in the line-up for the next reel, with a tall, straggly but romantic-looking man and waved at her. Ciara waved heartily back. She looks gorgeous, Amy thought, beaming at Ciara. Even though her new hair-do's wind-blown and all over the place with the storm, she looks so much happier than when I first saw her.

Amy had given up caring that her own hair-do was all over the place now too, she was having so much fun.

"*Wheee!*" she swung around with Zack again, buoyed up by a fifth gin-and-tonic. "And around we go!"

Outside there was another clap of thunder, then a lightning bolt. The microphone squealed with the sudden power surge. And then suddenly the doors burst open.

The band stopped playing. Art Callaghan was standing in the doorway dripping wet.

"Does anybody know where the doctor is?" Art gasped.

All eyes turned to Ciara.

"I'm here, Art."

"Jesus! What the hell are you doing here? I thought you'd be at home!" he yelled.

Ciara looked humiliated. She walked towards him. She stood in front of him, as if at a loss as to what to say in front of the entire island, and then she seemed to snap. "How dare you speak to me like that!" she barked.

Poor Gearóid stood aside, looking shocked. And everyone was staring at her. "Just who do you think you are?" she shrieked at Art. "I barely even know you! You've no business coming in here and speaking to me like that! I can go exactly where I like and when I like. And with whoever I like! So you can apologise immediately for the way you've spoken to me!"

Art stood still for a moment, looking at Ciara, and then at the man she was dancing with. And then he said with a very cold voice, "I think my father's dead."

"I only slipped up to the céilí for an hour!" Ciara panted as she ran after Art up the hill.

"Yes, but it was the exact hour when my father died, wasn't it? You told me you'd be home! I believed you! I believed you'd be there!"

"I know – but it was so frightening when the storm began. And Gearóid wanted to go out."

"Gearóid? Jesus, I ran all the way down to Marina's house for you! Have you any idea what that was like, finding you weren't there?"

"I'm sorry!" Ciara yelled against the storm. "I just – I

wanted to pop out for a few minutes to the ceilí. It's – I was bored and poor Gearóid . . ."

"But my father's dead! He could have been resuscitated if you'd been there! We could have saved his life!"

I can't believe we're having this argument running up a hill in the lashings of rain, she thought. "I'm sorry!" she screamed against the howling wind. "I honestly didn't plan on going out tonight. It was just sort of a spontaneous thing!"

I can't believe I'm apologising to this man for going out, she thought. This is exactly like the kind of row I'd have had with Dessie, except that this time I've actually instigated it!

But there wasn't any more time to analyse it now.

"I can't believe we had to run all the way back to your house to get your bag and then up to the pub again – what were you thinking, going out without your stuff?" he bellowed at her as another rumble of thunder hit the skies.

"You told me this was a quiet place where nothing happens!" she roared back.

They burst into the door of the pub and he led the way into the back where Jimmy Seán's room was. Tomás was alone in the bar, looking curiously very guilty, but they hadn't time to think why.

Jimmy Seán was lying on his bed. He was very, very still. Art sobbed as Ciara knelt down on the bed beside his dad. She felt his hands. Warm. His carotid pulse – barely palpable. But there was a pulse.

"He's not dead," she said. "Art, his heart's still going! He's not dead."

"What do you mean, he's not dead?" He knelt down beside her. "I thought – he isn't breathing, Ciara! He must be dead!"

She was busy examining Jimmy Seán's chest.

"Ciara, what the hell happened to him? Is he in a coma? Ciara, talk to me!"

She took out her stethoscope. "He isn't breathing, Art. It's a respiratory arrest."

"Oh for fuck's sake, Ciara! Do something! Please!"

She thumped Jimmy Seán's chest. He remained very still. Then she looked at Art. "How many morphine tablets did he take today?"

"What?"

"You heard me!"

"How many – Jesus! I don't know!" Art shoved his fingers up into his hair.

"Get the bottle out!" Ciara yelled.

The bottle was empty.

"All right," she said. She opened up her bag. It was extraordinary that she happened to have Naloxone on her, but she did. Working in a city brings certain habits – and carrying Naloxone as an emergency drug was second nature. It's just that Inish Rua was the last place on earth she'd ever thought she'd need it.

She drew up a large syringe and attached a large-gauge needle. "Tear open his shirt!" she commanded Art.

Counting five ribs down and running her finger from the midpoint of the collar bone, she took a very deep breath. Then she plunged the needle through the intercostal space, right into the tip of Jimmy Seán's heart.

"There," she said. "Let's just see if this works."

They both remained kneeling beside the bed, leaning back on their heels watching Jimmy Seán. They were very still. In the silence she could hear Art's breath. She reached out and took his hand. He closed his eyes. And he squeezed hers back.

"Please, God," she heard him mutter, "let him come back to life!"

Jimmy Seán's face pinked up. His lips moved.

"Dad!" yelled Art.

Jimmy Seán fluttered his eyes. Ciara rubbed his breastbone vigorously.

"What the fuck!" yelled Jimmy Seán, struggling to get Ciara off him. He looked at Art. "Who the hell are you?" Then he looked at Ciara. "Oh, hello, Maureen."

"How do you think he managed to take the full bottle?"

Art sat opposite her at the table where they sat drinking tea. Jimmy Seán was sitting in front of the telly, wrapped in a blanket, sulking over a cup of milk. Tomás was reluctantly running the bar. Most of the islanders had come in from the céilí and the bar was hopping with the sound of Wolftone and Liam who were strumming out punk-rock hits from Wolftone's days with Niall and the Nihilists. The electricity had completely gone now. In the candle-light, Art's face was creased with exhaustion.

Art sighed. "It wasn't exactly my idea, you know, the overdose of morphine. He's a law unto himself. I guess he just went into the bathroom and helped himself."

"But you are supposed to be looking after him."

"It's not as easy as you think." He shook his head. "There's the bar to manage. And Tomás keeps screwing up – selling drink to the teenagers behind my back. Dad just takes off and goes around and I can't keep him under lock and key –"

"Art, he could have died."

He looked away. His eyes were filling up. "I know he could," he said eventually. "I know he could."

She said nothing for a long, long time. And then she

said, "Art, is there a tiny tiny part of you that wonders if he didn't exactly really mind too much if he did?"

Art looked at her, desperately unhappy. "He is difficult, Ciara. But I know he wants to die. And I love him too. I came all the way back here from America to look after him. And now – jeez, I've really screwed things up tonight, haven't I?"

"No," she said very firmly. "You haven't screwed up in the slightest. You found me, didn't you? And he's still alive. And we saved his life. So definitely not a screw-up. Not this time, anyway," she smiled gently at him.

"I meant –" He stopped. He had about to say, *I mean I've screwed things up between me and you*, but thought better of it. She clearly wasn't interested in him. She'd had a date at the céilí, Gearóid that crazy-looking artist who was married to Marina but whom everyone knew was living aimlessly in a shed in Marina's garden. If Gearóid and Ciara were going to hit it off, well then, fair play to him. He deserved a bit of happiness after years of lonely marriage to Marina, Art supposed. "I meant, thanks for saving his life."

They sat in silence for a few moments.

"What brought you out to this island, Ciara?" He poured her out more tea. "It's miles from anywhere. You could do a lot better than this."

"Locum work."

"No – seriously. I know that Marina's job doesn't exactly pay."

She looked away.

"You can tell me," he said. "Look, everybody here is running away from something or someone here. You think I don't know that?"

"Even you?"

"Guilty." He put his hand on his heart. "Bad divorce," he said.

"Oh."

"So?" He held her eyes with his. "Your story is –?"

The kitchen door burst open. "Doctor?"

"Yes." She stood up.

"Doctor, it's Stiofán!" the two teenage girls said together.

"He's throwing up all over the place!" said Lauren.

"He's got alcoholic poisoning!" gasped Niamh.

"He's drunk two naggins of vodka!" wailed Lauren. "He's puking up his ring!"

"Coming now!" and Ciara grabbed her bag and followed them, without even saying goodbye.

Pierce Fox had had enough of the céili. Most of the islanders were absolutely slaughtered and had moved the party over to the pub. They'd be busy in Tí Jimmy Sheáin for the rest of the night and he'd have the entire house to himself.

Pierce had a much better party planned – and it was time to move it on up. He picked his Barbour jacket up and raised his eyebrows at Maggie and Gemma.

"Coming, girls?" He winked at them.

Ciara gave Stiofán an injection to stop him vomiting, wrapped him up in tinfoil and a sleeping bag to prevent hypothermia and gave strict instructions to Lauren and Niamh to keep him quiet.

"Where's the Bean an Tí?" she asked.

"Oh, God, please don't tell Mrs Delahunty that Stiofán and Luke bought drink!" begged Lauren and Niamh.

"Where is she, anyway, the Bean an Tí?" asked Ciara.

"She isn't home from the Céilí yet – or maybe she's up at the Big House – don't know – just don't tell her we've been drinking. Please, doctor. Please don't tell. She'd tell our parents!"

Ciara looked at them, both terrified, and at Liam and poor semi-conscious Stiofán again.

"All right," she said. "I won't."

"Little bit of charlie?"

Gemma smiled at Pierce. "You go first," she purred.

Pierce hoovered up the line of coke he'd just cut up and unbuttoned his shirt. He dropped it on the floor, waltzing over to the two girls on the bed with his erection bouncing in front of him like a baguette.

Maggie couldn't believe what they were about to do. She'd done a lot of crazy wild things in her life, but she hadn't yet done a threesome – not since she was in college anyway and that didn't count because one of the guys was only in the bed because he was unconscious. And this was all Gemma's idea! Mousy little Gemma, Maggie thought, watching Pierce rubbing his nose. Who'd have thought? The thunder wrapped around Atlantis like a battering ram. A zip of lightning streaked across the sky, crackling with electricity, and a thunderbolt cracked across the trees and the rain belted on every window of the house.

Maggie peeled her bra off and let it drop on the floor, then slid towards the other two. Gemma was sitting on Pierce's face. Maggie took Pierce's erection in her hand, and climbed across him, slipping it inside her. Oh! She heard Pierce groan. She straddled him with her legs, riding him like a bucking bronco. Gemma's face was right opposite hers now. She reached out and slid a finger underneath the back of Gemma's pale pink bra, unhooking it and letting it fall off revealing tiny, pert breasts. Maggie kissed Gemma all the way up her neck and then she kissed her open lips. With Pierce thrusting up inside her, it was the hottest thing she'd ever done.

And then Gemma suddenly pulled back.

"What's wrong?" said Maggie.

Gemma stared at her. "He's – oh my God."

They both stared at him.

"He's still hard," said Maggie.

But something had gone very, very wrong.

"Maggie," Gemma said. "He's stopped breathing!"

"Oh, Jesus!" Maggie leaped off Pierce. She covered her face with her hands. "Oh, Christ! Gemma, listen to his heart!"

Gemma lay her ear onto his chest and listened as hard as she could.

But Pierce Fox was absolutely dead.

"I smothered him! I killed him!" Gemma wailed.

Maggie stared at her. "Oh, Gemma. You didn't kill him. We both did."

"I can't understand where everybody's gone." Liam looked around the almost empty hall in dismay. "Half the crowd from Atlantis have disappeared. Ciara's gone. Amy and Zack have disappeared. Marguerite has disappeared as well. Setanta – Joy – where the hell is everyone now?"

Trish clapped her arm around his drooping shoulders. "Liam, it's not your fault. The whole island has been turned upside down by a storm, and Jimmy Seán nearly died. I'll stay behind and help you to clear up. And then, I've got something that'll cheer both of us up."

"What the hell are we going to do?" Gemma sobbed.

Maggie sat on the chaise longue. It was an absolute nightmare. Pierce Fox was dead. Dead! And in his own bedroom, coked out of his brain with only her and Gemma to witness it. Bloody hell. Of all the things that could go wrong, Maggie thought, there is absolutely nothing that could be worse than this.

"Gemma," she eventually said. "We are going to have to get the doctor up."

"All right," Gemma said. "You go for the doctor. I'll tidy up the place here. Get rid of – you know. Evidence."

Chapter Thirty

"Um – did he take anything before he died?" Ciara asked. "Er – drugs? Alcohol? I mean, I know he was at the céilí, but had he a lot of drink taken?"

Maggie stood beside the bed. Gemma, sitting in the corner on the lady chair, was convulsed with sobs.

Maggie shook her head. "I've no idea. We just found him like this."

"Found him? How?"

"We, er, we were supposed to be looking over the contracts. Er – for the book – er –"

"At midnight? In the middle of a power cut? After being at the céilí all night? With a skinful of booze on you?"

Maggie blushed furiously. This Doctor Ciara Love was no *daw*.

Ciara looked solemnly at her. "Maggie, it's all right, you know. I know you didn't kill him. I'm just a doctor. I only want to make sure we cover everything."

"What do we do now? Oh, stop crying, Gemma!" Maggie barked.

"Yeah, stop crying, Gemma," Ciara said. Then she turned to Maggie again. "Well, we'll have to inform the coroner first thing. He'll need to do a post mortem of course."

Maggie nodded.

"The phone lines are out," Gemma sobbed.

"Don't worry, there's a radio for emergencies in the doctor's surgery. I'll let the gardaí on the mainland know. They'll contact the coroner and they'll have to come over anyway to transfer his body out of here and to the mortuary." Ciara thought quickly again. "What about family?" She looked from Maggie to Gemma. "Is there someone we should ask the guards to tell?"

But who was Pierce Fox's family? The only family Maggie knew about was Gabriel – and his relationship to Pierce was a secret. And as for Nola Connaughton – probably best to leave it up to Gemma to tell *her*, Maggie thought.

"Do either of you know who his family are?" Ciara asked.

"He has none," came Gemma's small tear-soaked voice. "He's a bachelor, no kids, no siblings, parents dead." Then she looked up at both of them. "But there is someone," she said in a much quieter voice. "Someone here."

"Who?" Maggie asked, although she already knew the answer.

"He's got a son here, on the island."

"Who?" said Ciara.

Maggie looked astonished. "*What*?"

Gemma sobbed again.

"Come on Gemma, spit it out," Maggie then said impatiently. "Tell us all about his son."

"Setanta Lynch," said Gemma. "Setanta is his son. Only he doesn't know it yet."

Maggie's jaw dropped. "*What*? How on earth do *you* know *that*?"

But Gemma said nothing.

"All right," Ciara was saying, oblivious to the bombshell Gemma had just dropped. "Well, best say nothing yet to Setanta till the coroner's been contacted. But meanwhile, I'll get the Guards and you two go downstairs and let the others know what's happened." Ciara moved rapidly away towards the door. "Are you coming, Maggie?"

"Setanta Lynch?" Maggie stood there very still. "Gemma, how *do* you really know that Setanta's his son?"

"I – looked through his private stuff. When you went to get Ciara. I – I knew it might be my last chance to open it before the house would be full of police and coroners and so I opened the top drawer of his bureau. It's where he keeps his private things he's never let me see. He keeps the keys under his pillow – but now that he's dead, I couldn't resist. And I found –"

"Go on!" Ciara and Maggie both demanded.

"Setanta's original long-version birth certificate."

Maggie had to sit down again. "Oh my God! Gemma, that's incredible. What does it say?"

"It says that Setanta's father is Pierce Fox. Was Pierce Fox. And his mother is a – oh, I can't remember exactly – um –"

"Get the birth certificate!" Maggie urged her. "I want to see!"

"Does it matter?" asked Ciara. "Can't we give the poor dead man some privacy?"

The others looked at one another. "You're right," Maggie eventually said. "We'll have plenty of time to think about all that. And we have to decide which of us gets to tell Setanta that we've found out."

"I'll tell him," Gemma said. The others looked at her. "I am Pierce's lawyer, after all. It probably has legal implications. Wills and things. I'll talk to Setanta in the morning and explain everything."

"Everything?" said Maggie. "Are you joking? Gemma, how on earth are you going to explain to Setanta why exactly you were looking in Pierce's private papers? And how it came about that you were the one who found him dead?"

"Oh Christ. I hadn't thought of that."

"Well, think harder, Sherlock. And meanwhile, I'm going down to talk to the others."

They left the apartments, leaving the door unlocked behind them.

Across the hills, thunder crashed like machine-gun fire.

The best thing to do was to get everybody round the table as soon as they came in from the pub. In the candle-light, the jolly kitchen was a flickering cavern of despair. Maggie and Gemma sat and waited for the others to get home from the pub, and one by one they staggered in, giggling and yelling in noisy drunken voices to be greeted by the three solemn faces sitting round one of Pierce Fox's crystal decanters, toasting a dead man with his best Armagnac.

"Hey!" said Joy, stumbling slightly as she came in. "Why so morose, you lot?"

"Sit down, Joy," Maggie said. "We've got some dreadful news."

"News?"

"Let's wait till everyone gets here."

There was another clap of thunder and Setanta and Wolftone came lumbering in, singing "Some Say The Devil Is Dead" at the top of their lungs.

"Somebody die?" quipped Wolftone at the sight of their faces.

"Wolfie, sit down and behave yourself," said Joy. "The girls have something to say."

Then Marguerite arrived wrapped in a silver pashmina. "I find the thunder so frightening, don't you?" Marguerite was saying. "I miss my husband so much on stormy nights like this." She was followed by Trish and Liam MacDara who were giggling like schoolkids.

"What about Amy and Zack? Where are they?" asked Joy.

There were a few sly looks around the table. "Oh well," said Maggie. "We can let them know in the morning, I guess."

"Let them know what?" said Trish.

All eyes were on Maggie, but Gemma decided that seeing as Maggie was looking guiltier than ever since Setanta walked in, it might be better if she spoke.

"Let them know," she said simply, "that when I went up to Mr Fox's apartments tonight to finalise the draft of a legal contract I'd been working on, I found that Pierce Fox was dead."

Chapter Thirty-one

The residents of Inish Rua awoke to utter devastation. The island had been so battered by the storm that several trees were down. The smaller boats had been lifted at the little harbour and smashed against the giant stones of the pier like tinderboxes. The sign outside the *Gruaig Deas by Nóirín* had been whipped away and tossed up into the hills. Trish's garden was destroyed – strewn with broken plants and glass. The conservatory was in pieces.

Ciara woke to hear a sharp knocking at her door, and jumped out of bed, pulling her anorak around her. Oh God, not another emergency! Not after she'd been up till all hours with first Jimmy Seán and then Stiofán and then Pierce!

But it was Gearóid. Standing on her doorstep, his trousers dripping wet. And in the daylight, she looked past him to the end of the garden and saw exactly why. The sea had come up over the land, and in one great big gulp had swallowed up the entire ground floor of Gearóid's little barn.

"Oh, Gearóid! Oh, I'm so sorry!" she cried, opening up her arms to him.

They looked out at the underwater barn in dismay.

"Are the paintings all right?"

He nodded. "They are upstairs. It's only the ground floor that flooded."

"Well, come on in." She held the door open for him. "You'll have to stay in here. At least till your own house dries out."

On his face, a look of palpable dread. "What if Marina finds out?"

"Don't worry," she said. "I'm sure she'll understand once she hears about what happened to your little house."

He looked anxious. "I'll make sure I'm no trouble to you. I'll help with everything around the house."

"You don't have to do that."

"You'll be busy with the police."

"Mrs Freeman takes care of the house."

He shook his head. "There's too much going on in the Big House since Pierce Fox died. Let me take care of things here for you."

She smiled. "You are the sweetest man."

"Mr Pierce Fox?" said Sam Smith, the county coroner to Detective Inspector Nigel Lawlor. "The business tycoon? *Dead?*"

"Yes. Doctor on the island's just been on the phone. Fox died in his bed in the middle of the night. Of natural causes. But a coroner's PM, of course. So, thought I'd ring you first thing."

"Of course. And the last attending physician was –?"

"A Doctor Ciara Love."

"Pierce Fox? The multi-millionaire? *Dead*?" Garda Siobhán Green could hardly believe her ears. "Died in his sleep? Sure that fella hardly ever slept a wink!"

"That's what the coroner says. He'll do a PM for us tomorrow night, he says. We'll get the helicopter over as soon as the wind dies down a little. The island got a terrible hammering from the storm."

"I suppose they think he must have died of shock or something –" Garda Siobhán Green's voice trailed off. Even as the words came out of her mouth, she knew she couldn't really believe them herself.

"There's no shock that would kill that fella," Nigel snorted back.

Siobhán had to agree. "I'll let the Garda press office know so they can get a statement organised – or do you want to do that?"

"Actually, I do," Inspector Nigel Lawlor replied. There wasn't often he got to be at the heart of a big public story. And this story was definitely going to be very, very big.

"So," Ciara said to Trish at the breakfast table. "I've informed the police and they are on their way with the Garda helicopter and a body bag."

Trish nodded gloomily. Then she sat bolt upright. "Gardaí? Oh, bloody hell, Ciara! I hadn't thought of that!"

"What?"

"My bloody herbs, that's what!"

Ciara opened her mouth to speak, but Trish had already bolted.

A half hour later, Ciara walked over to the helipad to greet the police. Sam Smith, the coroner from the mainland had come over too. The police helicopter landed, its blades sending trees sideways in the wind. Ciara went out to meet it.

Trish was ripping up every single herb that grew in her greenhouse, even those that hadn't been damaged by the storm, and stuffing them as fast as she possibly could into a massive compost bin.

Amy woke up to find her nose buried in Zack's armpit which smelt mildly of asparagus. Outside a helicopter was landing on the lawn.

"Oh, my God, what time is it?" she groaned. Her head was full of pain. Oh, hungover to bits! Jesus, that helicopter was very loud. Who the hell was landing a helicopter at this hour? It was still dark, it wasn't even the crack of dawn! She sat bolt upright, and then looked carefully at Zack. In the very grey light of morning, he looked softer and more childish than ever.

Oh, God, what have I got into now? she thought in despair. In bed with Zack Rowley – this is not what was supposed to happen at all! Oh, bloody hell, hell, hell. She swung her legs out of the bed and grabbed the dress she'd been wearing last night and started pulling it on.

"Hey, what about good morning?" Zack murmured sleepily.

"Er, yes. Morning," Amy muttered. She was mortified. How on earth had she ended up in bed with Zack – I mean, she didn't even fancy him! And the sex was – well, he was awfully sweet but there was absolutely no chemistry between them at all. His body was too *soft* or something – he was too hairless, too bland, too mild in his lovemaking – in fact, now that you come to think about it, she'd had to do all the work herself.

Zack, of course, had had a whale of a time, with plenty of "ooh, baby!"s – but it hadn't worked. She'd only really gone through with it because – well, why on earth had she? To make herself feel better? Oh, God, how absolutely, utterly horribly wrong that was! What the hell am I doing here? she thought, zipping up her dress and catching her fingernails in the zipper. Ouch! See, there's my punishment. I'm a hundred times worse than Marguerite. She may well flirt all day with Setanta but she's terribly loyal to her husband – and I've actually got into bed with someone just because he fancies me. Just to make myself feel better. It's pure self-gratification. It's like a dog rubbing himself up against a sofa. It's – it's almost as bad as Pierce Fox! I'm disgusting, she thought.

"What's the hurry, Amy?" Zack fingered her dress. "Come back to bed, darling, why don't you?"

She almost jumped out of her skin at the touch of his hand on her back. "I've gotta go, Zack. I – we shouldn't have done this. I'm married," she muttered furiously.

"Yeah, I know. Me too," he said.

"You are?" she whipped around. "You never said!"

"I know. I just – hoped it wasn't going to be an issue."

"Oh, Zack. Of course it's an issue! What about your flipping wife, for God's sake? Don't you love her?"

"Of course I do. I adore her. But – well, you're gorgeous, Amy. And I wanted to comfort you. You seemed so upset, yesterday."

"Oh, don't be so stupid!"

A flood of guilt washed through her. She had been upset. She'd used him to comfort her, to make her feel better about her failing marriage to Terence, to console her for her appalling desire for Setanta, and to feel protected against the wickedness of Pierce Fox. And now she felt more guilty than ever. Zack didn't deserve to be used like that. But on the other hand, he was being pretty wicked too, wasn't he? Zack was cheating on his wife as well.

"What the hell happens to everybody out here?" she muttered furiously, fixing her tights and pulling her boots on. "It's as if we've all become different people. You come out to this island and your entire life is turned upside down."

"Maybe it was the storm," said Zack, looking very morose.

"Maybe it was just plain old-fashioned wickedness." She stood up. "I'm so sorry, Zack. You are lovely but I've got to go."

"All right," he said. And then he sat up. "Amy – do you see what's written on the side of that helicopter?"

They both stared out of the window.

"Jesus!" Amy breathed. "I do! It's the gardaí. What on earth could have happened?"

Zack sucked in his breath. "Something pretty big must have happened here last night, that's what."

"So, I'll bring you up to the apartments to where the body is," Ciara said, "And then do you want me to give a written report or will the coroner's examination do?"

They'd reached the landing to Pierce's apartment and to her astonishment, Ciara found the door was locked.

"God, that's funny," she said. "This is locked. We didn't lock it. Um –" She rattled at the handle.

"Well, someone did," Inspector Nigel Lawlor replied, studying Ciara's face. "Doors don't lock themselves."

"Unless this is self-locking from the inside?" She rattled the handle again.

"Does anybody have a key?" he asked.

She looked at him. "I'll have to ask Trish."

Ciara came back up the stairs ten minutes later, panting, with a set of keys. "Trish is busy in the greenhouse – it got destroyed in the storm so she's ripping all her plants out in some sort of hissy fit, God knows why – but I found these in her office – 'Master Keys' it says. None of them are labelled, but let's just try them all."

But none of them fitted. Pierce Fox's chamber was impenetrable.

"Only one thing to do then, isn't there?" Nigel looked at her. "But first, this lock needs finger-printing. This handle, and those keys."

"What?" Ciara's face went pale.

"Yup." Nigel looked as though he were beginning to enjoy himself. "Doors that lock themselves do need to be finger-printed. And then after we've broken into the room, we might need to dust the place down too. What do you think, Siobhán?"

Garda Siobhán Green looked very eager. "I'll get a kit prepared."

Eventually, having got a hammer from the toolshed and on Nigel's insistence dusted down the handle, they burst into the room.

The scene that greeted them of Pierce Fox's death chamber was not the one they had expected.

"Oh, Christ," Inspector Nigel Lawlor said.

"Shit," breathed Garda Siobhán Green.

"Holy Mother of Jesus and all the saints!" Sam Smyth the coroner said.

"Bloody hell!" Ciara gasped.

On the sumptuous fur-clad four-poster lay Pierce Fox. With a gunshot wound in his chest.

"Natural causes – not," said Nigel eventually, walking around to view the corpse.

"How did – I just don't understand!" Ciara spluttered. "I was the one who found him dead! I mean, the two other women did – but I diagnosed him dead. But he hadn't been shot. He was as dead as a door-nail at midnight and not a spot of a bullet wound – he'd clearly just passed away!"

Siobhán put a gentle hand on her shoulder. "Anything different from the last time you were in this room?"

Ciara looked around her, half dazed. In the daylight, everything looked different. Apart from the fact that there was a dead man in the bed, this time with a huge bullet wound in his chest –

But wait!

"There is no bleeding from underneath the wound," Ciara said very slowly, looking at Sam Smith. Sam was nodding. "That fur counterpane is quite clean beneath him. A shot at close range like that which was going to kill him would have had to burst a major vessel, heart or a lung, at least. The bed would have flooded with blood."

"So?" Nigel looked at her.

"So," Sam Smith said, "That means – doesn't it – that he was shot–"

"*After he was dead.*" All three of them finished his sentence for him in a chorus.

Chapter Thirty-two

The police set up an incident room in the drawing room on the ground floor of the main house. Serviced by tea and biscuits by a very demure Yvonne Delahunty, the gardaí proceeded to fingerprint and photograph every resident of Atlantis. Given the fact that Pierce seemed to have been shot after he was dead, Nigel couldn't launch a full-scale murder investigation until after the results of the PM. It was certainly a crime to deface a deceased body, but it wasn't actually a murder if the person had been shot after they were already dead.

Pierce Fox's apartments had been sealed off and were undergoing forensic examination. And everyone who lived on Inish Rua had to give a statement to the police. It was going to take days.

The police were terribly grateful to Yvonne Delahunty, who moved gracefully around making sure that those who were still reeling with the shock of everything were being well looked after. Mrs Freeman was struggling, following the destruction of the gardens, to provide people with enough vegetables for their meals, but thankfully Liam was helping out with stuff from his own gardens. Trish was spending all her time destroying every plant in her entire greenhouse.

Father Glen Cassidy came pedalling up to the house the morning the gardaí first arrived, to say a prayer over the body before they took it away in the helicopter for PM. He'd wait to hear from the family about the funeral, he said, wondering why Gemma and Maggie had given him such a funny look when he said that.

Setanta had disappeared into his studio, and was speaking to no one.

"Here's a coffee. You've been working at that like a lunatic. You need a break."

Trish looked up from her position on all fours, arms covered in mud, face splashed like a leopard.

"Come on," Liam reached out a hand to her. "Let's sit down on that bench and take a break." Following Wolftone's example, he'd thrown a splash of Tullamore Dew in her coffee. To settle her nerves.

With the gardaí now running an incident room in her house, Trish had become a basket-case. The police had brought over a team of detectives who had lined up all the residents first thing in the morning and finger-printed everyone. The police were combing the island for the weapon – presumed to be the rifle which was missing from its position on Pierce's bedroom wall.

Trish took the cup. "You are an angel." She surveyed the disaster of her garden. "Jesus, Liam, what a fucking mess!"

Liam's face went bright red. "I'll help. Let me help."

"You don't have to. I can fix it."

"But I want to help."

"You can't."

"Trish —"

"I can't ask you to help. It would be illegal." She hung her head. "I wouldn't do that to you. If anyone's going down for this, it'll be me."

"I'd do anything for you, Trish."

"Paint your face bright blue?"

"Anything."

"Destroy my illegal marijuana farm a half hour before the cops arrive?"

"Anything."

"Fly to Timbuktu?"

"And back again."

She looked at him. "Do you think we should though? Fly to Timbuktu, I mean? What if the cops do figure out what was growing in the greenhouse?" She chewed her mud-crusted nails. "I could be facing a very nasty time."

He thought about it for a while. All his life he'd longed to live in a place like this – simple, wholesome, organic, ancient, mystical, gentle and safe. The inner city where he'd done his teacher-training had been so full of drugs and violence and crime – and yet, ultimately, Inish Rua had turned out to be the most dangerous place he'd ever been. And in all his years of living in the inner city, where there was a murder reported almost every night, Liam had never had to face a murder on his own doorstep. And yet –

"I think, when all of this dies down – sorry about the pun – but despite everything that's happened, I'd really much rather stay out here with you, than run away again.

And if we do a proper job on the herb garden, well, they'll never guess, will they?"

She smiled. "And get a polytunnel, next time?"

He nodded. "Less dangerous than glass, if it all blows down."

"So," Detective Inspector Nigel Lawlor began, setting the tape recorder carefully on the table, "let's begin. Where were you on the night that Pierce Fox died? From the beginning, please. And take your time."

Ciara drew a breath. "I was in the house earlier on. Just on my own. The doctor's house. And the storm began – it was terribly noisy and frightening. Desperate wind. And – well, it was a bit lonely down there, I suppose. So I decided to go up to the céilí. And then – er –"

"Who was at the céilí?"

"Well, everyone. Pierce Fox, of course, with Gemma and Maggie, the musicians were there, Nóirín the *Gruagaire*, Glen the priest, even Mrs Freeman was dancing with Nóirín – what?" she asked Siobhán suddenly.

Siobhán hadn't been able to help smiling at this one. The image of Nóirín the *Gruagaire* and Mrs Freeman bust-to-bust, waltzing around to Wolftone O'Neill and Liam MacDara's céilí band was too much, even for her.

"What happened after the céilí?" Nigel hadn't blinked.

"After the céilí, I went up to the pub with everyone."

He raised a pair of wiry eyebrows. "A doctor on duty? In the pub?"

"Yes. I wasn't drinking. I had a cup of tea. With the publican, Art Callaghan."

"And then?"

"Then, somebody came down from the Big House and asked me to come up."

"Who?"

"Maggie Hennelly, the writer. Pierce Fox's biographer," she said.

"What about the other girl? The lawyer? Where was she?"

Ciara thought. "I don't know, actually. I met her later on. She came up to the room with Maggie and me. She had been with – er – been writing up legal documents she said, when Fox – when he – er – died. But she must have been somewhere else while Maggie came down to the pub."

"What time was it when you left the pub?"

"About half past twelve, I guess – maybe even one o'clock."

"Were they still serving drink?" asked Nigel.

Ciara felt her face burning again. Art and his dad had kept the pub open until all hours, and she'd assumed that nobody was worried about after-hours drinking on Inish Rua. But she didn't want to be the one who shopped Art and Jimmy Seán to the police.

"I – I was drinking tea."

The two police looked at one another.

"When you arrived at Mr Fox's apartments, to examine the body, did you notice the rifle hanging on the wall?" Nigel asked her.

"I can't remember."

"Oh, come on! You're not as dim as that!"

Ciara blushed furiously. "It's not a question of being dim. I'm a doctor. A man had died. I wasn't thinking about a gun. I assumed he'd had a heart attack."

"Without his clothes on? Lying flat on his fur bed?" Nigel's voice rose.

"I've told you! He was naked, yes – and he was dead. But there was no gunshot wound!"

There was a solid silence.

"What did you do after you left the céilí, between the hours of ten and midnight?"

"I – attended to a patient."

"Who?"

"A Jimmy Seán Callaghan, owner of the pub."

"Why?"

"That's confidential." Ciara blushed furiously again.

"Doctor, this is a murder enquiry. There is no such thing as confidential. There are two kinds of information you can give us – the kind where you help the police with their enquiry, and the kind you withhold, which is an offence against the State and so I will then immediately place you under arrest on suspicion of murder. So, again, I'm going to ask you – what was your reason for attending to Jimmy Seán Callaghan, owner of the pub?"

She felt weak. "He – he took an overdose." Her voice was coming out as if it belonged to someone else. "And I'd given him some morphine – the day before. For his back pain. But he took too much of it." She felt blood zinging in her ears. "He responded to Naloxone though, and came around. Then I had a cup of tea with the son, Art Callaghan, and then when Maggie arrived with the news about Pierce, I went immediately to the Big House." Her face was fire-engine red.

Their faces looked incredulous.

It was one complication too far. And as for Stiofán and the alcoholic poisoning – if she told the cops about that they'd probably close down Tí Jimmy Sheáin.

"What did you do after you found the dead body?"

"I diagnosed the death. Then I went downstairs with the other two women. They wanted to tell – to tell Setanta and the other residents about what happened to Pierce. I went back to the doctor's house and radioed the police."

"Who do you think shot Pierce Fox?"

"I've absolutely no idea."

"You must have some idea. You found the body dead. No gunshot wound you say. You leave the body and go downstairs with the other two women to break the news to the residents. Meanwhile you slip off again – ostensibly to radio the police. But nobody knew really where you went, did they?"

"What?"

"Nobody witnessed you going straight back to your house to radio the police. You had plenty of time to go back up to the body again while the other women were downstairs. How long did it take for everyone to arrive from the pub? An hour? Two? Who would have seen you slip back up?"

"I went back to the doctor's house," Ciara whispered. "To radio the police."

"The call came in at –" Nigel consulted his notes. "Eight this morning. You left the house at –?"

"After midnight – I don't know – maybe one or two?"

"You left the pub after midnight. You arrived at Atlantis at between half past twelve and one. You radioed the police at eight a.m. So again, I'm going to ask you, who saw you go back to your house, and who knows you couldn't have shot Pierce Fox?"

Ciara felt the blood drain from her face. This couldn't be happening – could it? They couldn't actually think she could have shot him herself, could they?

Eventually she replied, "No one knows. Absolutely no one."

Nigel slapped a big hairy freckled hand down on the table top in triumph.

"You must have had strong feelings about him," Siobhán said in a softer voice. "Pierce Fox. He's the reason your husband disappeared, isn't he?"

Ciara felt hot tears prick her eyes. It was as if her entire life had gone full circle. No matter where she went, Dessie would come back to haunt her.

"But I'd never met Pierce before I came here! He owned the island, owned this house, I'm just a locum doctor here. Dessie disappeared – but it had nothing to do with Pierce!"

"Except that Dessie was Pierce's lawyer, wasn't he? Dessie conveyanced all Pierce's property deals, didn't he? And then after Dessie embezzled Pierce's money, Dessie had to disappear. If it hadn't been for Pierce, you wouldn't have lost your husband. Isn't that the truth?"

"What?" she whispered. And then she felt a hot, liquid taste in her dry mouth. "I think I'm going to be sick." She grasped the edge of the table with both hands.

"Come on," Siobhán said. "You've had enough upset for one day. We can pick this conversation up again afterwards. And perhaps, when we've interviewed all the others, we'll be able to find someone who saw you going back to your own house at the time you said you did. Isn't that right?"

Ciara nodded, trying to agree. But inside her heart had almost turned to stone.

"So?" Nigel asked Siobhán after Ciara had left.

"She's lying. About everything. The whole story is a load of bollocks. Either that or she's as mad as a brush."

"My thoughts exactly," Nigel said.

Chapter Thirty-three

Marguerite was trembling so much that her rows of bangles on her plump arms were jangling like sleigh-bells.

"You are very upset, aren't you?" Garda Siobhán Green said, handing her a cup of tea from the beautiful china set that Yvonne had laid out. "Would you like a biscuit? This carrot cake is delicious too."

"I couldn't eat a thing!" said Marguerite. "I haven't slept, I haven't played the cello, my hands can't stop shaking – I can't believe that this is happening! It's so appalling!"

"It's very hard." Siobhán looked right into Marguerite's eyes. "So, let's start at the very beginning. When did you first meet Pierce Fox?"

Marguerite gave a little sob and then straightened her shoulders. "It was about two years ago – he has a corporate box at Covent Garden of course – and he came backstage to greet me. He was a huge fan of my music." She let a giant tear fall.

"You're a violinist, aren't you?" Nigel consulted his list.

"Cello. It was the Elgar Concerto! He adored my music." Marguerite sobbed again.

"What?"

"The concert! That night that Pierce and I first met."

"What did you think of him?"

"I thought that he was such a warm individual. He was so generous to all of us. He was a great patron of the arts. It's an unbelievable tragedy! I can't believe he's gone."

"How often have you come to stay at this house?"

"Every year since then – several times. It's a marvellous retreat – so tranquil." She shuddered. "Until this nightmare, of course."

"He treated you well?"

"All of us. He was so generous to artists."

"So did he have any enemies then?"

"I don't know what you mean!"

"Mrs Coyle –"

"Ms."

"Single lady? It says here on my list you're married –"

"Oh, I am absolutely married. But I perform in my maiden name. It's how people have come to know me. I've been performing since I was a student, you see."

Nigel scowled. It was some fucking performance all right. Ten past twelve in the day and only two of this lot interviewed for statements. He leaned his elbows on the table and looked more sternly at Marguerite. "Ms Coyle –"

"Marguerite, Officer."

"Marguerite. Who do you think might have done this? Shot Mr Fox? Your friend. Who would have wanted to kill him? Of all the people who knew him here?"

Marguerite licked her lips. She took a very deep breath.

Nigel couldn't help noticing her bosom heaving like two luxurious pillows.

Marguerite lowered her eyes. "Some of the guests were less appreciative than others."

"Like who?"

She looked at him. "Wolftone O'Neill, for one. He positively hated Pierce."

Nigel raised his bristly eyebrows again. "How so?"

"The other night at dinner. He launched an attack on Pierce – oh, we were playing some silly party game – and Pierce asked Wolftone if he'd ever been in the IRA. And then he accused Pierce of financial corruption, or something ridiculous like that. It was appallingly bad manners. He implied that Pierce was guilty of, oh, insider trading or something. I don't know – I don't understand these financial kinds of things. I'm a creative person." She waved an arm.

"I see. And was there an argument?"

"Yes. A huge one. Wolftone was furious with Pierce."

"Why?"

"Because he humiliated him. That was the point of the game. It was called Humiliation."

Nigel and Siobhán gave each other an incredulous look.

"And have you spoken to Wolftone since the row? I mean, before Pierce died," Siobhán asked.

"Yes. I talked to him last night. There was a céilí where he was playing the bodhrán. He asked me to play – but it wasn't my sort of music." She shuddered.

"And what did he say? About Pierce. Did he at any stage discuss his feelings about Pierce with you?"

Marguerite said nothing for a moment. Then she looked at Siobhán and whispered, "Yes."

"And what did he say?"

"He pointed at Pierce who was dancing with Gemma and Maggie, and he said –" Marguerite closed her eyes. "His language was foul."

Siobhán's voice was very patient. "What did he say, Marguerite?"

"He said," Marguerite drew a breath. "He said: 'There's that dirty hoorin' cunt. I'd kill the bastard if I could get my hands on him'."

The atmosphere in Atlantis house was like static electricity. Everyone was on edge. Trish was barely speaking, couldn't maintain eye contact with anyone and was spending a lot of time pretending to be busy, staying out of everyone's way. Mrs Freeman had gone into overdrive in the kitchen, sleeves rolled up, cooking up a storm. The team of police and forensic detectives were the next best thing to having an army to feed and she was in her element. She was preparing an enormous Irish stew with what appeared to be an entire sheep. Gemma was helping out, only too happy to be distracting herself by offering to scrape an absolute mountain of carrots. Amy was peeling buckets of onions, eyes swimming with tears.

Ciara left Atlantis after her interview with the police and half-walked half-ran down to the village. She didn't know where to turn. Half of her wanted to go up to Art to tell him everything that had happened, but she wasn't sure what he'd think of her any more. She ought to see how Jimmy Seán was doing, but felt terrible about breaking his confidentiality to the police by telling them about Jimmy Seán's overdose. The police had raided Tí Jimmy Sheáin, accusing Art of serving under-age drinkers – Ciara wondered who had told them about that – and Tomás had done a runner, so Art would be managing the pub on his own from now on. Ciara had probably just completely ruined his life.

But the connection the police had made between Dessie and Pierce had thrown her for six. Stumbling along the stoney little path, she barely noticed how beautiful the day was, how still the sea after the storm, how silent the trees. Inside her head, it might as well have been thunder and lightning.

Perhaps the best thing was to go back to the surgery and try to get on with the job she'd come out here to do. She could open up the surgery and air it a bit after the storm, see if any patients needed seeing. People would still need a doctor, even if Pierce Fox was dead. Wouldn't they?

She decided to go home – home? Was that what you'd call it now? But it was the only place she had. And the peaceful life she'd desperately wanted – all up in tatters! The island ripped up by the storm. Her reputation shot to hell again. What on earth is wrong with me? she thought desperately. Do I bring these kinds of disasters upon myself? Everything was in a complete heap! Why me? What on earth am I doing that everything I touch turns to death?

Pushing in the door, she was immediately hit by a horrible smell of something burning. Plastic. Burning plastic. What the blazes – ?

"Gearóid?" she went into the kitchen very cautiously. The smell of burning plastic was horrible. Gearóid was sitting all alone at the table with a bottle of wine that he'd appeared to have almost fully drunk, looking very ashamed.

"What on earth are you up to, Gearóid?"

"I decided to do the ironing," he said, blushing furiously. "What?"

His eyes were watery with unaccustomed drink. "I was trying to help, you see. With the housework, you know. And so I found a pile of clothes you'd washed – the stuff that was hanging above the range – and I tried to iron them. Just to help a bit. And then I ironed your bra."

He lifted up the stinking iron and showed her, glued to the bottom of it, a congealed lump of molten nylon, black as sin.

Ciara burst out laughing. There was nothing else to do. Gearóid grinned and then eventually began to laugh as well, and they could barely breathe they laughed so much, bent double.

"Ow, ow, ow!" gasped Ciara, clutching onto her sides. "Stop making me laugh, Gearóid!" she shrieked, but Gearóid roared with laughter, tears rolling down his face.

"Holy Mother of God, what is that smell?"

They turned around. Gearóid's mouth opened.

Ciara stood and stared. The woman who was standing in the doorway was nothing like she'd imagined. She was small and terribly pretty with jet-black hair cut in a neat smooth bob. She was wearing casual, sporty clothing, a sort of urban track-suit thing with a very clean pair of runners underneath.

"Marina? Is that you?" gaped Gearóid.

"Of course it's me. Who the feck else would it be." She turned to Ciara. "Is is true, then?" Marina De Barra said. "I heard you found him and you telephoned the police. So, is he really dead?"

"So now, Mrs Amy Shanahan of –"

"Churchtown, County Dublin."

"How long have you known Pierce Fox?'

"Oh, I only met him here the other day, when I arrived. I knew nothing about him previously."

"Nothing?"

"No."

"Well now, I think we all know that's impossible, isn't it?" Siobhán Green smiled at her.

Amy blushed. "I'd *heard* of him, of course."

"And you were invited here because –"

"Oh, I won the invitation. I won a short story competition. In one of Pierce Fox's newspapers, the *Sunday Sentinel*."

"So, how well did you know him, then?"

"Oh, God, not at all. We met at dinner, played party games, then I saw him at the céilí the other night – but we didn't speak."

"Ever?"

"Well, not really. No."

"Did you dance with him?"

"Oh, no."

Siobhán narrowed her eyes and consulted her notes. "People saw you both dancing together."

Amy opened her mouth and shut it again.

"Again, I'll ask you – did you dance together?"

"It was a set reel – we would have swung like all the couples did. I was coupled with Zack. We had to exchange partners all the time. But I wasn't dancing *with* Pierce and I didn't speak to him all night."

"Why not?"

"I – I – what do you mean, why not?"

"You were his guest, weren't you? Why didn't you speak to him all night?"

"I – I never got the chance." Amy felt as though her chest were about to explode. This Garda Siobhán Green was a thundering bitch! At least the other cop was much nicer. Nigel – he'd a kind of chubby, freckly boyish look about him. And he was kind of cute – in a country hayseed kind of way. Nigel looked at Siobhán Green who signalled him to take over.

"Who do you think killed him, Amy?" Nigel asked her very gently now.

"I – God, I've no idea. It could be anyone."

"Anyone?" Siobhán sighed impatiently. "Be more specific. Who were his enemies – in this house?"

Amy looked at both of them and then took a breath. "Setanta and Wolftone. They obviously hated him. They made that pretty clear. They started up a huge row with him in front of everyone. And Joy wasn't too keen on him either – she often said he was far more slippery than he appeared. Trish tended to ignore him – I think she despised him more than anyone really. Maggie pretended to like him but I could see right through her – she was using him. And Gemma – well, I bet she couldn't stand him really. She was getting paid to be nice to him, but you could see that she loathed working for him really. Zack didn't seem to have any strong feelings – but I have to say, that's probably because he didn't know what I knew –"

"Which is what?"

She looked away.

"Amy," Nigel said very gently now, "Of all the people staying in the house with Pierce who do you think hated him the most – enough to kill him, that is?"

Amy stared at him. "God, that's an easy one." They looked at her impatiently.

"Well, Amy? You heard us. Who hated him enough to kill him?" Nigel asked. "Which one of you hated Pierce Fox?"

"I did," she replied.

There was a very long silence. "Is that a confession?" Nigel eventually asked.

"God, no. I didn't kill him – but I wish I had done."

"You say you wish you'd killed a man whom you also say you barely knew?"

"I'll tell you one thing I do know about Pierce Fox," Amy said. "He deserved to die."

"How often have you stayed at Atlantis?" Nigel asked Setanta.

Setanta looked away, bored. "Off and on," he said.

"Mr Fox's lawyer says that you are one of the main reasons he set up the artists' retreat – because he admired your work so much."

Setanta snorted. "No, he fucking didn't. He just liked licking up to artists and he liked to be seen to be a man of culture – but he was just a vulgar philistine."

"He has a painting of yours in his bedroom," Siobhán said.

"Yeah, of course he does. That painting's worth a fortune – and it's deeply erotic. Why wouldn't you have something that's all about sex and money hanging in the room where you jerk off?"

Nigel felt his heckles rise. This arrogant layabout artist was not impressing him much. "Not a big fan of Pierce Fox then, are you?"

"Not in the slightest."

"So why come here? Why feed off him like this?"

Setanta's bitter green eyes softened. "Because of the

island. Because it's so perfect. Because I can't stay away – I paint like a lunatic when I come here, or sculpt, or whatever. It's the only place I feel I can work." He looked at his hands. "It's like my hands take on a sort of power of their own when I'm here. I can't explain it." When he looked back up at them his eyes were full of pain.

"Would your hands take on the power to lift a rifle off the wall and shoot your host?" asked Nigel.

Setanta laughed. "Chance would be a fine thing."

"So you admit you planned to kill him?"

He shrugged. "We all hated him. He was a monster. But I didn't fire the gun, if that what you think. Although, fair balls to whoever did."

"Did you hear the shot that night?"

Setanta shook his head. "Nobody did. There was thunder and lightning – I guess whoever shot him took advantage of that."

"What about Wolftone O'Neill? Could he have shot Pierce Fox?"

Setanta laughed again. "He could barely stand up straight that night, never mind fire a gun."

"But he hated Fox, didn't he?"

"Of course. Everybody hated him."

"Where were you between half past twelve and two o'clock?"

"In the pub. Getting rat-arsed."

"Who was with you?"

"Half the island. Like I said, I'd have loved to kill him. But I didn't. Somebody got there first."

"So, who've we got so far?" Nigel examined Siobhán's careful notes.

"Amy Shanahan – clearly admits motive. And intent. So do Setanta and Wolftone. Ciara is obviously lying about where she was when Fox died, and trying to cover up the connection between Dessie Moriarty and Pierce. Marguerite seems to be telling the truth – but she's the only one who seemed to like Pierce Fox! And then the kitchen staff – Mrs Freeman has an alibi, was at the céilí with Nóirín and didn't come back to the house. Everyone can vouch for that. So, who's left? Zack – no alibi – so we still need to interview him. Trish – no alibi. We still haven't taken her statement. And Yvonne – well, God love her she's been an absolute saint running around all day looking after the lads. We'll get a statement off her when she's feeling up to it."

Nigel frowned. He was going to have to tighten up the stories of the main suspects and see who would break when he pushed them. Somebody had gone back up to Fox's room after the céilí. And it wasn't to write up legal contracts. Preliminary word from the post-mortem told him that Fox had died with a stomach full of booze, pills, and a bladder full of cocaine.

There were two suspects whom he was very much looking forward to interviewing – Maggie and Gemma. And he couldn't wait to see what the results of fingerprints turned up.

Chapter Thirty-four

"So, I turn my back for five minutes and you manage to drive my teetotaller husband to drink and to kill Pierce Fox?"

Ciara stared at her. "I – I didn't kill him, Marina!" she stammered.

Marina smiled. "God, I'm only joking, girl. Get a grip on yourself. Tell us," she said softly, nodding to indicate Gearóid who had resumed his default position of shuffling around the gardens. He was busy bailing seawater out of his garden shed. "How did you get himself to come back into the house?"

"The sea drove him in," Ciara replied. She looked carefully at the other woman. Despite what she'd come to know about Marina during the past week, she could see that underneath there was a vulnerability about the woman that surprised her. Her toughness was like a mask. "I guess I assumed you wouldn't mind while you were away. I had a difficult marriage too," she said very cautiously to Marina. "I know what it's like not to get along."

Marina sighed. "We did. At first. We were madly in love. He's a wonderful painter, you know."

"I do know. He's been teaching me."

"Has he?" Marina's sea-green eyes lit up. She really was very beautiful, Ciara thought. She had such a sweet little face, those sharp, moss-green eyes and surprisingly merry smile. Although her skin was rough and blobby round the nose from years of heavy drinking.

"He's a sweet, sweet man, Marina. What happened between you two?"

Marina looked away. "It really wasn't between us two – but something happened between me and someone else, a long long time ago."

"An affair?"

"Well, aren't you the nosy one!"

Ciara blushed. "I'm sorry. But this place has been a bit too crazy over the past two days. I've brought a suicide attempt back to life, I've treated alcoholic poisoning in a teenager, and I've diagnosed a heart attack that turned into a murder enquiry. I came out here for a rest, you know." She smiled weakly at Marina.

Marina nodded. "Yeah, I know. And I know all about your husband, too, Ciara," she said softly. "It was all over the papers as you know. And I guessed when you first answered my ad. Medical circles are notoriously gossipy. I just wanted to say I'm awfully sorry about Des."

Ciara said nothing. Then she asked, "Sorry for him?"

"No, sorry for you. It must have been a nightmare."

"Yes," she said. "The problem is it still is."

"It's easy to fall in love with the wrong man, isn't it?"

Marina said. "I've often been afraid that kind of nightmare can go on forever. But after death there's always closure, isn't there?" She looked anxiously at Ciara.

Ciara frowned. "Marina," she said, "You weren't in Las Vegas just now, weren't you?"

Marina looked down. "Great liar, aren't I?"

"Marina, my husband drank. I didn't do anything about it. I just tried to avoid noticing it. And it led to all sorts of problems for him. He had huge debts. He gambled vast amounts. And ultimately, he disappeared. Once you start hiding your problems from yourself, everything unravels."

Marina sighed. "There's a sorrow in my heart that nothing will ever heal, Ciara. There's something Gearóid will never forgive me for."

"Is is something to do with Pierce Fox?"

Marina took a breath. It was so painful to talk about but she knew she had to start somewhere. And it was one of her twelve steps – number ten to be exact: *Will continue to take personal inventory and when we are wrong will promptly admit it.*

"I had an affair with Pierce – twenty-eight years ago," she began. "I thought he loved me – of course, he did no such thing. He was in love with the island though. He came over as a young fella on a boat, camping with two friends above the beach –" she nodded out towards the sea. "He was a wild thing. Gorgeous-looking. And I was a student. Love at first sight. Lost my virginity in a summer's tent."

Ciara nodded. Love at first sight – yup, been there. "But that was so long ago – why does it bother Gearóid now?"

319

"Because Gearóid and I were engaged to be married. Oh, Gearóid didn't know at the time that I'd slept with Pierce – but when I became pregnant I broke off the engagement because I had to go away to have the baby in secret. That broke Gearóid's heart. He couldn't understand where I'd gone. I pretended I had to go to Derry to do a medical attachment at the hospital. In truth, I was staying with a family and placing Pierce Fox's child in an orphanage." Marina's face crumpled up with grief.

"Oh, Marina, how awful for you!"

Marina said nothing for a moment. Then she carried on, "Eventually, I came back. And Gearóid forgave me. He and I were married shortly afterwards. And we carried on living here on the island. But I could not recover from the grief. We had two children of our own. But with each pregnancy I became worse and worse. The depression is like a black cloud that sits on your shoulders and just blocks you from even being able to breathe." She drew her shoulders back and sniffed deeply, eyes shiny again. "There's nothing so painful as having to get to know yourself."

"I know," Ciara said. "Does Gearóid know about the other child?"

"Child?" Marina gave a long sigh. "He's no child now! He'll be twenty-nine this spring! But, yes, eventually I did tell Gearóid. And so we tried to trace him – Gearóid wasn't keen, but I had to find out where he is."

"Do you know where he is?"

Marina shook her head. "There isn't a day goes by I don't think about him. But I've contacted the adoption societies – the orphanage has since closed down, all the nuns are dead – and none of them can put me in touch with him. That is to say, they have found him and told him that his birth mother wants to make contact but he isn't interested –" her voice broke. "He doesn't want to know who I am," she finished. "And who can blame him? He had a desperate life – brought up in a children's home. I abandoned him." She looked up at Ciara with eyes that were tight with pain. "I can't forgive myself, Gearóid can't forgive me for lying and my son will never know."

"Oh, Marina! Oh, that's so terribly sad!"

"But I'm going to do something about it now. I can't go on like this for another thirty years. I have to allow myself to heal. I've been having Reiki healing," she announced, much more confidently, "and apparently the angels know that one day my son will find me."

Ciara smiled. "How come you came back to the island so soon?"

Marina stared at her. "To go to the funeral, of course!"

"So, let's go through this again."

Nigel Lawlor liked Gemma Goodbody. He liked her vulnerable sweet nature, he liked her professionalism, he liked the fact that he *felt* he could actually believe her.

But her story wasn't adding up.

"You came home from the céilí with Mr Fox and Maggie Hennelly his biographer at approximately ten p.m. Despite the late hour, you had a legal document to get Mr Fox to sign, pertaining to the biographer, and the three of you went up to the study at half past ten to attend to that."

"I know," Gemma smiled very sweetly at him. "It seems to be an odd thing to be doing so late at night, but Mr Fox was a workaholic. We had so many things to cover earlier that day – he was considering several mergers and acquisitions, there were major investments that were still under negotiation and then there was Maggie's autobiography. They had decided that the autobiography needed to be written in time for the summer market. Maggie was very keen to sign the contracts while she was still out here so we decided we'd get that out of the way before having to get back to business."

"I see. And so you three went up to the study, and sat – where?"

"At the table – he used a sort of parlour table as a desk for three-way meetings. The table in the bay window."

"Negative for fingerprints," Siobhán Green interjected. "All three sets."

Gemma's face went purple. "The table must have been cleaned."

"By a dead person? I don't think so."

"Well, you said yourself that somebody had locked the door to the apartment after we left."

"The person who locked the door is our chief suspect," Nigel said plonkingly and Gemma pursed her lips. "However," he continued, "you say sat at this parlour table and read the contracts for the biography until –"

"Well, I'd say it took about an hour or so."

"Was there drink taken?"

"We all had a night-cap, yes."

"Just the one?"

"We were working."

"I see. So then, you finished up your work at about –?"

"It was well before midnight."

"Could you hear the storm?'

"Yes. The rain was awful, there was thunder and lightning."

"Didn't distract you? Up in the height of that apartment, overlooking that spooky lake, thunder clapping through the hills, lightning lashing the place out of it?"

Gemma looked very cool. "We were busy. Mr Fox is – was – very dedicated to his work. He – you wouldn't get distracted. There was business to attend to."

"I see." Nigel paused.

Gemma sat very still, waiting calmly for him to speak.

"So," he carried on, "What happened after you finished up working?"

"We all said goodnight."

"Was Mr Fox drunk?"

"Absolutely not."

"Was anybody using drugs?"

"*Excuse me?*"

"We found drugs in his stomach, traces of cocaine in the nasal passages, and a positive urine test on PM."

Gemma opened her mouth in shock. "Oh, my God!" she said, gaping at the two of them. "That's unbelievable! What a shock! Good lord! You know, you work for someone every day and you have absolutely no idea what their private life is like."

"When did you find out that Mr Fox had died?"

"When I got up in the morning. I went up to his apartment to begin work for the day – and well, you know the rest."

"At what time did you enter the apartment?"

"I suppose it – gosh, I can't remember."

"Had he been shot?"

"It appears so."

"So this would have been at – what time?"

"I don't know when he was shot."

"No – you found him dead at what time?"

"Um. Let's see. I suppose it was about nine – er – half-past eight or so this morning."

"You found the body?"

"Maggie and I did."

"State your full name for the record."

"Margaret Elizabeth Hennelly."

"Is this your statement, Maggie? '*I, Margaret Elizabeth Hennelly, left the céilí on Inish Rua at approximately twelve midnight. I arrived at Atlantis House at half past twelve to find a group of residents gathered in the kitchen. Among those residents were Setanta Lynch, Wolftone O'Neill, Trish Lenihan, Gemma Goodbody, Zachary Rowley, Joy Jackson and there was one other musician, Liam MacDara, who had come back from the céilí with Wolftone. We all sat down at the kitchen table because Gemma Goodbody had something to say to us. Most of the residents were drunk, including myself. I had drunk six pints of Guinness at the céilí and was quite intoxicated. Gemma Goodbody was clearly intoxicated as well. She announced that Pierce Fox had died, but that Doctor Ciara Love had gone to radio the police and we should all just go to bed and try to sleep because the police would be here in the morning. We talked for at least two hours that night about what could have happened to Mr Fox. Nobody was tired. We didn't want to sleep. We were all very upset to hear that Mr Fox had died. I eventually went to my rooms at approximately four a.m. I didn't hear any gunshots, nor did I hear anything unusual. I understand that Doctor Love opened up the apartments for the police at nine o'clock in the morning and that a dead body was found, the body of Mr Fox and he had been shot. I am unaware of any enemies that Mr Pierce Fox might have had. This is my statement as I can best recall it. Signed, Margaret Elizabeth Hennelly.'"*

Chapter Thirty-five

Glen was in a state of shock. The population of the entire island was going about with their mouths hanging open. The hills were peppered with forensic police examining the gorse bushes and peering under rocks. The lake was being dragged by a sub-aqua squad. And in the clear, blue skies above Inish Rua, the helicopters circled like vultures.

Sky news had sent a helicopter clattering across the skies by the time the Garda forensic team had arrived, and Glen sat excitedly watching the news unfold on the hour, every hour.

How appalling to have a murder on the island! How terrifying to think that someone amongst them could have shot Mr Pierce Fox! But at the same time how thrilling to have the island as the number one story on Sky News!

"Peanut?" Nóirín the *Gruagaire* asked Glen, passing him a bowl. They sat glued to the television, munching their way through a giant bag of goodies. In all the excitement, they held their own little party.

"Terence, it's me."

"Amy! Oh, thank God you called! What on earth is happening out there?"

"Pierce Fox was shot. In the middle of the night. It's horrendous."

"Amy, are you going to be safe?"

"Who knows? Whoever shot him is probably still here. But the police won't let us leave. We've all had to give a statement, fingerprints and things, and some of us have to go back and be interviewed again. The house is full of detectives and they are working around the clock, so I guess it's pretty safe. I mean, I don't think the murderer will strike again."

"I'm coming over."

"Terence, you can't."

"I can and I will."

"What about the kids?"

"They're coming too."

"Oh, Terence. Be realistic. The place is crawling with police, the helicopters are going like the clappers overhead, the kids would hate it here." There was a pause. She could hear him breathing heavily on the phone.

"They miss you, Amy. And I miss you too."

She felt her heart crumple. "Terence," she groaned, "I miss you all as well!" Her face burnt with shame. Only hours ago she'd left Zack's bed. But she did miss Terence. Even though he was such a control freak and he'd broken her heart by refusing to allow her to speak to the children. "I just miss my family."

She felt a solid hand on her shoulder. Zack turned her around and handed her a tissue and a cup of tea. She turned to smile at him.

"They miss you too, Amy," Terence said down the

phone. "I shouldn't have been so prickly the past week. Here, talk to Holly."

"Oh, can I?"

"Mama! Daddy says you were on the telly but I couldn't see you."

"Oh, darling! I've missed you so much! Oh, but guess what? Guess who's here – who can't wait to meet you and June?" She looked at Zack who was beaming with pride. "You know *Emerald The Dragon*?"

"We've got the prints back on the bedroom, study, bathroom, hallway, door and the computer." Siobhán Green handed Nigel a printed report.

"And?"

"Several sets of prints were found. Gemma's and Maggie's from the bedroom, as to be expected. Mrs Delahunty the housekeeper too. And the victim's of course. And Doctor Love, her prints are on the woodwork of the bed frame. But there are two sets of prints that have no explanation. Two of the people we've interviewed who deny ever having been in Fox's apartment have left prints there."

Nigel took a breath and flipped open Siobhán's report. Then he read the list of names again. "Well, well, well," he said. "This is going to be very sticky for someone."

"Again, Ms Coyle, I'm going to ask you – how do you explain why your fingerprints were found *all over Mr Pierce Fox's bedroom*?"

But Marguerite was hyperventilating. "I need a paper bag!" she flapped her hands which rattled like sabres. "I can't breathe! I'm going to pass out!"

"No, you're not," snapped Siobhán Green, handing her

a brown envelope. "Now get a grip. You were in the room at some stage. We know that. Your prints are all over the bed frame. On the whiskey decanter. On the bathroom sink, toilet, the window frame, and the light switches. So, why don't you tell us why and when you were in his room, before we have to arrest you on suspicion of murder?"

But Marguerite fell to the floor, in a dead faint.

"Oh, for Christ's sake! This is ridiculous! Pick her up. Put her to bed for half an hour under Garda surveillance and bring the next one in."

Nigel had had enough. There wasn't a single suspect amongst them who could keep their story straight.

Doctor Ciara Love, who'd contacted the police, was lying. Amy Shanahan was clearly lying too. Marguerite Coyle who'd appeared to be so innocent, was now the most devious of them all. Zack Rowley had absolutely no alibi if Amy Shanahan was to believed. Zack had provided an alibi for Amy – but Amy looked as guilty as hell. Amy had quite brazenly admitted motive. And her prints were all over the room. Setanta Lynch had motive, opportunity, and no alibi. Wolftone was the same. Maggie and Gemma had completely conflicting stories and so either one or both of them were lying too.

Trish Lenihan and Liam MacDara were both clearly lying – about what, Nigel had absolutely no idea, but their faces were as red as beetroots. And both Setanta Lynch and Wolftone O'Neill had openly admitted both motive and – if Amy, Trish and Marguerite were to be believed – intent. But then, Amy was obviously not to be believed – her prints were all over the computer, and Marguerite had lied as well and was trying to wriggle out of her statement by faking a fainting attack. And Trish was definitely hiding something.

It was going to be another very long night.

Chapter Thirty-six

"We have to talk to Setanta, Gem."

Gemma and Maggie had holed up in Tí Jimmy Sheáin. The safest thing was to get out of sight altogether. The police were everywhere, and the discovery that Pierce Fox's security system meant that every single room had CCTV and that some of them were bugged for sound as well had delighted the police who were trawling furiously through recordings.

Unfortunately, the landings up to Fox's apartments weren't on film – and neither was his bedroom. It was the only room that Fox kept to himself.

Except that Gemma had been busy too.

"He's been in his studio all day refusing to talk to anyone – he's in terrible form," Maggie said. "He hasn't spoken to anybody since the shooting. It's as if his whole personality has changed."

"He still doesn't know he's Pierce Fox's son. We have to tell him, Mags."

"How? I can't break that kind of news to someone I barely know."

Gemma looked around the pub. In the other corner Ciara was sitting quietly talking to Art Callaghan.

"What else does it say on the birth cert?"

"It says – place of birth the Madonna Mother and Child Home Letterkenny, father unknown, mother Maureen Lynch of Inish Rua – and that's all. And then this little hand-written note that was in the same envelope, in this spidery hand-writing: '*Pierce, it's over now. I've done what you wanted me to do. Your son is forever gone. M'.*'"

"Then maybe his mother is alive. Maybe we should get in touch with her. She must still live on the island."

"Maybe. Maybe not. Let's ask someone who lives here. Art!" Gemma called across the room. She got up and went over to them and sat down. "Hi, Ciara. Art, do you know anybody who lives or lived on the island called Maureen Lynch?"

Art shook his head. "Never heard of her. How are things up in the Big House?" Maggie had come across to join them too.

"That name's so familiar though. Maureen Lynch, Maureen Lynch," Ciara said, thinking out loud to Gemma. "It's a funny coincidence, but when Jimmy Seán died the other night –"

"Huh?" Gemma and Maggie both gaped. "Someone else died?"

Ciara smiled. "When he came back to life, that is." She winked at Art. "He called *me* Maureen. It was funny, wasn't it?" She looked at Art.

"Maureen was the name of the other doctor here," said Art. "At least that's what Dad and all the older people called her."

331

"The only doctor I know is called Marina," Ciara said.

"Máirín is what they say in Irish," Art explained.

"Marina – Máirín. Is she called Marina Lynch?" Gemma asked.

"No," Ciara said. "Her name is De Barra."

"But could she have *been* a Lynch?"

Ciara shrugged. "Can't say. I've only just got to know her. She's – she's been ill though. She's not ready to go back to work."

Art looked suddenly very interested. "Does this mean you'll be staying on?" he asked.

Ciara smiled a shy smile at him. "I guess. For a while, at least."

Just then Jimmy Seán shuffled in from behind the bar where he'd been sleeping in the kitchen. "Máirín Lynch. That woman was an awful slut."

"Dad!" Art looked shamefaced. "That's an awful thing to say about your doctor."

"Why was she a slut, Jimmy Seán?" Maggie asked, excited.

"Ah, sure, she'd had opened her legs to anyone with a bit of money in the old days. She got her punishment though. Her bastard child died." Then he pointed at Art. "Who the hell are you and what are you doing in my house?"

Art sighed. "It's me, Dad. It's your son, Art. And I'm serving customers in the pub." He got up to attend to Jimmy Seán.

The three girls looked at one another.

"Maggie," Gemma said very quietly to her, "we need to look at the stuff I removed from Pierce's room again."

Ciara gaped. "You did what? There's more stuff that you removed?"

"Gemma!" Maggie was in awe.

"The police were coming – they'd keep everything if I hadn't got there first," said Gemma very quietly so as not to be overheard by Art. "When you went to get Ciara I had a gander through his filing cabinet – the top drawer of that mahogany bureau, the one he never let me open. That's where I found Setanta's birth certificate. And the other letter from Maureen. But there was lots of other stuff, two whole folders of things and when I had a good rummage that's where I also found the other birth certificate and the copies of the adoption form. Maggie, you were right. Pierce has another son."

"So – he had two abandoned children." Maggie could hardly believe her ears. There were two complete stories – here was a birth certificate from Setanta's birth, one male child born to a mother Maureen Lynch in a home in Letterkenny in the early 1980s, and another birth certificate, belonging to a male child, born in Mayo the exact same year, a baby who's been called Dorroch Blain.

Maggie pointed at her laptop. "Have we still got Internet access?"

Gemma opened it up.

"Google Nola Connaughton," said Maggie. "Find out her maiden name."

The three women held their breath while Gemma typed. "There! Born Nola Ann Blain, Kiltimagh County Mayo, 1962. There it is. This must be the birth certificate of her child with Pierce Fox. A little boy they called Dorroch." Gemma looked at Maggie and Ciara. "He must have been adopted."

"He was," Maggie said, nodding slowly at Gemma.

"His name is now Gabriel Kelly. He's become an actor. And he knows all about Pierce."

The other two gaped in astonishment. "But he's famous!" Ciara said.

"Even I've heard of him," said Gemma.

"Why didn't you say something before?" Ciara asked Maggie.

"Because I wasn't one hundred per cent sure. It was a rumour I'd heard – it was gossip really. I met Gabriel's publicist in London and he told me that Gabriel had been contacted by Nola and was getting to know her, and that she'd told him his father was Pierce. But none of them wanted to go public. They wanted to protect Nola's political career as well as Gabriel's."

"And," Gemma softly interjected, "more importantly, Pierce wanted to protect himself."

"How?" Ciara gaped.

"Well, Pierce got huge political favours all his life from Nola Connaughton. And now I can see why. She probably helped him out so that he would never tell anyone that she'd had this son with him and then given him away. It's a form of blackmail, but it worked." Gemma looked solemnly at the other two. "It must have broken her heart."

The three of them sat silently for a few minutes. On the desk in Maggie's room, the two birth certificates of Pierce Fox's abandoned sons. And another thick file that was his will.

"Do you think we should read it?" Gemma picked up the will.

Maggie and Ciara grinned at one another. "Yeah, go on!"

Gemma opened up the file. The other two sat very still.

"Um. It says. It says. It –" she was rifling through each page.

"Go on!"

Gemma looked at them. "He's left everything to his sons. That's what it says."

"Everything?"

"Yes. The only thing is – and nobody but me knows this – Pierce Fox is completely bankrupt. More than bankrupt, actually. He owns nothing. Everything is in debt, mortgaged to banks everywhere. He owes millions and that's why he was finding it so difficult to get the legal wherewithal to buy Jet Éire. At the time of his death, his only real asset was this island. It's all he had left to give."

There was a rumbling in the distance. A rumble that grew closer. A whirring, buzzing noise that was now all too familiar.

"Another helicopter." Maggie got up to look out of the window at the skies. "Probably another news station showing boring footage of the island all over the news. Oh, no. It's landing. Godalmighty! Will you look at that!"

The helicopter grew louder and the three women watched as, out of the grey mid-Atlantic skies, it descended like a giant pink balloon.

"Who on earth flies a pink helicopter out here?" Ciara said.

Just then Trish stuck her head around the door. "Girls, something awful's happened."

"What?"

"Amy Shanahan's been arrested for murder."

Chapter Thirty-seven

The police were keeping Amy under house arrest in the front drawing room until they could get another helicopter over. The arrival of Gabriel Kelly's bright fuchsia pink helicopter the previous day, on the only helipad on Inish Rua had caused them no end of disgruntlement, but Gabriel Kelly and his publicist Eddie Mannion were oblivious. Eddie was thrilled to see Maggie again.

Gabriel and Eddie sat in the big kitchen with Mrs Freeman and Joy, who fed them scones and banana cake and sat open-mouthed while they regaled them with the lowdown on their trip over from the States. The crowds of paparazzi at the airport, the constant phone-calls Eddie was having to field from the press. Gabriel was having a complete emotional meltdown about the horrendous shock it had been to discover Pierce had died.

"Talk about a fairy tale of new york," Wolftone grumbled, furious that the others were getting all the attention, and that Mrs Freeman's enormous supply of cakes and scones were being wolfed by Eddie and Gabriel.

It struck Ciara that this was the first time in all her stay she'd seen Mrs Freeman silenced – but she was far too interested in Gabriel to give it too much attention.

"It's just a nightmare! An absolute nightmare! Losing my birth father before I'd even got to meet him!" Gabriel sobbed. "I can't be-*lieve* this is happening to me. And only two months to go before the Golden Globes!"

Eddie took the plate of scones away. "That's enough scones, sweetheart. You'll only regret it, you know. He's terribly upset," Eddie nodded at the sympathetic faces of Mrs Freeman and Joy. "He always gains a few pounds when he's upset." He took the butter away from Gabriel too, and helped himself to a giant slice of banana bread.

"Have a bit of butter on that," Mrs Freeman suggested.

"Oh, thank you," Eddie spread a thick wodge of it. "I'm always famished in the Irish winter time, aren't you?"

"I think I'd like to go to the chapel," Gabriel sobbed. "I need to get in touch with my spiritual side. I'd like to pray to Saint Tristan for the soul of my birth father."

"Oh, sure, Father Glen will be up any minute now," Mrs Freeman said, reaching out to squeeze Gabriel's hand. "You'll get on very well with him, Gabriel, so you will."

Terence arrived later on that day. He was allowed to see Amy, while the children were encouraged to keep themselves busy. Trish took Holly and June up to her own apartments and gave them crayons and paints to play with and Zack read to them from *Emerald the Dragon*. Holly and June were having an absolute ball.

"Amy – you've got to get out of this mess! How on earth could they think you could have murdered him?'

Amy shook her head. Her face was white. She sat very still, hands clenched on her lap in an upright chair.

"Haven't you got an alibi?"

"Not really." She looked up at him. "I left the céilí just like everyone else, but came home. I talked to Zack for an hour and then went straight to bed."

"So why do they think you are lying?"

"Because," Amy sighed. "A whole load of reasons. Zack pretended to the police that I was with him all night – um, we used to help each other with stories. He's writing a new one about a dragon called Andraste and he found it a great help to talk to me, because Holly and June are his readers, you know. So he told them that I was with him all night. But at that stage, I'd already told them I wasn't. So they wouldn't believe him. It was stupid of him to make that up anyway – he was trying to protect me I guess."

Terence frowned. "Why would he do that?"

"Because I'm the only one who's got no alibi."

Terence sighed. "But you don't even know how to fire a gun!"

"I know! It's ludicrous. They've made a huge mistake."

"Amy, darling, you'd need to have a motive to have shot Pierce Fox. Even I know that. What did you say to them that would make them think you'd ever kill someone?"

Amy looked away. "I told them that I hated him. And that he deserved to die."

"Oh Amy! Why on earth did you tell them that?"

"And they found my fingerprints. On his computer."

"Oh, for Pete's sake!" He grabbed her by the shoulders. "Amy! What the hell were you up to?"

She looked at him. "I – I went up to his room. Because of what the others said. At dinner. Setanta and Wolftone.

338

We were playing a daft game – Humiliation, it's called – and each of us had to name an experience we'd never had and get points from everyone in the room who'd had the experience."

"Huh? This is what artists get up to?"

She bit her lip and tears began to well her eyes. "I don't know. It – it was just daft. Anyway, I said I'd never been to New York. And so I was winning because everyone had. And then I nominated Setanta to go next. And he said he'd never taken money for work he wasn't proud of. And that started a horrible row with Pierce. And Setanta accused Pierce of investing in an arms factory in Derry. And Pierce got very defensive because Setanta was investigating his financial affairs as part of a sort of an environmental campaign. And then Wolftone accused Fox of political corruption – and of insider dealing with Leinster Bank. And then I thought of you."

Terence sat very still and stared at her. And then he said in a very quiet voice. "Amy – you didn't do anything daft, did you?"

"The day before the céilí, I was alone in the house. So I went up to his rooms. I wanted to see what they were like. To see inside the life of the man who'd ruined your bank. Who'd ruined your life. Who'd ruined our family, Terence." She looked up at him. "We were happy once, you and I. When you had a job. You knew who you were. I could write." She stood up and began to pace the room. "And then everything went wrong. You were blamed for the bank losing millions. You lost your job. You were at home all day. I lost my ability to write. I had to find out the truth behind everything that went wrong in our world. So that I could move on, you see."

"So you pried into Fox's affairs –"

"I looked at his computer."

Terence stood up to face her, shoving his hands in his hair. "Jesus! Leaving prints everywhere! Oh, Amy! And –"

"He collected films of us. Of all of us. He had a film of me – undressing, getting in the shower, washing myself, getting dried again. He had CCTV all over the house and he filmed us. Me, Gemma and Maggie of course, Marguerite – he even had a film of me on the toilet, Terence! I found it on his computer. In a file with my name on it. I think he used the secret films of us as porn."

Terence sat very still for a moment. And then he said, "Is that why you told the police that you'd have loved to kill him?"

She sat down again. "Pretty much."

"Do they know why you left prints on the computer?"

She shook her head. "It doesn't matter. They don't believe me anyway. They think I had another motive. And they need to find someone to blame for the shot."

He put his head in his hands. "Something has to get us out of all of this." He looked at her. "I'll get you a lawyer. I'll talk to Gemma – see what she suggests."

"Terence, I'm so sorry that I've got you into all of this. But I thought it might help you if you actually knew why you lost your job at the bank. That it wasn't all your fault. Because Pierce Fox was gambling banking shares all the time. He was dumping shares after he got his government investment and then buying them back via another company – and that's what caused the bank to lose billions. It wasn't all your over-selling mortgages to life-insurance customers."

Terence had his head in his hands. Eventually he looked up. "Amy. I've been so unhappy."

"I know."

"I've felt so useless and rejected since becoming unemployed."

"I know! That's why I wanted you to see it wasn't all your fault. That bastard got the better of all of us."

"Amy, I've been so lonely and miserable at home. But I wanted to prove to myself that I could be some sort of super-dad. I thought if I turned my whole life into being a massively successful dad and really being in charge there, that it wouldn't matter that my department at the bank had gone down the toilet. But – looks like I messed up there as well!"

"Terence, you just took it all too seriously."

He shook his head. "I was jealous of you – because you're the parent the girls really want to be with. Even when I lost my job and had to be at home all day, they still wanted to be with you."

"But they pestered me all the time! I couldn't get a thing written."

"I thought if I kept them away from you then they'd eventually want to be with me more. They'd see me as the number-one parent. And I would be important again. But it doesn't work that way with kids, does it?"

She shook her head. "Come here," she said, and he took her in his arms. "We can work this out together, you know."

"Gemma, we absolutely have to show them the recording."

"I – we – I don't know. It's just so awful!" Gemma was purple with shame.

"But Gemma," Maggie shook her head, "listen to what Terence is saying. Amy could go to jail if we don't."

"I know! But, oh, that doesn't make it easier!" Gemma moaned.

"I know." Maggie squeezed her hand. "But we have to tell them. It's the right thing to do. Let's go and show them the video together. And I'll be there for you. And you for me. We've done nothing illegal. We are doing the right thing. Amy can't go down and we have the information that will set her free."

Father Glen Cassidy couldn't wait to see who owned the big pink helicopter. He was straight up to Nóirín the *Gruagaire* to see what she knew.

"Pierce Fox has a son?" Glen gasped. "An actor in America? My oh my!"

Nóirín sucked her teeth. "Given away at birth, the *créatúirín*!" She sighed. "But a lovely actor, by all accounts. And tipped for a prize at the Golden Globe Awards in the spring, they say. Would you like a blow-dry, Father Glen?"

Glen smoothed his black hair and checked his appearance in the grubby mirror. He could do with a bit of a tidy-up, actually. With celebrities on the island and all.

"Ah, sure, why not, Nóirín? Why not indeed?" And he settled back into the chair with a copy of the latest *Scoop!* magazine that Maggie had dropped over earlier in the week. *I really ought to take out a subscription, Glen* thought, *if only for the interior design.*

"So," Nigel Lawlor looked solemnly at Maggie and Gemma across the table in the incident room, "let me get this right. This video was made by yourselves, of yourselves, during the night that Pierce Fox died. And it is only now that you are bringing it to the police as evidence. Have I got that right?"

Gemma's face was beginning to crumble so Maggie spoke first.

"Detective Lawlor. Gemma and I are *sooooo* embarrassed to have to bring this recording to you – but we have no choice. We were with Pierce Fox when he died. And this digital recording was made by Pierce – for his own use. Only Gemma and I took the camera away when we heard the police were coming. We are very sorry that we tampered with the evidence, and very sorry that we lied in our statements, but when you view the recording, you'll see exactly why. But please, I am begging you, keep this recording as discreetly as you can. It is a very compromising recording, as far as Gemma and myself are concerned."

Nigel looked wearily at them. What a pair of loopers! This place gets crazier and crazier by the hour. He looked at Siobhán. She was looking pretty intrigued.

"All right," he took the camera from Maggie. "Let's have a look at this."

Gemma was cringing as they hooked the camera up to the computer monitor.

Maggie took her hand. "It's for the best, Gem," she whispered while Gemma looked as though she were about to die.

The screen came to life. And to the two women's agonising embarrassment, and the (first) astonishment, and (undisguisable) then amusement of Detective Nigel Lawlor and Garda Siobhán Green, Pierce Fox's private recording of his cocaine-fuelled threesome with Maggie and Gemma was replayed.

"There – that's the bit where we realised he'd died," Maggie muttered, beetroot-faced, pointing at the screen. The computer screen was hopping with the moans and groans of Pierce Fox's final hour, Maggie and Gemma's little shrieks of glee, and the background of thunder and lightning like a medieval Mystery play. Nigel's eyes were glued to it. Siobhán didn't seem to know where to look.

"Jesus!" Nigel whistled eventually.

Gemma had her face in her hands.

"And see – here's where we try to resuscitate him – and we can't – see? Gemma knew first aid but she realised he was dead."

The two police officers looked incredulously at Gemma who wouldn't show her face.

Maggie carried on. "And now here, you see me going to get Ciara the doctor." The recording went on. "Now, nothing happening for a while."

"Is that it?" Nigel's voice was dry.

"Well, we didn't stop the recording. I mean, after that, we just come back up with Ciara – shall I fast-forward?"

"Oh God, please do!"

They watched the screen flicker and jump – and then Siobhán shouted "Stop!"

"What?"

"I saw something – go back!"

The images reversed. Seeing herself panicking and running about the room naked was even more humiliating for Maggie when it was shown backwards, but she had to maintain dignity. Either that, or just lie down and die on the spot.

"Look! There – somebody looked in!"

They slowed the replay down. Frame by frame. God, this is so humiliating! Maggie cringed a thousand times. Gemma had her head in her arms on the table. She couldn't look at any of it.

"Now." Siobhán pointed at the screen. "Look. See? There's the door. Look, in this picture, it's closed. Now, you're in the way of the camera. There you are. It's all you. Can't see the door any more. Just you. Just you. But look. If we flip forward to this one – there – it's open. Somebody looked in, while you were – um – *doing it*, Maggie." Siobhán looked at her. "Somebody was watching. And then they left."

"Oh, shit!" Maggie groaned. "Or – is that good? Does that mean that – that there's another suspect?"

Siobhán looked at Nigel. Gemma eventually looked up.

"Well," Siobhán said very slowly, "if somebody watched you having your – er – threesome, then somebody watched him die. And that somebody *could* have come back up and shot him after you'd left the room then, couldn't he? Or she?"

"But – do you still think it was Amy then? Because if you do, then this whole humiliating screening has been in vain!"

The two police looked at Maggie kindly. "Well, you did the right thing by showing it to us. Even if – it doesn't make flattering footage." Nigel had the decency to look embarrassed for her. "But, unfortunately, no. This footage certainly doesn't give us any evidence we need to release Amy. Because she is still our chief suspect. She has motive, opportunity, and has admitted intent."

And then Siobhán's mobile phone rang. She turned away from them to answer it. They tried to politely talk among themselves while she took the call, but both Maggie and Gemma felt sick. They'd been forced to re-live the most awful night of their lives on video, and it was all in vain. Amy was still under arrest, suspected of murder.

And then Siobhán hung up the phone. "We've got the post-mortem report back, Nigel." She looked at him and then the two women.

"And?" Nigel said.

"The pathologist confirms that Pierce Fox *was* already dead when he was shot." Siobhán looked, blushing, at both Gemma and Maggie. "It appears that he died of a Viagra overdose."

There was one set of prints in Pierce Fox's bedroom that were unaccounted for, and Siobhán Green was determined to get a confession.

"Now, there'll be no fainting this time. Correct?"

Marguerite sulked. This was grotesquely unfair! It was perfectly obvious that she could have no way been involved in this horrendous act. She glared at Siobhán who eyeballed her across the table.

"So, I want you to describe as slowly as you like in your own words, what your exact movements were the day before and the night that Pierce Fox died."

Marguerite looked plaintively at Nigel. But Nigel's face was a stone. She shuddered. "I have already told you about the night when he died. I came back from the céilí with everyone else and found that he was already dead. Gemma and Maggie announced it to all of us. And prior to that I was with the musicians – so there is no reason for you to suspect me."

"It's just that new evidence has come to light – pertaining to a prior medical condition that Mr Fox may have had. Unknown to him. Which may have contributed to his death. We feel – the pathologist feels – that there may have been a sort of heart attack. But that we need to know if he was engaged in any kind of – er – activity during the day. Before he died. And so, I'm asking you again, Marguerite, did you or did you not go to Pierce Fox's bedroom on the day he died?"

Marguerite's face was as white as a ghost. Her lip trembled. She clenched her hands together and twirled her rings around.

Siobhán raised her eyebrows. "I'm waiting, Marguerite."

Eventually Marguerite gave a little sob. "We loved one another *very* much!"

Siobhán nodded very slowly. "Go on."

Marguerite's shoulders heaved. "We had to keep our affair a secret. People would have talked. I'm very well known, of course. And married. I adore my husband – I could never hurt him! You have to believe me!" She looked at Nigel's stony face for sympathy – and drew a blank.

"So?" Siobhán was becoming impatient but she sensed she was getting somewhere. "Were you with him on the day he died?"

Marguerite sobbed again. "We had to meet in secret. It was terribly romantic. He was such a lonely man, but he found a connection with me that neither of us could explain. He felt that my musical soul could *feed* his longing, somehow."

Siobhán wanted to puke, but she nodded very sympathetically at Marguerite. *Hurry up, you stupid vain twit!* "Your musical soul could feed his longing. Yes. And so – did your musical soul feed his longing, at –" she glanced down at the pathologist's report, "somewhere between twelve midday and six p.m.? Because that's when the first quantity of – ahem – Viagra was ingested, we think." Siobhán coughed politely and looked up at her again.

Marguerite burst into tears. "All I can think," she wailed, "is how relieved I am that he didn't die in my arms, and that he lived to love me just one last time!"

Chapter Thirty-eight

Amy, Terence, and the children left in the Garda helicopter for the mainland.

And night fell.

"Can you believe he's dead?" Marina said to Gearóid. "All this time – his shadow hanging over us – and now it's gone." She looked up at her husband. Dear, lonely Gearóid. Sad, moochy Gearóid. Crazy, artist, Gearóid. "Do you still love me, Gearóid?"

He looked at her. The girl he'd married despite the fact that she'd disappeared for six months before the wedding without telling him why. The girl who had him bewildered and heartbroken. The girl who'd laughed and been so full of honesty and life, who'd become a lonely, desperate woman. The girl he'd fallen in love with despite the fact that she'd never got over someone else. The woman who'd borne him two wonderful children – but had never seen her own boy again. She had lived beside him and not with him.

She had healed broken bones and broken hearts all across the island but couldn't heal herself.

And yet – she did look different now. Her face was softer. Her eyes – her bright mossy green eyes like a summer's field on Inish Rua. He loved her so much it hurt.

"You're everything to me," he told her. "You always have been, Marina."

"I need you to stand with me," she said.

"And then I want 'Nearer My God To Thee'," Gabriel was saying, "And 'The Lord Is My Shepherd'." He sobbed dramatically and wiped another tear.

Glen nodded. "Anything – more modern?" He cocked his head on one side.

"Modern?"

"Well, Dolly Parton has a wonderful song, 'I Will Always Love You'."

Gabriel raised his eyebrows. "Dolly?"

Glen nodded in encouragement. "I've often heard it sung at funerals. I think sometimes people like to have some modern secular music. It helps them to identify with the emotions," he said, confidingly.

"Oh, Glen! I don't know what I'd have done without you," Gabriel sighed.

With Marina back in the house, Ciara didn't like to hang around in the evenings really any more. Marina and Gearóid needed to get back into their own rhythm of things. And Atlantis House was full of police and in any case she'd spent enough time there over the past few days.

What she really wanted to do was go up to the pub and sit around chatting to Art. But since Pierce Fox had died, she hadn't had the courage to go up to talk to him again. She'd ruined Jimmy Seán's business, and she'd ruined Art's life. And if that weren't enough to put him off, the suspicions the cops had of her certainly would. What if Art got wind of that? More Dessie disgrace to land on her again!

But there was one small event that had stuck in her mind, in between all the chaos of the thunderstorm, and the hasty exit from the céilí to resuscitate Jimmy Seán, and then Stiofán's alcoholic poisoning, and then Pierce Fox. There was an image sellotaped onto her memory in the middle of that crazy night. One small image but it was a very strong one.

It was the look on Art's face when he'd come into the céilí. He'd stood in the doorway, dripping wet, no coat on despite the storm, and she'd caught a glimpse of something in him – just the way he'd watched her for an instant before she'd lost her temper and made such a fool of herself. He'd just stood still and watched her – watched what she was doing. She'd been dancing with Gearóid, of course. Two and fro, in and out, and she'd been laughing and actually for the first time in, oh, maybe two years, she'd been happy. And he'd stood there watching her. He'd observed her happiness as if he'd wanted to photograph it in his mind – and then he'd suddenly switched his expression, as if he'd just remembered what he'd come there for. But she couldn't forget.

She couldn't stop seeing that instant snapshot of a look he'd had, the way he'd taken his mental photograph of her. And knowing it – knowing he'd wanted to watch her, the way she laughed, the happiness of her – there was something in that instant that reminded her of what it felt like to be loved. And the thought of it both exhilarated and terrified her.

She decided to go out for a walk to clear her head. She took a torch from the conservatory and put her anorak on and stepped out of the house. She walked briskly for a few hundred yards until she got to the top of the hill. And then she stopped. She looked up the road, and she looked down the road. Up the road to the pub – down the road back to Marina's house again. The only way to go was to go up.

She didn't want to make a fool of herself. She didn't want to get in Art's way – he had enough trouble keeping Jimmy Seán under control. Jimmy Seán was deteriorating – that was quite obvious now. But she could pop up to the pub to ask about him, and she had offered to do a house call if Art ever needed it. But what would she come to say? It was well after dark, the pub would be filling up with locals.

On the other hand, Jimmy Seán did tend to sleep all day and get up at night – so it wouldn't look too weird to pop in at this hour, would it?

Art was strong – he was capable and got things done. He didn't make a great big deal of everything. He was just there. She could just go into the pub and sit down and have a drink, a Coca Cola or something, chat to the locals or something. And if Art wanted to talk to her, well and good. And if Jimmy Seán was up and about, she could check on him. There was no harm in that. And if it all came to nothing, well, so what? She was no worse off than when she'd started.

Tí Jimmy Sheáin was hopping. Everyone on the island had plenty to talk about – the pink helicopter that had landed and dropped off Gabriel Kelly – the movie-star no less! – who was actually Pierce Fox's long-lost son! 'Twas a pity he never knew him when he was alive! And then the police everywhere – and the helicopters from Sky News that had been circling all day. Never had Inish Rua buzzed with so much excitement.

Nóirín the *Gruagaire* was pinned to the bar, gossiping about how Father Glen was above in the parish house arranging the funeral with Mr Fox's son.

Gabriel was a little dotey, Nóirín the *Gruagaire* said.

Art knew from the very minute Ciara walked into the pub that she'd entered. It was weird – but he felt a sort of sigh come into the room as she did. He watched her cautiously move into the room, her shyness as she approached a group she recognised. He waved at her across the crowded room and she gave a small wave back, smiling generously. He watched her join Setanta who was sitting at a table with Maggie and some of the others from Atlantis House.

He watched her for a while. Her shyness fascinated him. She'd seemed so unsophisticated when he'd first met her – struggling with her suitcase – and she'd been so solemn, and kinda *in on herself* when he'd brought his dad up to the surgery to see her. But she was so smart. She'd brought his dad back to life. She'd known exactly what to do. And she was gentle and yet – she was also kinda tough. The combination of that was what was so attractive about her.

She sat with the others in a group and yet she always seemed to be outside of things. He watched the way the others laughed and talked and watched Ciara's face as she listened to them. She listened to people. She had a soul that cared – that was why he couldn't stop staring at her. He could see in her a kind of person who gave everything –

and kept nothing for herself. No wonder she always looked so lost.

"Tomás," he said to the barman. "I need you to do me a favour. Mind the bar for the rest of the night. I'm taking the night off."

"Fuck's sake," Tomás muttered.

"Tomás, you're lucky you still have a job. You owe me one."

Jimmy was pottering in the back kitchen, cursing away as usual.

Art approached Nóirín the *Gruagaire* who was propping up the bar with Wolftone.

"Nóirín – would you keep an eye on Dad out the back for me tonight? There's a bottle of whiskey in it for you – and your guest," he added, noticing Wolftone's eyes light up.

Then he went across the room and touched Ciara on the shoulder. "I need a favour from you, again, I'm afraid."

She looked up from the group. "Is it your dad, Art? I was going to ask you about him. I thought he might be troubled again tonight."

"No," he said, studying her. "It's me. I need to do something. Will you come and help?"

"Nigel," Siobhán Green handed him a cup of tea, "get that down you. It looks like we've got some very important evidence now. You aren't going to believe what we've found at the very end of the film."

"I had an inkling over the years that there was something about Pierce and me and yet it never dawned on me that it might be him – who'd be my father, I mean." Setanta said to Maggie and Gemma. In the background, Nóirín and Wolftone had started a sing-song. "He was so different to anything I could have possibly have imagined as my dad."

"But your mum might be still alive, Setanta. Don't you want to contact her?" Maggie looked at Gemma.

But Setanta shook his head. "Not just now," he said. "It's too painful at the moment. I still have a lot of things to get my head around. Maybe in the future, sometime. I do know she's been trying to contact me – only I didn't respond when the adoption society contacted me. I don't want to have to meet her yet. Maybe some day. Maybe I will. I just want to keep on sculpting for the moment. I want to finish the sculpture of Andraste."

Maggie nodded. "I understand. But – what about Fox's other son? Gabriel Kelly? He's your brother, isn't he? And he's staying on the island. Don't you want to meet him now?"

Setanta's eyes were full of anxiety. And then he sighed. "I know how to find him. But I don't feel like a brother to him. It's another world, isn't it?"

"Maybe you'll work something out in your art," Gemma softly suggested.

"Yeah. Maybe I will. Hey," he grinned at the two women, "at least I don't ever have to leave the island now! It appears I own half of it."

"So. There she is. The shooter. She comes in. Cold as ice. Takes the shotgun up. Cocks it – she knows what she's doing with it. Experienced shooter. And then she points it straight into his chest, right into his heart – or where she thinks it is. The pathologist actually said she missed the heart and if he'd been alive when she'd shot he might have survived. She shot him in the stomach, actually, and just through a bit of lung and spleen. But she shoots him – there. And now – cool as a cucumber. She walks away. Taking the gun with her."

"And have we searched her house?"

"The gardaí are on their way."

Art handed a shoulder-bag to Ciara.

"What's this?"

"Tripod," he replied. "And you hold this. We'll need it to see our way." He handed her a torch.

"Tripod, for –"

"My telescope. Which is here –" he picked up a large case.

"Wow! That looks heavy. What are we going to do with this?"

"You'll see. Just follow me." He looked at her and smiled. "You saved Dad's life. I want to give you something in return. I want to give you something beautiful that will be with you for the rest of your life."

She walked beside him and they didn't talk, just listened to the baa-ing in the fields and the shuffle of cows in the black night. The roar of the sea beyond the beach and the crunch of stones on the path. They climbed the hill – Ciara held the torch he'd given her and they followed its little moonlike beam up a sheep-worn path that wound around the top of the village and away off into the flat-rocked hills that climbed up and up until they could begin to hear the sea again at the other side of the island. The north-west side. The side that faced America.

Ciara panted as she climbed. "Wow! I didn't realise you

could climb all the way up here. Isn't it dangerous?" she gasped, noticing the foamy sea that was beneath them now as they walked along the cliff path with just a thin moon and the stars to light their way. The bobbing torchlight helped – but only just.

"Not to me – I've been coming up here all my life. I grew up here. This walk is like the back of my hand. We're nearly there now. It's all much flatter from here on."

And so they came to a shallower incline, and she was aware of the ocean's roar beneath them and an end to the little path. "That's as far as the sheep would come," he said. "But just a little more over these rocks and you'll see the most wonderful sight in all the universe."

She plodded on obediently. "It's such a pity it's so dark, isn't it," she was saying. "We can hardly see a thing."

"That's because you are only looking down. Now – here we are. Let's put the stuff down. And see – I want you to look up." He touched the back of her head lightly. And she tilted up her face to the sky. And all above them, the universe exploded.

"Oh, wow! It's like the sky is alive," she gasped.

"Look," he said. "Look at that moon. Our moon. What do you see?"

"A – a thin crescent. A mean, thin little moon," she said. "And beneath it a very bright star. What is it?"

He touched her hair. "It isn't a star at all. It's a planet. It's Venus."

"The goddess of love!"

He laughed. "That's right. Look at the way she's hanging in the sky – as if she's just passing underneath the moon? She won't do that again for another hundred years. So you're looking at something very special. Jupiter's just to their right above them, chaperoning the pair. We'll put the telescope up here," he said, opening up the tripod, "and then if we turn it to the east, I'll show you Saturn."

She watched him assemble the telescope, fixing the eyepiece for her, adjusting the sights.

"Now. Look up there. And tell me what you see."

At first – nothing. And then the focus adjusted. And then – a thin line, streaking through the disc of Saturn's gas.

"I can't believe it!"

"You should be able to see two of Saturn's moons. Aren't they beautiful?"

"They're the most beautiful thing I've ever seen!" She shivered.

"Cold?"

"No."

He took his scarf off and wrapped it around her neck.

Looking up at the universe, seeing the planets so intimately – something so far away that could at the same time, if you looked at it in the right way, seem to be so near, so familiar – it was as if suddenly, the world made sense.

As if we are at the centre of the universe, thought Ciara, but it is so much more important than we are.

"When you look up at the skies like this," she said, "it's as if nothing else matters. Isn't it?"

He nodded. She felt his breath warm on her hair. He was standing right behind her, sheltering her from the icy wind. "That's what I've always thought. There's something deeply consoling in being reminded of our own insignificance. To know that the universe goes on with or without us. That we are part of an infinitely bigger plan."

358

She turned to look at him. His face was only inches from her own. "Art, do you believe in afterlives?"

He looked up towards the night. "Look!" He pointed at a constellation of stars. "That's the Hyades. It's a hundred and fifty light years away. Do you know what that means?"

Ciara laughed. "That it's very, very far away?"

He grinned at her. "Very smart. But not exactly the point. What it really means is that the light you are looking at – the starlight – was emitted a hundred and fifty years ago. So that light – those very photons – are a hundred and fifty years old. And there, that little cluster is called Pleiades. It's called after seven women, seven nymphs, followers of Artemis the huntress. Orion was so smitten by their beauty that he began to chase them, but they outsmarted him. And see, there: there he still is, chasing them helplessly across the sky."

"It's magnificent."

"Some of the stars are millions of light years away – so they are millions of years old. You could be looking at the light that burst out of a sun that happened way, way before human history. Before life on our planet even began. You could be looking at light that may no longer exist – that very star could have burnt out years ago. But the light that you see is still there to guide you." He looked at her again, and stroked her hair off her forehead, where it was falling in the way of the eyepiece. "That's what I believe in. That's what I know. That we are a part of all of that. Isn't that enough wonderment for one lifetime? When you think about the randomness of the universe and the randomness of life, then what we know and can experience is enough to be in awe of."

She leaned against his shoulder. "When you put it that way, it's incredible."

"When you think about the conditions that are necessary for life to exist on any planet – the correct concentration of oxygen in the atmosphere, the correct distance from the sun, the correct amount of water – and to think that we have a planet with the correct conditions for life, and not only that, intelligent life, and not only that but life we can experience and are aware of."

"We are very very lucky, aren't we? To have even a tiny part of all of that?"

"Try telling that to my dad though!" Art grinned at her, brushing her hair off her face again.

She looked at him, excited. "Why don't we bring him up here? To see the stars? Or even on the beach – you could set up the telescope there. It might cheer him up."

Art shook his head. "I've tried. He can't concentrate on it. He gets too confused and disoriented as it is. He needs something children could enjoy to help him to concentrate."

Ciara's face lit up and she beamed at him. "Then I know exactly what would help."

Stiofán, Luke, Niamh and Lauren were astonished to find four gardaí on the doorstep of Yvonne Delahunty's house.

"She isn't here," Lauren explained. She let the police come in.

"She hasn't been here all day," said Niamh, as the police began to search each of the rooms.

"We actually don't know where she is. Did you try the priest?" said Stiofán.

Luke looked at him and they both shrugged at one

another. Thank God their parents were coming out to collect them in the morning. They'd had enough of this weird place for a lifetime.

Yvonne Delahunty, it appeared, had left the island. And not a single fisherman was admitting to having lent her a boat.

"Two of the ban gardaí are going to stay in the house with you until your parents get here in the morning," Nigel explained.

As if the four teenagers were going to sleep a wink, he thought to himself.

Mrs Yvonne Delahunty, Bean An Tí. And shooter of the multi-millionaire business tycoon, Pierce Fox. Who would have thought it for a minute?

Chapter Thirty-nine

Gabriel wanted to have Pierce Fox cremated, and as there were no specific instructions in the will, Gemma couldn't see why he shouldn't. The will would be read in due course after the arrangements, but Gemma had read it and discussed its contents with both Gabriel and Setanta separately. Neither of the two brothers wanted to meet just yet. Setanta was studiously avoiding Gabriel by spending all his time working on his sculpture of Andraste. And Gabriel was spending all his time at Father Glen's parish house.

The body was cremated on the mainland. Gabriel was in no hurry to collect the ashes.

On the morning of the prayer service, the grey skies above Inish Rua were a rattle of helicopters again. There were garda helicopters as well as those from Sky News, and the Tánaiste Nola Connaughton arrived in the government helicopter wearing a fur coat.

"And no knickers, I'll bet," whispered Mrs Freeman to Wolftone, as Nola Connaughton entered the chapel of St

Tristan's and genuflected, then marched straight up to the top of the aisle where the two front rows were reserved for dignitaries. Gabriel took Nola's arm and steered her to the front row which he and Eddie had lined with all their hottest bachelor friends.

Setanta sat with Maggie and Gemma.

"You will speak to Gabriel after the funeral, won't you?" Maggie squeezed his hand.

Setanta shrugged. "It's not a funeral. It's a prayer service. But I'll go over and say hello. Maybe."

Wolftone was playing the guitar – a plaintive rendition of "Pretty Vacant" in a flamenco style, which nobody recognised except himself.

Nóirín the *Gruagaire* was accompanying him on the organ – completely unaware that he was not playing "Nearer My God To Thee", which was what she was playing. Marguerite had agreed to sing Dolly Parton's "I Will Always Love You", and had been practising in a wobbly contralto all morning.

As darkness began to fall outside, Glen lit the chapel with candles. As soon as Marguerite's voice began to fill the chapel, everyone wanted to join in – which wasn't too difficult – even Marguerite was glad to be able to carol away without having to worry too much about being on show. After the chaotic past few days, filling the hills with song in a bunch of keys was a blessed relief.

Then they sang "The Sound Of Silence", as loudly as they could, and the seagulls screamed along above them in approval.

And then Glen invited prayers – free prayers, Gabriel had decided. Anyone could contribute a prayer. Each of the congregation would hold hands with one another and could close their eyes or open them and people could speak and pray for whatever they wanted.

"Let us pray for peace on our island," Glen began. "Lord, hear us!" and the congregation chorused in approval with "Lord, graciously hear us!"

"Let us pray for an end to violence," added Gabriel, and they all echoed him again, "Lord, graciously hear us!"

"Let us pray that whoever shot Pierce Fox doesn't really to go to jail," said Jimmy Seán.

There was a very uncomfortable silence.

"Because," Jimmy Seán added, "The jails are full enough and it wouldn't do any good. At all at all. Sure, 'twas only the one shooting. And wasn't he already dead? Lord, hear us!"

Silence. Coughs. Shuffles of feet.

"Lord, graciously hear us!" Glen waved his hands at the congregation, nodding to encourage them to join in.

"Let us pray for Amy, who got out of jail thanks be to God, and for Mrs Delahunty, who is missing but not forgotten. May we wish her a safe journey wherever she is," began Mrs Freeman. "God help her, she'd an awful life. Sure didn't her own husband die in the same way – shot himself years ago with a gun, just like Mr Pierce Fox did? Lord, hear us!"

There were a few embarrassed looks, but none of disapproval.

"Lord, graciously hear us!" the congregation dutifully replied.

"Let us pray for more clear nights," suggested Art. "Nights without clouds or rain – nights when we can only see the stars and be reminded of who we really are and of our place in this great universe. Lord, hear us!"

Ciara squeezed his hand, and the congregation chorused with approval. And then they fell to silence again.

There was a sound of someone clearing their throat.

"Let us pray for love." Marina De Barra's voice came softly from the back of the chapel. She cleared her throat again and then spoke very soft and low. "Let us pray that we will always love one another, and be true to the things we care about. Lord, hear us!"

The others rumbled in response.

"Let us pray for Gabriel, that he might be nominated for a Golden Globe," suggested Eddie.

"Lord, hear us!" beamed Father Glen.

"Lord, graciously hear us!" the congregation boomed.

"Let us pray," Setanta's voice quavered from the other side of the church, "that this island will always be a place of peace and beauty. That everyone who comes here will find their true selves. And that the art we make here will bring truth – and beauty to the world. Lord, hear us?" He looked around him helplessly. He didn't know why he'd said it. It just – he'd felt he had to say something. In the candle-light, the twilight chapel, it had just come out of him and he stood trembling, his words still hanging in the silence of the night. All eyes were on him.

"Lord, graciously hear us!"

He searched the faces of the other mourners in the chapel. His brother Gabriel – he blinked at him and Gabriel nodded back. And so Setanta acknowledged the face of a man who shared so much and yet had shared nothing with him. The priest and the people who lived on this island – an island that he felt drawn to, unable to live without, organically connected with – as if he'd been born here, unable to move, unable to remove its clay from his fingers, unable to explain the effect its mysticism had on his hands.

From the other side of the chapel Marina De Barra had

looked up suddenly to see who was the young man who'd just spoken. His voice was unmistakably familiar. It was as if the cold finger of death had run itself along her spine, just hearing the words he spoke. And she found she was looking right into the face of someone she thought she'd never see again.

She clutched Gearóid's hand. "I – I –" she whispered.

"What?" he examined her face. "You look as though you've just seen a ghost."

"I have," she said. And sat down heavily. The whole world had begun to spin before her eyes.

Through the little crowds that were milling around the chapel entrance she pushed her way, barely excusing herself when she bumped into people. He was standing with his back to her, amid a group of young women from the Big House but she butted in anyway. She placed a hand on his shoulder – he was quite small, actually. Not like his father at all. Not a whole lot taller than herself. But she knew that it was him. She just knew it. All of it. It had to be.

And then he turned around.

His face was beautiful.

"You have my eyes!" she said, tears spilling out of them. "And you have his mouth, you know."

He said nothing. And then asked her, "Your name was Maureen Lynch?"

And she gave a low moan and stumbled, her head falling into his chest.

Chapter Forty

Everyone was leaving the island. There were boats ferrying over and back with poets and writers and musicians. Gabriel was leaving in his pink helicopter at eleven – and taking Father Glen with him.

"He needs a holiday after all the commotion," Nóirín the *Gruagaire* said to Art, as he served her a pint after breakfast. "Do you think, will you ever go back to America yourself, Art, *a stór?*"

Art watched the foamy head filter itself off from the black beer underneath. Back to America – it seemed to be such a foreign idea to him now. He never thought he'd feel at home again here – and yet, now he couldn't imagine what it would be like to leave. Now that he'd met Ciara, all he could focus on during the past few days was how on earth he was going to be able to persuade her to stay.

But looking after a sleepy little bar on a remote island, with a cantankerous old man who wandered around all night wasn't much to tempt anyone, especially not a young, beautiful, smart woman like Ciara Love. No matter how romantic you tried to make it. One starry night didn't make a universe. Did it?

"Gearóid," Ciara said. "There's something I'd like you and Setanta to do for me. As artists. I'd like you to help me to do something for a friend. A patient of Marina's actually."

Setanta shrugged. "Depends on what it is."

Gearóid smiled. "No bother. Whatever you like. If I'd be any use to anyone."

Marina poked him in the shoulder as she passed. "Stop feeling sorry for yourself." She sat down at the table with them. "What is it you want them to do, Ciara?"

Ciara looked at her. "Jimmy Seán is becoming very difficult – with the dementia."

Marina nodded, pouring tea.

"He gets up at night," Ciara continued. "And sleeps in the day. And he needs something to occupy himself. He needs something – with meaning." She looked at Gearóid. "And so I wonder – would you show him how to paint?"

Gearóid sat and said nothing. And then said, "I will. If he can get up the loft."

Amy sat in her small study in the front bedroom of the three-bedroom semi-detached house in Churchtown and looked at what she'd written. Outside, on the little street, she could hear the sounds of Holly and June shrieking with laughter as they careered up and down on their trikes. Downstairs, the gentle tinkle of Terence emptying the dishwasher. A radio in the background. The smell of beefburgers grilling for tea.

Chapter Forty-one

Three months later.

"And we're live from the red carpet at the Golden Globes ceremony and here's one very special actor who's just been nominated for his amazing role in Blood Not Tears *– Gabriel Kelly, can we talk to you a moment? Because everyone in Ireland is so excited about your nomination."*

"Certainly! It's a pleasure."

"First I have to say how much I absolutely adored the film – thought it was fab – you were fab, wasn't he, Maggie?"

"Superb! He was superb!"

"And we know you had a very deep personal tragedy this year and that it's been really really tough for you –"

"Yes. That's true."

"Do you feel that this is the sort of film you are most comfortable with? Because we know you started off on the stage in a production of Playboy of the Western World, *which is very different from the sort of work you're doing*

now. And then you were whisked off into a glittering television role before you could almost catch your breath – and now this amazing film. Are you comfortable going straight from theatre to playing these Hollywood tough-guy parts, or do you think you'll want to do an Irish film next time?"

"I've absolutely loved working on this film. Martin Scorsese is a genius and I'm so privileged to have been able to work with him. It's been a remarkable journey and I've been incredibly lucky. My co-actors Meryl Streep and George Clooney are such professionals. And I admire Quincey Mertz as a screenwriter so much – he brings out the best in everyone."

"Well, that's great, Gabriel. And we absolutely wish you the best of luck, don't we, Maggie?"

"Hugs!"

"Ooh, you got a hug off him! She got a hug off Gabriel Kelly, everyone! Hollywood's hottest bachelor! Lucky girl!"

"Course I did!"

"Of course, you're his official biographer now, aren't you? You're the one who broke the story of his relationship with his birth father, and your book about the whole Pierce Fox story is coming out –"

"At the end of next month."

"Fantastic! What's it called again?"

"Foxblood."

"And you've sold the movie rights already, haven't you?"

"Yes, a major studio has just optioned the rights."

"Fantastic. Well, we'd better go to a quick ad break and then see you back here in a few minutes. You're watching me, Georgina Ní Bhrollacháin."

"And I'm Maggie Hennelly."

"Reporting live for Entertainment Ireland from the Golden Globes in California! See you soon!"

"Good old Maggie," said Amy, curling her feet up underneath her knees and cuddling closer to Terence on the couch. "She's actually got a much better book deal out of this than she could ever have done while he was alive."

Terence kissed the top of her head. "How's your own book coming along?"

"It's going well. Should be finished soon."

He nestled into her hair. "I'm so proud of you."

The whole of Inish Rua was gathered in Tí Jimmy Sheáin to watch the Golden Globes.

"There's Gabriel!" Nóirín the *Gruagaire* clapped her hands in glee, almost knocking over Wolftone's pint.

"Oh, and there's Father Glen! In the seat beside him!" The islanders gawped at the television and then began to gossip happily amongst themselves. "Doesn't he look well?" "Fair play to Gabriel for inviting him to the awards!" "Isn't he a dark horse, not letting on he was going to America!" "And we thought he was only gone on a retreat!"

"Shhhh! I want to hear the nominations!" Trish motioned suddenly to everyone to be quiet. Liam, parked beside her at the bar, wrapped an arm protectively around her shoulders.

"Doesn't Gabriel look gorgeous," sighed Joy. "Although, he's not a bit as good-looking as you, Setanta," she added, squeezing Setanta's hand.

Julia Roberts was reading the nominations.

"The nominations are: Brad Pitt, for Colonel Seed; *Leonardo Di Caprio for* One Day In Your Life; *Ed Norton for* Shudder; *Gabriel Kelly for* Blood Not Tears. *And the Golden Globe Award goes to . . ."*

The whole of Inish Rua held its breath.

"Gabriel Kelly, for Blood Not Tears*!"*

Wolftone and Nóirín the *Gruagaire* leaped into the air and began to dance around the pub. *"Here we go, here we go, here we go!"*

Marina and Gearóid kissed one another. Joy and Setanta hugged one another. And then kissed. A French kiss, to Joy's astonishment and – well, joy.

"Setanta!" she gasped, and then kissed him back.

Trish and Liam were snogging the faces off one another.

"Shhhh! We have to hear him make his speech!" Trish broke away from Liam's frantic mouth, her own face covered in saliva.

"Shhhhh!" and the entire island held its breath again.

"Thank you! Oh, thank you so much! You can't imagine how much this means to me. I can't believe how lucky I am to win this award for my first film. It's been an absolute dream. And this year has been a very turbulent one for me, and I want to thank Martin Scorsese and all of my co-actors from the bottom of my heart for being there for me during this tremendous journey. As many of you will know, I discovered my birth mother and birth father this year, and discovered that my life is even more dramatic than I'd thought it could ever turn out to be! I'd only just begun to know my birth parents when my birth father died. But something else happened when he died. I discovered the love of an individual who has changed everything for me. Who has made me complete. And so I dedicate this award to the people of Inish Rua, thank you for giving me hope. Thank you for giving me love. And thank you for giving me Glen. I adore you, Glen. You are my award. You are the love of my life."

The bar in Tí Jimmy Sheáin became so suddenly quiet

you could have heard the sea – if you were listening. You could hear the gulls muttering on the black cliffs – if you were remotely interested. You could have heard a pin drop – except for the fact that the television was still on and there was a standing ovation of applause going on for Gabriel Kelly who was now descending the stage with his Golden Globe and wrapping his arms around his lover, Father Glen Cassidy of the parish of St Tristan on the island of Inish Rua, and kissing him full on the mouth before waving at the crowd again and sitting down.

"*Aaaagh!*" gasped Nóirín the *Gruagaire*. There was another very long silence.

"Doesn't surprise me in the least," said Joy eventually.

Setanta grinned from ear to ear. "Fair play to him. He won't be back to the parish again though, I guess."

"'Tis very hard to keep a priest on Inish Rua," Mrs Freeman said. "'Tis an awful desperate very lonely life."

Jimmy Seán Callaghan laughed until he cried.

It's long past midnight and the stars are everywhere. The whole of Inish Rua is wrapped in a cloak of stars. Everyone is still busy celebrating Gabriel's Golden Globe in the pub at Tí Jimmy Sheáin. Jimmy Seán himself will go to bed at approximately four a.m. after painting for several hours during the night. He is up in Gearóid's loft, painting a picture of the stars. Great swirls of blue and green and yellow on a deep navy background. He paints the stars every night – every painting more or less the same, but he paints what he sees. He paints whatever matters to him now.

Jimmy Seán will die tomorrow morning, very peacefully in his sleep. But Ciara and Art don't know it yet, because they are quite occupied with one another.

"Hey, we forgot to watch the film awards," says Ciara, nuzzling into Art's neck.

"Ah, crap. Oh, so what. We'll find out if he won tomorrow," says Art, rolling on top of her again. "I don't really care, do you? There's only one thing on my mind right now . . ."

Epilogue

Island Of A Thousand Stars.
A Novel By Amy Shanahan

They'd say that when you went out to the island you either turned back and went home again the very same day or you might never leave. Perhaps it was the wet fog that rolled in off the Atlantic that captured you, a fog that smothered the landscape like a ghost, putting all the boats to dock for days. Perhaps the wickedness of the sea trapped you there while it pounded every beach and cliff with waves that whipped the trawlers away from landing at the harbour for a month. Or perhaps you fell in love — with Inish Rua itself, with its solid silence, its empty strands, its ferocious cliffs, its rough hills moist with heather, munched quietly by black-faced, tough-nosed sheep. Perhaps you met someone there who needed you — or you needed them. Perhaps you had nowhere else to be. Or perhaps, when you'd been there long enough, you weren't sure why you couldn't leave — but you stayed. To see what would happen next.

If you enjoyed *Dead Wicked*
by Juliet Bressan why not try
Entanglement also published by Poolbeg?
Here's a sneak preview of Chapter One.

Entanglement

Juliet Bressan

1

Tuesday Morning, 4.a.m.

"Doctor Gilmore to the labour ward. Labour ward, Kate. Come urgently, please. Labour ward, Kate, thank you."

She was wide awake. She had the light switched on almost before the bleeper's siren had finished. But Doctor Kate Gilmore was quite used to switching from dreamless deepest sleep to a hyper-alert state of wakefulness, then jumping out of bed and grabbing her clogs to make it down into the labour ward in under a minute. The transition was almost automatic to her now, after seven years of obstetric training.

She slipped swiftly out of the single on-call bed and ran her fingers through her short dark hair that sleep had left all askew. Kate kept her hair deliberately short and in an almost boyish haircut, because it was so much easier to leap out of bed and be in the labour ward in seconds if she didn't have to brush it down. The tight short cut suited her smooth olive skin and heart-shaped face with its wide cheekbones, enhancing her elfin neat appearance.

She quickly smoothed her sleep-creased theatre scrubs across her chest, feeling underneath the bed for clogs while the labour ward sister's low-toned voice summoned her across the pager back to work. She checked her watch. It was almost four o'clock. When she'd been getting into bed, it had said three. She'd only had an hour's sleep.

Kate strode very rapidly now, down the shockingly bright corridor towards the labour ward. It was never a good idea to *run* anywhere in clogs, and the kind of doctors who *ran* about the hospital rather than walked were generally the headless-chicken type. And that was the last thing Kate would ever have wanted anyone to think about her.

Natasha, the labour-ward midwife, was standing at the nurses' station with the patient's notes all ready for Kate.

"What's the story?" Kate raised her eyebrows and kept on walking briskly, towards the room that the midwife had indicated. The room was full of noise of oxygen hissing, trolley cot sides clanging, instructions being called.

"Twenty-nine-year-old para 0 plus II at thirty-four weeks with PV bleed and low BP," said Natasha. "Foetal heart right down. It looks like an abruption."

Kate took the case notes out of the midwife's hand and whipped them open. The file was empty of written notes. "Unbooked patient, yes?"

The midwife indicated yes. Kate bit her lip and flipped the case file over and went straight to the labour chart. Probably a drug addict or undocumented migrant, if she was unbooked. She stood a moment studying the labour notes and then the tocograph, while the midwife tended to the woman who was on the trolley, lying on her side, desperately inhaling nitrous-oxide gas.

"Hello there, I'm Kate Gilmore. I'm the doctor on duty tonight. It seems that you will need to go to theatre straight away now, I'm afraid, Mrs . . ." Kate flipped the chart over to the front. "Mrs – Le Normand." She turned to Natasha. "French?" she mouthed.

"She gave us a next-of-kin address in Switzerland," the midwife said quietly, while she checked the continuous-blood-pressure monitor.

Kate nodded, watching the midwife work. Natasha took another large pad from underneath the trolley while she spoke quietly to the woman.

Kate quickly calculated the extent of this emergency. The blood pressure was dropping. But there was a foetal heart of ninety-five.

Kate glanced at Natasha. "Looks like the placental haemorrhage is concealed."

Natasha nodded back. It was time to go to theatre.

Kate let the midwife slide out of the way and then stepped up to the woman on the trolley, showing her the consent form to sign.

"*Bonjour, Madame. Pardon, je ne parle pas Français. Je suis médecin.* Can you please sign the consent form for Caesarean section? *Nous voulons prendre le bébé, vers le . . . le . . .*"

Mme Le Normand was nodding in between deep moans, the black mask clamped firmly to her face. It was impossible to see much of her behind the mask but her long brown hair was soaked with sweat and her skin was very pale.

"I can speak English!" she said breathlessly – and with a mild American accent, Kate thought.

"Good. Thank you." Kate touched the woman gently

on her arm. "Madame, I need to take the baby out immediately. Can you just sign the consent form here? Thank you."

The woman grasped the pen and signed the line that Kate had marked with a generous X.

"Thank you," said Kate. "Very good. Thank you." She turned to speak to the midwife again. "BP?"

"A hundred over forty now."

"Okay. Good." Kate snapped the case notes shut and placed them on the trolley at the woman's feet. "Let's go. Have we grouped and cross-matched blood?"

"Six units and twenty of fresh frozen plasma on the way."

"Foetal heart?"

"Almost down to eighty-five."

Kate frowned.

"Nick Farrelly is in theatre already," Natasha added.

"Good." Kate stood back to let them out. Nick was the anaesthetist she liked to work with best.

Kate put a hand out to touch the woman's arm very briefly as they pushed the trolley into the lift. "Don't worry, I am going to deliver your baby very quickly now."

But the woman's hands were shaking as she held the rubber mask to her face, dark hair sticking to her neck with sweat. She groaned and Kate met Natasha's eyes as the lift door closed between them.

Kate turned rapidly to take the stairs. Thirty-four weeks. In this hospital, without the placental bleed the baby would have been a good enough gestation to deliver in the labour ward. But with the mother in shock the situation was much more severe. Everything depended on keeping the mother as well as possible now. She took the stairs two steps at a time, wooden clogs tapping loudly in the night.

Kate pulled a cotton theatre hat out of the box that was in the hallway just outside the operating room and grabbed a mask to tie around her mouth. There was the sound of metal clanging against metal, instruments being unwrapped, nurses' voices over one another. She stood back to let Natasha leave and then pulled two plastic shoe-covers over her clogs before walking backwards into the operating theatre, letting the doors flap shut behind her.

At four o'clock in the morning, gynae theatre was alive, crashing with the noise and light – nurses flapping drapes, the wheeze of anaesthetic machines, the snarl of suction. The patient was already parked and undergoing anaesthetic, in the centre of the long wide room. Kate caught the familiar earthy smell of iodine and sour liquor that was the night-time delivery smell of new birth.

Across the theatre underneath the window the nurses were quickly unwrapping and counting instruments and towels. Normally, as soon as you walked into this theatre you were struck by the beautiful view over the Dublin Mountains through the long wide windows on the far wall. Tonight, the sky was thickly black outside.

Nick Farrelly the anaesthetist was working rapidly, fixing Mme Le Normand with a central line.

"Hi, Nick. Glad you're on tonight. This is a tricky case here. Unbooked patient. Is Paeds out of bed yet?"

God damn it – Nick mustn't have been able to get another vein if he was going straight into the major vessel just above the heart. The woman must be quite shut down.

"Shit, Nick, does she need a central line already?" Kate said quietly over her shoulder as she passed him on her way to the scrub area. Not waiting for his reply, she whacked the two taps on at the scrub sink and began to briskly lather up.

"Aw, I don't know, but who's going to wait around to find out?" Nick grinned at her over his shoulder and Kate smiled back at him from the scrub room through the glass.

"I just love putting clever things in, you know." He shrugged his shoulders while he taped the central line in place, briskly attaching it to the IV. Despite the tension Kate couldn't help smiling at Nick while she scrubbed her fingernails. Nick worked very briskly but he was always very careful and neat, with his black-rimmed glasses and slightly protruding, ever-smiling teeth. Everybody loved Nick Farrelly, the anaesthetist.

"Well, do something even cleverer and get her oxygen sats in good nick for me, there's a good man," Kate called to him over the noise of the nurse's counting.

"Paeds on the way, Kate – Ronan's nearly here." Nick was starting up another unit of fresh frozen plasma. "And the patient's under. We are all ready for you now, Kate."

Kate spread her arms out to the theatre nurse who opened out the gown, twirling her around to tie the wrap-around while she snapped on rubber gloves from the box that was kept specially for her on the window-ledge beside the scrub sink. Kate Gilmore was the only member of the hospital theatre staff who needed sterile gloves in a size *extra small*.

"How's the patient's oxygen saturation, Nick?" Kate asked him now, as she took the scalpel from the theatre nurse. One neat swipe and the skin was open. Kate clamped the incision open and the uterus was visible instantly. "Okay, opening up the uterus now . . . suction please and we can get a look in . . ." The suction vacutainer was filling rapidly. "Christ, Nick, we're going to need a lot more volume. Look at the loss just since we've started and there's more going down there . . . gosh, this is a small baby for thirty-four weeks, Sharon." Kate looked up at the theatre nurse who stood by with a green towel draped across her arms, ready to take the newborn.

"Is the Paeds here yet?" Kate went on, talking rapidly as she worked. "Oh, good. Hi, Ronan. Brilliant. Very tiny baby, Ronan. Here we go. A bit still as well. Heart rate is right down." Kate neatly clamped and cut the cord. "Okay, there you are, she's all yours." She handed the silent, slippery newborn child to Sharon Guinness who whisked the child away towards the paediatric station in the green theatre towel.

"I'll rub her up for you, Ronan, and then I think you'll have to intubate." Sharon Guinness wiped the baby carefully and placed her on the resuscitaire for Ronan Clare the paediatrician to examine.

"How's the Apgar, Ronan?" Kate called over to him, but he did not reply.

I'm rushing him, thought Kate. Steady on. Take your time. Ronan's in charge there now.

She checked Nick Farrelly's eyes over his theatre mask for signs of worry. Behind his black-rimmed spectacles, Nick looked his usual placid self. But then Nick was never jumpy or emotional. Kate slid her hand around the cavity one more time, desperately trying to make sure she had it emptied completely. The uterus was empty all right but it was boggy and unresponsive.

Kate could feel her heart begin to thump.

"This placenta is all over the place," she said, looking at Nick.

"Okay, Kate, no problem, honey." Nick looked at her, reassuring her with calm eyes behind his glasses. "You just work away. I've got her saturated enough for the moment. But I'd stick another unit of packed red cells on now, Sharon, and maybe some ergometrine?"

"Apgar four at one minute," said Ronan. "But don't worry, she's responding to oxygen by mask. And crying now. There you go, little baby!" He rubbed the tiny infant's chest to make her gasp. "She's really pinking up now."

"Good man, Ronan!" Sharon nodded over to him.

They were needing all the signs of life that they could find.

The theatre went silent for a moment. Kate removed the last remnants of the torn placenta and handed it to Sharon to weigh.

The familiar warm-blood dampness of the crash gynae theatre was soaking into her gown and she scolded herself inwardly yet again for forgetting to put a rubber apron on. She would be soaked in this woman's blood afterwards. And her scrubs (which she had slept in) would be soaked right through.

Kate was always forgetting to get a rubber apron on for a crash section. It was the one mistake she consistently made, and the only person who suffered for it was herself, and now she'd have to take another shower before she could get back into bed tonight. And it was already nearly time to get up again.

She stood back to examine her work and check the progress of contraction. There was no contraction happening. The woman's uterus lay where she'd placed it outside the abdomen on the green drape like a limp hoodie, its open mouth tiny now that the small newborn person it had housed had been delivered.

Kate glanced sharply at Nick, to see if the anaesthetist had noticed. "Nick, what do you think about the blood loss? I can't seem to get stasis from this uterus at all."

Nick squinted at the volume that had already gathered in the vacutainer. It was almost four litres. It was more than enough to need a hysterectomy and if they didn't make a very quick decision, the woman would no longer be able to tolerate the numbers of units of fresh frozen plasma and the packed red cells and would start using up all her blood-clotting factors – which could be fatal.

Nick looked at Kate now, and she searched his face to see what he was thinking.

"How many units of packed red cells has she had?" she asked him.

"Four."

"In what length of time?"

"In twenty minutes."

"If we keep going, there is a risk of disseminated intravascular coagulopathy, isn't there? And then we'll lose her altogether."

"Of course there is. Isn't she contracting down at all?"

"We've given two infusions of oxytocin," said Sharon Guinness, shooting a warning glance at Kate who was desperately squeezing on the uterus. "Kate, the fluids are just flying in and they're flying right out again through that uterine wall."

"Kate. You can squeeze it all you want, but if it keeps on bleeding –"

"I know, Nick." Kate spoke quietly but her mouth felt as though it were full of cotton wool. "Sharon," she said, "is her husband still outside?"

Sharon looked questioningly at the others.

"Does anybody know where this lady's husband is?" Kate's voice was sharper now. "Or partner? Did she come in with someone, or come in alone?"

In the echoey theatre her voice was shrill with nerves. Steady on, she told herself. This is a team decision. Nobody is alone here. And this is about life and death. Do the right thing, and do it well. That's all you need to do. She flared her nostrils to calm her eyes and breathed a deep, liquor-scented breath.

Ronan Clare the paediatrician was happy with the baby's Apgar now and was settling her up underneath the lights. The baby seemed to be breathing spontaneously, her tiny head fast asleep beside the continuous-oxygen mask that Ronan had set beside her. Ronan usually liked to avoid intubation if at all possible at resuscitation, pushing babies hard to breathe on their own.

"Good little girl, that's a good baby, take a big deep breath, and have some nice cold oxygen." Ronan chatted to the baby while he held the mask in front of her face.

Normally Kate would smile to hear Ronan yapping away behind her as she worked, but tonight her face was frozen.

"I'll pop outside, shall I, and see if there's anybody with her?" Ronan offered. "Thanks, Ronan," said Kate. "Please do that."

"Sharon, you just keep an eye on *le bébé*," said Ronan.

Sharon's expression of anxiety as she passed Kate on the way over to the resuscitaire said it all. They would have to make a quick decision, and every second counted now. Above the theatre masks, four pairs of eyes blinked, searching one another for an answer.

"We'll give her one more unit," said Kate, "and then if

there's no stasis after two more minutes we'll make a decision then."

It was a plan, at any rate. And it was a decision.

Kate stood still for a moment, waiting for the packed red cells to run in through Nick Farrelly's central line. God help her, thought Kate, while she tried to pack the woman's still-flaccid uterus again with yet another towel.

An unknown patient, here on holidays, having a disastrous delivery in a strange hospital. Please God, let there be a husband outside! She felt her neck becoming tense; her nostrils flared. Every second was an agony.

Kate tried to rub a contraction up again and packed the uterus with another towel. It was as flaccid as a burst balloon.

"Shall we have some music on?" Sharon suggested. "How about a bit of Lyric FM?"

"That would be lovely, Sharon," Kate smiled at her gratefully.

Nick began to hum along with Mozart's Clarinet Concerto. They stood silently, waiting. Blood and liquor dripping from the soaked green drapes into the bucket underneath, running off the operating table like a thick black rain. Mozart and the hum of theatre lights, and the wheeze of ventilation machines.

Ronan poked his head around the doorway of the theatre. "She is alone," he said. "I checked with them downstairs too. They have a phone number for her next of kin and they've been ringing it all night. They got through and left a message earlier but now there's no reply. They think she was visiting Dublin on business."

"Her sats are very low now, Kate. And the BP is not responding." Nick's brown eyes looked at her solidly.

"Okay, Nick. Thanks. I appreciate that." Kate looked at Sharon.

"Do you want to ring the Prof?" Sharon asked her.

"There isn't time," Kate heard Nick quietly say.

"All right," she said. She turned to the trolley and changed her gloves briskly for new dry ones. Size extra small.

"Let's go then, Nick. Clamp by two then, please, Sharon?"

The theatre nurse handed her forceps, and she tied off the uterine vessels one by one.

They worked rapidly, heads bent together, her dark hair under one theatre hat, Sharon's strawberry curls like a cherubic halo under hers. Four gloved hands moving swiftly as they passed sutures and clamps, in silence – the only noise the wheezing of machines, the snarl of suction, and the Mozart lightly in the background.

"Don't you just love the clarinet?" said Kate. Although they couldn't see her mouth behind the paper mask, her eyes revealed the creases of a clearly very distressed smile. She held her hand out to Sharon for the scalpel.

"Don't worry, Kate, you're doing the right thing," Nick told her. Behind his glasses, dark brown eyes full of kindness.

Sharon closed her eyes and opened them again, looking at Kate above the theatre mask as if to send her a small silent message of goodwill.

Kate lifted the woman's womb away from her anaesthetised body, for good.

Tuesday morning, 5.45 a.m.

"Prof, it's Kate Gilmore."

"Kate."

"Prof – we had a very difficult delivery in theatre just now. Unbooked patient Para II. She's stable now. But we've had to do a hysterectomy."

There was a very long pause.

"Is the infant alive?"

"Yes. Apgar four and nine. Thirty-four weeks. Patient is in ICU."

There was a longer pause.

"I'll see you soon, then."

Leaning against the wall, she replaced the receiver. Her green operating gown discarded, she sat down. She sat for half an hour alone in crumpled, stained pale-blue theatre scrubs in the dressing-room, exhaustion over-whelming her like a wave.

Professor Dennis Crowe arrived into the ICU at seven smelling of a musky aftershave and soap. He and Kate sat side by side at the big desk in the nurses' station while the sisters did their round. He calmly read through her theatre notes, picking through them like a haystack in which a vitally important needle might be found. He ran a finger over the labour chart as he silently scrutinised each word she'd written in her theatre notes, taking what she assumed were mental notes. This was Professor Crowe's idea of debriefing. Silent scrutiny followed by withdrawal. She sat patiently and waited for him to get through the notes. The noise of an unanswered phone punctuating the silence made her jump. The wheeze of a computer printing methodically in the background grated on her nerves.

"We'll need to present this to the M and M on Thursday," said the Prof.

Every tough delivery was audited in a question-and-answer style presentation by the entire maternity hospital staff at a meeting called the monthly Morbidity and Mortality meeting. Evidence-based medicine was what it was all about. And a pretty good thing it was too, Kate usually felt, and normally she looked forward to her monthly task of presenting the hospital statistics for these meetings. But now, after this disastrous delivery, the last thing she wanted in the entire world was to have to go through last night's events in theatre in front of the staff of the entire hospital.

"Yes, of course," she said. But her heart was as low as it could be. "I'll get a PowerPoint demonstration ready tomorrow," she said, wondering in her over-tiredness how she'd summon up the energy to even *look* at a computer screen. And then suddenly something caught her eye – Jesus, was this even the right chart? Yes. Of course it was. But surely . . . she'd been convinced that she'd delivered a Para *two* last night – and yet this chart was yellow – which meant it was the woman's first pregnancy. This didn't make sense. She was sure the midwife had said that the woman had been on her third pregnancy and midwives didn't make those kinds of mistakes – unless – was there any chance that she could have made that kind of mistake herself? She shook her head and tried to focus her memory on the events of last night – but her over-tired state of fuzziness was drawing a complete blank. The chart the professor was holding was a yellow one, primagravida. And then she noticed, there at the top right-hand corner of the theatre notes, in the midwife's handwriting: Para 0 +II. Two previous pregnancies – both miscarriages.

She glanced sideways at the Prof's face to try to read his thoughts and desperately tried to re-run last night's events of the emergency in the labour ward – to see if she could remember what she'd read in the admission notes. She *seemed* to remember Natasha saying to her that the patient was a Para II – which *would* have meant two live births. Kate closed her eyes for a moment and tried as hard as possible to remember what she'd heard the midwife say. But fifteen hours later and after only one hour's sleep it was all a fuzzy blur.

Perhaps it had been a language problem, she thought, glancing sideways at the Professor's face again as his finger underlined the words *Para 0 plus II*. Perhaps the patient had misunderstood, she thought, and we muddled the history in the emergency last night. Even with perfect English, in a state of distress *she* might have got things slightly mixed up.

But Professor Crowe had a face that told her nothing. He continued to read through the notes with one finger underlining each word, as if he were marking an exam. The only sound that she could hear while he read was his breathing, deep exhalations through his nostrils that sounded like a wind tunnel. That, and the thumping of her heart.

Mme Le Normand was under heavy post-op sedation and Kate would only be able to speak to her properly when she'd woken up. And the most important thing Kate would have to tell her was that she wouldn't be able to have any more pregnancies.

Kate leaned her elbows on the desk and rubbed her temples with her eyes closed. Talking to the patient about the delivery and having to explain everything that went wrong was a major anxiety to face. But having to present it in front of the entire staff – that was like having to rub her own nose into it.

"All right," said Dennis Crowe eventually, standing up. "You've done enough. I'll go and see the patient." And he turned to march away, carrying the case notes with him underneath his arm, as if they were a weapon.

Tuesday evening, 7 p.m.

All she could hear all day long going around in her head was Mozart's Clarinet Concerto, second movement. Normally it would have been a beautiful piece of music to have fastened into the brain, but today it was like a toothache that wouldn't go away.

Kate decided to take one last run through the charts in ICU while the nurses were busy. In the quiet of the nurses' station while the evening medicine trolley was going round she flipped through the trolley full of files. It was very difficult to concentrate now. The familiar buzzing feeling in her cheeks and hairline meant that she was not only running short on sleep but running short on patience too. She clenched her jaw and steadied herself to read the case notes on the patient one more time. But her mind didn't seem to be able to absorb the information any more.

She shivered and yawned widely and noisily, and then wondered if she ought to just go home and try to forget about everything till morning when she'd had some sleep. It was after seven, the traffic would be hell outside and she couldn't do much more tonight. And yet she felt that she couldn't leave the hospital.

If only there were someone she could talk to about all this, about how awful she was feeling now – that was all she needed, someone who knew the significance of what she'd been through but who'd want to make her feel instantly better. She'd been trying to ring her husband Dave all day. But Dave was an anaesthetist doing a list on the other side of the hospital, and he was uncontactable.

It was pitch dark outside now and a light rain was beginning to streak the window just above the nurses' station. Freezing out tonight, Kate thought, her head spinning with the tiredness. Kate had plenty of good friends in the maternity hospital and everyone had been so kind to her today, knowing what had happened for her in the gynae theatre last night. But what she really wanted was to be able to talk it through with someone she loved.

And Dave seemed to be held back later and later every evening these days as the cases in his theatre piled up because of bed shortages and he always seemed to have someone difficult in ICU himself. It was still worth trying to give him one last bell, though. She dialled his mobile number from the ward, just in case he'd already left and might be on his way home.

But Dave's mobile was still switched off.

Kate stood a moment by the desk in the nurses' station and gathered her thoughts together. She would still have to go back down to the on-call room to get her bag anyway and then head out into the carpark and   face the blustery December night. Perhaps Dave was still in theatre. Perhaps he'd been caught up in an emergency too.

She yawned and then shivered again suddenly. She could ring the ENT theatre of course, on the other side of the hospital where Dave had been doing a list earlier on, and see what stage they were at and ask if he was still in there. But that would mean going through the petty nosey-parker theatre porters again, who took messages down all wrong and got people's names mixed up and pretended that they couldn't recognise anybody in a theatre mask. It might be more trouble than it was worth.

"Jesus, are you still at it? And I thought *I* had no life!" Ronan Clare grinned at her as he ambled into the office.

She smiled. "I have a life all right, Ronan – it's just a bit rubbish at the moment, that's all."

Poor Ronan had been up all night too and Baby Le Normand was struggling as well.

"How is the French – I mean Swiss baby, Ro?" she asked him now.

Ronan shrugged his drooping shoulders and sat down in the nurses' station, putting his feet up on the desk. "Quite up and down, really, now. IV feeding, which is to be expected. But he, oh no, it's a she – she was actually a bit more shocked than I'd realised. Jittery today, and we had to do an X-ray. And we might be ventilating in an hour. I'm waiting to hear back from the lab about the blood gases and then I'll decide – but I've a feeling that we'll be intubating and going for full-on ventilation."

"Oh. I'm so sorry, Ronan. That's a bummer. Are you knackered out?" Kate could feel the clang of anxiety come over her again. She closed her eyes for just a moment. Thursday M and M to prepare tomorrow – having to talk to the Prof today was bad enough – what if the baby doesn't do well either? But that's not my problem, she carefully reminded herself. The Paeds are responsible there from now on. I've kept my patient alive, we delivered a live infant. I've got to keep on telling myself that.

She opened her eyes brightly instead, to smile at Ronan.

"I guess there's no point in worrying any more about it for tonight," she said. "We should just go home and get some rest, Ro. I feel like have done enough for this week anyway."

"Well, I could do with a pint but I'm not going home for a while – do you want to pop over for one later on when I've got the baby settled?" he asked her hopefully.

Poor Ronan is so sweet, she thought. But I'm not up for hospital gossip now. It's been a hell of a night and a very long day trying to make it right again. She shook her head.

"I'm going to go on home, Ro. Try to see my husband, get something to eat and hit the sack. But maybe later in the week, if you're still around?"

"That would be great." Ronan nodded and yawned at the same time. He suddenly beamed. "Let's go to the Clarence after the meeting on Thursday night and get absolutely pissed!"

Kate laughed and clapped him on the back.

Ronan looked up at her. "You did the right thing, Kate, you had no choice. Last night, I mean. It was really tough on you."

"Yeah, I know." She sat down again with him. "My head's all over the place, Ronan. I'm sure this case has gone as well as we could have expected in the circumstances, but I can't seem to think straight any more. The other thing is that I won't feel better about it until I've talked to the patient to counsel her. Prof went to talk to her this afternoon but she's still very heavily sedated. She won't be taking a lot of it in yet." She looked at him. "Ronan, I'm normally quite good at talking to patients, aren't I? I mean, I'm good at breaking bad news to patients, aren't I?"

"You're the best. You put a lot of time into it," Ronan grinned. "And I know a lot of Obs and Gynaes who wouldn't, so I'm sure it will all go well."

"You're a pal," she said, squeezing his hand where it rested on the table.

But the truth was that she had never felt more alone. What she longed for more than anything was to have somebody at home who would talk her through her horrendous night, who'd know exactly what to say to make everything all right again, who'd understand completely all the tough decisions doctors have to make and who would love her for it – and that person should have been Dave. But Dave just wasn't there for her in that way any more. He was completely absorbed in his own work issues. And here she was, staying back late at work when she could hardly think any more, just to have someone to talk to.

Kate normally felt quite confident about her career, about her ability to get things right – but the more responsibility she had at work, the more tough decisions she was going to have to make. And although she didn't want to be a wimp, there were some things that happened in hospital life that were almost impossible to deal with without support. Colleagues just weren't the same. They couldn't be detached and still supportive at the same time because they were also involved in the case. Dave was the one person who could have been there for her – another doctor, an anaesthetist, someone who had known her all her life, someone who loved her no matter what, someone who understood the responsibility for life and death. But Dave was the one person who wasn't there for her tonight. And the empty hole that left in her confidence was beginning to yawn wider.

"Here," Ronan put his arms around her, "give us a hug, Katie-cakes."

He took the wind out of her with his crushing bear hug and Kate squealed, wriggling away.

"I'll see you in the morning. But thanks for the pep talk, Ronan." She was about to add, "I really need somebody to talk to now" but that made her sound pathetic.

"Don't mention it!" Ronan waved at her and pulled the *Lancet* towards him, putting up his feet again. "Jesus," he yawned again and grumbled in a tired voice. "When is that flipping lab going to ring me with that baby's sats?"

"You won't be able to have any more children, I'm afraid. We did the best we could but sometimes things happen during emergencies that are out of our control."

Marianne Le Normand looked at the head of the man that was talking to her – and saw two of them. He was speaking English.

This is – yes, I am in the hospital in Dublin. The baby – yes. That's the nurse. She's the one who told me about the baby. I have had the baby. The baby has been born, and it's a girl. The nurse who told me, that's her over there – and she said I'd see the baby soon. It's in a special place. A special baby place. The nurse has blonde hair, strawberry blonde, that's what the Americans call it, reddish gold, like a Botticelli painting. She's so beautiful. And this place. It's very noisy, this place now, and what's this tubing on my hand? Oh. Medical equipment. But the man is speaking again. His head is saying things. Both his heads are, actually.

"Things go wrong very quickly in obstetrics."

His mouth is moving – both his mouths – and saying the words.

"You will need some more time to come to terms with it. But the main thing is that the baby is quite well and that you are making progress too. We'll answer any questions that you ask."

Well. That's very nice of them.

Her lips were trying to move but she didn't seem to be able to operate them fully. She tried to speak – "Mweeh!" – but no, that wasn't a real word at all. Not in any language.

Try again, Marianne. Say something nice to the doctor, now.

"Thank you, *docteur*." She smiled at both his heads and then, with relief, they merged back into one. But the one head had horns growing out of it.

What? What's happening to his head? No, that's not horns. That's his soul, it's a halo around his head. Oh! And the nurse has one too. Well.

That's beautiful.

She closed her eyes.

"We'll talk to her when her husband gets here, too," she heard the man's voice say.

"He'll be here tomorrow night," said the nurse.

In her sleep, she stepped onto a boat, gently, gently, with her newborn baby in her arms.

Veronique.

Her name is Veronique.

And the boat rocked both of them together.

The carpark was almost empty when Kate scuttled across it in her duffle coat, head down against the icy drizzle. She beeped her pale grey Mini Cooper open and slammed herself inside, rubbing her hands against the cold before she started up the engine.

A blast of music boomed Kate's small car across the empty carpark in the hard night rain. Kate always left the radio on whenever she parked her car – she liked the fact that as soon as she turned the key in the ignition, music played. Starting up the engine and the radio at the same time would run down the battery, Dave would grumble furiously at her if she left the radio on in *his* car. But in her own car, she could leave whatever the hell she liked on, and do whatever she wanted to the battery.

'Cos I know how I feel about you now! sang the Sugababes and Kate waved her head in time to the music, singing as loudly as she could as she swung the Mini out into the traffic jam, trying to put the hospital and the ICU and Mme Le Normand and the disastrous night on call that she had had as far away from her memory as was possible.

POOLBEG WISHES TO
THANK YOU

for buying a Poolbeg book.
As a loyal customer we will give you
10% OFF (and free postage*)
on any book bought on our website
www.poolbeg.com

Select the book(s) you wish to buy
and click to checkout.

Then click on the 'Add a Coupon' button
(located under 'Checkout') and enter
this coupon code

 USMWR15173

POOLBEG   (Not valid with any other offer!)   POOLBEG

WHY NOT JOIN OUR MAILING LIST
@ www.poolbeg.com and get some
fantastic offers on Poolbeg books

*See website for details

Also by Poolbeg.com

Snow White Turtle Doves

Juliet Bressan

Isabella swaps Dublin for Manhattan to find herself and lose Harry. Harry, with whom she had been primary school classmates, teenage sweethearts, university lovers and a not-quite-grown-up couple.

Harry, who is so caught up in anti-war demonstrations that he fails to organise a life for the two of them. Harry, a committed but penniless "revolutionary activist". Harry, whom she loves and misses and must learn to live without.

Harry loves Isabella totally. Except for the bit of him that loves Sinead. Sinead loves Harry. And Sinead wants desperately to help her friend Moussa, a doctor living amidst the fear and devastation of the fighting in Fallujah.

The lives of Isabella, Harry and Sinead are haunted by the horrors of the war in Iraq, culminating in a tragedy that will change lives forever.

978-1-84223-328-3